THESE
HOLLOW
VOWS

BY LEXI RYAN

HODDER

First published in Great Britain in 2021 by Hodder & Stoughton
An Hachette UK company

This paperback edition published in 2022

1

A CIP catalogue record for this title is available from the British Library

Hardback ISBN 978 1 529 37691 3
Trade Paperback ISBN 978 1 529 37692 0
Paperback ISBN 978 1 529 37695 1
eBook ISBN 978 1 529 37693 7

Printed and bound in Great Britain by Clays Ltd, Elcograf S.p.A.

Hodder & Stoughton policy is to use papers that are natural, renewable
and recyclable products and made from wood grown in sustainable
forests. The logging and manufacturing processes are expected to
conform to the environmental regulations of the country of origin.

Hodder & Stoughton Ltd
Carmelite House
50 Victoria Embankment
London EC4Y 0DZ

www.hodder.co.uk

FOR BRIAN —
THEY'RE ALL FOR YOU.

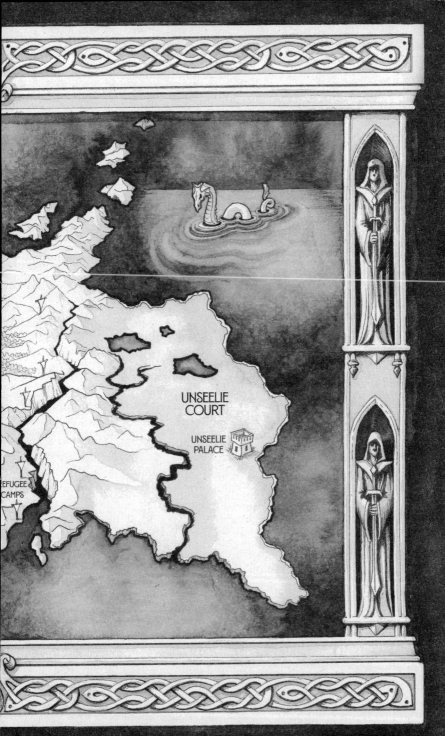

CHAPTER ONE

COOL SHADOWS WASH over my sweaty skin, welcoming me, disguising me. I could revel in the darkness — happily lie under the stars and let the night air unravel my knotted, overworked muscles — but I won't waste tonight on rest or fleeting pleasure. These are the hours of spies and thieves. They're *my* hours.

I slide two hairpins into the lock, my chapped fingers dancing over them like the strings of a viola. This is a song I've rehearsed a thousand times, a hymn I've played in my most desperate moments. Better to pray to deft fingers, to shadows and camouflage, than to the old gods. Better to steal than to starve.

Frogs sing in the distance, and their chorus nearly covers the satisfying click of the lock releasing. The servant door into Creighton Gorst's manor house swings open.

Gorst has business elsewhere tonight. I made sure of it. Nevertheless, I scan my surroundings for any sign of him or his staff. Most of the wealthy keep guards on duty, but a few — like Gorst — are so paranoid that they don't even trust those in their inner circle to be unaccompanied near their vaults. I've been waiting for a night like this for months.

I pad down the stone stairwell into the cellar. The temperature drops with each step, but my skin is flushed from adrenaline and the climb over his property walls, and I welcome the chill that skates across my skin.

At the base of the stairs, a glowstone senses my movements and kicks on, dimly illuminating the floor. I disable it with a gash of my knife along its soft center, blanketing the room in a darkness so complete that I can hardly make out my own hand in front of my face. *Good.* I'm more comfortable moving in the dark, anyway.

Following the walls around the periphery of the cellar with my hands, I reach the cool steel of the vault door. I blindly examine it with my fingertips — three locks, but none too complex. They yield to my blade and pins. In less than five minutes I have the door open and can already feel relief loosening my muscles. We'll make this month's payment. Madame Vivias won't be able to enforce more penalties this time.

My smile of triumph is short-lived as I catch sight of the symbols etched on the threshold. That quickly, the rush from my success ebbs.

Gorst's vault is protected by wards.

Of course it is.

A rich man paranoid enough to forgo sentries would be a poor man very quickly if he didn't employ a little magic to guard his wealth.

Tonight's mission is dangerous, and I can't risk forgetting that for even a moment. I only steal from those who have more than they need, but with wealth comes power — the power to have thieves like me executed if we're caught.

2

I sidestep the markings and pull a starworm from my satchel. Its silky-wet skin is slippery between my fingers, but I lead it to my wrist, wincing when it latches on. As it slowly draws a trickle of blood from my veins, its skin glows, lighting the ground before me. I hate losing the darkness, but I need to see the symbols. Sinking to my haunches, I trace every line and curve, confirming their shape and intent. *Clever magic, indeed.*

These runes wouldn't keep me out of the vault. They'd let me in and lock me there, make me a prisoner until the master of the manor could deal with me. A common thief schooled only in protection runes might make the mistake of thinking the wards were faulty when he passed them. A common thief would find himself locked inside. Good thing I'm anything but common.

I scour my mind for an appropriate counterspell. I'm no mage. I might like to be, if my fate had been different and my days weren't so full of scrubbing floors and cleaning up after my spoiled cousins. I don't have the time or the coin to spare on training, so I'll never be able to carry magic at my fingertips with spells, potions, and rituals. I'm lucky to have a friend who's taught me what he can. Lucky to know just how to get out of this vault when I've taken what I need.

I slide my knife from my belt and bite my cheek as I drag the blade across the palm opposite the starworm. The sharp pain makes my head spin and pushes every thought from my head. For too many moments I teeter, my body begging to give in to the reprieve of unconsciousness.

Breathe, Abriella. You have to breathe. You can't trade oxygen for courage.

The memory of my mother's voice has me dragging air into my lungs. What is wrong with me tonight? I'm normally not so squeamish about blood or pain. But I'm exhausted and hungry after working all day with no break. I'm dehydrated.

I'm running out of time.

I dip my finger into the blood welling in my palm and carefully draw the counterspell runes atop those etched into stone. I wipe my bloody palm on my pants and study my work carefully before rising.

I don't let myself hold my breath as I cross the threshold, immediately passing the symbols in each direction to make sure my runes are working. When I step into the vault, I cast the light from the starworm across the space and gasp.

Creighton Gorst's vault is bigger than my bedroom. The walls are lined with shelves holding raqon coinbags, jewels, and shining weapons. My hands itch to take as much as I can carry, but I won't. If I let my desperation get the best of me, he'll know someone was here. Perhaps he will anyway. Maybe I underestimate the drunkard's ability to account for the wealth he's amassed dealing in pleasure and flesh, but if I'm lucky, he'll never know that someone breached his wards.

I knew Gorst was rich, but I didn't expect riches like these. Prostitution and drink make wealthy men, but *this* wealthy? I scan the shelves and instinctively reach out when I spot the only explanation. I hover my hand over a stack of life deeds but yank back at the magical heat radiating from them.

Had I been born into a different life, I would have very much liked to become a powerful mage for contracts like this alone. I would unravel the magic that binds these lives to evil men like Gorst. I'd gather my resources and free as many girls as I could before I was caught and executed. Even knowing that I don't have the skill to undo the magic in those documents, it's all I can do to leave them where they sit. Everything in me screams that I should at least *try*.

You can't save them.

I force myself to step away. Choosing a cluttered shelf where a missing coinbag might go unnoticed, I scan for markings. None. Maybe Gorst should pay me to teach him how to truly guard his treasure. I lift a single pouch and peek inside to check the contents — more than enough raqon for our payment. Maybe enough for next month's as well.

He has all this wealth. Will he really notice if I take more?

I scan the shelves and carefully choose two more bags that are tucked behind unorganized piles of treasure. I knew Gorst was despicable, but this is the kind of wealth that people of Fairscape see only if they do business with faeries. With that realization, each of those magical contracts takes on a new meaning. It's bad enough that he can make those people do his bidding, bad enough that they'll spend their lives paying an impossible debt, but if Gorst deals with the fae, he's shipping humans off to another realm to spend their lives as slaves. *Or worse.*

There are three stacks of contracts. I can't risk touching them, but I make myself look at each pile. *Someday* I'm going to buy my freedom, and once my sister isn't relying on me, I'll come back here. Someday I'll find a way.

My gaze snags on the stack closest to the vault door and the name on top. I reread the name and the date the payment is due in full. Once. Twice. Three times. My chest ratchets tighter each time. I don't believe in the old gods, but I send up a prayer anyway at the sight of that name, that child's scrawl. At tomorrow's date highlighted with a streak of her own blood.

Steps sound overhead, the booming of men's boots, and I hear a deep voice. I can't make out his words from down here, but I don't need to understand what he's saying to know that I need to run.

My satchel is heavy with my stolen goods, and I clutch it to my side so it won't clang against my hip as I race out of the vault. I lift the starworm off my wrist, gasping as it fights me, trying for more blood.

"Patience," I whisper, guiding him to the floor. The leech crawls across the threshold, cleaning away my blood with its tiny tongue.

More steps above. Then laughter and the sound of clinking glasses. He's not alone, but if I'm lucky, everyone up there will be too intoxicated to notice me slip out.

"Hurry, hurry," I whisper to the starworm. I need to close the vault, but if I leave my blood behind, I'll risk Gorst knowing someone was here. Or worse — taking a sample to a mage and tracing it back to me.

The voices come closer, then steps on the stairs.

I have no choice. I wrench the starworm from his bloody feast and slip him into my satchel.

I splash water from my canteen onto the stones before I swing the vault closed.

"I'll get a new bottle," Gorst shouts from the top of the cellar stairs. I know that voice too well. I used to clean his brothel. I mopped his floors and scrubbed his toilets until a month ago, when he tried to corner me into working for him in a very different capacity.

I've spent the last nine years living by two rules: I don't steal from those who give me honest work, and I don't work for those who steal from me. That night, I added a new rule to the list: I don't work for those who try to blackmail me into prostitution.

Every scuff of his boots brings him closer, but I keep my movements smooth and steady.

I latch one lock. *Snick.*

Scuff, scuff.

The second lock. *Snick.*

Scuff, scuff.

The third —

"What the hell?"

Snick.

"These glowstones are worthless," he grumbles from the foot of the stairs.

I keep my breathing shallow and press myself against the wall, where the darkness is deepest.

"You coming or not?" A female voice from the top of the stairs. She giggles. "We found the other bottle, Creighton. Come on!"

"I'm coming."

I count his steps back up and inch closer to the stairs as he stumbles his way toward the top. He's drunk. Perhaps luck is on my side tonight.

Listening carefully, I track their progress through the manor house until there's no more noise in the servants' quarters above me and the sounds all come from the front of the house. I can't risk opening the vault again to remove the rest of my blood. Not tonight.

I pad silently up the stairs, retracing the steps that brought me here.

I don't register the extent of the tension locking my muscles until I'm out of the house and it leaves me in a rush. Under the cool night sky, I'm hit by a wave of exhaustion. I won't stop now, but I've pushed myself too hard this week and I can't deny my body much longer.

I need sleep. Food. And in the morning, maybe even a few mindless minutes of watching Sebastian train in the courtyard behind Madame Vivias's. That might be better than sleep *or* food.

The thought is like a shot of adrenaline to my system, pushing me to finish what I need to do. The shadows guide me out of the manor — a meandering path around trees and shrubs, dodging the moonlight as if this is a game.

The gates to the front are wide-open, and though my weary muscles beg me to take that easy exit, I can't risk it. I pull the rope from my satchel and toss it over the perimeter wall of Gorst's property. The fibers bite into my chapped hands, and my arms scream with each pull to the top.

I jump down on the other side, landing on soft knees. My sister says I'm like a cat because of the way I've always jumped from trees and roofs without getting hurt. I think of myself more like a shadow, unnoticed and more useful than people bother to notice.

I'm a ten-minute walk from home and am nearly limping under the weight of what I've stolen. It would be so easy to hand Madame Vivias what she's due, climb into bed, and sleep for twelve hours.

But I can't. Not after what I saw on that last stack of contracts.

I turn away from home and head down the alley past the dress shop where my sister Jas works. Around the corner from Gorst's tavern and behind an overflowing bin of trash, I slip past the entrance to the city's "family housing." What a joke. The four-story building has twelve two-room units and one shared bath and kitchen on each floor. It's shelter, and better than many have, but after seeing Gorst's massive estate, the inequity disgusts me.

My friend Nik's door is ajar, and there's sobbing coming from inside. Through the crack, I can see her daughter, Fawn, curled up against the wall, rocking, her shoulders shaking. Fawn has the same dark skin and curls as her mom. Once, Nik told me that everything changed for her when her daughter was born — that from that moment on, all that mattered to her was being the best mother she could be, even if it meant crossing lines she'd never want her own daughter to cross.

I push inside, and Fawn startles. "Shh. It's just me, baby," I whisper, sinking to my haunches. "Where's your mama?"

She lifts her head, and tears stream down her cheeks. Her sobs grow louder and harder, her whole body shaking and teetering as if she's trying to hold still through the gusts of an invisible storm. "I'm out of time," Fawn says.

I don't ask what she means. I already know. I hear footsteps and turn to see Nik standing behind me, her arms crossed, horror on her face.

"She did it to save me," Nik says, her voice raspy, as if she's been crying but has dried her tears through sheer will. "She got money from Gorst to buy me medicine from the healer."

"You were dying," Fawn says, angrily swiping at her tears. She looks at me. "I didn't have a choice."

"You did. You should've told me. I wouldn't have let you sign that contract."

I reach for my friend's hand and squeeze. The thing about desperation is that it steals the right choice from our list of options. Nik knows this as well as anyone.

"I'll give myself in your place, Fawny. Got it?" Nik says. There's a quiet resolve in my friend's expression that breaks my heart.

"And what happens to me then?" Fawn asks.

I wish she wasn't old enough to understand that by going in her place, her mother would be sentencing her to a fate that could be worse. No one in Fairscape wants an extra mouth to feed. The only people who can afford charity are too greedy to bother.

"Can you take her, Brie?" Nik asks. "You know I wouldn't ask if I had a choice. Take her."

I shake my head. I want to, but if Madame Vivias found Fawn living in the cellar with us, there would be horrible consequences —and not just for Jas and me. For Fawn too. "There has to be someone else."

"There's no one else, and you know it," Nik says, but there's no bite in her words, only resignation.

"How much does she owe?"

Nik winces and looks away. "Too much."

"How. Much."

"Eight thousand raqon."

The number makes me flinch. That's two months' payment to Madame Vivias, even including all her "penalties." I don't know how much I got from Gorst's vault tonight, but there's a good chance I have enough in my satchel to cover it.

Fawn looks at me with those big eyes she was named for, begging me to save her. If I don't do this, it's the end of Nik's life and possibly the end of Fawn's. Best-case scenario, Fawn ends up as some rich noblewoman's handmaiden. And worst? I can't let myself think the worst.

Nik wanted better for her daughter. A chance to be better, to have better. If I miss this payment to Madame V, it's just more of the same for me. Our debt is too deep, our lives too entangled with the witch we were stuck with when Uncle Devlin died. The contents of this satchel can't save me and Jas, but they can save Fawn and Nik.

I reach into my bag and pull out two pouches. "Here."

Nik's eyes widen. "Where did you get this?"

"It doesn't matter. Take it."

Wide-eyed and slack-jawed, Nik peers into the bags before shaking her head. "Brie, you can't."

"I can and I will."

Nik stares at me for a long beat, and in her eyes I see her

desperation warring with her fear for me. Finally she pulls me into her arms and squeezes me tight. "I'll repay you. Someday. Somehow. I swear it."

"You owe me nothing." I pull out of her arms, eager to get home and clean up. Desperate to sleep. "You would've done the same for me and Jas if you could have."

Her eyes fill with tears, and I watch one spill over and down her cheek, smearing her makeup as it goes. Her gratitude morphs to worry as she spots my bloody hand. "What happened?"

I make a fist to hide my sliced palm. "It's nothing. Just a cut."

"Just a cut? It's an infection waiting to happen." She nods to her bedroom. "Come with me. I can help."

Knowing she won't let me go without a fight, I follow her into the tiny room where there's a rickety dresser and the bed she and her daughter share. I sit on the edge of the bed and watch as she shuts the door behind her and gathers supplies.

She sinks to her haunches in front of me and paints a salve on my cut. "You got this getting that money." It's not a question, so I don't bother with a lie. "Are you okay?"

I try to hold still as the salve seeps into my skin. The flesh itches where it knits together. "I'm fine. I just need some dinner and a nap."

Dark, incredulous eyes flash to mine. "A *nap?* Brie, you're so run-down I'm not sure anything but a coma would refresh you."

I laugh—or try to. It sounds more like a pathetic mewl. *So tired.*

"Another payment due to your aunt?"

"Tomorrow." I swallow hard at the thought. I'm seventeen, but I'm magically bound to a contract that will, at this rate, keep me in Madame Vivias's debt for the rest of my life. When my sister and I signed ourselves into servitude nine years ago, Uncle Devlin had just died and Mom had abandoned us. The payments Madame V required then seemed reasonable—and much better than the uncertain fate of an orphan—but we were little girls who didn't understand things like compound interest or the insidious trap of her penalties. Just as Fawn didn't truly understand the contract she'd signed with Gorst.

"And thanks to us," Nik says, reaching for the gauze, "you're going to be short again."

"Worth it," I whisper.

Nik squeezes her eyes shut. "This world is so screwed up." There's no way Fawn can hear us unless she's listening at the door, but Nik lowers her voice anyway. "I have a friend who could give you work."

I frown. "What kind of work?" There's none that can earn me the kind of money I need. None except— "I might as well work for Creighton Gorst if I'm going to do that."

"Creighton would take half your earnings." Nik wraps my hand and gives me a sad smile. "There are fae who pay a premium for the company of a beautiful human and more if you'll bind yourself to them. Far more than Creighton can offer."

"Faeries?" I shake my head. I'd sooner get involved with Creighton's handsy clients than give myself over to a faerie. My people used to believe the faeries were our guardians. Before they

13

split the sky and opened the portals, the fae visited at twilight in their spirit forms — just a shadow or an outline in the trees that looked like something living.

My people called them angels. They'd kneel and pray for the angels to stay close, to protect them, to watch over their sick children. But when the portals opened and the angels were finally here, they didn't protect us at all.

Because the fae aren't angels. They're demons, and they came to exploit us, to steal babies and use humans as their slaves and their breeding stock. They tricked thousands into signing over their lives to fight in their wars. Only when the Magical Seven of Elora, the seven most powerful mages from this world, came together did we guard the portals against them. Now they can take a human life only if it's fairly purchased or freely given — a magical safeguard that the clever faeries have created a hundred workarounds for. In practice, this protects only the rich and powerful.

"Better than nothing," say so many who support the Seven. "It's a start." Or worse, "If people don't want to be sold to the fae, they shouldn't take on so much debt."

"Why would they pay when they can just glamour women into giving them whatever they want?" I ask Nik.

"Keep your voice down!" She cranes her neck to check that the door behind her is still closed. "Not everything you hear about them is true. And my friend can —"

"It's out of the question. I'll find another way." If I know anything, it's that I'll never trust the fae.

"I'm worried about you," Nik says. "In this world, the only

14

power we have is in our autonomy. Don't let anyone back you into a corner. Don't let your desperation make decisions for you."

Like it did for Fawn. "I won't," I promise, but it feels hollow, as if my voice already knows it's a lie. I'm working all the time and stealing as much as I can get away with, but I can't keep up.

Even if I were okay with selling my body — and I'm not — I don't want anything to do with the fae. I don't care how much money they offer. There are more important things in life than money. Even more important things than freedom — like taking care of your two little girls and not abandoning them so you can run off with your faerie lover.

"I hear you, girl," Madame Vivias says the second my hand hits the knob for the basement.

I squeeze my eyes shut. I should've come in through the cellar door. It's after midnight, and I have no energy for whatever task she's planning to give me. Lowering my head, I turn to her and give a brief curtsey. "Good evening, Aunt V."

"Good evening. Tomorrow's the full moon."

"Yes, ma'am."

"You have my money?"

I keep my gaze leveled on the hand propped on her hip — a sparkling ring on every finger. Any one of those rings could cover this month's payment. I don't lift my head. I won't give her the satisfaction of seeing the fear in my eyes. "I'll have it tomorrow, ma'am."

She's silent for so long that I dare to lift my gaze to hers. She's

15

adjusting the thick strands of glittering jewels hanging from her neck and scowling at me. "If you don't have it today, what are the chances you'll have it tomorrow?"

Not very good. But until it's officially too late, I won't admit it. Every time we're short, our contract grows longer and our payment higher. It's a vicious cycle we can't seem to escape. "I'll pay you tomorrow, ma'am."

"Abriella!" The shrill cry comes from the stairs, and I have to fight my flinch at my cousin Cassia's voice. "My dresses need washing!"

"There are fresh dresses in your room," I say. "I pressed them this morning."

"None of those will do. I don't have anything to wear to dinner tomorrow night."

"My room needs cleaning," Stella, her sister, says, because gods forbid I do more for one spoiled cousin than the other. "The last time she did it, she barely spent any time in there, and it's beginning to feel grimy."

Madame V arches a brow and turns back to me. "You heard them, girl. Get to work."

Sleep will have to wait a few more hours. I pull back my shoulders and turn toward my cousins' rooms.

CHAPTER TWO

THE SECOND I STEP into our shared bedroom in the cellar, Jas launches herself at me. "Brie! You're home!" Our bedroom is little more than a storage room with a bed in it. I found the cinderblock walls claustrophobic when Madame V first moved us down here, but now we've made the space our own. One of Jas's handsewn tapestries hangs over the bed, and our assortment of personal trinkets — odd stones and shiny scraps of cloth that have value only to us — decorate the top of the rickety dresser.

I hug my sister tight, breathing in the fresh linen scent of her. She might be only three years younger than I am, but in some ways she'll always be the toddler I wrapped in my arms to rescue from the house fire.

Jas pulls back and grins. Her brown eyes are bright, and her sleek chestnut hair is bound in a knot on top of her head. My sister is my opposite — all soft beauty, like her cheerful personality. I'm all hard angles and stubborn will, with hair the color of a blazing fire, much like the rage I carry inside me.

"I heard you up there," she says. "I would've come to help, but

17

I was working on new dresses for Stella and Cassia." She nods at the gowns now hanging on the stand in the corner.

"What's wrong with the eighty other dresses they have?"

"They'll *never do!*" she says in a mock-falsetto imitation of our cousins.

I would've thought I was too exhausted for it, but I laugh. Whatever the losses of my day, whatever new penalties tomorrow's missed payment will bring, I'm glad to be home. To be here with Jas, who's unusually chipper for this late hour. I narrow my eyes. "What has you so excited?"

"Didn't you hear?" She has the absolute worst poker face, and her big smile reveals that she has some exciting news.

I've been working all day. Other than my short visit with Nik and Fawn tonight, I haven't talked to anyone. The kind of people I work for believe the help should be neither seen nor heard. "Hear what?"

She's practically bouncing. "In one day's time, Queen Arya will open the doors to the Court of the Sun. She's giving humans safe passage to Faerie to attend the celebration at her castle."

"What? Why?"

"She wants to find a human bride for her son."

I grunt out a disgusted huff. "Of course she does." The fae are good at many things, but reproducing isn't one of them, and without offspring, their lines die off—especially when so many immortals were lost in the Great Fae War. *Good riddance.*

"You really didn't hear about it? It's all the girls at work were talking about today. A Faerie Ball. We're swamped with rush orders for new dresses."

"You'll have to remind me to stay far away from the portals."

She giggles at my cynicism. "Brie! This is the *Seelie Court*. The good faeries! The faeries of light and joy."

"You don't know that," I snap. "You don't know they're good."

Her smile falls away. *I'm a jerk.*

The last thing I want to do right now is pick a fight. "Sorry. I'm just tired." So *tired*.

"Look at your hands." She runs her thumb across my cracked knuckles where the skin is raw from cleaning compounds. "Do you really want to be stuck in this basement for the rest of our lives?"

"Anyone who goes to that court has a death wish, Jas. You know as well as I do that there are no *good* faeries. Just degrees of evil and cruel."

"Not so different from humans then." She drops my hands. "I heard you and Madame V talking. I know the next payment is coming due, and despite your efforts to keep me in the dark —"

"I don't want you to worry." All I truly want is to protect her, my sweet sister with her optimism and joy, who loves me even when I'm a hateful grump. I'm not sure I deserve her.

"I know the contract as well as you do," she says. "She keeps adding those penalties, and we're never going to escape her without some sort of miracle."

"And the miracle you're counting on is beneficent faeries? I think we'd be better off going to the gambling underground and trying our luck at cards."

She turns to a lavender dress in the corner and smooths the fabric of the deep neckline. "One of the girls I work with has a cousin whose friend fell in love with a golden fae lord. She comes back and visits with her family. She's happy."

"It's always a friend of a friend—do you notice that?" I try to keep the bite out of my tone this time. "No one who tells these stories actually *knows* the person who's supposedly lucked out with the good faeries."

She turns away from the dress to frown at me. "There are more good faeries than bad, just like humans."

I'm not convinced that's true of either. "Even so, a *ball*? Like, with dresses and fancy stuff? Faerie nonsense aside, I'm supposed to try to impress some stuck-up noble prince? Can't you just hang me by my toenails instead?"

She rolls her eyes and sits on the edge of the bed. "You don't have to go, but *I* want to."

I recognize the stubborn edge to her voice. She's going to go whether I want her to or not. I don't even have to take a full step to sink onto the bed beside her. I fall to my back and stare at the ceiling. "I don't like it."

"I thought you two might still be up."

Jas and I both whip around, and the sight of Sebastian's broad frame filling the doorway sends the small amount of adrenaline I have left zipping through me. My heart pounds a little faster, my blood runs a little hotter, and longing clenches my stomach in its fist. Sebastian is just a friend, he'd never see a scrappy thing like me as more than that, but no matter how many times I lecture my heart, it refuses to listen.

He ducks his head and leans against the frame, his sea-green eyes scanning the space as if he hasn't been here hundreds of times before. Madame V moved us down here not long after Uncle Devlin died, claiming we'd have more privacy this way. Even then, we knew that the cold, dark room with concrete walls, no windows, and space for little more than a shared double bed and a dresser was an attempt to put us in our place.

Jas and I are short enough that the ceiling height isn't a problem, but Sebastian's over six feet tall and has smacked his head more than once. Not that it keeps him from visiting. He's been sneaking down here for the last two years, since he started his apprenticeship with Mage Trifen next door. He's the one who unlocks the door and sneaks us food and water when our cousins are feeling cruel and lock us in.

"Still up," I say, yawning despite the burst of energy I felt at his arrival, "but not for long."

"What don't you like?" he asks, his brow creasing with his frown. "What were you talking about when I came in?"

"Jas wants to become some faerie prince's bride," I say, scooting over on the bed to make room for him.

My sister's cheeks flame red. "Thanks a lot, Brie."

Sebastian sits between me and Jas before reaching out with one long leg to kick the door closed. He murmurs an incantation and snaps his fingers, giving a self-satisfied smirk when the lock on our side slides into place. *Mage showoff.*

My cousins have made more than one crack about Sebastian's friendship with me and Jas. They blackmailed us for months the first time they caught him down here, but I know they're just bitter that Sebastian, a lowly apprentice mage, won't waste his time looking in their direction. What Sebastian lacks in money and family connections, he makes up for in good looks—tall and broad-shouldered, gleaming white hair he keeps tied back at the base of his neck, and eyes like the raging sea. He's the most beautiful man I've ever seen.

Objectively speaking, of course.

Sebastian leaves in two days for another part of his apprenticeship, and I won't be able to look forward to these late-night visits—the brightest spot in my life next to Jas. He's taken trips before, but his training will keep him away for months this time. I'm dreading it.

"I don't want to be a faerie prince's bride," Jas says, pulling my thoughts back to the matter at hand. She shakes her head. "I just . . . It's not that."

I arch a brow. "Really? Why *else* would you want to go?" When she looks at her hands, realization hits me so hard it forces the breath from my lungs. "You're hoping to find our mother."

"If the stories she told us are true and the faerie she loved was a noble, they'd be expected to attend the ball."

"And what *then*, Jas? You think she's going to see us and change her mind about what kind of mother she is? She *abandoned* us."

"She knew we wouldn't be safe in Faerie."

When I flash her a hard look, she holds up her hands.

"She had a terrible choice to make, and I'm not saying she did the right thing. I'm not even saying she isn't selfish. I'm just saying that she *is* our mother, and if she knew about our lives, about the contract with Madame V . . ." She shakes her head. "I don't know. Maybe she doesn't have any money. Maybe this lord she said loved her so much has no money, no lands, nothing that could help us. But maybe he does. And maybe she's been living under the assumption that we're happy and cared for."

My stomach knots. I don't know how Jas maintains so much *hope* when everything about our life should have beaten it out of her by now. "If she really cared, wouldn't she have checked on us sometime in the last nine years?"

She swallows. "Then we'll use guilt to our best advantage. Maybe she doesn't care but will feel obligated to help us. We have to try. We can't keep living like this." She takes my other hand this time and frowns at the bandage. "*You* can't keep living like this."

I bite back an objection. She's right that something needs to change, but I'm not the kind of girl who looks to Faerie for answers. I turn to Sebastian. "You're being awfully quiet."

He stands and attempts to pace in the three feet of space between the bed and the door. If his face weren't creased with worry, it might be comical. "It's dangerous."

Jas throws up her hands. "Thousands of humans are going to be there, dying for the chance to be a faerie prince's bride."

"*Dying* being the key word," I mutter. But she's right. Though some will sneer at the girls planning to go, at least twice as many will put on their finest clothes and line up in hopes of becoming a faerie princess.

"The golden queen is powerful," Sebastian says, putting his hands behind his head in his typical *thinking* posture. "She'll use her magic to protect the humans in her palace, but I don't like the idea of you two going to Faerie and poking around looking for your mother. There are too many creatures over there who would love to snatch you at the first opportunity to fulfill their nefarious cravings."

I giggle at the ceiling and roll to my side to look at my sister. "Remember the time Cassia snuck into the golden queen's solstice celebration and that goblin stole all her hair?"

Jas laughs. "Oh gods, she could not pull off a bald head. And the wigs V bought her while it grew back . . ."

"Atrocious." I sigh. If it makes me shallow and catty to talk about my cousins this way, I don't care. They've made our lives miserable from the moment Mother put us under Uncle Devlin's charge. They're cruel girls who wish the worst for everyone but themselves. It's hard *not* to delight in the occasional poor fortune of someone like that.

"I'm talking about creatures much worse than *goblins*," Sebastian says. He knows goblins don't scare us. They're the messengers between the realms, the only creatures from either who are allowed to freely travel between them. We're used to goblins. Even Madame Vivias has a house goblin who lives under the second-story stairs. He's a greedy little thing who holds secrets ransom and has a disturbing collection of human hair.

"I know," I say, because he's right about what lives in Faerie. Evil fae, wild beasts, and monsters we've never imagined. There's a reason our realms are kept separate — and maybe even a reason our mother left us behind.

In a lower voice he adds, "If a faerie from the shadow court got his hands on you . . ."

"Make no bargains or ties with the silver eyes," Jas and I

24

singsong together. Because, yes, the shadow fae are so dangerous that they teach children songs about them.

"I think we should risk it," Jas says. "I know it's dangerous, but it would be *more* dangerous if I had blind faith in the queen's protection. I'm going to go with my eyes open, and I'm going to find Mother."

"Do you really think you can find her in the middle of the masses that'll show up for this thing?" I ask.

"It's only one castle to search rather than an entire realm." She shrugs. "And even if we can't find our mother there, imagine what treasure we might find, Brie."

So much of what I know about Faerie comes from the bedtime stories Mother liked to whisper as we drifted off to sleep.

Once upon a time, a golden faerie princess fell in love with the shadow king, but their kingdoms had battled for hundreds of years and her parents were sworn enemies of the king and his kingdom . . .

The rest of what I know about Faerie comes from legends everyone knows—pieces of truth and superstition that humans pass through the generations. One of those pieces is of the Seelie queen and the jewels she hoards.

"You're crazy if you think her sentries will allow you any-where near her treasures," Sebastian says, spotting the smile that's curved my lips.

"They won't *allow* anyone," Jas says, her words measured as she studies me. "I know only one person who could search her grounds undetected."

Sebastian shakes his head. "Impossible."

25

I smile. "But it would be so *fun* to try."

He arches a brow at me then turns to frown at Jas. "You see what you've done?"

"She's right," I say. "I could do it." And if the thrill that rushes through my blood at the thought of stealing from fae nobility is more satisfying than the prospect of finding my mother, so what?

"You two are forgetting one possibility." Sebastian slides down the wall and onto the floor, props his elbows on his knees, and looks back and forth between us.

"What?" Jas says, annoyed.

His steady gaze meets mine, and I see the worry there.

I reach for Jas's hand and squeeze. "He means that maybe Mom is dead. Maybe that's why she never came back."

Jas shrugs. "One can hope. It's the only excusable reason for not returning for us." She says it with such lightness, I might believe it if I didn't know her so well. But I know Jas better than anyone, and she doesn't hope that our mother is dead. No, she'd rather forgive the woman for abandoning us during our most formative years than accept that she won't ever see her again.

Personally, I don't hope. Not ever. Hope is addictive, and you start relying on it. In a world this cruel, I won't be caught needing a crutch.

"It would be nice to know," I admit. "But I'm still not convinced a visit to Faerie is in our best interests. We *are* humans. Even Mother, for all her romanticizing of the fae, warned that their realm was dangerous."

Jas bites her lip, her eyes dancing. "But *maybe*—"

"I can't decide right now." I've put off sleep too long, and

26

exhaustion falls over me like a heavy blanket. Yawning, I stretch my arms over my head before curling up on my side. "Someone blow out the candles. Or don't. I don't care. I'm sleeping."

"Abriella! Jasalyn!" Cassia calls from upstairs. "There's a *bug* in my room!"

"I'll get it," Jas says, squeezing my arm. "You sleep."

"Thanks, sis," I say without opening my eyes. I'm faintly aware of her leaving the room, the sound of her feet on the steps, then the soft puff of breath as the candles are extinguished.

"Good night, Brie," Sebastian says softly.

"Good night," I mumble, half asleep.

But then there's a hand on my forehead, smoothing back my hair, and the tickle of lips against my ear. "Don't go to the ball."

I smile. It's sweet that he's so concerned. "Don't worry. I want nothing to do with that place."

Then a kiss. Lips on my forehead — there and gone in a breath.

I open my eyes to see Sebastian's silhouette shrinking toward the cellar door.

And now I'm wide-awake.

———

The click of raqon clanging together gives me a stomachache. Each month, for nine years, Jas and I have counted out our money to give to Madame Vivias. Sometimes we've had enough. Sometimes we had more than we needed and headed into the next month with a head start. But too often we've fallen short. With each short month, all the following payments increased and the penalties compounded until, without what I could steal, it became impossible to scrape together what we owe.

27

"How much?" Jas asks, voice shaking.

"We're seventeen hundred short."

She flinches. I hate that she understands what this means for us. I want to save her from that. Maybe I need her to be the one who always believes in the best when I can't. The idea of this world beating that out of her makes the pain in my stomach sharper.

"We have to go to Faerie," she says softly.

I shake my head. "Sebastian's right. It's too dangerous."

She swallows. "For humans, yes." She lifts her gaze from the pile of raqon on the bed and meets my eyes. "But what if we attended as fae? We could buy potions for an elven glamour from Mage Trifen so we'd look like fae nobility. Wouldn't that be an added protection?"

I drag my fingers through the coins; the *tinking* is a delicious torture. We're killing ourselves to get out of this contract, but the hole sinks faster than we can climb. Something has to change. "Let's do it," I say, nodding. "Let's try."

She grins so widely I know I never had a chance of denying her. I love my sister, and if searching for Mother will make her feel that she's done her part in obtaining our freedom, then we'll make it happen.

"We'll need dresses," she says. "To fit in!" she adds at my cringe. She pulls a bolt of muslin out from under the bed and practically squeaks with delight. "I've wanted to make a dress for you *forever.*"

"Well, don't get used to it," I say. Still, I can't help but smile.

"When I'm done with you, Prince Ronan won't be able to take his eyes off you — whether you want him to or not."

I strip down to my underwear and let her wrap me in the muslin she uses to plan our cousins' new dresses. She has me pinned into a mockup of a dress when there's a rapping at the door.

Three taps. Pause. Two taps. Sebastian's signature knock.

"Come in!" Jas and I call out in unison. Her hands pause their pinning at my waist.

We both turn to the door as it swings open. When Sebastian sees me, his eyes go wide and he throws a hand over his eyes. "Sorry, I . . . Sorry."

"I'm decent." I laugh at his pink cheeks. "Come on in."

"Shut the door behind you," Jas says, speaking low. "We don't need Madame V coming in here."

Sebastian gives a curt nod and steps into our room, shutting the door as requested. "You look really nice," he tells me. The words come out strangled, as if he's not sure how to give me a compliment. And why would he? I don't know if he's ever seen me in anything fancier than cleaning scrubs or the fitted black pants I favor for excursions into the night.

"Thanks." I consider the thin brown fabric pinned around me. He's just being kind. I don't look *nice*. Just . . . awkward.

"Wait until you see it in the proper fabric — think a thin velvet the color of the deepest emerald," Jas says, smiling up at me. "You'll be stunning."

It's my turn to blush. I keep my head bowed so Sebastian won't notice.

I can't believe I'm actually excited about this gown. Jas knows how I feel about dresses and not being able to move freely, so she designed mine as loose-legged pants that'll pass as a skirt when I stand. On top is a sleeveless fitted bodice that dips a little too low for my taste. It's the kind of outfit our cousins would kill for — or at the very least whine and beg for until we gave it up.

"What's the occasion?" Sebastian asks.

Jas resumes her task of fitting the muslin at my hips and sticks a pin in her mouth as she adjusts the seams, leaving me to speak.

Guilt rushes through me at the memory of Sebastian's sweet kiss on my forehead last night, his request that we not go. "We don't have a choice, Sebastian," I say gently. "If there's any chance —"

"You're not serious." Sebastian's gaze swivels between me and Jas before landing on me. "But you *hate* the fae. Tell me how anything good can come of this. And don't tell me you're going to steal from the queen. I'll tell you now, that's a death sentence."

"I'll be careful." I hate the disappointment in his eyes. "We have to do something."

He stares at me, his jaw ticking and those wild sea eyes bright with his frustration. When I'm convinced he's going to say more, he turns on his heel and storms out of our room.

I lunge forward to rush after him, but Jas grabs my arm. "The dress."

"Help me," I squeak desperately. I don't know what I'm going to say to Sebastian. I've promised Jas we'll go to the ball, and I won't back out now, but Sebastian's been my rock for two years and I can't stand the idea of him being angry.

Jas works quickly to remove the right pins so I can step out of the thin cotton. I pull on a pair of slacks and a tank before rushing up the cellar stairs and into the courtyard that Madame V shares with Mage Trifen.

A shock of white in my periphery catches my attention. Sebastian's sitting on the stoop just outside the courtyard, his big hands sharpening the tip of his staff.

My stomach always goes wild at the sight of him — not just a little flip-flop, but a full-on tumble down a hill that never ends.

Unlike my cousins, I was too busy *surviving* my adolescence to have crushes or worry about falling in love. But then Sebastian moved in next door, and the first moment I saw him, I felt something different . . . in my stomach. In my lungs. All along my skin.

The first time he smiled at me, it was as if my chest opened up, as if my heart were trying to reach out and grab him. Somehow I got around my awkwardness, we became friends, and I got to see him almost every morning. We didn't spend a lot of time together — just enough that he became a bright spot — and his smile got me through my fair share of hard days.

He's not smiling now.

I lower myself onto the stoop beside him, tucking my knees to my chest and wrapping my arms around my legs. I sit there for long minutes. He sharpens his staff to a deadly point, and I watch. We let the birds in the courtyard do all the talking.

I'm not good at feelings. I'm good at working and *doing*, and the only person I've ever been any good at sharing my emotions with is Jas. No one else has ever mattered enough to be worth the effort.

"I'm sorry," I finally say. It's not enough, and it only brushes

31

against what I want to explain — that we're running out of options, that I love how much he values our safety, that I'll do everything in my power to come back home — if only because I desperately want to see him again.

Sebastian lifts his head, and those sea-green eyes seem to see right through me. He searches my face. "Do you have *any* idea how dangerous it is for humans in Faerie?"

"Sure I do, but —"

"So *don't go.*"

My fingers itch to reach out and touch him. To stroke the side of his jaw or grab his muscled forearms. He's never hinted that he has the same feelings for me that I harbor for him, so I've never allowed myself that sort of connection with him. I've never had the courage to risk rejection, keeping my feelings secret from everyone — even Jas. "If our debt gets much worse, we'll never escape it. Even now, it would take . . ."

He squeezes his eyes shut. I know he hates that he can't help us. He's given us money before, but he's only an apprentice. He doesn't have the resources to make a dent in what we owe to Madame V.

When he opens his eyes, he studies me for a long time. So long that my cheeks heat. My skin tingles. My breath comes short as I wait for his soft lips to find their way toward mine.

"Just hold off a little longer," he finally says. "Just hold off until I can help. Someday I'll end your contract. I'll free you from her."

I know he believes it, but —

"I promise we'll be safe," I say. It's not the promise he wants, so I stand and wipe my sweaty palms on my pants. I was foolish to think he might kiss me, foolish to focus on that when we're arguing about something so important. "I have to go get ready for work."

There's something in his eyes I've never seen before. Desperation.

I walk away because I understand that emotion all too well.

I've taken three steps when he says, "What if he's not what you think?"

I stop and turn back to see him stand. "What?"

"Prince Ronan. What if you end up . . . what if you realize you could *like* him?"

I shake my head. "Bash, I'm not going in hopes of becoming a faerie princess. I'm not that girl."

"But if he isn't what you expect . . . if he's *better* than you've let yourself believe?"

I fold my arms. "Are you worried I'm going to fall for a *faerie*?" *Are you worried I'll forget you? Because I promise I won't. I couldn't.*

"Abriella . . ."

"What?"

His throat bobs as he swallows. "Just promise me you'll do everything you can to be safe. If you go to the ball, you'll be under the queen's protection, but if you wander off her land, that protection no longer applies."

"I know how it works, Sebastian. I promise."

With a single step, he closes the distance between us. He touches my cheek with two fingers and tucks an errant lock of hair behind my ear. I'm entranced by the sensation of his rough calluses against my skin.

A cackling laughter cleaves the air behind me. I spin around to see Cassia standing in the courtyard, her hands on her hips. Her blond hair is piled in carefully pinned curls on top of her head, and her breasts nearly spill from her mint green dress. "Here I thought you'd be crying and moaning, but you aren't losing any tears over her at all, are you?"

What is she blathering about now?

Sebastian puts a comforting hand on my arm, and I just shake my head, prepared to ignore my cousin's jealous nonsense.

"Now that little sister's out of the way, you can finally score the hunky apprentice? Is that how this works?"

I roll my eyes. "What are you talking about?"

She grins, blue eyes bright. "You don't know? You're officially too far behind on your payments, and Mother has had enough. Bakken just took Jasalyn to the faerie traders." She makes fists with both hands and then opens them dramatically. "Poof! Gone. Just like that."

CHAPTER THREE

I BARGE INTO MADAME VIVIAS'S OFFICE, sending the door slamming against the wall so hard the pictures rattle on the walls. "Where is she?"

My aunt doesn't even startle. She puts down her pen and pats her head, adjusting the perfect bun of dark hair she spells to keep lustrous and thick. "Hello, Abriella. Congratulations on your freedom."

"*No*," I breathe, but I see it — the pile of ash on the corner of her desk, all that remains of a magical contract once it's fulfilled. "Why?"

"I had to cut my losses at some point." She folds her arms across her chest and leans back in her chair. "I could've done this months ago, but I was waiting to see if you could catch up."

I feel like someone's squeezed all the air out of me and I'm held in a grip so tight I can't fill my lungs. I didn't realize I was hoping that Cassia was lying. I didn't realize I was . . . *hoping*.

Madame V waves a hand, as if this is all as trivial as who will prepare dinner, not about my sister's life. "Your sister will be just fine in Faerie. I'm sure she'll charm everyone there, just like she did here."

"You've made her a *slave*. They'll work her to death or torture her for their own amusement . . . or . . ." I can't even say the rest, can't begin to enumerate the other horrific possibilities. *This isn't happening.*

"Don't be so dramatic. It's really the best future she could ask for, considering the hole you two have dug for yourselves. What was she going to do? Spend her life scrubbing floors like you? Maybe sell herself to men looking for cheap pleasure?"

"You should've warned me. I would've—"

"What? *Stolen* the balance of your debt?" The arch of her brow suggests that she knows all my secrets. "Even you couldn't manage that, Abriella. Frankly, you're lucky I've looked the other way all these years. I could have turned you in for your illegal deeds."

"But you didn't. You took the money, no matter how I got it. You've made *thousands* every month off that unfair contract, and you sold her anyway." My body burns with anger, my blood boiling with rage that threatens to spill over.

"Come now. You're being ridiculous. They'll ply her with faerie wine and it will all seem like a dream."

I feel like I'm vibrating. I want to tear off her jewelry and turn it to dust with my bare hands. I want to rage and scream until I wake up and learn this was all a terrible nightmare.

"Jasalyn's sacrifice released you from your debt today—be glad."

"Where?" I demand. "Where did they take her?" I'll find her. I'll search their entire godsforsaken realm to get my sister back.

"Maybe she'll fall in love with a faerie lord," she says, ignoring my question. "Maybe she'll live happily ever after, like in those stories your mother always liked to tell." Disgust drips from every one of her words. I don't want any part of me to be like Madame Vivias. But this we share — her disgust, her judgment. I hate my mother for abandoning us, for leaving us with her brother just so she could be closer to her faerie lover. For sentencing us to a life that led to this.

"If Jas dies, I hope her death haunts your every waking moment," I whisper. "If she's hurt, I pray that fortune cuts you twice as deep."

"Now you sound like one of *them*, throwing curses around on good people."

"Good people don't sell girls to the fae."

She cackles. "Have you seen the world we live in, Abriella? Have you seen the realities I've saved you from by keeping you under this roof? Maybe your sister is the lucky one. Maybe you should be wishing you could've gone in her place." She waves toward the door. "Now, out. Go enjoy your freedom. But unless you want to sign a rental contract, you'll need to find a new place to sleep, effective immediately."

I wouldn't stay here another night if she paid me, but I don't bother responding. I pull her office door shut and rush down the stairs to the cellar.

Our bedroom looks just as it always does. Jas's sewing kit sits open against the wall. She must have been working when Bakken took her. The muslin mockup of my dress is folded on the foot of the bed, and I clutch it to my chest, ignoring the stinging pinch of the pins poking me from the fabric.

I crawl on the bed and curl onto my side. I'm too tired to cry, too stunned, but my eyes burn. *She's really gone.*

The door clicks, hinges creaking as it swings open, then whooshes shut again. I feel his presence without having to look. The mattress shifts as Sebastian sinks onto the bed, lying on his side to face me. He takes my chin in his hand, tipping my face up so I meet his eyes. "Hey . . ." He wipes my tears away with his thumb. "It's true, then?"

I can only stare at him — at those eyes like the stormy sea, at the wrinkle between his brows that reveals more of his worry and fear than his words likely will.

"Brie?"

"It's true." I swallow, trying to keep my voice steady. "Madame V sold her."

He squeezes his eyes shut and mutters a curse. "Another year," he whispers, his jaw hardening. "Another year, and I would've been able to free you myself."

"This isn't on you, Bash. You can't blame yourself for what Madame V did."

He blows out a long breath and opens his eyes, pulling one of my hands off the muslin to grip between both of his. "Please promise me you won't go searching for her. I can't bear to think what might happen to you if you went to Faerie."

"What about what's happening to Jas there now?"

"Just give me a chance. Let me try to figure this out."

Sebastian leaves tomorrow for the next part of his apprentice-ship. I don't know what he thinks he can do for her, but I nod. I won't deny his help, even if I don't believe he can save her.

He releases my hand and looks around the room I've shared with my baby sister for the past nine years. "Where will you go?" he asks.

I don't have much in the way of possessions. I could pack up everything and be out of here by sunset. "My friend Nik owes me a favor. I'll stay with her." *Until I can come up with a plan to get Jas back.*

Nik will feel awful about what Madame V did, maybe even blame herself, but I know in my gut that if we hadn't missed today's payment, we would have missed another in the future. The money I gave Nik couldn't have saved Jas when a soulless witch held her life in her hands.

"I am so sorry," he says, his eyes searching my face.

"Me too."

"I promised Mage Trifen I'd help with his next client. Will you be okay if I go? I'll come find you later."

I nod, and another tear escapes. Sebastian watches it roll down my cheek before following its path with his thumb. The touch is so gentle it makes me want to wrap my arms around his waist and curl into him, to bury my face in his chest and pretend none of this is happening.

Instead, I say goodbye, happy to see him go, if only so I can make a plan.

Madame Vivias's house goblin lives under the stairs by the kitchen. I knock softly with one hand and pull the tie from my hair with the other.

Goblins love human hair, teeth, and nails — collect them the way the Seelie queen is rumored to collect jewels. If I'm going to get any information out of Bakken, it'll be by using my hair. I can only hope that denying him all these years has made him want it that much more.

He yanks the door open on my second knock, and the faint odor of rotting fruit wafts from his tiny room. Bakken is a typical house goblin — short and barrel-bellied, with spindly limbs and thin lips that can't quite close around his pointed teeth. His bulging eyes widen greedily when he spots my hair. I rarely leave it down, and never around goblins. "Good day, Fire Girl. How may I help you?"

I ignore the nickname he's used for me since the day we moved in with Uncle Devlin and I met Bakken for the first time. He took my hand in both of his and leered at the scar on my wrist — the only evidence left of the burns that should have killed me. That day, I was shocked that he knew about the fire and my unlikely survival, when I knew nothing about him. I didn't know then that goblins deal in stories — in histories, secrets, and information. They make it their business to know. "Take me to my sister."

He blinks several times, as if trying to process my request, before shaking his head. "It doesn't work like that."

"Cassia said you're the one who took her to the traders' market. I need you to tell me who bought her — how to save her." My heart is racing too fast, and it's all I can do not to look over my shoulder to make sure that Madame V is still in her office. She wouldn't want me talking to Bakken and would probably find a way to make me pay for the privilege — or to deny me entirely out of spite. If I don't talk to him now, I may never have another chance. "Please."

"There is a price." Licking his lips with a pointed tongue, he closes the distance between us. He glances down the hall in each direction before pulling me into his tiny room and closing the door behind me. When it clicks shut, he drags one of those long, pointed nails through my hair, from my ear all the way down to my shoulder. Revulsion crawls over my skin, but I don't let myself back away. He releases a gleeful giggle. "Such a fascinating red. As if your hair took on the color of the fire that day."

"Take me to whoever bought Jasalyn."

He frowns. "But why?"

"I want to . . . I'll buy her back." I'll have to raid Gorst's vaults again to have any chance of finding enough money. Maybe even clear them out this time. But it'll be worth it.

"Not everything is about money, mortal." Bakken narrows his eyes and cocks his head to the side. "In this world of yours, I'd think you'd be glad to have one less mouth to feed, but you look . . . heartbroken? Curious."

I clench my fists at my sides. Goblins are known for their ability to move between the realms and for collecting information. They're *not* known for their compassion. *"Where?"*

"Let it go, Fire Girl. You don't want the fate that awaits you in Faerie."

"I *want* my sister back. Tell me where you took her. Please."

41

"What will you give me for that information?"

The word *anything* sits on the tip of my tongue like a piece of sour fruit. I want to spit it out, but goblins are very literal. I know better than to offer more than I can give. "A lock of my hair."

"Ah, but I'd prefer to have *all* of your hair." He reaches out, but drops his hand before touching me. "It would make such a beautiful scarf. What could I make with a mere lock?"

"What could you make with *nothing?*"

He grins, but I see the greed in his eyes, the glint of desperation. "Show me how much."

I take some between my fingers and hold it out for his inspection. "From here," I say, pointing to a spot on the lock just beneath my eye, "to the end." Jas used to wear her hair with shorter pieces that framed her face. I always loved the way it drew attention to her eyes. But I wouldn't dare let Bakken know I won't miss what I'm offering; he'd only demand more.

"Yes, that'll do." Before I can draw another breath, he has a knife in his hand, and he takes my hair with one slice of his blade.

I bite back my gasp at his speed. "Tell me."

"I brought her to the king's emissary in the traders' market who was to escort her to the king. Madame Vivias couldn't refuse the sum the traders offered."

The king? My blood turns to ice in my veins, and I freeze all the way to my bones. "What king?"

"The emissary took her to His Highness, King Mordeus," he says, "who paid a great deal to purchase your sister's life."

No. It can't be. Buying or stealing my sister back from some random faerie is one thing, but getting her back from a fae king

42

—from Mordeus, the Unseelie ruler, the shadow king himself? Where mortals consider the Seelie to be the "good" fae, the Unseelie kingdom is most dangerous and most lethal to humans. Their king has a reputation for finding pleasure in torturing creatures of all kinds. Humans who go to that kingdom rarely come back. If they do, they return as catatonic husks of themselves. On the other hand, this is the king who has countless human slaves. Perhaps he wouldn't even notice if she went missing. "One human girl's as good as the next. Why didn't the king buy one of those girls who *wants* to go to Faerie?"

"Because he wants Jasalyn Kincaid, sister of the Fire Girl, daughter of the beautiful mortal who—"

"I know who my sister is," I snap. This has to be a nightmare. It doesn't make sense. "Why does he want her? Why Jasalyn?"

"It's not mine to question the king. Perhaps he wants to make her his queen." His sigh might pass for dreamy if his expression weren't so . . . *hungry.* "Maybe he just loves her beautiful chestnut hair."

"If he doesn't want money, what does he want? What kind of payment can I offer?"

He taps one long, dirty fingernail against his front teeth. "King Mordeus cares for nothing more than securing his seat on the throne."

I shake my head. "He's the *king.* Why would he need to secure anything?"

"But some say he isn't, not truly. Mordeus stole the throne from his brother many years ago and waits for the day when his nephew—Prince Finnian, son of King Oberon and rightful heir to the Throne of Shadows — emerges from exile to claim his crown. His subjects wait too. Some have pledged loyalty to the king and will fight to keep him in power. Others believe that the Unseelie Court is dying because of Mordeus's trickery and that it won't recover until the rightful heir is on the throne with Oberon's crown."

I normally wouldn't care at all about Faerie politics, but I make myself tuck this information away in case it proves useful later. "What does this have to do with getting Jas back?"

His lips peel back from his yellowed, pointy teeth in a smile. "Do not underestimate King Mordeus. He does nothing by accident. Every choice he makes is about power — *his* power."

I can't wrap my head around it. Jasalyn's never had dealings with the fae — at least none that I know of. What kind of power could the king get by enslaving her? Could this have something to do with our mother? But that doesn't make sense. If, for some reason, the king requested her for our mother, wouldn't she want both her daughters, not just her youngest? And why would she suddenly care about us after nine years? "Take me to my sister. Please."

Bakken focuses on the lock of my cut hair in his fingers and strokes it lovingly. "The Unseelie kingdom is a dangerous place for a human girl, even for a Fire Girl. You're better off forgetting about your sister and enjoying your newfound freedom."

"That's not an option."

He tucks my hair into a pocket. "I cannot take you, but for another lock, I can *tell* you."

I don't even think before offering him a nearly identical lock from the opposite side.

His eyes dance as he slices it off. "At midnight, the river portal will open for the celebration of the Seelie prince's birth. There you can enter the Seelie Court and find the queen's secret portal to the Court of the Moon. It opens only once each day, when the clock strikes midnight."

This makes me pause. "Why would the Seelie queen have a portal to the Unseelie Court? I thought they were sworn enemies."

Bakken's stroking his new lock of hair and barely paying any attention to me. He answers absently, the way one hums a tune they've heard a thousand times. "Once, the golden queen was but a princess. She loved Oberon, the shadow king, and sacrificed dearly for a way to see him in secret. Her kingdom had been at war with the Court of the Moon for centuries, and her parents would have never allowed her to visit."

I frown. That's the tale my mother used to tell us at bedtime — the golden princess and the shadow king. "I thought that story was just legend. It's true?"

"Where do you think legends begin, if not from truth?"

Suddenly I wish I could remember more of Mother's stories, but it's been so long and I've recalled them with so much resentment for years. I shake my head, focusing on the issue at hand. "Where's the portal?"

"You'll find it in her childhood wardrobe — a massive armoire marked with wings on each door. She's never been able to bring herself to destroy it."

I swallow hard. Go to the Seelie Court, find the queen's secret portal to enter the most dangerous place in Faerie, find my sister, and rescue her from a power-hungry king. *Child's play.*

Bakken's eyes flick to mine, and he frowns. He reaches into his pocket and pulls out a bracelet made of fine silver threads. He offers it to me with an open hand. "Take it. No one but you will be able to see it or feel it on your wrist."

I've heard of goblin bracelets, but I've never seen one. The silver threads are so fine they're nearly invisible, but they glitter in the candlelight.

"Each thread represents a story of Faerie. Stories are power, Fire Girl. If you need me, simply break a thread, and I'll appear."

"If I break one of these" — I finger the threads gently before meeting his gaze — "you'll help me?"

He nods. "Yes. Though I cannot save you from mortal peril, so don't bother with it if you're to become some beast's next meal. But with information, for travel within the realm, I can help."

"At what cost?"

His grin is more devious than comforting. "But a lock of hair. Or teeth if you'd prefer."

My hand shakes as I take it from him. "What if I break a thread by accident?"

"Goblin threads don't break accidentally. There must be intent."

I slide the bracelet over my hand, and it magically tightens around my wrist. "Thank you, Bakken." I reach for the door and step into the hall.

"Fire Girl!" Bakken says, stopping me. "Remember, the shadow king is clever. He'll play you against your fate for his own benefit."

Play me against my fate? What does that even mean? *Faerie riddles.* "I don't believe in fate, Bakken. All I care about is my sister."

"Ah yes, and the king knows that."

CHAPTER FOUR

"You need to tell Sebastian your plan," Nik says, leaning against the side of Mage Trifen's house.

"Is that why you brought me here?"

I had moved out of Madame V's this morning and gone straight to Nik, who patiently listened to my panicked story and half-baked plan before insisting that I follow her to Mage Trifen's for a sleeping tonic. The portal doesn't open until midnight, she reasoned, and I wouldn't be any good if I didn't get some rest before then.

Now the sun inches toward the horizon, and it feels as if time is moving both too fast and too slow. If it were up to me, I would already be searching Faerie for my sister, but I'm scared I won't be strong enough or smart enough once I get there. I'm so scared I'll fail.

"I brought you for the tonic," she says, patting her purse, "but I do think you should tell him. Maybe he could go with you."

I shake my head. "He'll get in the way trying to protect me. And anyway, he leaves for the next portion of his apprenticeship tomorrow. I won't ruin that for him."

Frowning, she straightens. "I don't like you doing this alone. I don't like that you're doing this at all."

"Would you go if you were in my shoes? If it were Fawn who'd been sold to the Unseelie king?"

Her dark eyes glitter with tears, and she swallows. "In a heartbeat."

"Then you know I have no choice."

"I imagine you've done many things because you had no choice," she says softly. She toys with a dark curl and seems to consider this before adding, "I need to ask you something."

"Okay."

She looks down the alley in each direction, and even though we're the only ones out here, she lowers her voice when she speaks. "That money you gave me for Fawn's contract . . . did you steal it from Gorst?"

My stomach plummets. How would she know that? "Do I look that stupid?"

She narrows her eyes at me. "Brie."

I rub the back of my neck, where all my tension from the last twenty-four hours seems to have coiled into one big knot. "Wouldn't it be better if you didn't know where I got it?" I can't believe that was only last night. So much has happened since then — my whole world tipped on its axis.

She purses her lips. "*Someone* broke into Gorst's house, got past his wards, and raided his vault. He's pissed."

"I imagine so."

"Whoever it was left blood behind," she whispers. "And it's

only a matter of time until his mage finds the match — finds the thief."

Shit. I've been so busy dealing with everything else that I'd forgotten about the blood. "Gorst is the least of my worries."

"Yeah? Well, you'd better hope the magic works slowly, or you may never get the chance to enter that portal."

"Brie?" Sebastian calls, coming down the alley from the courtyard.

"We'll talk later," Nik says, giving me a sad smile and squeezing my wrist before backing away. "I'll see you at home. Until then, watch your back."

"Thanks, Nik." With a deep breath, I turn to face Sebastian. My heart squeezes at the sight of him. He's wearing a white tunic with dark leather pants that are fitted to his powerful thighs, and his white hair glows faintly golden in the sunlight.

"Master Trifen said you were looking for me."

I swallow the knot of emotion in my throat. I want to tell him my plan and warn him that we may never see each other again. I hate deceiving him, but I don't see a better alternative. "I wanted to see you before you go."

Sebastian steps closer and takes my hands in each of his, squeezing. "I wouldn't have left without saying goodbye."

"I know." I scan his face, memorizing every inch. His eyes are more blue than green in the setting sun. *I may never see those eyes again.*

He reaches into his pocket and draws out a necklace with a crystal pendant. "I made you something."

"Bash . . ." The chain is a simple, finely woven silver, but the crystal is flawless. "It's . . . the most beautiful thing I've ever seen."

"Then it suits you." His voice is hoarse, and the heartbreaking tenderness in his eyes grates against my conscience. "It's an amulet of protection. If I can't be here to protect you myself, then . . ." He flinches, as if the thought causes him physical pain, then gently guides the necklace over my head. "Promise me you'll always wear it."

"I promise." It falls between my breasts and glitters in the sunlight. I clutch it in my fist. "When do you leave?"

"First thing in the morning." His gaze goes to the sky, as if checking to make sure he hasn't run out of time.

"Thank you for being such a good friend. I don't know if I would've made it through the last two years without you."

"Don't do that." He shakes his head. "Don't act like you won't see me again."

I drop my gaze to my feet, staring at my battered black boots instead of letting him look into my eyes, where I fear the truth is written.

He tilts my face up to his. "There's so much I still need to tell you."

"Like what?"

He scans my face again and again. "About my past . . . about me."

I open my mouth and snap it shut again. Sebastian's never talked about his family. He never wanted to share anything about his life before he moved to Fairscape, and I never pushed.

"I'll do everything in my power to see you again," he says softly. "But I'm not ready to leave you yet." His hands are big and warm. I've secretly imagined him touching me like this so many times, but nothing I dreamed up could compare with the sensation of his callused fingers sliding behind my neck and into my hair as his gaze drops to my mouth. "Is there anything you need to tell me? Anything I should know before I leave tomorrow?"

Does he mean about my feelings for him? Or does he suspect that I'll be headed to a different realm at midnight, risking everything on the unlikely chance that I can save my sister? "Sebastian, you're my best fr —"

Before I can finish the word, he lowers his head. Soft lips find mine, and I gasp against him. Electricity buzzes through me, waking me up, zapping between us, making this kiss feel like it could light all of Fairscape, all of Elora.

When his tongue sweeps across my lips and then inside my mouth, I kiss him back with everything I have. Everything I am. I can feel his worry in his kiss, and I wonder if he can feel my fear. I have to save my sister, but I don't want to die. I don't want to lose him either.

My emotions are a muddled mess, somehow heightened by his kiss. When he pulls away, I'm lightheaded, the rug pulled out from under me. I've been falling for Sebastian for two years, and all this time I believed my feelings were unrequited. And now, when I may never see him again, I learn that they're not. Fate is toying with me.

"Wait for me," he whispers.

I won't. I can't. And I feel a stab of guilt at how good his words feel anyway. I can't let my feelings for Sebastian blur my focus. All that matters is getting to Jas.

———✦———

"Brie." A whisper in my ear as the mare runs faster and faster, carrying Mom and me toward the beach. "Brie, they're coming."

My heart races, and my hair flies in wild wisps around my face. Mom's wedding band bites into my little finger as she grips the reins.

"Brie." The breeze turns hot, and smoke fills the air, stinging my throat. "Abriella, wake up!"

My eyes burn as I crawl across the floor on my hands and knees. The acrid smoke snakes its way into my lungs, and fire dances all around me. Heat licks my skin. Flames dart out and sear my bare legs. Jasalyn smiles up at me, blinking through the smoke. I sweep her off the bed, but she's too heavy for my skinny arms to hold, and I fall back under her weight. I grip her tighter, and she disintegrates into a pile of ash.

"Brie!" Someone shakes me *hard*.

I force my eyes open. Force air into my lungs.

The room is dark and cool. There's no fire, save for a single flame flickering atop a candle on the bedside table. Nik crouches beside me on the floor, still in the skintight dress she wore to meet her client.

"What is it?" Sleep threatens to drag me under again, thanks to the tonic Nik gave me after dinner.

"Gorst is here for you."

I press my hand to my mouth and spring to my feet. Fawn is curled on her side in the bed, her stuffed rabbit clutched to her chest. My stomach cramps at the thought of Gorst tearing this little girl's home apart because of me.

The booming knock on the door seems to shake the whole apartment, and I spin to Nik with wide eyes. "Stall for me. I'll sneak out the window."

She nods, one step ahead of me. "I put one of my dresses in your bag." She looks toward the door when the knock sounds again. "It's nothing as fine as what your sister could make, but it'll help you blend in with all the girls going to the ball."

"Thank you." I hug her tightly. "I owe you."

"If you don't open this door, we'll knock it down!" a deep voice calls.

"I'm coming!" Nik shouts. Her voice doesn't betray any of the fear on her face. Then, to me, "The portals should open in less than an hour. Be safe and come back to us, you hear? Fawn needs her aunt Brie."

My eyes burn, so I just nod and sling my bag over my shoulder.

Nik stomps toward the door. The fear sloughs off her with each step, replaced with bravado. "Who do you think you are, pounding on my door in the middle of the night?"

I close the bedroom door as quietly as possible, then pull the pillows and blankets from my mat and place them neatly on the bed.

"We've been told that Abriella Kincaid is staying here," the deep voice says.

"Well, you've been told wrong. It's just me and my daughter."

After kicking the mat under the bed, I blow out the candle. The blanket of darkness is a reassuring balm to my senses.

"If you don't mind, ma'am, we'd like to see for ourselves."

Nik huffs. "I *do* mind. My daughter is sleeping."

I pull myself out the window and shut it behind me just as light pours into the bedroom from the main part of her unit. I run down the alley, then cut across to another, zigzagging in a path they'd never suspect. The night is bright under the full moon, and I avoid the main streets, sticking to the darker, narrower paths between buildings to remain unseen, pressing myself against walls and between trash barrels when need be. I run and run and run, sweating, lungs burning. I don't stop until I'm safely ensconced in the woods at the edge of town.

There's already a line of young women tittering excitedly in the flood of moonlight at the river's edge. Some are dressed in elaborate ball gowns, others in simple cotton frocks that are likely the nicest thing they own. They're all waiting for the portal to open, staring at the riverbank as if it's their own personal path to salvation. *Fools.*

Avoiding the crowds and the moonlight, I head to the dense grove of trees beyond. Blindly, I strip off my clothes, peeling my shirt and pants from my sweat-drenched limbs before searching the satchel for the dress Nik packed. The fabric is thin and silky, and when I pull it over my head, it slides like cool water over my skin.

I clutch the crystal at my neck. I don't know how well amulets of protection work, but I escaped Gorst's men tonight. If this necklace can get me to Faerie safely, I may never take it off.

I huddle against a tree, hidden by the darkness, and watch the moon climb higher in the sky until, finally, gasps and delighted laughter drift toward me.

"It's opened."

"The portal has opened!"

"The golden queen welcomes us!"

"Prince Ronan awaits!"

I tuck my amulet into my dress and slowly emerge from the shadows, stepping into the line of women. We wait our turn to walk through the portal. I clutch my hands to resist the urge to smooth my hair and wipe the sweat off my brow. If I keep my head down, maybe they won't notice that I'm not dressed as finely as they are.

I'm not like these women. I've never wanted to be a faerie princess, never dreamed of the day I could dance with the immortals at one of their legendary balls. But tonight I recognize my luck. Once I'm on the other side of the portal, Gorst's men can't touch me.

With that thought, I lift my head to see the woman in front of me step off the bank and into the sheer five-foot drop to the river — only to vanish into thin air.

"Go on now," the woman behind me says. "It's your turn. Don't hold up the line."

"I just . . . jump?" I ask.

She laughs. "No, silly. If you jump, you'll fall right into the river. You have to walk to the portal above the water. You must believe it's there, or it won't work."

I gape at the rushing river beyond the bank. Fear climbs on my back and weighs me down.

56

"Go on," she says. "What's the worst that can happen?"

"I fall into the water, get pulled under, and have the rapids beat my body against the rocks until I drown?"

She laughs as if I just said something hilarious. "Go on now."

"Right. Just *believe*." So simple.

"Have any of you ladies seen a redheaded young woman with a scar on her wrist?" someone asks farther down the line. "She's a thief, and we have a cash reward for the first person who helps us find her."

The woman behind me drops her gaze to my wrist.

I press my palm to my amulet, and I don't just walk over the riverbank. I run.

CHAPTER FIVE

My back teeth clang together as I slam onto my knees. Pain radiates up my legs, and when I open my eyes, a clear moonlit sky shines above me. I scramble to my feet and turn back to the river, but it's gone. The forest beyond is also gone. The only trees are far in the distance. All around me, streams of women appear out of thin air, arriving from portals all over Elora.

This is it. This is Faerie. I made it.

An undeniable energy buzzes along my skin. As if the air is different here, as if it's charged — an electric spiderweb waiting to trap humans like flies.

I scan the faces around me, looking for any sign of the woman who looked eager to turn me in for the reward. I can't find her in the crowd — not that she could do much on this side of the portal. Instead, I see young women rushing happily toward a golden footbridge that leads to a mammoth castle. Golden spires line the horizon, poking up into the night sky. The stone walls shimmer in the starlight. Mother described it just like this in our bedtime stories — castle walls of crushed quartz, floors of marble, the night sky an endless blanket of shimmering stars.

When we were younger, Jas and I used to dream of this place. It was like a game. We'd imagine running away to Faerie through the solstice portal and finding Mother. We'd describe how excited she'd be to see us and list the countless reasons that had kept her from returning. As the years passed and Mother never visited, when she never returned to free us from our contract, the game held less and less appeal for me. I didn't want to think of my mother, or the reasons she'd failed us. I didn't want to talk about her anymore, and imagining a reunion made my stomach hurt.

But now that I'm here, I can't help but wonder if she is too, if she survived this dangerous land all these years, if she's . . . happy.

I'm at least a hundred yards from the footbridge and castle gates, but even this far back, swarms of women line up eagerly. I expected the crowd to be overwhelming, but I never could have imagined this. Women push past one another to take their place in line. Their desperation makes me equal parts sad and on my guard.

"Oh, girl," the woman behind me says. "You won't get in like that."

I stiffen as I turn to her. "What do you mean I won't get in?"

She frowns, looking me over, then pulls a handkerchief from her purse. I don't know how I look, but *she* is radiant — a canary yellow dress with a fitted bodice and full skirt, her dark hair falling in perfect bouncing curls over her shoulders.

I look down at myself for the first time since Nik woke me. The silk dress she gave me is a bright red that nearly matches my hair. It sags at my chest and clings to the sharp angles of my hips before flaring out above my knees. The thin fabric exposes every underfed angle of my body, from my jutting hipbones to my sunken stomach. On Nik, its simplicity is probably sultry and seductive. On me, it looks a bit pathetic and ragged. Normally I don't have time to worry about things as superficial as appearance, but next to this glowing woman I feel self-conscious.

"Don't worry. I'll help," she says, offering the handkerchief to me. "Let's get you cleaned up."

My arms are streaked and smudged with dirt. When I pressed into the shadows in the alley, I was thinking of hiding, of surviving, not of cleanliness. "Thank you." I accept the soft fabric and gently wipe the dirt from my skin. "I guess I was in such a rush to get here, I didn't even realize." Beneath the filth, pink scratches — from running through the brush in the woods — crisscross up and down my arms. I'm not exactly a picture of beauty. "What do you mean they won't let me in? Don't they let everyone in?"

She digs into her purse again and pulls out a small bottle of ointment. "Even as massive as the queen's castle is, it isn't large enough to hold all the women who will show up for a chance at the prince's hand." She takes the handkerchief back and squeezes a bit of the opaque ointment onto it. She dabs it on a particularly ugly abrasion on my shoulder, and I watch the skin heal and return to a healthy ivory hue.

"I'm so sorry, but I can't pay you for this."

With a smile, she continues the application down my arm. "I won't need your money once I'm Prince Ronan's bride." She winks at me like it's a joke and only I am privy to the punch line. "My name's Pretha."

60

I swallow, still not sure what I did to deserve this kindness. "Abriella."

"That's a beautiful name." She moves to my other arm.

"Thanks." I scan the long line ahead of us. "How do they decide who gets in?"

"The majority of women will be sent home before they ever set foot in the castle. The guards at the door make the first cut on appearance alone." She must see the disgust on my face, because she says, "I know. Shallow, right? But they're looking for a healthy, beautiful human bride for their prince."

The line moves slowly, and though I'm itching to get inside the castle and start searching, I'm grateful for the extra time. I never considered that I might not get past the doors.

"There." She finishes the last scrape on my wrist. "And now . . . may I work on your face?" She pulls out a small mirror and turns it so I can see myself.

My face is no better than my arms were, but worse than the dirt and scrapes are the circles under my eyes and the hollows of my cheeks. *Healthy* isn't the word that comes to mind when I look at my reflection.

Pretha dabs at my face with a clean cloth, then draws cosmetics from the endless depths of her purse. She lines my eyes with kohl, coats my lashes, brightens my cheeks with rouge, and paints my lips a deep red. When I look into the mirror again, my only familiar feature is my curly red hair. "You're quite an artist," I say, dabbing at my skin where the bags beneath my eyes used to be. "Are you sure you didn't use magic on me?"

She laughs. "There's nothing wrong with a little magic to enhance your natural beauty."

I should expect the hairbrush that appears in her hand, but when she starts to work on my hair, I burst into laughter. "If that brush can tame my curls, you might qualify to join Elora's Seven."

"I wouldn't dare mute your wild beauty. It's what will draw the prince's eye to you." She gathers my curls into a crystal barrette on top of my head and arranges them carefully around my face.

I try to smile like a girl who's anxious to have a faerie prince's attention. The truth is, once I'm finally inside, I want the opposite.

When she's done fussing with my hair, she steps back and cocks her head to the side. "Now the dress?"

The line is slowly creeping forward, and the moon is making its way across the sky. At this rate we'll be in line until the sun rises. Maybe even after. "I suppose you have a needle and thread in those pockets, and you'll be sewing this into something fancier?"

"Pssh." She waves a hand. "I'm no seamstress."

The word is a punch to the gut, a reminder that makes my smile fall away. "Me neither."

She frowns, not missing the change in my mood. "Did I say something?"

"No, it's nothing. My sister was . . . *is* a seamstress. That's all."

Her eyes soften. "I'm so sorry. What happened to her?"

"She's been sold into slavery."

Something flashes in her eyes, and for a second I think she might roar in rage on my behalf, but then she blinks and it's gone. "And is that why you're here?"

I sigh. I need a friend, but I can't risk telling this stranger my plans. "I imagine every girl in this line has dreams of what she could accomplish with the power and privilege of a faerie princess."

"Hmm." She opens her palm and shows me a fistful of pins. "May I?"

"I thought you said you weren't a seamstress." I watch as she places the pins side by side around my waist. I turn slowly, allowing her to continue behind my back.

"I'm not, but the woman who enchanted these pins is." She slips a final pin in place, closing the circle, then snaps her fingers.

Just like that, the dress isn't the one I slipped into in the forest. This is a ball gown, lovelier than anything I've ever worn, maybe even lovelier than anything Jas ever created. The full skirt sweeps the grass as I walk. Rosebuds are sewn into it along the hem and up one side, as if the skirt itself were some sort of magical trellis. The fitted bodice has boning that makes my nonexistent chest swell above the sweetheart neckline. It just barely covers my amulet.

I'm busy admiring my new gown, so it's not until Pretha taps me on the shoulder that I realize we've crossed the bridge. We've finally made it to the castle gates.

I don't know what I expected to see, but there's a party on the lush green lawn. Creatures of all kinds meander around the grounds. Faeries that look like butterflies with translucent wings and tiny, humanoid bodies flit through the crowd, their wings humming like a flute on the breeze. Red-skinned fire fae with glowing eyes dance around a bonfire, spinning human partners between each other so fast my eyes can hardly track their movements. The elven fae nobility meander throughout the crowd, and were it not for their pointed ears and ethereal grace, they could almost blend in with the humans — not that they'd want to.

"Getting closer." Pretha squeezes my hand, and I feel an unexpected rush of affection.

"Why are you being so nice to me?"

"Maybe I need a friend too."

How does she know *I* need a friend? No one has ever thought that about me. If anything, I come across as cold and standoffish. A loner with no desire to change her stripes. "Well . . . thank you. For everything." I bite the inside of my lip as I study my dress again. It's beautiful, and with any luck it'll help me get inside, but what about after that? I can't sneak through dark hallways in this skirt.

"You don't like it," she says. She's not defensive or pouting, just observing, almost curious.

"I'm not used to clothes that restrict my movement. I mean, I've been taught all my life to be on my guard in Faerie, and if I need to run or something . . ."

She lifts her chin. "A smart girl."

I cringe. "Or an ungrateful wretch?"

"The pins are still at the top of the skirt. Remove a single pin, and the spell is undone. The dress will take on its original form."

I graze the top of my skirt with my fingertips until I feel one of the pins. "Perfect. Thank you."

We make idle conversation for hours as the line inches closer and closer to the castle doors. The whole time, I take in as much detail as I can about my surroundings, ignoring my aching feet and growling stomach to study the fae in the yard and the sentries on patrol around the perimeter.

There's no doubt in my mind that the easiest way into this castle is through the front doors, but my chances are looking more and more slim by the time we reach them. The sun is high in the sky, and I've watched dozens of women being sent away through the portal beside the sentries and very few being allowed entry into the castle.

"Good luck," Pretha whispers as I step forward.

The male by the door has pointed ears and bright blue eyes. He looks me over, shrugs, and waves me inside. I turn back to Pretha. "How will I pay you back for all this?"

She grins. "Oh, I'll think of something before we meet again."

As I step inside, another elven faerie takes me by the arm and leads me down a sparkling hallway. I'm dazzled by the crystal chandeliers overhead and the way the light bounces off the shining floors.

I risk a glance over my shoulder to see if my new friend is following, but instead I see an unfamiliar face trailing several paces behind. Has Pretha been sent home? Guilt gnaws at me. After all she did to help me, it's unfair that I was allowed in and she wasn't. I should have let her go first — maybe persuaded the guards if they told her to leave through the portal.

"Straight ahead. Enjoy the celebration," my escort says curtly. Before I can reply, he releases me and heads back the way we came.

I take several steps forward and gasp as I step into a ballroom as big as a square block in Fairscape. Late-morning light floods in from two-story floor-to-ceiling windows, and humans and faeries alike mill all around the shining marble floors. I slowly make my way into the room, merging with the crowd as I study the space.

"Why did she have to send Jasalyn away before she could finish my dress?" a familiar voice whines from somewhere behind me. *Cassia.*

My heart stumbles into a gallop. *No. Please no.*

"At least you had something appropriate," Stella says. "I had to bribe one of the girls at the seamstress for this, and they nearly sent me away without anything."

Of course Cassia and Stella came to the ball. That was probably why they insisted that Jas make them new dresses. They're just the kind of idiots who'd believe they could become faerie princesses.

I keep my head bowed and weave my way through the crowd and away from them. I don't want to consider what will happen if they spot me. They'd do everything in their power to get me thrown out of here, and they'd laugh about it if they knew I was trying to save Jas.

In my rush to get across the ballroom, I bump into a broad male figure. "So sorry. Excuse me." I don't look up, but keep walking forward.

"Are you okay?" His voice is deep and melodic. Something tugs in me at the sound, and I can't resist turning back to him.

My breath catches at the sight of a tall male with light brown skin. This is no simple faerie. He's *stunning*. His dark hair hangs to his angular jawline in a shaggy mop of curls. His silver eyes glow like moonlight and are framed by thick, dark lashes. If he were a human, I'd guess him to be in his early twenties, but there's something about his posture and the hard lines of his face that make him seem much, much older. His full, lush mouth tilts in a frown as he studies me, then offers a hand. "A dance, milady?"

"What? No." I have to stay focused. I don't need this gorgeous fae male distracting me.

His eyes widen, as if he's never been rejected before. With those looks, I wouldn't be surprised. "Then perhaps a walk in the gardens?"

"Back off. I'm not interested in —"

The sound of my cousins' laughter approaches, and I peek over my shoulder to see them coming closer.

"Fine. Let's dance," I blurt, shoving my hand into his.

His lips twitch, but he accepts my hand and leads me onto the dance floor. "It would be my pleasure."

From a stage at the front of the room a full orchestra plays a heart-rending melody. The song isn't one I've ever heard, but it makes my limbs ache to match the rhythm, to move with the beat.

The male I'm dancing with holds my gaze as he leads me across the floor. Chandeliers glitter above us, orbs of light floating on a soft breeze. Something about the dance — about the way we sway together — reminds me of how free I feel when I move through the dark. It's relaxing and intoxicating all at once. It's a high I don't want to let go. And when he studies my face and whispers, "So beautiful," I can't remember a single worry.

The song changes, and another faerie cuts in, taking my hand before the silver-eyed male can lead me off the floor.

Could it hurt? To indulge in another dance before I risk

everything in my search for my sister? Could it hurt to give myself just a few moments to imagine a life where every day wasn't a struggle, where I could live like these faeries — dancing and drinking wine, laughing over petty nonsense?

My body and the song become one, and as the orchestra picks up the beat — as the bows move faster over the strings and the flutist's fingers race over the keys — my muscles anticipate every note and rhythm. I'm passed from one partner to the next, and I feel as graceful as the fae. I dance and dance and dance until I can hardly breathe, until my lungs burn and my feet ache.

The faces of my partners are a blur. I don't care who or what they are as I'm lifted away from my problems and out of my wretched life by this magical movement and song.

Smiling and feeling lighter than I have in months, my hips swish to the beat, my shoulders rolling languidly. Before I know it, I'm in the center of the floor, dancing and letting faerie after faerie lead me. I lift my arms over my head and wave them in the air to the beat. The tremendous weight of all my responsibilities lifts from my shoulders. I'm free for the first time in years. Maybe for the first time ever. This dance *is* freedom.

Someone shoves a glass of wine in my hand, and I contemplate the liquid while I continue to move. I feel so good, and I know the wine will make me feel even better. All I have to do is *drink.*

Something nudges the back of my mind. Something about this wine. Something I'm supposed to remember. But . . . I lift it to my lips. I want more dancing, more joy, more delicious *freedom.* The goblet is yanked away before it can touch my lips, and then I'm wrapped in strong arms and pulled off the dance floor.

I fight against him, trying to return to where I belong — to the music, the beat, the comforting sway of hips and blur of motion, the quickening arpeggio.

"Enough," he whispers in my ear.

"No." The word is a plea.

He drags me away from the dancers and the lovely melody and into a quiet hallway outside the ballroom. At the end of the corridor, a window reveals the sun sinking into the horizon, casting the land in the yellow-orange glow of twilight.

The music loosens its grip on my mind, and I swallow hard as my senses return. Drop by drop, like water filling a cup, my thoughts fall back into order.

Jas. I need to save Jas.

I'm trapped in a faerie's hold. My arms are pinned to my sides. He's too strong. Too big. I can't fight him.

"You need to catch your breath," he says against my ear.

I yank out of the male's arms and spin on him. It's the silver-eyed faerie I first danced with. "Is that . . ." I force myself to draw in a deep breath and stare dumbfounded at the window at the end of the hall. "Is that sunset?"

He scoffs, narrowing his eyes at me. "Did time get away from you?"

I squeeze my eyes shut, cursing myself. I should've known better, but I let myself be drugged by their music. I lost *hours* that I was supposed to be using to search the castle — to get to Jas. And I almost drank faerie wine. *Fool.* "I'm fine."

"You are *now.*" He nods to my wrist. "That's an interesting scar."

My heart squeezes at the reminder of Jas. She always called my scar my "moon and sun." One side looks like a crescent moon and the other a glowing sun. "I was caught in a fire as a child. I'm lucky I survived." I snap my mouth shut. I don't need to tell him anything, but his charm nearly unravels me. He can't seem to take his eyes off the mark.

"But was it —" He snaps his gaze down the hall, tensing. "The queen is coming."

I don't know if that's supposed to be a warning or if he simply doesn't want me to miss it. I wave toward the ballroom. "Please, return to the party."

His eyes flash. "Don't let her see your scar."

What? Why? I don't have a chance to ask, because he bows from the hips — a *full bow* from a fae noble, a gesture reserved for their highest ranks. Then he disappears into the crowd inside the ballroom doors. Part of me wants to follow him and demand that he explain what he means about my scar, but I won't risk returning to the ballroom and that music. I can't waste any more time.

I pull a pin from my skirt, and the dress falls away, leaving me in the simple thin silk I arrived in. I back into the shadows, breathing a sigh of relief that the encounter is over, even as I catch myself replaying what it felt like to dance in his arms and the look on his face when he whispered *So beautiful.* Did he mean the music? The dance? Why do I want to believe he was talking about me? Why do I *care?*

Then I hear it — heavy steps coming my way. A dozen sentries come into view, marching in step on either side of a robed elven female wearing a sparkling golden crown.

Even I am awed by the sight of her, Arya, golden queen, ruler of the Court of the Sun. Her hair shines like spun gold, and her skin glows like morning sunlight reflecting off the water. And her eyes . . . her eyes don't match the rest of her. The blue should be stunning, but instead it strikes me as empty — lonely.

Once upon a time, a golden faerie princess fell in love with the shadow king . . .

Did the king break her heart?

Shaking my head, I force myself to focus. The silver-eyed male was right about one thing: I can't let the queen or her sentries see me. I need to stay hidden so I can sneak through the castle while the rest of her palace is distracted by the ball.

I look down at my hands, and my breath catches. My hands, my legs, my body — there's nothing but shadow. I wave my hand in front of my face, but it's not there. I'm . . . invisible?

I stumble back into the wall — and fall right through it, into a flood of sunlight in a bustling kitchen.

"What do you think you're doing in here?" a muscular dwarf in a chef's hat growls at me. He has an enormous swine-shaped snout and curved ivory horns.

I scramble to my feet, staring at the wall I'm pretty sure I just fell *through*.

"You come to steal food from my kitchen?" He swats my back with a spoon, and my skin stings. "Get outta here, ya wildling."

"Yes, sir," I murmur. I find the nearest exit and rush out of the room, emerging into a long hall different from the one where I spotted the queen. Candles flicker from sconces every few feet, but there are no windows, and the shadows are plentiful.

71

I reach into a shadow and watch as my shaking hand disappears.

Is this some strange reaction to being in Faerie? Does my skill for blending in the normal world become an actual ability to disappear in this one?

Voices float toward me from a room down the hall, and I step into the shadows, willing myself to disappear as I listen.

"They're expecting the prince *tonight*," a deep voice says.

"Yes, sir, I understand," another male replies, this voice squeaky. "But Prince Ronan is still away. As you know, he isn't keen to return home and is less keen to choose a bride."

"Then *find him*," the first says. "If you make me deliver bad news to our queen, I'll be greatly displeased."

The palace is overflowing with women ready to offer their lives to the Seelie prince, and he couldn't be bothered to show? How typical of a faerie. Egotistical nonsense.

The males step out of the room and head toward me. They're tall, graceful, noble fae dressed in yellow-and-gray uniforms — from the queen's guard, perhaps?

I stay in the shadows, praying I'm invisible to them as well and not just to myself. They walk past me, and I hold my breath as one brushes my stomach with his elbow.

When they turn around a corner, I allow myself to breathe again. Carefully, I peek inside the room they emerged from. It's an office that has two desks, stacks of books, and maps on the walls, but what interests me most is the window and the fading sunlight.

I need to find that wardrobe. I've already lost too much time.

I found it. Deep in the lower levels of the palace, in a far back corner of a storage room, I found an oversize armoire with wings painted on the doors.

The queen's castle is vast and filled with fae and far more light than is convenient for a girl whose skills revolve around shadows and darkness. There are very few corridors or rooms that don't have someone nearby, but I roamed through every space I could, searching. I could've saved myself hours if I'd thought to start in the storage rooms, but considering the size of the palace, it's a miracle I found it at all.

It's dark and cool down here, and I'm so tired I want to curl into a corner and sleep for a week. I've been awake nearly twenty-four hours, and my muscles ache from the hours I was sucked into the faerie dances. But I can't stop now. I need to get to the Unseelie Court. My sister's name rings again and again through my mind, reminding me of what's at stake and giving me the energy I need to keep going.

As I throw open the doors to the wardrobe, I realize that I don't know what I'm looking for. It is — at least in appearance — an ordinary piece of furniture, a place to store clothing. Although I didn't expect flashing lights spelling out *Magic portal! Step this way at midnight to find your sister!* I thought there'd be some sign as to how I could use the thing.

Of course there's nothing remotely obvious. Bakken described the wings for me, but perhaps there's more than one wardrobe matching that description. What if the queen finally did destroy the portal, and this is nothing more than an ordinary wardrobe?

I open all the drawers and run my hands along the walls and

back. No passageway, no hidden compartments or false back. Maybe this is like the portal at the river, and you have to enter and *believe.*

But enter where? How?

There's a low, husky laugh behind me that makes me spin around.

I don't see anyone at first, but then an orb of fae light appears, floating in the air toward me, and a tall, dark-haired male emerges from the shadows. I recognize his silver eyes immediately.

I reach for the dagger I don't have on my hip. I knew I wouldn't be able to get into the castle if I had weapons, and against my better judgment, I'd come into this dangerous realm completely unarmed. If I were wise, I would've made my first stop at the queen's armory and *then* begun my search for the portal. No — if I were wise, I'd have made Bakken tell me how to go directly to the Unseelie Court. If I don't figure out this portal quickly, I'll have to hide in this castle a full day before it opens again.

I'm running out of time.

"Did you follow me?" I demand.

"A fascinating human comes to Prince Ronan's ball and some-how sneaks around the palace undetected — of course I'm follow-ing you."

Not completely undetected, apparently. Not if he followed me here.

"I'm wholly intrigued," he says, but he doesn't sound intrigued. He sounds irritated.

I freeze, waiting for him to call the sentries, to lunge for me and drag me to the dungeon — *something.* But he doesn't make a move, and I realize belatedly that this male with his silver eyes and dark hair isn't one of the golden fae nobility. *Don't make bargains or ties with the silver eyes.* He's from the Court of the Moon. "Who are you?"

He chuckles. "I'd ask you the same thing."

I lift my chin. If he's not one of the queen's court, he won't know that I don't belong here. "I'm a handmaiden for Queen Arya, sent down here to retrieve something for her."

Folding his arms, he cocks his head. "You don't look like any of Queen Arya's girls."

"And you've met them all?"

"I suppose not." He looks me over. "But I consider myself familiar with the humans in her court."

"Perhaps you're not as knowledgeable as you think." I know better than to talk back to a faerie. I should *run,* not speak. And yet I'm drawn to him — something about him calls me to move closer, not run away. Power purrs in my blood, a trace of the same high I felt when we danced.

Why did no one tell me that humans have powers in Faerie?

He smirks, stepping forward, and with just that step I'm too aware of how large he is. He's dressed in fine black pants and a matching tunic that looks like it's made of velvet, but his shoulders are broad like a warrior's. And here I am without any defenses.

You can walk through walls, Brie. You're not stuck.

And with that mental reassurance, I take a deep breath and let him study me. As if I have nothing to hide.

"If you wanted to pose as one of Arya's handmaids, you should've at least bothered to learn what colors she dresses them in." I can only interpret the shaking of his chest as a silent chuckle. "Or to know that she'd never take on a handmaiden more beautiful than she is."

My cheeks heat at that, and I have to fight the urge to look down at myself. I'd half convinced myself that I'd imagined him saying those words when we danced. This gorgeous male thinks *I* am beautiful? Of course, with Pretha's magical cosmetics, anyone would look lovelier, but if he wants me to believe he thinks I'm more beautiful than the queen, he must be trying to flatter me. "What do you want?"

"I'd love to know who you are."

"I've just told you."

"You're no handmaiden, and I've lived long enough to know a thief when I see one." He shakes his head. "But I can't figure out what it is you're trying to steal. What do you think she's hiding in that wardrobe?"

I fold my arms, not bothering to answer.

"Maybe you're looking for something we both want," he says. "Maybe we can help each other. Tell me what you need, beautiful thief."

My story nearly leaps off my tongue — there's something charming about this male that would make it easy to tell him whatever he wants to know — but I bite it back. Of course he's charming. He's fae. Worse, Unseelie. They're born with charm and deadly cruelty.

He's probably powerful enough to compel me to talk, and I can't risk that. My chest goes tight, my breathing shallow. I feel trapped — pinned under that scrutinizing gaze that seems to miss nothing.

The palace bells ring, and the walls seem to shake with it. *Bells.*

"What time is it?"

"Nearly midnight." He meets my gaze. "Somewhere you need to be?"

I look into his eyes, and for a moment I can't remember why I need to rush away. I've never seen eyes like this — silver flecked with white. They're extraordinary, and they match the rest of him. Captivating. The kind of unexpected beauty that entrances. Dangerous.

The chimes continue. *Six. Seven. Eight times.*

I stumble back. "I have to go." *Nine. Ten.*

His nostrils flare as he draws in a breath. "Let me help you." *Eleven.*

In a panicked rush, I hurl myself into the wardrobe. *Twelve.*

I lunge toward the back wall, but I don't walk through. I fall down — right into a massive ebony four-poster bed in an elegantly appointed bedroom. Around me, half a dozen sentries stand with hands on their blades.

I look around in a panic. *Where am I?*

A single sentry steps forward. "Abriella Kincaid, come with us. King Mordeus awaits your arrival."

CHAPTER SIX

MY BODY LOCKS UP IN TERROR. The guards surrounding me are thickly muscled, with curling horns on their heads and forked tongues that dart out every few seconds like a frog's would. Although I know the beautiful elven fae nobility are just as deadly as any, the sight of these sentries makes me want to run and hide.

I wish I could disappear or become shadow, but any power I had in the queen's palace eludes me now. A clawed hand closes around my wrist, and I yank my arm away. "Stop!"

"No one makes the king wait."

"I will speak to him only if I remain unharmed."

The sentry holding my wrist snorts, unswayed by my threat, and two more like him step forward and grab my other arm.

"Release me." My bravado turns to panic. "Let me go now, and I promise to follow you."

Two of the guards exchange a look of amused bafflement. The third laughs and tells the others, "She thinks we trust her."

Their hands pinch my arms and wrists as they lead me out of the room and down a dimly lit hallway. My panic rises with every turn.

They're going to take me to the king, and he will throw me into a dungeon. They're going to enslave me, just as they've enslaved so many humans. But worse than knowing that my own life is over is knowing that I failed to rescue Jas.

Suddenly they pull me into a room that is brighter than every hallway we've been in before. Globes of light dance high above my head to the rhythm of the music. Faeries of all kinds dance under the moonlight that shines in through a domed glass ceiling.

The Court of the Moon is beautiful beyond imagining, and the gathering before me is no drunken reverie. I pictured human sacrifices above great bonfires, torture in every corner, and curdling screams of pain. But this? This is a *ball*, as lovely as the one happening at the golden court, and though the guards escorting me are terrifying, the elven fae in their fine attire are as lovely as the nobility in the queen's palace.

We enter, and the sentries drag me forward, as if they've been awaiting my arrival. The crowd hushes, then parts, revealing a polished ebony throne sitting atop a dais at the opposite end of the room. And standing beside it, his arms crossed, is a male who could be no other than King Mordeus.

Even from across the room I can see his silver eyes. He fixes them on me as I approach. Arrogance and entitlement roll off him in waves. He stands with his legs wide, oozing power and confidence. His dark hair is tied back at the nape of his neck save for two white braids that hang free, framing his sharp jaw and high cheekbones. If it weren't for the cruelty gleaming in those eyes, I might call him beautiful. But those eyes . . .

A sharp chill runs through me. This is the male who bought

my sister as if she were an item to be owned. This is a ruler who will stop at nothing to get what he believes is his.

He holds up a hand, and the music stops. The crowd falls silent. He crooks a finger. "Bring her to me."

The sentries obey, dragging me to the dais faster than my feet will follow.

"Abriella, the Fire Girl," the king says, his calculating eyes roaming over me possessively. "No one told me how pretty the human thief is."

I want to spit and claw at him. This piece of evil may have already hurt Jasalyn — or worse. Maybe he sees that on my face because as the guards shove me forward, he laughs.

I stumble, but when I right myself, a sentry knocks me in the back of the knees, and I slam into the cold marble floor. "You will bow before His Majesty, King of the Shadows, Lord of the Night, Ruler of the Stars."

Pain radiates up my legs, and when I try to stand, I can't. Invisible bonds force me to kneel before this wicked king.

Anger flares through me, as hot as the fire from my nightmares. For a beat, darkness floods the room, so thick that nothing is visible in any direction.

I gasp, and it's gone. Is the king showing off? Trying to prove his power to a lowly human girl?

"Impressive," the king says, smiling down on me. "So impressive."

Is he complimenting his own magic? I lift my chin. They can force me to my knees, but I will fight them before I bow to their king.

"They said it couldn't be done," the king says. "They said no human could move through the Golden Palace undetected. But *I* knew. You're special."

"Where's my sister?" My words are but a hiss of steam from the rage that boils inside me.

The king's smile could be described as nothing but welcoming — the comforting expression of a friend who wants you to know that everything will be okay — but no smile can hide the ice in his eyes. "Your sister is safe. For now."

"Why do you want her? You're a faerie king. You can have anyone you choose. There are countless human women who would line up for a chance to be with you." *The fools,* I add silently.

I wonder if he hears my thoughts, because he smirks and chuckles quietly. "I don't want your sister."

"Then why—"

"I want *you.*"

I yank against the invisible bonds. "That makes no sense."

"Doesn't it?"

"If you wanted me, why did you buy *her?*"

"Would you have come to me if I'd asked? Would you have done my bidding if I'd bought *your* contract instead of hers?" His gleaming eyes lock onto me with such intensity, I feel like he's studying my soul. "No, a girl like you wouldn't help me, not even to save her own life. But if you had to help, if your sister's life depended on it . . ."

"Why would you need *my* help? You're a faerie king. I'm a mortal girl."

"Abriella, even you know you're far more than that." He toys with the end of one of his white braids. "You managed to sneak through the golden queen's castle and wander her hallways. You found her portal and came through undetected. You have impressed even me, the Lord of the Night. I believe you can do a job for me that no one else can."

"I doubt it," I spit, then wish I could yank the words back. As long as he has my sister, I'm at his mercy, and he knows it. If this *job* is the only leverage I have to free Jas, I need him to believe I can do whatever he asks. "I won't do anything as long as you have my sister prisoner. Send her home and I'll talk to you about whatever help you need from me."

"Home? You mean send her back to that moldy cellar beneath the witch's cottage?" He laughs again, and this time the whole court laughs behind me. *I hate them all.* "You expect me to believe that if I release your sister, you will give your services freely?"

"You expect *me* to believe you'll release her if I help you?"

He nods. "Of course. Yet you don't have a choice but to believe. I think we can make a deal—a bargain if you will. In return for your services, I'll let your sister go. I'll send her home safely. But *only* after you return what the golden court has stolen."

"Why not do this job yourself? You're the all-powerful Lord of the Night."

He grins, and again I'm rocked by his sinister beauty. "Thank you for the compliment, but I won't abandon my throne to be an errand boy."

I nod toward the sentry standing beside me. "Then send one of your guards."

"This is not a job for a faerie." He steeples his fingers and taps them together. "Queen Arya's son is searching for a bride, a *human* bride. I believe Prince Ronan will find you quite to his liking."

"What does the prince have to do with—"

He stops my words with a wave of his hand. Literally *stops* them. I'm moving my mouth, but no words are coming out. I grab my throat and glare at him with all the hate in my heart.

"Tomorrow," the king continues, "the prince will choose a dozen young women to stay at the Golden Palace as potential brides. You'll offer yourself as his bride and infiltrate my enemy's court. While you're trying to win young Ronan's hand, you'll retrieve some of my belongings that the queen has had for a bit too long now." Another smile. "You will need to win the young prince's heart and his trust to gain access to the magical artifacts that have been stolen from my court—you must bring all three to me if you want your sister to return home."

Suddenly the magical gag on my voice is released. A cry slips from my lips before I can stop it. "You're mad. I don't know the first thing about winning a faerie's heart." And even if I did . . . *Shudder.* The idea of seducing a faerie makes my stomach churn. "What makes you so sure he'll choose me out of the hundreds clamoring for the chance?"

The king laughs. "You need to understand that nothing in my realm is a coincidence, human. If you present yourself to the prince, he will do everything in his power to keep you close. He will give you the access you need."

"I couldn't even *pretend* to care for a faerie—"

"Do you want your sister back or not?" he snaps. His smile slips, revealing the fringes of a dangerous temper.

I swallow. "How do I know you even have her? How do I know this isn't all a trick?"

He pulls a tiny pink swatch of fabric from his pocket and tosses it in front of me. "This is the best I can do."

I choke back a sob and snatch the scrap of Jas's sewing smock from the floor. "Let me see her."

"You want me to trust Elora's most talented thief with my most valuable possession? I wouldn't dare. However"—he clasps his hands together and steps forward—"the first artifact you retrieve for me will allow you to see your sister. It's a magical mirror. In it, you can see whatever you wish."

"You want me to trust a mirror?"

He arches a brow as if to say, *You want me to trust you?*

"Let me see my sister, and then we can discuss this task you have for me." What if he doesn't have her? What if he's hurting her right now? What if she's already gone? The thought makes the simmering rage steam in my blood. "You've gone to a lot of trouble to get me here, so the least you can do is take me to my sister. This isn't negotiable."

"You think *you're* in position to negotiate?"

I yank against my invisible bonds again. When they don't budge, I spit at him. Mordeus's eyes flash and his nostrils flare. He lifts his open hand in my direction and sends a ball of darkness rolling toward me.

I jerk away from it, but I'm too late. The moment it hits me, I find myself in a brightly lit room that smells faintly of mildew and urine. My thin dress does nothing to insulate me from the ice-cold stone floor, and my teeth chatter as I push to my feet.

Where am I?

There are no windows, no doors. At least none that I can see. Just four stone walls, a stone floor, and blinding light that seems to pour from the ceiling. Does the shadow court use *light* to torture their prisoners?

Shaking — half with cold, half with rage — I walk the perimeter of the room, pushing against the walls, searching for cracks between stones, anything, but I don't see a way out.

I wrap my arms around myself and squint against the light as I try to make out a trapdoor above me. This must be some sort of oubliette, but all I can see above me is blinding brightness. "Hello?" My voice echoes off the stone. "Is anyone there?"

No answer.

"I demand to speak with the king!"

No answer.

I kick the wall, and pain lashes through my foot. "Get me out of here!"

No answer.

I stare at my hands, willing them to disappear into shadow the way they did at the castle, but there's no shadow here. There's no darkness to hide in or slip through.

I slide down the wall and wrap my arms around my legs. I'm so tired. I haven't slept since the few hours I got on Nik's floor before running from Gorst's men, and a full day has passed since I came through the portal.

I don't have the energy for tears, and my rage ate up what little I did have. I'm drained from my journey, but I refuse to believe I'm stuck. I didn't come all this way for nothing.

I rest my head on my knees and close my eyes. I imagine my sister curled in a ball in a room much like this one, crying herself to sleep. I think of the tenderness in Sebastian's eyes as he gave me the crystal pendant of protection. When he returns to Fairscape, what will he think when I'm not there?

I'm two places at once. Two people at once. I'm the sleeping would-be rescuer curled against the wall in Mordeus's oubliette, the girl who failed to save her sister. And I'm the eight-year-old protector, the girl who's snuggled under the blankets with my little sister, spoon-feeding her hope so she doesn't drown in the sadness.

Dreams can be so strange. I know I'm dreaming, but I don't want to wake up. Because Jas is with me in this dream. And if she's with me, she's safe.

We're in the upstairs bedroom that we shared before Uncle Devlin died, and I wipe away her tears as she cries. She's missing Mother tonight. I am too, but my grief will only intensify hers, so I lock it up tight and brush her chestnut hair from her eyes.

"I miss her," Jas says on a shaky sob.

"I bet she misses us too," I whisper. "So much that she's planning a way to come get us."

Jas sniffles. "Tell me a story?"

I sweep her hair from her face and weave a story of faerie castles and elven royalty. The story comes, and I feel like it's important, but it's almost like I'm watching myself from a distance. I can't make out my own words. They're as fuzzy as a murmur from another room.

Jas grips my hand, and I know I've gotten to an exciting part. "Now what?" she asks.

"The cruel king waits for the day the princess of shadows will come to his castle." I'd forgotten this tale — one our mother told us only once, the night before she left for Faerie. "The false king knew she could command the shadows, but he didn't know that her big heart and her endless love would cost him his throne."

Jasalyn closes her eyes, and her face softens with sleep. I don't know if she's dreaming or half awake when she says, "The prince will help you find me."

I blink away from her to the darkness at the foot of the bed. The silver-eyed male I saw at the ball is there and then gone, flickering like a fading, precious memory.

"Who told you that story?" he asks. He's more shadow than corporeal.

I sit up and smile at him, oddly comforted by his appearance and my sister's words. I feel safe here, under the intense gaze of this faerie who is all but a stranger to me. I feel less alone. *The prince will help you find me.* I climb out of bed and tuck the blankets around Jas. "Our mother told us many stories."

"Then why do you feel so powerless?"

Suddenly our bedroom becomes the cold, doorless, windowless cell in the evil king's castle. And I remember. *I'm a prisoner. This is a dream.* "Because I am."

Something like anger flashes in those silver eyes, and then I'm standing beneath a vast, starry sky, the moon a comforting beacon over my shoulder.

The silver-eyed faerie fully materializes, as if strengthened by the starlight. His dark curls are pulled back from his face and his brow is creased with worry. "You're only powerless if you believe you are." He sneers as he looks me over, and in his eyes I see a reflection of starlight. "We don't have much time."

"What?"

"He won't let you go — he won't release *either of you* — until you agree. I'll help you get her back. Come find me."

"You're Unseelie. Why would I want your help? You're probably working for him."

His eyes flash. "Never. I swear it on my magic." He blinks and turns his head. "They're coming."

He disappears, and the dark night around me is erased by too-bright light.

"Wake up, Fire Girl." The command is followed by a dry cackle, and I open my eyes.

A goblin stands in the center of the cell. He grins down at me, his gnarled fingers extended toward my hair, his bulging eyes bright with excitement. But I'm still half in my dreamworld and can barely focus on the creature before me.

Why did I dream of that faerie? He had seemed so real. Why hadn't I dreamed of Sebastian giving me advice — or Jasalyn? Or anyone I knew?

The goblin offers his hand, pulling me from my thoughts.

"The king believes a night's sleep may have made you change your mind. We go to him now."

My instinct is to refuse, but what will that accomplish?

Nodding, I take his bony hand. I'm still crouched on the ground when we appear in the throne room again. Unlike last night, the room is empty except for Mordeus, who stands before his throne like he's been pacing. Despite the bright morning sun pouring in through the windows and the domed glass ceiling, the space seems bigger and colder.

"Has the mortal reconsidered my offer?" King Mordeus asks his goblin, his eyes hard. A ruler who doesn't tolerate being refused.

My stomach hurts, but I force myself to take one deep breath after another. I don't trust faeries, and I specifically don't trust this one, but I do trust my dreams. *I swear it on my magic.* Did my mother once tell me that a faerie can't break a promise made on their power? I have to believe that my subconscious pulled this information from my memories for a reason.

I push myself off the floor only to be bound by those invisible chains again. I have to bite my lip to keep from snarling at him. "I have reconsidered."

Pretend I want to marry the prince so I can infiltrate the castle, steal a few magical faerie artifacts, and free my sister. I can do this.

"If I retrieve these three artifacts and return them to . . ." I hesitate. I don't want to give anything to this male who thinks human girls are objects to be purchased, and some instinct has me subtly reworking his terms. "If I return the artifacts to the

Unseelie Court, you will return my sister safely to a location of my choice in the human realm." It's not a question. These are my terms.

His silver eyes glow. He knows he's won. "You have my word, Fire Girl."

"Swear it on your power."

He flinches, and his features harden for a beat before he replaces his friendly mask. "Who told you about *that?*"

I shrug. "Everyone knows," I lie. "Unfortunately, it's the only way I can trust you."

"Fine. With one caveat. If you tell anyone from the Seelie Court about this arrangement, our bargain is over and I'll give your sister to my goblins as a solstice gift. Do you understand?"

Who would I tell? The only soul I trust in this realm is Jasalyn. "I understand."

He smiles. "We have a deal then. Once the three artifacts are returned to my court where they belong, I will send your sister safely back to a location of your choice in the human realm."

"Alive," I snap. It seems like *safe* should cover that, but I won't allow him to work a loophole.

"Alive. I swear it on my power." With a snap of his fingers, a silver-gilded mirror appears in his hand. "This is a replica of the Mirror of Discovery. When you find it, replace it with this so the queen won't know it's missing."

"What happens when she realizes it's a fake?"

He shakes his head. "Only one with Unseelie blood can tell the difference."

"Where will I find this mirror?"

He shrugs. "All I know is that Arya has hidden it away in the Seelie Court. You may have to search to get your hands on it, but that shouldn't be a problem for someone who found her portal." He smirks and offers me the mirror. "You may stand."

I shift experimentally and find that the invisible bonds have slipped away. Standing, I realize I'm still clutching the scrap of Jas's smock in one hand. I take the mirror in the other, willing myself not to shake. "Will I bring it to you through the portal once I've found it?"

"The portal's been . . . disabled." His goblin laughs, and Mordeus smirks in his direction. "My goblin will retrieve you and it when the time is right."

I don't enjoy feeling like the butt of a joke, but I let my pride get the best of me last night and lost hours — hours I could have been searching for the mirror. If I get to take my sister home, they can laugh at me all they want. "What are the other two artifacts?"

"Focus on one task at a time, my girl. I will tell you the second when I have the first." He claps his hands, and a trio of elven fae females appear around me. They share the king's pale skin but have short, light blue hair. "Dress Abriella for the Seelie Court. Make her look like his future queen, then return her to the Golden Palace."

The three females bow their heads in acquiescence. "Yes, Your Majesty," they say in unison. One takes my arm, and I follow them toward a door in the back of the room.

"Abriella," the king says. I stop and turn to him, meeting his eyes. "When you meet Prince Ronan, remember that you need him. Hold his trust, or you will be unable to infiltrate his court."

"I understand my mission."

He spreads his fingers, and a ball of darkness bleeds like an inkblot between them. "You'll be fine if you remember what's at stake." The ball of darkness shifts until it's not darkness at all, but an image of Jasalyn and me sitting on the floor at Madame V's. She's in her pajamas, and she looks like she just crawled out of bed. The smile on her face makes me step closer to that image, despite the man holding it.

He adds, "Or, I should say . . . *who*."

CHAPTER SEVEN

"THERE HAS TO BE ANOTHER WAY," I say, stepping away from the goblin at my door. After I was given an opportunity to bathe and the king's servants dressed me like a doll, King Mordeus sent his goblin to escort me to the queen's palace. I don't care to put that much trust in a creature who has wiped drool from his mouth twice since I came into his view.

"King Mordeus long ago destroyed his brother Oberon's portal to the Seelie lands," one handmaiden says.

"Can I take a carriage or . . . a horse?"

The handmaidens exchange surprised glances. "It's a week's journey on our fastest steed, milady."

At first I nearly snorted every time they call me *lady*. That's one thing I've never been accused of being, but after hours of having them fuss over me, I'm more annoyed by the title than anything else.

King Mordeus's goblin grumbles under his breath, then offers his hand again. I get it. Not only can goblins move freely between and within realms, they can do so instantaneously. They choose to go somewhere, and they simply *appear* there. Next to the knowledge they hoard, it's their greatest power. My gaze lands on the bracelet at my wrist. As the faeries washed me, I confirmed Bakken's promise that the bracelet was visible only to me. Now I'm tempted to use it. I would so much rather have Bakken transport me than this unknown goblin, but I don't want to waste a thread — or, truthfully, unnecessarily lose any more of my hair. I'm supposed to seduce a prince, and my wild red curls are the best physical attribute I have on my side. I take a deep breath and a step forward. "Okay."

The goblin takes my hand. His skin is leathery against mine, but before I can think on it too long, the world falls away. This isn't like the sensation of appearing before the king from my cell. This is like moving down and up and out all at once — then I'm jerked to a halt, my head whipping back. I'm surrounded by rows of neatly tended flower beds, and the golden queen's castle gleams in the evening light.

"I leave you here," the goblin says, releasing my hand.

I turn to ask how I'm to summon him after I retrieve the mirror, but he's already gone.

The castle is as bustling as it was when I first arrived in Faerie, with humans and faeries of all kinds milling about beyond and within the gates. I graze my fingers across the amulet that hangs between my breasts and start toward the footbridge. The handmaidens who dressed me had asked about the amulet and suggested that I trade it out for pearls, but I refused. I don't know if Sebastian's magic works in this realm, but even if it doesn't, the feel of the cool crystal between my breasts brings me comfort.

Sebastian. My chest pinches, and I allow myself a moment of self-pity. I close my eyes and remember his kiss, his sea-green eyes. It's hard to believe that only a few days ago my debt to Madame V and my secret crush on the mage's apprentice were the most complicated problems in my life.

I don't know if I'll ever see Sebastian again, but if I do, I hope he can forgive me for whatever actions I'll have to take to make Prince Ronan trust me.

"Brie? Is that you?"

I turn toward the familiar voice and see Sebastian striding toward me, as if my thoughts alone summoned him. I nearly fall to my knees in relief at the sight of his beautiful face. He's dressed in dark brown leather pants and a vest, a long sword strapped to his back, as if it's just another day in Fairscape and he's ready to train in Mage Trifen's courtyard. But then I take in his pointed ears, glowing skin, and the sharper angles of his features. He looks every bit like the noble fae I saw dancing inside the queen's castle last night.

He must have gotten a potion from Mage Trifen — I considered it myself before realizing I could never afford such a thing, and I didn't have the time to steal the funds.

"Bash," I whisper.

He pulls me into his arms. His heat is a comfort I thought I'd never experience again. "It *is* you."

When I pull back to study him, a combination of awe and frustration taint his perfectly handsome face. "I would never have believed you could pass for a faerie," I say, skimming my fingertips across his beautiful cheekbones. "Your glamour is flawless. If I didn't know you, I wouldn't doubt that you belong here."

He flinches at this, and his throat bobs as he swallows. "When I heard Gorst's men were looking for you, I went to Nik. She told me you were gone. She wouldn't tell me where you went, but she didn't have to. I knew you'd come for Jas." He pulls me into his chest again and exhales heavily. "I've been searching the Seelie Court all day, and I couldn't find you. Damnit, Brie, where have you been?"

I fish the amulet out of my dress and show it to him. "I'm safe. See?"

He runs his big hands up and down my arms and looks over every inch of me. After pulling my hair back in a series of braids gathered into a bun atop my head, the Unseelie handmaidens had dressed me in a sleeveless gown of layer after layer of yellow satin. The fabric hugs my figure from the sweetheart neckline down through my hips and flares out to where it sweeps the ground around my yellow-slippered feet. When they showed me my reflection, I thought I looked like a giant tulip. The maids insisted that the prince would find me irresistible like this, and I had no reason not to trust them.

But maybe Prince Ronan isn't the only one with a weakness for tulips. Sebastian is speechless as he takes me in. His eyes return to my face again and again, as if he's trying to convince himself that I'm okay. "You look . . ." He squeezes the back of his neck and flashes me a boyish grin. "Let's just say I can't imagine that you've been able to get around unnoticed."

I swallow but can't help my blush at the compliment. "I managed."

"I've been so worried."

"I'm fine." It's on the tip of my tongue to tell him the truth, but what did the king say about talking about our deal? Was it only the Seelie I can't tell or did he forbid me to tell anyone? I think it's just the Seelie, but what happens if one of them overhears me telling Sebastian? "You shouldn't have come looking for me. What about your apprenticeship?"

He studies my face, tracing the edge of my jaw with his thumb. "Nothing matters as much as you."

I rest my cheek against his chest, curl into him, and hold tight. Maybe it makes me weak, but I'm desperately grateful that he's here. Because I'm tired. Because I'm scared.

Because I'm ashamed.

I'm ashamed that part of me wants to go home — that I wish I could leave this place and these awful creatures. Ashamed that I wish I didn't have to be the one to rescue my sister.

The king was right about one thing. I am a great thief. I can steal just about anything. But a faerie prince's heart? I wouldn't know where to start.

I should feel lucky that the king isn't asking anything worse from me, but instead I feel primed for failure. I would rather have ventured into the depths of the Unseelie wilds — fought and evaded terrible monsters to steal magical treasures. I would've had more confidence in my ability to do that, but this? Pretending I want to be a faerie's bride and beating out other women for the honor? Even in the prettiest dress, I wouldn't know how to do that.

Sebastian steps back and cups my face in one big hand. "Tell me where you've been."

I shake my head. I can't tell him about the king. I can't risk it. "I've been looking for Jas. My search led me . . . away from the queen's lands."

He closes his eyes and shakes his head. "My amulet can't protect you from the worst of the shadow court. You have no idea how dangerous they are. If an Unseelie fae had seen you, they would have taken you. They could have bound you as a slave. Worse."

I hate that my choice hurts him. How can I explain? If anyone understands what Jas means to me, it's Sebastian. "I won't go home until I find her. But *you* should. This isn't your fight, Bash."

He scans the lush gardens around us and curses under his breath. "I need more time," he says, more to himself than to me.

I put my hand on his arm, all too aware of the strength and warmth beneath my fingers. "For what?"

"To do what I should have done months ago." He swallows. "Walk with me?"

I cast a long look at the castle. I need to go in and present myself as a potential bride for the prince before he's chosen his twelve.

"Just for a few minutes," Sebastian says. He tucks a loose curl behind my ear. "Can you give me that?" His smile is like sunlight on my icy heart. I can't deny him this — not when it's so simple.

Turning, he stoops and plucks the bud of an orange day lily from the garden. It blooms in his palm, and I gasp. "I've never seen you do that."

"My mother loves day lilies. When I'd leave you to go home, my best friend would mock me for staring at them. He knew they reminded me of your hair, but in truth they don't compare." He tucks the flower into my hair, and I allow myself a beat to close my eyes. The feel of his rough fingertips on the shell of my ear sends a shiver through me. How can I be so greedy for more of his touches — more of these long glances and tenderly spoken words — when Jas needs me?

"You never talked about your family." I shake my head. "I should have asked more questions."

"I never gave you the chance." He adjusts the flower one last time before dropping his hand. "I was raised in privilege and power. And I couldn't always trust that those around me truly cared."

This surprises me. Not everyone is lucky enough to be a mage's apprentice, of course, but any family with significant power would consider the position beneath them. "What kind of power?"

"Ruling power. The kind I'll be expected to take on myself." He takes my hand in his and studies my fingers in his palm. The glamour may have sharpened some of his features, but it left his calluses untouched. "Soon."

Frowning, I curl my fingers, squeezing his fingertips in my palm. "Then why have you been studying to be a mage?"

"The skills are useful, and I . . . In truth, I needed to get away."

That's when it clicks. "You weren't really leaving for another part of your apprenticeship, were you? You were going home."

He nods and searches my face. "I wanted to ask you to go with me, but I knew you wouldn't want the life I could offer you."

My heart soars and aches all at once. "Why would you say that?" Does he think I'd be that picky? Or was it because he knew I'd never leave Jas behind and didn't think he could take us both?

He blows out a breath. "I still can't believe she sold her."

I return my cheek to its resting place on his chest, relishing the feel of his heat and strength. Maybe Sebastian can't save Jas or protect me from this task I must take on, but there's something comforting in his embrace. Part of me wants to believe I could put my problems in his capable hands and he would be able to fix everything. "It's not your fault."

"It *is* my fault that I never told you how I feel. And now I'm afraid I'm too late." His gaze flashes away, and I follow it to see a group of yellow-and-gray-clad guardsmen marching out of the castle. *Yellow*, I realize, like my dress. One of the queen's banner colors.

When I look back up at Sebastian, he's staring at my mouth.

I lift my hand, cupping his jaw in invitation. Slowly — so slowly it's nearly painful — he lowers his mouth to mine. His lips are soft, but I slide my hand into his hair and the kiss turns searching. Time stutters to a stop. The sun stalls on the horizon, the birds quiet, and the breeze stills in the flowers. Nothing in the world exists but his mouth and mine, and my heart aches as I try to memorize every perfect second. This could be our last kiss.

How can I make another man fall in love with me when I have always been in love with *this* man?

When he pulls away, my knees are weak and the world comes back into focus too slowly.

"Please forgive me," he whispers.

"You have nothing to apologize for." I almost smile. "I'm pretty sure *I* kissed *you*."

"His Royal Highness, Prince Ronan, is needed in the throne room," a guard says, too near us.

I jerk away to scan the gardens. Is the prince nearby? Did he see me kissing Sebastian? If he did, how will he ever believe I want *him*?

Foolish and reckless, Brie. Get it together.

But no one is in the garden except Sebastian, the guards, and me. The guards watch Sebastian expectantly, and Sebastian watches me.

"Sir, excuse me," one of the queen's garrison says, "but it's time to go. They await you inside. The selection was to begin hours ago."

"Tell my mother I will join her shortly." His voice is tight and sharp, and my muddled brain scrambles to make sense of his words.

The sentinel shifts awkwardly from one leg to another and looks to his fellow guardsmen. "Your Highness —"

Sebastian sets his jaw. "Leave us."

I'm vaguely aware of the sound of feet marching away on the garden's flagstone path, but I can't take my eyes off my friend. I blink at him. "Your *mother?*" Prince Ronan. They addressed him as *Prince Ronan.* And *Your Highness.* "Bash, I don't understand. What kind of glamour is this? Why do they think you're the prince?"

He takes my hand and gently squeezes my fingertips. "Because I am."

I step back, yanking my hand away. "That's not funny."

"Brie, listen to me. I couldn't tell you, not when I knew how you felt about my kind. I wanted to, but —"

"No." I shake my head wildly. "No, you're a normal human. You can't be —"

"Please. Just give me a chance to explain."

I've backed away without realizing it and find myself in the shadow of a willow tree.

"Brie?" He mutters a curse and spins in place. "Abriella? *Please.*"

I look at my hands, but they're not there. Somehow I've become invisible again — become the shadows, like before.

I don't question it. I just *run.* Through the gardens, beyond the castle gates, and into thick fog. My lungs burn and my legs ache, but I don't stop — not when the landscape changes from the impossible perfection of the palace grounds to something like a ruin, not when my limbs appear again, whatever magic made me invisible falling away. I don't slow down until the fog is as thick as a storm cloud and the sun is so low in the sky that the last fingers of light barely brush the horizon.

I lean against a broken marble column and sink to the ground. I don't even realize I'm crying until my cheeks are wet and my breath comes in hiccupping gasps.

He lied to me. He made me believe he was someone he wasn't.

I was prepared to steal from a spoiled prince. I wouldn't hesitate to deceive a faerie to save my sister, and I wasn't the slightest bit concerned about my heart. But Prince Ronan isn't just a faerie. He's Sebastian, and I don't know how I'm supposed to pretend I can forgive him — pretend I want to *marry* him.

When you meet Prince Ronan, remember that you need him. Hold his trust, or you will be unable to infiltrate his court.

The king's words from this morning ring in my head. He didn't tell me to *earn* the prince's trust. He told me to *hold* it. And yesterday he told me that there are no coincidences in Faerie. *That's* why he wanted me for this mission. He knows. *Somehow,* King Mordeus knows about my relationship with Sebastian, and he's using me because of it.

I don't know what upsets me more — the idea of hiding my heartache and pretending that Sebastian's lies are forgivable or the possibility that playing this part with Sebastian might break me in a way I can never come back from.

But what choice do I have? I ran because I panicked, but if I had been thinking clearly, I would have stayed with the prince — used our relationship as a way in. I will give up *anything* to save Jas. My pride. My heart. My life.

I have to go back. I have to convince Sebastian that I still want him. I push off the ground and brush the tears from my cheeks. Turning around, I step through rubble to find my path back to the palace.

A robed, hooded figure steps out of the fog. I tense until familiar dark eyes meet mine. My shoulders sag, and a soft breeze of relief washes over me, leaving exhaustion in its wake. *I know her.*

Another figure — tall and menacing, with glowing red eyes that leer at me from under his hood — appears behind her. I open my mouth to warn her, but before I can get out a sound, sleep swallows me whole and I fall to the ground.

CHAPTER EIGHT

I'M JOSTLED AWAKE TO FIND myself being carried over someone's shoulder like a bag of grain. I bite back a cry of panic and force myself to take three deep breaths to calm my racing heart. *Be smart, Brie.*

I'm pretty sure I left smart behind the moment I ran from the safety of the Seelie queen's grounds with no plan and no weapons. And now I've been captured.

If I had to guess from the meaty hands on the back of my skirt and the height of my captor alone, it's a male that carries me. But the woman I saw before I collapsed — she was someone I thought I could trust.

"Get the door," the male holding me grumbles. "She'll wake up any minute."

"Such a brute," says a melodic voice ahead. *Pretha,* the beautiful woman who helped me get into the queen's castle. I know she's the same person, but she looks different from the woman I stood in line with. She has the same pretty brown eyes and dark hair, but she has sharply pointed ears and that ethereal glow all the noble fae seem to have. "You didn't have to knock her out," she says.

"I don't deal well with hysterical mortals," the male says as he adjusts me on his shoulder.

The door opens, and loud music pours out. Trying to keep my body loose so my captor won't know I'm awake, I scan my surroundings as he steps inside. With the exception of the clientele, the tavern isn't all that different from Gorst's place in Fairscape. The place reeks of stale beer and is so loud it makes my ears ache. In every direction, couples of all kinds dance together. A lithe sprite with translucent wings and a barely there scrap of dress lets a troll tuck a gold coin between her breasts. A young elf in leather riding gear strokes his burley dance partner's Mohawk as they grind against each other. Females and males alike dance on the counters, swinging around poles to the crowd's chorusing approval. A busty fire fae in tight black leather leans against the wall to my left and pinches Pretha's ass as she passes.

Pretha smacks her hand away. "I'm working," she shouts.

The male carrying me chuckles. "You might make time for that, Pretha," he says. "If you don't, I might. You know what they say about fire fae."

"You're such a pig, Kane," Pretha shouts.

She leads the way through a throng of dancing bodies, then turns suddenly and catches me watching her from under Kane's arm. "And there's our girl." Yes, she looks just like the woman who offered to be my friend, but her ears aren't the only thing that's changed. She now has silver webbing tattooed across her forehead. It resembles the cracks of a broken mirror.

With no reason to pretend anymore, I squirm in the giant male's hold. "Put me down."

Pretha winks at me, then pushes past two sentries and through a heavy wooden door, revealing a sparsely furnished office illuminated only from the street lanterns outside the windows.

I'm dropped to my feet. As my eyes adjust to the dark room, I finally get a look at the male who was carrying me. Everything about him is terrifying. He's massive, with broad, muscular shoulders and thickly muscled arms. He stands at least seven feet tall, even taller if you measure the horns that curl toward the back of his head. His eyes are black where the whites should be, with blazing red pupils. His long hair and trim beard are red, and he wears a hoop in one pointed ear.

"I think she likes you, Kane," Pretha says. "Either that or you're so ugly you've scared her speechless."

"You found her," says a deep, melodious voice behind me.

I whip around, drawn to the owner of that voice, and bite back a gasp at the sight of the male before me. He's lounging on a chaise with one leg stretched long and the other bent at the knee. His dark curls have been tied back like they were in my dream, and he holds a book in his big hands. The office is large, yet he seems to fill it, with his size, with his piercing silver eyes, with his presence.

My captor shoves me forward. I stumble and fall to my knees before a menacing shadow faerie for the second time in as many days.

I hate this place.

"She was running from the castle," Pretha says.

I glare at her. *"You."*

She lifts her robe off the floor and gives a little curtsy. "Abriella, I told you we'd meet again."

"What do you want from me?"

"I want —" She huffs, scanning the space. "Why is it so dark in here?" She snaps her fingers, and the wall sconces around the office blaze to life. "Better." She turns back to me with a satisfied smile. "I want to help you. Nothing's changed since yesterday in that regard."

"You made me think you were a human," I spit, and there's more anger in the words than there should be. Pretha was a virtual stranger, but her sin is the same as Sebastian's, and it feels good to have somewhere to direct the hurt eating at my chest. "You're a vile liar."

The male lounging in the chaise laughs. "That's fresh coming from the human who claimed to be Arya's handmaiden."

I narrow my eyes at him. I don't like that this strange male is showing up again, and I like even less that I dreamed about him.

Nothing in Faerie is coincidence.

"I don't think she has control of her power," Pretha says, all grace as she steps toward me and tenderly tucks my hair behind my ears.

I yank away. "Don't touch me."

"Or her emotions." She tears her disapproving gaze away from me to meet the eyes of the male in the chair. "I think she's actually in love with the golden prince."

My cheeks go hot. I hate that these faeries are talking about me, speculating about my feelings. "You don't know anything about me."

The male in the chair tsks. "Let her be, Pretha. I'll take it from here."

107

Pretha bristles. "Finn—"

Finn. Finally a name for the enigmatic silver-eyed elf.

"Leave us." The words are softer than the ones he spoke before, but they are full of authority and leave no doubt as to who's in charge of this little trio.

Pretha tenses, and I know she doesn't want to obey, but she gives a sharp nod and leaves the office. The horned brute trails behind her.

I watch them go.

"Rough night?" Finn asks me. Such a casual question, as if we're chatting over tea and his people didn't knock me unconscious to drag me in here.

I glare at him. "Who are you—other than some Unseelie kidnapper? I hope you realize that no one's going to pay a ransom for me."

He arches a dark brow. "*Oh?* It seems you know more about me than you let on. What else do you know?"

Dangerous. This faerie is dangerous, and I need to stop antagonizing him and focus on getting out of here. "Nothing. I know nothing."

He lifts his chin. "I'm curious. Why are you so sure I'm Unseelie?"

"Your eyes."

"What about them?"

"Everyone knows that the Unseelie have silver eyes. *Don't make bargains or ties with the silver eyes,*" I say, parroting the rhyme we sang as children. *And what a lovely job I've done following* that *age-old wisdom.*

He grunts. "That's the most ridiculous thing I've ever heard. You were taught that the entire Unseelie Court has eyes like mine?"

"Don't they?"

"No. Only very few." And even as he says it, I think of the sentries at Mordeus's castle. Did they have silver eyes? I don't remember. And is Pretha Unseelie? Her eyes are brown. And Kane's were that creepy black and red.

"Am I free to leave now?"

His eyes go wide in faux innocence. "And where would you go? You aren't sure you want to return to your friend, even if you do wish you hadn't been so rash in running away from him."

I press my lips into a thin line and lift my chin. "You can read my mind?"

His laugh is dark. "No. I don't need to read your mind to know your worries, though that would be a useful talent. Your emotions are written all over your face. You're not sure you can play the part Mordeus needs you to."

What's his connection to Mordeus? Is he working for him? "What do you know?"

"Enough." With a deep breath he unfolds himself from the chair. He crosses the room to a small bar nestled in the corner of the office, and I take advantage of having his back to me to study him. His presence gobbles up the space. But it's not just his height or his muscular body that gives the effect. Finn has the aura of a leader who commands the attention of everyone around him. I wonder what kind of power he has that he, an Unseelie, can be here in the Seelie Court.

He uncorks a bottle and pours two glasses. The pale yellow liquid bubbles as it hits the glass. My mouth waters at the fruity aroma, but when he turns around again and offers one to me, I shake my head. I can't imagine any situation where I'd accept wine from a male I just met — hello, *stranger danger* — but faerie wine? He must think I'm a complete fool.

With a careless shrug he sets my glass on a long table by the windows. As he drinks from his, he closes his eyes. "I understand that your sweet, golden prince hurt your feelings with his deception, but if you truly wish to save your sister, you need to do what Mordeus asks."

He'd said the same thing in my dream. "You're Unseelie," I say. "Of course you want me to help your king."

"He's not *my* king," he snaps, and the sharp declaration echoes off the office walls. "He will never be my king," he adds, softer now.

"Why are you in the golden court? I thought the Unseelie weren't welcome in Seelie territory."

"I'll make you a deal. I'll answer that question if you answer one of mine."

The word *deal* triggers my defense mechanisms, but I'm too tired and emotionally wrung out to worry about all the ways I could potentially be manipulated by a deal with a faerie. "What's your question?"

"What do you know about the faerie who gave you your magic?"

I frown. "What magic?"

He takes another sip of his wine and studies me with those mercurial eyes. "I'll admit that it's been many years since I've ventured to the human realm, but would you have me believe that humans can now walk through walls and turn themselves to shadow?"

I shake my head. "It's just some strange reaction to being in a magical place."

Finn tilts his head. "I don't know what I find more interesting. The lie or that you truly *want* to believe it." His lips curl, but there's no amusement in his smile. Only disgust. "You know already, though. You know that the powers you have in my realm aren't so new. You've been using them for years."

A dry laugh bursts from my lips. "If you say so."

"You're a thief. A good one, too."

How do these shadow fae know so much about me? "If I do have powers — and I'm not saying I do — why would you assume someone *gave* them to me?"

He narrows his eyes and lowers his voice. "Because humans don't have magic unless it's granted to them by a magical creature powerful enough to do so."

"Witches have magic. And mages."

"No. Witches and mages *use* magic. Symbols, spells, potions. Some humans are able to *use* magic, but they do not *have* it. Not like you do. *You* are a human who can wield darkness. You can become shadow and walk through walls — without spells or potions, without ritual. The magic is part of you, and the only way that's possible is if a faerie granted it to you."

"I don't know where it came from," I admit. Because he's right. There's part of me that knew long before coming to Faerie that my skills in night and shadow aren't normal — that they're something special. I open my mouth, considering telling him more, then snap it shut. His people have proved that they can't be trusted. "Your turn."

He studies his wine for so long I think he won't answer. "Mordeus is my uncle."

That's the moment his name clicks into place for me. Bakken told me that Prince Finnian was the rightful heir to the Throne of Shadows — this is *that* Finn? "You're the prince." It's not even a question. It explains everything. The way he moves, the way his friends defer to him, the way he feels like the most important person in the room, whether I want to believe he is or not. Yes, everything about Finn screams royalty. *Power.*

He lifts his eyes to meet mine. "You might have noticed the resemblance."

The silver eyes. It's not all shadow fae who have those silver eyes. Only the royal family.

"I don't reside in my own court, because good old Uncle Mord wants me dead. Heartwarming, isn't it?"

"What did you do?"

He grunts, as if my ignorance is amusing. "I was *born,* and that was enough to threaten his claim to the power he's craved since his own father bestowed the crown upon *my* father. As for why I'm in the Seelie Court . . . I'm here temporarily, and" — he smirks — "*covertly.* I prefer the Wild Fae Lands to the golden queen's territory, but there are matters here that require my attention."

My mind reels with a hundred questions, but only one repeatedly shuffles to the top. "Why are you telling me this? What do you want from me?"

"I know Mordeus has your sister, and I know what he's demanding from you in exchange for her." He sips his wine. "I want to teach you how to use your gifts to protect yourself in this land. I want to help you."

That's what he'd said in my dream. *I'll help you get her back. Come find me.*

"You keep saying that, but why should I believe you?" I back toward the door. "Your people abducted me and brought me here against my will, and you want me to *trust* you?"

His silver eyes flash and his mouth draws into a thin, tight line. "You chose to trust Mordeus by taking his deal."

"I don't have a *choice.* At least I understand what Mordeus wants from me and why. Am I supposed to believe that you want to help a human girl out of the goodness of your heart?"

He takes a menacing step forward, anger clear in every line of that beautiful face. "I want to help you because it helps my court. Every member of my court is weaker as long as our magical artifacts are missing. As long as the golden queen ..." His nostrils flare, and he takes several shallow breaths, as if suffering some sudden, invisible pain. "They are vulnerable as long as the power of the courts is out of balance."

"You expect me to believe that? You stand there in fine clothes, drinking fancy wine in a tavern in the Seelie Court. Poor, exiled prince. It seems like you're fighting *really hard* to get Mordeus off the throne."

The wineglass shatters to dust in his hand, and my body locks up in fear at the evidence of how dangerous he is. Calmly, he brushes his hands together, letting the drops of wine and glass dust fall away. "Take my help, mortal."

"I don't need you."

His gaze flicks over me, and I flinch when I see darkness leaking off my hands like ink into a pool of water. "Have you shared the bond with anyone?" he asks.

As if I'd submit myself to faerie bonding. As if I'd give *anyone* that kind of control over my free will and my life. *Never.*

"Maybe someone back home," he says. "A friend or lover, *anyone?*"

It's on the tip of my tongue to spit that humans don't perform such absurd rituals. I don't even know how or if it would work between humans, but I bite back the denial. I know just enough about faerie bonds to know that there's some level of protection involved. If Finn believes that someone might be bonded to me, maybe he won't try to keep me here.

He stares at me for a long beat. "It's a simple question."

I shrug. "And I simply choose not to answer."

He mutters something under his breath. I can see the anger in his eyes, his efforts to keep his temper under control. "You need to understand that bonds have consequences and aren't as easily undone as you might think."

Is this self-righteous ass seriously going to lecture me about this? I fold my arms. "If I leave, will your friends come after me?"

"Are you planning to return to the queen's son?"

The words are a balled fist to the gut. *Queen Arya's son.* Prince Ronan.

Sebastian.

I have to close my eyes against the pain of it. The betrayal. I can't let myself think about him right now.

When I open them, I stare at the inky blackness around my hands. This reminder is just what I need. *I have power. I am not trapped here.*

Finn steps close, studying me as if I'm a rather interesting insect, his lips curved in a smirk.

I step toward the shadows between the wall sconces, desperate to disappear into them as the office door opens.

"Word came from the castle," Pretha says, letting the door swing shut behind her. "Prince Ronan has delayed his selection until tomorrow. We need to put a plan in place quickly and get her back there."

Finn folds his arms. "I'm not sure the girl *wants* to work with us." There's a challenge in his voice. As if I'm a child and he's working me through reverse psychology.

I press my back against the wall and will myself to push through it, to escape. Nothing happens. How did I use my power before?

Pretha crosses the room, heading toward me. "You can't do this alone," she tells me.

I shake my head. "You're wrong." I've been working alone my whole life. Nothing needs to change now. Like the inverse of a flickering lamp, I fade to shadow and back to my corporeal self.

Panicked, Pretha spins on Finn. "What's she doing?"

Shadow. Turn to shadow. My hand disappears and appears, but the wall behind me holds firm.

"Finn!" Pretha's eyes are wide. "She's going to escape."

Shadow. This time when my hand disappears, the rest of my arm goes too. I melt into the wall and stumble through it. My dress tangles in a rosebush on the outside of the tavern, proving once again that pants are the wiser clothing choice. I scramble upright, and the thorns rip my skirt and tear at my legs.

I can hear Finn and Pretha argue through the cracked window, but their angry words are muffled until Finn barks a final, clear command. "Let her go."

I hoist my dress up and run, but I don't know where I am and the fog is too thick to see the castle in the distance.

I know the forest was ahead of me when I fled Sebastian, but now it's to my left. I turn, putting my back to the woods, but nothing in that direction looks familiar.

The forest. I can hide there — I can turn myself to shadow and nothingness and hide until I can find my way back to the castle. *Because I have to go back to the castle.*

If Sebastian's delayed his selection, perhaps I can still make this work. There's still a chance to save Jas.

The forest is darker than any in Fairscape — the canopy of leaves dense and the lights of the homes beyond dimmer than those from my overpopulated part of the world. A horrible cry tears through the night, followed by a triumphant howl. I've never been scared of the dark, but I know enough to be scared of *this* dark. I don't know half of what lives in these trees. Maybe my shadows can hide me, but can they protect me?

The summer heat has gone with the sun, and I wrap my arms around myself as I scan the forest, my eyes adjusting to the darkness.

Another howl, this one closer, and terror trembles through my muscles. *You know that the powers you have in my realm aren't so new. You've been using them for years.*

Normal humans can't see in the dark like this. I knew that, didn't I? I just didn't want to admit it to myself, didn't want to admit that there was some piece of faerie inside me.

But knowing you have a tool is a far cry from knowing how to use it. I have no idea where I am. No idea which way to the castle. And no idea how to use my power to protect myself from whatever lives in these woods.

A low growl sounds from twenty yards away. I spin and freeze in terror. Gold-flecked, glowing blue eyes flash in the dark, and a black wolf with bared teeth slinks toward me.

CHAPTER NINE

NOT A WOLF. EVEN IN A CROUCH, this animal's head is nearly as high as I am tall. A tongue darts out between long, fanged teeth, and it prowls toward me one slow step at a time.

I have no weapons but my fickle magic and nowhere to hide but in a forest this creature undoubtedly knows better than I do.

The branches of an oak tree flare out above me, but the ones within my reach are spindly and look too weak to hold my weight. Several feet away is maple tree with sturdy lower branches. If I sprint and jump, I might be able to climb high enough before the wolf-thing can reach me.

A low snarl, and it creeps closer, as black as night, the promise of death in its eyes.

Take a deep breath and run, Brie.

Turning, I sprint forward, then cut to my left as fast as my dress will allow. The creature lunges toward me, moving too fast for something so massive. I jump, reaching as high as I can even as the feel of the beast's breath warms the skin on the back of my neck. My fingertips brush the branch, and the bark bites into my skin as I grapple for a better grip.

I curl my fingers to claws, trying to hold on, but I slip. Time moves in slow motion as I fall toward to the forest floor and the beast's snapping maw.

I kick hard, aiming to dislocate the creature's jaw and barely moving it.

Pain sears through me as those teeth sink into my calf, and I scream as the muscle is torn away. *I'm in over my head. I'm nothing against this place.*

Low growls sound behind the creature, and two wolves pounce on it. For one pain-blurred moment I think they might be trying to protect me, but I'm delirious, and the rational part of my mind knows they're probably fighting for territory.

Or fresh meat.

I try to stand as the smaller wolves work together to attack the beast, but the moment I put weight on my injured leg, I collapse to the forest floor.

I use the tree to pull myself back up, and a horrific roar rips through the forest. The wolves' attention snaps away from the beast for one long beat before they turn and run . . . leaving me alone with the black, snarling creature.

It moves slower now — blood oozing from bites on its back — but not slow enough to make up for my maimed leg. I scramble backwards, trying to put all my weight on my good side and crying out when I collapse again.

The beast lunges, jaws wide, and I know it's coming for my

neck. Before it can reach me, an invisible wind lifts it from the ground and throws it into a tree across the clearing.

The creature screeches and collapses on the forest floor with one final cry.

"Abriella." Sebastian is here, breathless. He scoops me up like I'm weightless and cradles me in his arms. "Brie? Are you okay?"

I nod against his chest, but I'm not okay. The pain in my leg is so blinding, nausea rolls through me, but it's nothing compared with the defeated ache in my chest. I am so unequipped to take on this vicious world.

"Brie, your leg." He shifts me in his arms, and I jerk away as he reaches for the wound. "Shh. Be still." With a touch of his hand, the pain disappears.

I'm shaking so hard, and I take deep breath after deep breath to calm myself.

Sebastian smooths my hair off my face, tucking the loose strands behind my ears, and I realize that he's the one who's shaking. "I wanted to give you space, but I should have come after you. I'm so sorry I didn't come sooner."

I swallow. He looks . . . devastated. No matter how much his deception hurts, this is still Sebastian. He's broken my trust, but my feelings for him haven't disappeared because of who his mother is. They haven't vanished because he can wield magic from within himself more effectively than anything he learned from Mage Trifen. "I'm okay."

He runs a finger across my cheek, and when he pulls it away, I see blood. "I'm taking you back to the palace to see my healers."

The pain is gone, but I feel *off*, as if I am losing my balance and slipping from existence, whether from Sebastian's magic or a reaction to the creature's bite. I need help. I need healers. I nod and cast one last look toward the body of the beast.

"I'm sorry I didn't come sooner," Sebastian says again. "I'm so sorry."

He carries me out of the forest to a clearing where a white stallion waits in the moonlight. Sebastian's big hands are gentle — reverent — as he lifts me onto the horse. When he climbs on behind me, I relish the solid strength of him and the reassuring heat of his skin through his tunic. If I close my eyes, I can pretend we're back in Fairscape and nothing has changed.

He wraps one arm around me, and taking the reins with his other hand, he urges the horse into a gallop.

With his breath in my ear, the steady beat of his heart against my back, the rhythm of the horse beneath me, my eyes grow heavier with every step. I'd slide off this horse if he weren't holding me. My muscles refuse to work. I melt into his heat, his protective embrace, and I resent myself for the weakness.

By the time we arrive at the castle, keeping my eyes open is a losing battle.

He positions my hands on the stallion's neck. "Hang on right there for a minute," he instructs. He swings off the horse and hops to the ground, immediately reaching for me. Even half conscious, with a numb leg, I'm aware of every point of contact as he pulls me into his arms. He smells like the salt of the sea and the leather of his vest and pants. I jostle against his chest as he runs through the castle doors with me in his arms.

"Am I dying?" I ask against his chest, but I'm so tired there's no urgency behind my words.

"The Barghest's saliva is slowing your heart rate. If we don't get you the antitoxin quickly . . ." He runs faster, and I close my eyes, unable to muster the energy to worry. I'm vaguely aware of the sound of people around us, quick steps on stone and doors opening and closing.

"A Barghest got her in the forest —" he says. "Call the healer."

I open my eyes as a set of double doors opens before us and Sebastian carries me to a large four-poster bed. The layers of soft white bedding look like something from a dream. I curl onto my side. I don't care about anything but sleep right now.

When I close my eyes, I see Jasalyn's smiling face, and grief rips through me.

"Tell Jas I'm sorry," I whisper.

"Don't —" He grips my shoulder in his warm, callused hand. "Don't talk like that."

But doesn't he know it's true? I can feel death in the poison snaking its way through my veins. I open my mouth. I need to speak but can't find the energy.

Promise me you'll find her.

My mouth won't form the words.

Sebastian grips my shoulder harder. "Hold on, Brie."

I don't know how long I lie there, fading in and out of consciousness. I hear Sebastian talking to someone. Maybe many someones. Commanding them to action, shouting when they move too slowly.

"She's lost a lot of blood," an unfamiliar voice says. "And the toxin is spreading. She might not be able to drink."

"Abriella . . ." Sebastian says. That hand on my shoulder again. So warm. So strong. My one safe place to land. Even now.

"Abriella, I need you to drink this."

Glass against my lips. Warm liquid spills onto my tongue, down my chin.

"Swallow, dammit! You have to swallow."

I choke, gag, and finally manage to swallow before my energy flags again and I go limp in his arms.

"Good," Sebastian murmurs. "Good girl."

"I need to heal this leg before she loses any more blood," the unfamiliar voice says.

"Do it," Sebastian snaps.

The scorching heat of healing hands pulls me back in time. Then and now blur together. *Mom's voice. Sebastian's. Wind chimes at midnight. A stranger's promises.*

My bedroom is ensconced in fire — my body wrapped around Jasalyn, protecting her from flames that feel like they are eating me alive.

I'm barely aware of Mother's voice. *Please save her.*

There's a cost.

I'll pay it. I want to open my eyes and tell her it will be okay, but I can't. Her desperate silence is broken by a gasp that makes my heart ache. *There has to be another way.*

I do this for you.

My mother's sobs fill my ears, and then the numbness fades away with the heat of healing hands on my burns.

Pain. Lashing, blinding, terrible pain.

A spool of cool relief. And . . . life—pumping through my veins and rushing through my limbs.

I spy my mother looking both relieved and wretched. As if she'd sold a part of herself.

———·———

When I open my eyes, I almost expect to see my mother as she was the day I woke up nine years ago, healed from my burns. But she's not the one who sits in the chair by this unfamiliar bed. It's Sebastian, with his pointed ears and delicate fae grace. He's covered in blood, and his eyes are closed.

"Bash?" My throat is ravaged, and his name comes out broken.

Sebastian jerks awake and releases a long breath as he studies me. "It's okay," he says softly, resting a hand on top of mine. "You're going to be okay. I'm here."

He's here. And curse me but it feels good to know so completely that it's true. For this moment at least, for *this* set of struggles, I'm not alone. "Thank you." My voice sounds scratchy. "How long was I out?"

"Only a few hours. How are you feeling?"

"I'm fine." My stomach churns at the sight of the blood on him. Not on me, though. I'm in a clean, light blue sleeping gown of the softest cotton.

Sebastian catches me studying the gown. "We tried to save your dress, but it was covered in blood and shredded in places."

"You dressed me?" A silly question, really, given everything else. But the thought of him dressing me in sleep clothes and cleaning the blood off me . . .

He shakes his head, and then his eyes go wide as he realizes what I'm asking. "One of the handmaids changed you. I didn't — it wasn't — I wouldn't . . ."

If I weren't so exhausted, I might laugh at the red creeping up his neck. "I wasn't worried about that," I say softly. He's taken such good care of me. "Were you hurt?"

"No." He waves a hand to indicate the bloodstains on his tunic. "This was all yours, courtesy of the Barghest. Luckily, my healer was available when we arrived."

The room spins. I squeeze my eyes shut to still it, but the smell of blood fills my nose. Seeing it puts me back in that forest again. That wolflike creature lunging toward me. "Barghest? That's what that thing was?"

"Some call it the death dog."

"Is it from the Unseelie Court?"

"There are death dogs in all courts, but some of the more powerful Unseelie have them as familiars — animals that have been magically tied to them and can do their unholy bidding."

Did Mordeus send that Barghest after me? No. That doesn't make sense. If he truly wants me to retrieve the stolen artifacts for his court, he wouldn't try to kill me with some mind-linked monster. But Finn . . . Did Finn attack me because I wouldn't work with him? "Was that one bonded to an Unseelie?"

Sebastian shakes his head. "I don't know."

"If those wolves hadn't shown up . . ." I would have been dead. I catch another whiff of my blood and have to turn my face into the pillow. "I'm sorry . . . Do you have something you could change into?"

He mutters a curse and jumps out of the chair. "Of course. I'm sorry." He turns his back to me as he works the buttons on his shirt.

"We need to talk," I say. "About what happens next."

Sebastian looks over his shoulder and meets my eyes. "You should rest first."

I shake my head and force myself to sit up. I've shown more weakness since coming to Faerie than I have in the last nine years, and it needs to stop now. "I'm fine."

"You're still recovering from a major injury. Don't push it." He turns to me, bare-chested and . . . beautiful.

The room spins again.

I want to hate him like this — his true self — but despite everything, I still find Sebastian as alluring as I did that first day I saw him training in the courtyard.

I force myself to look away from his sun-kissed skin and sculpted arms. "I'm well enough to talk, I think." I hear the sound of a drawer opening, and when I turn back to him, he's pulling a fresh shirt over his head.

I watch as the soft white fabric falls over his perfect golden skin. I hate that this attraction didn't fade alongside the trust I lost when I found out the truth.

If my emotions were a mess before he rescued me in the woods, they're a disaster now.

He settles back in the chair by the bed and leans forward, elbows on his knees. "Okay. We can talk, if that's what you want."

"You saved me." I swallow. The memory of my terror is still too close to the surface, and I shove it down. "Thank you."

"I'm sorry I didn't come sooner."

"I didn't expect you to come at all."

He flinches, as if I'd just smacked him. Then hangs his head. "I know you don't like who I am, but it doesn't change how I feel about you."

My guts twist. "I don't like that you *lied* about who you are."

His jaw hardens. Blowing out a breath, he smooths back his white hair and ties it with a strap of leather. "When should I have told you? I couldn't let anyone in Elora know the truth —I'd have been crucified. And by the time we were friends and I knew you well enough to trust you with the information, you'd made it clear how you felt about my home *and* my kind." He swallows. "Maybe it was selfish, but I couldn't stand the idea of giving you up."

"Were you ever going to tell me? Or were you going to lie to me forever? Was that the real reason you begged me not to go after Jas? Because you didn't want me learning the truth?"

"I *wanted* to tell you. So many times. But my reasons for wanting you to stay on your side of the portal were honest. This is a dangerous place for you." His gaze drops to my leg, and even though I'm healed, in clean clothes, and covered by blankets, I know he's seeing the damage the Barghest did. "Do you see now? Do you understand why it terrifies me to have you wandering around my world looking for your sister?"

When he lifts his eyes back to mine, I hold his gaze. "I won't abandon her."

"I'm not asking you to. I'm asking you to allow *me* to find her." When I don't answer, he takes my hand and squeezes my fingers against his palm. "I've canceled my obligations for the day, and after you get some sleep, I'll be escorting you home."

I jerk my hand away. "No."

"You could have died tonight. How would that've helped Jas?" He shakes his head. "When I find her, don't make me tell her that she's lost her only family."

"Bash—" I close my eyes, remembering. "Sorry. I mean, *Prince Ronan*."

"Don't." He shifts from the chair to the edge of bed, his warm thigh against my side. "Call me Sebastian. Like you always have. It's still my name—the one I prefer, at least. No one calls me Prince Ronan but my servants and my subjects."

The modest apprentice I mooned over for two years has *servants* and *subjects*.

I take a breath. *Remember your deal with Mordeus. Remember what you're here to do.* "Okay . . . Sebastian. I can't go home. Gorst's men are after me, and it's not safe for me there. Please let me stay. I'll be careful, but don't make me go home. There's nothing for me there." Even if Gorst's men weren't looking for me, I wouldn't go home without my sister, but maybe if I put the emphasis on my protection rather than rescuing Jas, he'll agree.

"I can't protect you outside these palace walls." But he did tonight. Against all odds, he was there when I needed him.

"I understand," I whisper.

"Brie . . ."

I can sense that he's grasping for another argument to send me home. I look around his opulent bedchamber as if seeing it for the first time, as if I haven't already explored nearly every inch of

128

this castle. I've been in here before. I just didn't know this was his room when I was searching it. "This is a big place, and I won't get in the way. Can't you find a little room for me? Isn't there some way I'd be allowed to stay?" I can practically see him thinking it through. I hold my breath.

"There's only one way," he says. "I don't think you'll like it."

I school my face into a mask of curiosity. I already know where this is going, and it's exactly what I need. "Tell me."

"This morning I will select a dozen women to stay at the castle. Twelve women who want to . . . marry me." He nearly coughs on the words. "Perhaps if I presented you to my mother as a potential bride . . ." I see it on his face. He's waiting for me to shoot him down. He has no idea about my deal with King Mordeus or that I *need* access to this castle, so of course he'd think I'd hate the idea.

"What would I need to do?"

He blows out a breath. "Learn about the court, go to some fussy dinners, maybe a party or two . . ." He gives a shy smile, and for a moment he looks so vulnerable that I forget he's not the human boy I fell for. "Pretend you like me."

Part of me wishes I would have to pretend, but my conflicting emotions are all too real. "If I acted like one of these potential brides, would I stay in the palace?"

"Yes. You would be in the guest wing with the other girls."

"And while I'm here" — *while I look for the artifacts the king requires* — "you'll look for Jas?"

"Yes, of course. Whether you stay or return to your home, I'll search for her." He brushes his thumb across my knuckles, then rests it there. "You have my word."

I stare at his hand on mine for a long time, pretending to think about his offer. In truth, it will chafe to watch him choose his bride, and being here will be a constant reminder of his deception and my feelings for him, however misguided. But it will all be worth it when I turn the relics over to the shadow king and take Jasalyn home. "I want to stay."

His brow furrows.

"What's that look about?" I ask.

"After you learned who I was and ran away, I didn't think you'd want anything to do with me. I thought I'd lost you forever. You staying here . . ." He shrugs. "Maybe it seems too good to be true."

I force myself to smile, but part of me is curling up in shame. If I stay, if I do this, I'm not just deceiving some random prince. I'll be deceiving my friend. I have reasons for my lies, but he had reasons for his too, and it didn't make it hurt any less when I found out the truth.

I shake my head, trying to shrug off the tangle of emotions.

"Take the night," he says. "Rest. Think it through. If you're at my palace, I can't allow you to sneak out and search for Jas. You have to decide if you can handle that."

"I'll be a prisoner?"

"You'll be protected." He toys with my hand, and the light touch of his fingertip against my palm sends a needy shiver through me. I blame it on conditioning, on habit. My body doesn't understand that Sebastian isn't who I thought he was. "I know it's not your style to step back and let someone else do the work, but I can't bend on this. It's too dangerous. If you'll promise not to search for Jas — to leave that to me — I'll keep you here as long as I possibly can."

"Okay," I whisper. "Thank you so much, Sebastian."

He tucks the blankets around me, but I can tell his thoughts are already elsewhere. "Now sleep."

CHAPTER TEN

I DREAM OF FIRE. Of baby Jas in my arms. I dream of my mother's desperate pleas for a stranger to heal me and the sound of her tears when he agrees. I dream of night so dark all I can see are the Barghest's fangs as it lunges for my neck. I dream of silver eyes, and of Jas at five, telling me to count while she hides. *Don't peek! The prince will help you find me.*

When I wake, I'm no longer in Sebastian's chambers. Light pours into the room from a massive wall of windows. Two servants busy themselves around me — one at the foot of the bed, preparing a small breakfast tray, and the other filling the tub inside an attached bathing room.

Did Sebastian carry me here or did he have a goblin move me? It shouldn't matter. *It doesn't matter.* But after the way he carried me into the castle in his arms last night, it's all too easy to imagine him moving me here while I slept. Too easy to imagine that tenderness in his eyes and him dipping to press a kiss to my cheek. I catch myself clinging to the image before shaking it away. *Not why I'm here.*

As I sit up in bed, the servant adjusts a bouquet of orange day lilies before turning to me. *A human.* She wears a plain blue dress that hangs loosely on her plump frame, her blond hair tied into a simple but sleek braid. I pat my own hair, which is no doubt wild from a night of restless sleep in a strange bed.

"Good morning, Miss Abriella. I'm Emmaline and that's Tess," the woman says, gesturing to the servant in the bathroom. "Would milady like a bath or breakfast first?"

I press a hand to my growling stomach. It's been far too long since I've had anything substantive to eat, and though I'm accustomed to going without food, I'm pushing even my limits. "Breakfast, please."

She beams at me as if I've just offered her a gift. "Good choice."

Tess emerges from the bathroom, wiping her hands on a beige smock. Twins, I realize when I see her blond braid and identical smile. "Would you like your meal in bed or at the table?"

"The table is fine." I throw my legs over the side of the bed and stretch, yawning. I was so tired and weak when I fell asleep last night, but this morning I feel better than I have in days — maybe months. The healer must have repaired more than the damage from the Barghest. "Do you have coffee?"

"Of course. The prince told us that you prefer coffee," Tess says. She bites back a smile, and she and Emmaline exchange a meaningful look. "And day lilies."

"We asked around," Emmaline says, leaning in conspiratorially. "He didn't request flowers to be brought to any of the other girls."

"Or assign any of them their own rooms yet," Tess adds, winking at me.

133

I don't have to fake my surprise and delight as I approach the table. I run a finger across a soft orange petal. A renegade butterfly flutters in my stomach as I remember Sebastian tucking the flower behind my ear. I don't want to feel anything for him, but how can I not?

I take a seat at the small table by the windows, pausing a moment to appreciate the heat of the sun on my face. I've always been too much of a night owl to care for mornings, but I'm so rested after a full night's sleep that I feel almost optimistic.

Channeling my inner Jasalyn. She'd be proud.

I take a sip from my mug. It's different from the brown water folks at home call coffee. This is thicker and more decadent. Layered — as if I can taste the sunshine that warmed the beans and the berries on the bush beside it. It's as if my love of coffee before was only about its potential and I'm finally tasting it as it should be. But even this can't distract me from the feast waiting for me. A plate full of pastries, colorful berries, a cup of creamy yogurt, and a platter of cured meats and cheeses. I take a flaky pastry from the tray and nearly moan as it melts on my tongue. I lose myself in the food as my maids busy themselves around me.

I've stuffed myself to the point of discomfort when I realize the maids have gone still behind me.

"Your Highness," they say in unison.

When I turn, they've both frozen in low curtsies in front of Sebastian, who gives them a curt nod and warm smile. In truth, I expected the human slaves in Faerie to be drugged or mindless and treated like disposable tools, but if the twins are representative of life for humans here, my assumptions were completely off base.

Maybe nothing is how I thought it was.

"Tess, Emmaline," he says, nodding to them. "How are you this morning?"

"Good, Your Highness," Tess says, standing.

"Happy to get to know Lady Abriella," Emmaline says.

These women don't look at Sebastian as if he's their jailer. Their expressions are closer to that of doting aunts. And Sebastian treats them to the same charming smile that made half of Fairscape fall for him.

"Could you ladies give me a moment alone with Lady Abriella?"

"Of course," they say in unison. They each dip into another brief curtsy and scurry away.

Sebastian waits until the door closes behind them before he turns to me. "How are you feeling this morning?" He runs appraising eyes over me, and I shift, suddenly self-conscious in my nightgown in a way I was too tired to be last night.

"I'm good." I wrap my arms around myself. "I just woke up half an hour ago. Good as new."

He nods, but I can tell this doesn't surprise him. He knew I was okay, or he wouldn't have let me out of his sight. That's not why he's here this morning. "What we talked about last night — do you really want to do this?"

I hold my breath and nod. *Please don't send me home. Please don't make me fail Jas.*

He rolls his shoulders back. "Okay then. You'll have to go before my mother and me this afternoon and state your wish to . . ." He clears his throat but doesn't finish.

"Marry you?" I ask.

135

He nods. "I know how you truly feel, of course, but my mother cannot."

"I understand."

He turns to the day lilies and adjusts them in the vase, avoiding my gaze. "I need to ask you a favor."

"What's that?"

He's quiet for so long, I begin to fidget with my silverware. When he does speak, his voice is lower than before. "Keep our history a secret. I don't want my mother knowing that we met before today. It would . . . skew her judgment of you."

There is no future for me and Sebastian, so this shouldn't hurt. But I can't deny the sharp twisting in my chest. "You don't want her to know where I came from. That I cleaned fancy houses instead of living in one?" That aside from thievery and hiding in the dark, I don't have any skills or talents to speak of.

"I don't want her to know anything that might make her question why you're really here." He swallows and turns back to me. There's a storm of worry brewing in those sea-green eyes. "Despite my better judgment, I don't *want* you to leave, Brie. I like the idea of having you around."

I wish you'd stop saying sweet things. "Do you think your mother will allow me to stay?"

"I'll insist. It'll be fine." He takes my hand and skims his thumb across my pulse point. Awareness shivers through me, but when I look down, my scar is gone. "What — did you . . ."

"It's a glamour," he says quickly.

I stare at that smooth skin on the inside of my wrist and frown. I like my scar. It's a reminder of who I am, where I came from, and what I will sacrifice for the people I love. It represents the only truly good things about me. "Is that necessary?"

"I'm afraid so." I hear the regret hanging on his soft words.

What kind of mother is she that she won't allow her son to marry a girl with so much as a small scar? "Okay. I understand."

"I have to go, but I will see you soon. Remember not to let on that you knew me before you arrived at the castle, and don't tell anyone details of your life. They can know your name and that you're from Fairscape, but that's enough."

I nod, and as I watch him go, my stomach clenches uncomfortably.

How can feeling unworthy of a position I never wanted make me feel so small?

I play my part. A human girl excited over the prospect of marrying a faerie prince.

I'm bathed, scrubbed, plucked, and moisturized to within an inch of my life. Tess and Emmaline ask me questions about home, about what I think of Sebastian, about what it's like to have his eye. I try to act like a regular human girl who's known luxuries rather than having provided them for others. I pretend I don't know more than I should about their prince — like the way he gravitates toward the outdoors when the sun is out, or the way the muscles in his back ripple when he swings a sword. For them, I pretend I don't know what it's like to feel those soft lips meet mine, and for myself I pretend I don't want to feel that again.

The entire morning is surreal. My maids treat me like I'm some beautiful princess from a foreign land, not the penniless human thief who lived in a cellar for the last nine years. If I'm honest, their doting is . . . *nice.* I've spent all my time going unnoticed, being unremarkable, and I'm surprised to find that there's some part of me that likes having them coo over the blazing red of my hair and the hazel eyes I've always found too plain.

They present me with half a dozen dresses of different shades and styles, each more lovely than the last. Jas would have swooned over the gowns as if they were priceless works of art, but all I can think is how much I'd rather wear pants. If I'd been in pants last night, I might've stood a chance when running from the Barghest. Now isn't the time, though. I need to dress in something the queen will find appropriate for her son's potential bride.

"Hair all up or half up?" Emmaline asks. She drops my curls and hides her delighted giggle behind her hand. "The prince thinks you're lovely either way, I'm sure."

I cock my head to the side, studying her in the mirror. "Why do you laugh like that when you talk about Prince Ronan liking me or asking you to do things for me? Is that uncommon with the fae?"

The maids exchange another long look. "Not with the fae," Tess says. "But Prince Ronan . . ."

Emmaline shakes her head subtly and offers me an apologetic smile. "We shouldn't say."

"I wish you would."

"It won't hurt anything," Tess says under her breath to her twin.

Emmaline bites back a smile, then lets it loose. "Our prince has been reluctant to choose a bride. He's been doing what he must because this is tradition, but he's not been involved in any of it. He alone has been responsible for all these delays in the ceremony."

"He didn't even show up the first night of the ball," Tess says. "Rumor has it he told his mother he wasn't ready, but she moved forward with it anyway. Eventually he had to comply, but he's been . . . distant."

"Until you showed up," Emmaline says, pinning a curl at the back of my head. "Now he's suddenly *very* interested in the process. So interested it seems he's already decided. *Make sure Abriella has coffee. Please prepare dresses for Abriella. Could you put a bouquet of day lilies on her breakfast tray?*"

"And of course he also gave you the nicest guest quarters," Tess adds.

"And the sweetest maids, it seems," I say softly.

The twins giggle happily at the compliment, but it's not just flattery. I know it's true. Sebastian has done all this for me and I'm not sure I deserve it.

I sit still as they finish my hair. They pull the top half of my hair back and pin it in place, but they leave the rest down, using special creams to tame my curls and make them hang perfectly.

These women want to be my friends. That simple kindness fills me with guilt as I imagine how I'll have to deceive them in the days ahead, but I lock up the feeling and push it aside. Starting now, I will use every tool at my disposal to get Mordeus his relics and free Jas.

Even these human servants' kindness.

Even Sebastian's blind trust.

CHAPTER ELEVEN

"LADY ABRIELLA KINCAID OF FAIRSCAPE," the steward calls from the doors of the throne room. "Her Majesty, Queen Arya of the Seelie Court, and His Royal Highness, Prince Ronan, will see you now."

I throw a glance over my shoulder at my maids. I need their confidence. They give me the smiles I'm looking for, and I take a fortifying breath, lift my soft white skirts, and follow the steward forward.

The queen's gray-and-yellow-clad guards line both sides of the path from the doors to the dais, where she sits on her throne in a yellow gown that sparkles in the sunlight. The jeweled golden crown atop her head looks heavy enough to break a neck, but she keeps her head high. Sebastian stands beside her, turned away as he speaks with the armed sentry nearest him. He looks nothing short of regal in his uniform of steely gray, a velvet yellow sash hanging across his body.

The space alone is intimidating — too big for so few people, too polished for a girl like me — and each step forward is an effort. But I realize that's the point. Any girl who doesn't feel worthy upon entering this room has no business becoming the Seelie princess.

When I reach the foot of the dais, I curtsy deeply. I wish Sebastian would look at me. I need some reassurance — any at all — that he's going to make sure I can stay, that it's going to be okay. But he's wrapped up in his discussion with his sentry. "Your Majesty," I say, standing. "Thank you for seeing me this afternoon."

As I speak, Sebastian whips around and blinks at me. He must not have been paying attention when they announced my name, because he looks surprised. Slowly, his gaze travels over me, and I feel my skin heat with each detail he observes. My hair curled and pinned neater than he's ever seen it, my eyes lined with kohl, my lips stained a dark crimson. His gaze sweeps across my bare shoulders and continues to the swell of décolletage above the dress's sweetheart neckline, over the bodice covered in glittering silver and gold crystals. My cheeks warm, and when his lips part and he draws in a ragged breath, my entire body warms.

My maids chose well when making their selections. *With just enough white, we can make you look like a bride without wearing a bridal gown.* I lift my chin, fighting the instinct to revel in the appreciation in those eyes. A week earlier, I could only dream of Sebastian looking at me like this. It's a struggle to remember that everything has changed. He's not the sweet, struggling apprentice next door. And I'm not an innocent girl looking to become faerie royalty.

"Tell me your name again, girl," the queen says.

I tear my gaze away from her son to look at the queen. "Abriella Kincaid," I answer. I don't use the title *lady* like her steward did. I'm no lady, and to pretend otherwise feels like an insult to a female I can't risk upsetting.

"Abriella. What a lovely name. Congratulations on making it this far. As you've seen, countless women have tried and were sent away. More will be sent home today. Tell me, why do you wish to marry my son?"

I open my mouth to answer, then snap it shut again. I was prepared for this question, of course, but in this moment my planned response strikes me as shallow. Sebastian seems to hold his breath as he waits for me to answer. I meet his eyes and imagine an alternate reality where Sebastian never had a secret identity. One where he became a mage and took me to meet his family.

"I can't claim to know your son well," I say. It's in line with the part I'm playing, but it's also true. "But I've met many males, young and old, powerful and powerless." My voice shakes a bit. "And yet Se — Prince Ronan is the only one who's ever made me feel special from his first smile and safe from his nearness alone."

The queen chuckles and looks to her son. "She sounds quite besotted with you." When she looks back to me, she rolls her eyes in an expression that is so young and so human it's almost difficult to believe that she's an immortal ruler. "*All* the girls feel that way, my dear. Don't feel too special."

Sebastian shifts uncomfortably, but he doesn't correct her. How could he if he doesn't want her to know we already have a relationship?

She arches a brow at her son. "Your thoughts, darling?"

Sebastian looks me over again before clearing his throat. "I've had the opportunity to speak with Abriella, and I wish her to stay. I . . . enjoy her company."

The queen smirks at her son as if to say *This one? Really?* "You would risk marrying a girl who may not be capable of bearing you children?"

"Mother," he says softly, warning in his tone.

"I won't apologize for noticing that she is quite thin." She taps her nails on the arm of her throne as she studies me. When she lifts her eyes to mine, I'm struck by the emptiness I find there. The sadness. Perhaps immortality does that to a person, but this seems like something more. "My son's bride will be expected to bear him children. Do you even menstruate regularly?"

I blanch. "Excuse me?"

"Your cycle? Do you have it? Or is it irregular due to" — she waves a hand to indicate my figure — "malnutrition?"

I open my mouth — to say what I'm not sure — but Sebastian speaks first. "I'm sure Lady Abriella isn't used to speaking freely of such things, Mother. She comes from a part of Elora where women are expected to keep such information private."

I'm not sure which part of Elora *doesn't* expect that. Girls are taught to dread their cycles, to never speak of them and hide every evidence of their existence. With all the trouble it brings — and risk of pregnancy high on that list when there's never enough food — menstruation is considered a curse more than a sign of good health.

"She forfeited any right to privacy when she decided she wanted to be your bride."

"I do," I blurt. "I mean, my monthly cycle is . . . It's normal." My cheeks are on fire. It looks like I got *something* right about the Seelie Court. This whole tradition is built entirely around human fertility. As if, as a woman, my only worth lies in my ability to give them offspring. It's a struggle to smile through this confirmation, but I do my best.

"Truly?" the queen asks. "If I ask my healer to examine you and he tells me you've lied —"

"Please, Mother," Sebastian says. "I'm sure that any gaps in Lady Abriella's nutrition can be corrected during her stay at the palace."

The queen brushes her fingers against her son's wrist but keeps her gaze narrowed on me. "My son's tender heart will make his future bride so very lucky. He gets it from his father. My Castan was full of compassion and goodness. Beloved by our people." She nods at me. "You may stay for now, Abriella. But see that you take full advantage of the meals while you're here, yes?" She smirks. "I will recommend that my healer visit you for a full physical in two weeks' time. Assuming that my son hasn't tired of you by then, of course."

I nod and curtsy. "Of course, Your Majesty." I don't dare look at Sebastian before I allow the queen's steward to escort me from the room. I'm too afraid the relief on my face will make the queen question my true intentions.

———·———

After locking my bedroom door, I pull up my sleeve and snap a thread of my goblin bracelet.

When Bakken appears, he's squinty-eyed and scowling.

I allowed my maids to ready me for bed, then waited for them to leave for the night, but every moment since the queen agreed to let me stay, I've been itching to start my search. At dinner, I remembered my goblin bracelet and realized that I might not have to search for the mirror.

Bakken blinks a few times, but his scowl turns to a smile when he takes me in. "Fire Girl, where is my payment?"

I pull out a knife I stole from my table setting tonight. I use it to slice off a lock of hair. Bakken yanks it from my grasp before I can offer it to him, quickly tucking it into the pouch at his waist. "Next time you call me, don't do it from inside this palace. I'm not welcome here."

"I need the Mirror of Discovery." I turn to my bed and pull the fake from beneath my mattress. "It looks like this, and the queen is said to have stolen it from the Unseelie during the war."

Bakken lifts his chin. "The queen keeps the mirror in the sunroom just off her bedchambers."

The night I searched the castle for the portal, I was never able to search her chambers. They were too brightly lit and well guarded.

Bakken holds the hair to his nose and inhales deeply, like an addict taking a hit.

I open my mouth to ask how I can get past her guards, but he snaps his fingers and disappears as suddenly as he appeared. I have to bite my fist to hold back a howl of frustration.

What a waste of a thread. What a waste of hair.

I unlock my door and crack it to peek down the hall. The guest wing of the castle is quiet but not dark. The corridors are dimly lit by soft orbs of light floating between each room. Quietly I leave my room and slowly close the door behind me.

I met the other eleven girls at dinner, but there's no sign of them now as I slip past their rooms. Is Sebastian inside with one of them? I tamp down the jealous thought and focus on my mission.

I might need to turn myself to shadow to get through certain parts of the palace, but I'll wait as long as I can. I'm not in full control of my power yet, and a girl suddenly appearing from shadow is much more conspicuous than one of Sebastian's potential brides wandering around the palace in the middle of the night.

The guest rooms are in their own wing, and by the time I reach the entrance to the wing with the royal chambers, the bones in my feet ache from the cold stones. I didn't think to put on slippers before I left my room.

Sebastian's room is to the left at the top of the stairs, but I turn right, toward the queen's chambers, only to scramble back a few steps at the sunlight filling her hall. No, not sunlight. The window at the end of the hall is still dark with night. It's as if these walls have been enchanted to glow like the sun. Queen Arya's guards stand watch every six feet down the hall. Even if I knew how to control my shadows long enough to sneak past these sentries, it wouldn't help. What good is becoming darkness where there is only light?

"Brie?" I turn to see Sebastian. His eyes flick down to my white nightgown and bare feet before he lifts his chin and trains his gaze on my face, ever the gentleman. "Are you looking for something?"

Yes. I'm looking for a magic mirror your mother had stolen

146

from the Unseelie Court. Would you fetch it for me? If only it could be that simple.

I sigh and deliver my preplanned lie. "I can't sleep. I was hoping to find a hot cup of tea in the kitchen, but" — I look around and shrug — "I'm afraid I've gotten lost."

I expect him to question this. Although I've not officially been shown the whole castle, I've been shown enough to know that the kitchen isn't in this direction. Or on this floor.

But Sebastian's too trusting for his own good. He gives me a sympathetic smile. "I can't sleep either. Come with me and we'll have some tea together."

We don't exchange a word on the way to the kitchen. Sebastian barely spares me a glance as he leads me into the large, empty space and puts a kettle on the stove. Just two nights earlier I'd fallen through the wall into this kitchen, and these gleaming countertops were covered in enough food to feed hundreds while servants bustled about in every direction. Tonight, there's no one here but us.

"Has something upset you?" I ask, leaning against the counter.

Sebastian pours steaming liquid from the stove into two mugs. He frowns as he passes me a mug. "Why do you ask that?"

"You've barely spoken to me since we headed down here, and I was surprised not to see you at dinner."

"I'm not upset. I'm preoccupied. I apologize for that." He blows out a breath. "I've just returned from a meeting with my contacts in the Unseelie Court." He slowly lifts his eyes to mine, and I see the torment there. "They still haven't found any sign of Jas."

I can't even register disappointment as panic has my lungs in a vice-grip. "You have spies in King Mordeus's court?" Does he know I was there yesterday? Does he know about the deal I made with the king? If Sebastian learns of our bargain through spies, will the king renege on his promises?

Sebastian shrugs, but his answer is clear. Yes, he has spies in the Unseelie Court. *Of course* he has spies. "I don't understand what he wants with her," he mutters.

There's my answer. Sebastian remains ignorant of my bargain with his enemy court. "None of your sources have any idea either?"

"Nothing helpful." He hesitates a beat. "Has he tried to contact you?"

"He hasn't. Do you think you could put me in touch with him?" It's what I would ask if my lie were true. "Maybe he'll tell me something about where he's keeping Jas. Or maybe he'll be interested in some sort of —"

"No." Sebastian's nostrils flare. "Absolutely not. Even if I thought he could be trusted — and I can't stress enough that he *cannot* — there's nothing he would ask of you that I would let you give." He curses and drags a hand through his hair. "This is such a mess."

He really is a wreck about not being able to find Jas. I may still be reluctant to trust Sebastian again, but he's doing everything he can to help my sister. It's impossible to stay angry with him. "Thank you," I say. He deserves at least that. "Thank you for trying to find her."

He opens his mouth, and I can tell he wants to say something, but he snaps it shut again and stares at his tea. "How was dinner?"

I bite back a smile. "It was definitely . . . interesting. Gods above and below, Bash, I think those women would skin me alive if they thought it would get them closer to you." I shake my head. Eleven beautiful, bright-eyed, healthy women, each more excited to be Sebastian's bride than the last. "You're really going to marry a stranger?"

His throat bobs as he swallows. "I hope whoever I marry isn't a stranger when the time comes."

"You're evading." I try to keep my tone light, but I see the weariness in his eyes.

He takes a sip of his tea. "It's tradition."

"What is? Choosing a bride like you'd choose a breeding mare?" And there goes my attempt to make nice.

"As awful as it might seem from your point of view, it is important that we continue the royal bloodline. I have no siblings, and my grandparents and great-grandparents were killed in the Great Fae War. My mother and I are the only royal Seelie blood remaining. Though some of my ancestors had the luxury of marrying for love and hoping to be blessed with children over time, I don't. Being born into privilege comes with responsibilities."

I bite my lip. I hate this conversation. I hate it because I can't hide my feelings on this, and I hate that I have feelings on the subject at all. "If you had the choice, would you prefer to marry a fae female — perhaps a member of the nobility?"

Sebastian puts his mug down and leans against the counter, folding his arms. "Honestly, I would prefer not to be thinking of marriage at all. I'm only twenty-one, which is considered very young among my kind. In an ideal world, I wouldn't be thinking of marriage for another decade or more, but my world isn't ideal. It's broken. And I find myself in the intimidating and humbling position of fixing it. Part of me would rather be back in Fairscape acting as a mage's apprentice, but I take my duty to my people seriously. No matter how much I want to, I don't get to think of marriage and bonding ceremonies with the same romantic notions my mother did when she was my age."

"Bonding? What's romantic about controlling someone?"

He tips his head to the side, and his brow furrows. "Why do you think it's about control?"

"Isn't bonding the way you imprison your slaves?"

He shakes his head. "None of my servants have been bonded to me. And while some fae have used the bond to lock humans into lifetimes of servitude, it was never intended to be used like that. Faeries have incorporated the bonding ceremony into their weddings since the beginning of time. Its origins are pure. Life-bonded fae have a sense of each other at all times. It's a heightened empathy that allows you to know when your partner is in danger or hurting. Bonded fae spouses are conscious of each other's needs always. They feel each other's pain and happiness like it's their own. It's quite beautiful, really."

"But that's not what happens when you're bonded to a human."

He rocks back on his heels and sighs. "The first faeries to bond with humans didn't know that it would be different. But you're right. It is. Humans aren't magical, so the bond is more like a one-way street. The human partner doesn't have the awareness of the other side of the bond the way a faerie would."

"And it gives faeries a degree of control over their humans,"

I say, unwilling to let him keep that piece unspoken. I shake my head. "I can't imagine why anyone would allow that."

"They can't control them the way you think. The human still has free will, but faeries who don't respect the bond have certainly used it to compel their humans."

"That sounds like control to me."

"But it's not." He rubs the back of his neck, thinking. "Imagine that I want you to sleep. If we were bonded, I couldn't force you to, but I could mentally do the equivalent of turning off the lights and wrapping you in a warm blanket. You still get to choose whether or not to close your eyes."

"What if your bride-to-be doesn't want the bond?"

He gives me a sad smile and holds my gaze as he touches my cheek. My skin tingles beneath his callused fingertips. "I think I'm looking at the only woman under this roof who would refuse to be bonded with me."

Does he want me to apologize for that? Does he expect me to change the way I feel about everything just because he's not who he pretended to be?

But he doesn't seem to need an answer, because he goes on. "It can still be beautiful — even between a faerie and a human. It's about protecting someone who's a piece of you. It's a gift that makes you the best partner possible by heightening your awareness of their . . . needs."

His gaze dips to the neckline of my nightgown, and my cheeks heat.

"It means a lot to you," I say.

"It does. And after my bride has children, she will drink

the Potion of Life, and the bond will work between us as it does between any two faeries."

"The Potion of Life?"

"That's the special magic we use to transform humans into fae. They become immortal. Surely you've heard of it."

I have, but I figured it was just another legend to convince humans to put their trust in capitalizing faeries. "What if your bride doesn't want to be a faerie?"

"Then I suppose I'll have to decide if I truly want her as my bride. It would be no easy thing to watch and feel my life-bonded partner die, knowing that I have centuries of life ahead of me." He straightens and backs away. "I'll take you to bed. You have an early start tomorrow."

CHAPTER TWELVE

LIVING IN THE CASTLE IS STRANGE. It *should* feel like a dream come true. Every day I am pampered, fed delicious foods, and dressed in beautiful gowns. Though I continue to try to convince my servants to find me pants, there's no real need for them amid this luxury. At night I sleep in a warm bed covered by the softest blankets.

I've never known a life like this and never thought I would, but I can't enjoy it. Every day that I fail to find the mirror is another day my sister is locked away. The king says she's safe, but what does *he* consider safe?

I've been at the castle for five nights, and despite the splendor, I'm ready to crawl out of my skin. I go to meals with the other girls, take dancing lessons, listen to long lectures about the history of the Seelie Court and the crimes of the lawless Unseelie. In short, I do what I must to continue this charade of being a potential bride while using every free moment to search for ways into the queen's chambers. I observe the guards and the comings and goings of the servants.

I may be temporarily stuck on the mirror, but I hope

153

everything I learn about the castle now will make my next task that much easier. The sooner I can finish this mission and get Jas home, the better.

I stare out my bedroom windows and scan the garden below. The day lilies stretch their heads to the sun and make me think of Sebastian. "Any word on when the prince will return?" I ask my maids. Sebastian's rarely at the castle, much to the girls' dismay, and I'm not sure how he's finding time to get to know his potential brides when he's gone so often.

"He's not away," Tess says, braiding my hair out of my face. "He's spending the day with one of the other girls."

Jealousy sits like a rock in my stomach. "Oh. A favorite, then?"

My face must give me away because Tess tsks and smiles at my reflection in the window. "You have nothing to worry about. Everyone knows he favors you."

And yet we haven't spoken since our discussion over tea in the kitchen. There's no reason he would spend his limited time with me when he knows I'm not interested in being his bride. I should be glad for that — I've had more time to search — but it's hard to let go of feelings I've harbored for Sebastian for two years.

"I'm sure he'll spend time with you soon," Tess says. She ties off the braid and starts on the other side. "And anyway, he probably knows you're not available."

"I'm not?"

"You'll meet your tutor today."

I frown. "Tutor? For what?"

"All the girls are assigned tutors. Should the young prince choose you as his bride, you'll need to be prepared. Your tutor will refine your habits and manners, attending to you on a personal level."

"Can't *you* do that?" I ask. I like my maids, and I've become accustomed to them. I don't want to have another person watching me.

Emmaline laughs from the bathroom, where she's cleaning the tub. "We are not *ladies*," she says, poking her head out the door. "Simply servants."

"But I bet you could teach me anything my tutor could."

The twins look at each other. I can't tell if they're amused or baffled by me. Perhaps both. "In any case," Tess says, "your tutor will arrive any minute. Her name is Eurelody, and she's worked with the queen's historians for over a century. You're lucky to have her."

Over a century. Maybe she'll know about the queen's schedule and when Arya's expected to travel away from the castle. If I can find a discreet way to inquire . . .

"Can we get you anything before we go?" Emmaline asks.

"No, I'm fine. Thank you."

I don't know why I assumed that Sebastian was out of the castle just because he hasn't been to see me. Maybe I offended him with my comments about his sacred traditions.

Or maybe he's trying to find a bride.

"Lost in thought, I see," a soft voice says behind me.

I turn to see a short, chubby faerie with rosy cheeks and pointed ears. Her translucent wings barely fit through the doorway. I make myself smile. It's not her fault that I have no interest in our time together. "Hello. You must be Eurelody. I'm Abriella."

The woman gives me a quick once-over and, seeming to find

155

my attire acceptable, turns back to the door. "Very good. Let's get out of the palace for a while, shall we?"

My breath catches. Until this moment, I hadn't realized how claustrophobic I was feeling being stuck inside these walls. After nearly dying in the forest, I didn't dare disobey Sebastian's order to stay within the palace gates, but surely I'll be safe if I'm with Eurelody.

She's already heading down the hall, and I have no choice but to follow. "Where are we going?"

She doesn't bother slowing or looking back at me as she answers. "If you want to be a princess, you need to meet your future subjects."

———

The carriage is comfortably appointed with cushions, and draperies across the windows for privacy. Eurelody and I sit knee to knee as we leave the castle grounds, and I'm well aware of her attention on me as I watch the changing landscape outside. I don't bother filling the silence, and neither does she. Instead, I focus on the rolling green hills, the forest in the distance, and the mountains beyond. Even knowing how dangerous those woods are, I can't help but find them lovely. Everything in Seelie territory glows with the lush green of late spring. I wonder if Unseelie territory is the same or if the shadow fae suffer perpetual winter.

Miles from the castle, we turn into a quaint village. The carriage jostles on the cobblestones, jarring me this way and that before coming to a sudden stop.

"We're here," Eurelody says.

Half-timbered houses line streets where faeries of all kinds hawk their wares to passersby. The smell of fresh bread and pastries fills the air from one merchant's cart. Another merchant pours a sample of wine for a patron while others sell flowers, beautiful fabrics, and jewelry.

Fairscape has a market like this. When I was a child, my mother would take us along when she ran errands for the wealthy family who employed her. They would send her for candles and clothing, for art for the walls of their massive home. If we behaved, Mother would buy us a tiny candy each. I used to imagine that we were shopping for ourselves, that *we* were the ones who could afford such luxuries.

"What are those little faeries?" I ask Eurelody, nodding to the tiny airborne creatures with butterfly wings.

"Hush, girl." She shakes her head and tugs me by the arm toward a narrow lane opposite the village market. Nearly identical houses line the road, and she leads me up the front steps of the third. The door creaks as it opens, and she drags me inside and throws herself against it to shut it. "Sprites," she says, wagging a finger at me, "do not like being called *little*."

"But they—"

"Are more powerful than they look and more spiteful than you can imagine," she says. "In fact, some call them *spites* for just that reason, but that's slang, and many sprites consider it derogatory. If you offend a sprite, you just might find yourself attacked by fire ants or with a swarm of bees charging at you."

"They're not *all* so spiteful," a deep voice says. "Some are quite docile."

I turn to my right and scramble backwards toward the door

when I spot the male emerging from a dimly lit room. *Kane.* The red-eyed, horned faerie who carried me over his shoulder to meet Finn.

I spin away from Kane and smile at my tutor. I don't know where we are, but I can't let one of Queen Arya's people think I've been associating with the enemy. "We should go."

Eurelody smiles at me, and then the air around her shimmers and her skin glows. Suddenly she's not Eurelody but *Pretha.* This faerie has many faces, it seems.

"Pretha . . . *you*—" I seethe.

She smiles in response and gives me a little curtsy. "So kind of you to remember me by name, Abriella."

"Where's Eurelody?"

"She left the queen's service years ago, but I show up in her form now and again to maintain easy access to the castle. The queen has so many in her service that she doesn't even notice that her old scholar is rarely researching."

My eyes dart to the door. Did the carriage we arrived in belong to Pretha or the queen? If I run outside, I can't assume that my driver will take me anywhere. "Give me one good reason I shouldn't return to the castle and tell them who you really are."

She rolls her eyes and turns to Kane. "Prince Ronan thinks she's so smart and so special, but if she truly were those things, I think she'd want to know *all* the reasons she shouldn't tell the queen, not just one."

"The prince is young and blinded by her beauty," Kane says. "The night she ran from the tavern, she proved how lacking she is in the intelligence department."

I fold my arms. "Insulting me will get you nowhere but the queen's oubliette."

This threat doesn't faze either of them. Instead, Pretha casually shrugs out of her robe and hangs it on the hook by the door. She adjusts her leather vest and the scabbard at her side. "I am not your enemy, Abriella."

"And yet the last time I got away from you, a death dog nearly made me his dinner. Am I supposed to believe that was a coincidence?"

"You think *I* sent the Barghest after you?" The silver webbing on her forehead seems to pulse with outrage.

"You, Finn, Kane? Does it make a difference?"

Kane grunts. "Why would we do that?"

"Because I refused to work with you. I'm not clueless. I know the Unseelie sometimes take Barghests as animal companions."

Kane barks out a laugh, then shakes his head and walks away. "I'll tell Finn she's here — and that she thinks we're murderers who command vicious and powerful monsters. Awesome start to a new partnership, I think he'll agree."

"Where would you get such an idea?" Pretha asks, ignoring Kane. "Did your prince tell you we were behind the Barghest?"

"He didn't have to."

"You wanted to leave, and we let you." Pretha frowns. "After you ran from the tavern, I followed you to the forest. Finn forbade me to follow you too closely. He just wanted to make sure you made it safely to wherever you were going."

"Oh? And did you tell him I was nearly torn to bits?"

"Yes." She cocks her head to the side. "It's a good thing those wolves came along to distract the creature."

"It's a good thing *Sebastian* came along to *save* me."

"So you've already forgiven your golden prince for his deceptions?" Finn says, stepping out of the dark hallway and into the foyer. I was so distracted by Pretha that I didn't hear his steps in the hall. Or maybe I wouldn't have even if I'd tried. He looks to Kane and Pretha. "I told you it would take less than a week. Looks like you each owe me five gold."

"We don't owe you a damn thing, Finn," Kane says, entering the foyer behind him. "The girl didn't answer the question."

"If she didn't trust that boy, she never would have gotten into that carriage with Pretha this morning," Finn says.

Pretha shakes her head. "She can trust him without forgiving him. They're entirely separate emotions."

They're betting on when I'll forgive Sebastian. *Rude.* "I'm glad this is all so amusing to you."

Finn's silver eyes harden and glitter like the surface of a frozen pond in the moonlight. "I assure you I'm not amused in the slightest," he says. "I'm impatient. Considering that my uncle has your sister, I'm surprised you aren't as well. But maybe you're content to enjoy the luxuries of palace life, busy preparing for your life as that boy's *princess.*"

"How dare you—" I shuffle back a step, spotting two sets of glowing silver eyes in the dark hallway. Two large wolves prowl forward and stop on either side of Finn.

Finn snaps his fingers, and the wolves sit, sniffing the air in my direction and whining quietly. They've healed since I saw them in the forest, but there is no doubt in my mind that these are the same animals that attacked the Barghest.

Their silver-and-gray coats were mottled with blood when they ran away, but today they are clean and shining, and . . . much larger than I remembered. They looked so much smaller compared with the Barghest, but now I can see just how massive they are. Even sitting, they're only a head shorter than I am.

My eyes flick to Finn. "They're yours?"

"In a manner of speaking," he says, absently scratching one behind the ear.

Pretha says, "I told you we aren't your enemy, Abriella."

The night it happened, I had wondered whether the wolves were just trying to get the Barghest out of the way so they could get to me. But looking at them now, panting happily at their master's affection, I know without a doubt that they saved me. If Sebastian hadn't shown up, they would have kept fighting — until the Barghest died or they did.

"Are they okay?"

"They are now," Finn says. "Thanks to my healer."

"What do you call them?"

"Dara and Luna," Finn says. The wolves' ears perk up at the sound of their names.

"May I?" I'm aware of all the eyes in the room on me as I inch forward and extend a tentative hand toward each. Finn mumbles a low command, and the wolves rise and approach me slowly. "Thank you," I say, kneeling in front of them and offering the back of my hands to smell. "You protected me."

The wolves lick my hands, then nuzzle my palms like big cats.

When I look up, there's something like confusion in Finn's eyes, but he blinks and it's gone, replaced by the steely cold I'm used to. "Why did they do it?" I ask.

"Because I asked them to."

"That was a terrible risk. They could have been killed."

Finn doesn't deny it. Instead he folds his arms and leans one shoulder against the wall. "They're very loyal, and now that they've protected you once, they would do it again."

Pretha sighs dramatically. "But it would be much better for everyone involved if you didn't go running off and need saving again."

Kane chuckles. "Maybe she likes being rescued by her prince. Sounds like he made quite an entrance when he returned to the palace — running inside with her in his arms and generally playing hero to her damsel in distress."

My cheeks heat at the picture he paints. I hate the idea that anyone sees me that way, but I don't bother asking how they know about what happened at the castle. Clearly everyone spies on everyone here. I direct my attention to Finn when I ask, "What do you want from me?"

"I told you before," he says, his voice a little rough, as if he's very, very tired. "We want to help you."

"Why would you want to help me when I'm working for the king who wants you dead?"

"You mean the *false* king," Kane says, his voice sharp.

Finn snaps his fingers, and his wolves obediently return to his side. "The missing relics make my court weaker. My people are suffering, and I will do anything I can to help them."

162

"Even if it means strengthening the . . . your uncle?" I smell something, and it's not honesty.

"Mordeus," Finn says with none of Kane's annoyance, "cannot get any more powerful unless he wears the crown."

I frown. "Where's the crown?"

"My father's crown has been missing from the Court of the Moon for too long now," Finn says. He pauses a beat. "I take it you haven't found the mirror yet?"

"I know where it is, but I haven't been able to get to it," I admit.

"And have you tried using your magic?" he asks. "You know, that thing that lets you walk through walls and magical wards as if they weren't even there?"

Jerk.

"How could she do that when she can't even control it?" Pretha asks, but Finn shoots her a look that shuts her up.

"No," I say, answering Finn's question. "Pretha's right. I don't have enough control. But that's not the problem. The queen keeps the mirror guarded and surrounded by light. Even if I had control over my powers, they would be useless there."

Kane snorts. "She has no idea, does she?"

"Stop talking about me like I'm not in the room," I snap. "And no idea about what?"

"No idea just how strong you are," Pretha says. She cocks her head to the side. "No idea what you're capable of."

"What if I told you," Finn says softly, "that your power is never useless. That you're strong enough to manifest darkness so complete that it would gobble up every bit of her light?"

"How do you know that?" I ask.

163

"We've been watching," Finn says with a shrug.

"What do you say, Brie?" Pretha asks. "Will you let us help you?"

I don't know if I can trust Finn and his people, but I can't afford to be discovered in my attempts to get the mirror. I can't afford to fail. I look at the wolves and make my decision.

"I'll work with you today. Teach me whatever I need to know so I can swap the mirrors."

Finn arches a dark brow. "The first thing you need to know is not to use the mirror. It's not a toy for human girls to play with, understood?"

Right. Because I'm just a lowly human and unworthy of his precious mirror. *Whatever.* "I thought you were going to teach me to use my powers so I can get into the queen's sunroom."

"Wait." Finn holds up a hand. "You didn't say the mirror was in her *sunroom.*"

I shrug. "Well, it is. And the hall that leads to her chambers is flooded with light. I assume she keeps her sunroom that way too?"

"The light is the least of your worries," Finn says.

Pretha's brow creases with her frown. "If the queen is keeping the mirror in her sacred sunroom, no one but the prince or the queen herself can remove it from its spot."

"What happens if they try?" I ask.

"Nothing," Finn says. "You can't take it. The items in the queen's sunroom are immovable even for the strongest hands or the gentlest touch. You will find, Princess, that the real magic in our world is tied up in free will. Not even the strongest fae — or the greatest thief — can take that which can only be given freely."

164

"Is there a counterspell?" I ask.

"Everything has a counterspell," Kane says.

Finn looks to Pretha, who shakes her head. "I don't know it," she says, "but I'll do some digging and see what I can find out. In the meantime, we'll have to think of another way."

I don't have time to wait for Pretha to research a counterspell.

No one but the prince or the queen herself can remove items from the sunroom. "It's okay. I know what to do," I say softly, and honestly, I'm not sure why I didn't think of it before.

"Kill the queen?" Kane asks, his hand going to the dagger on his hip. "Me first."

Finn shakes his head at his . . . his friend? His sentry? "She would carve you up and stake you to the front lawn as an example."

Kane scowls.

I sigh. "If the only way to get the mirror is to have the queen or the prince give it to me, I will ask Prince Ronan to retrieve it for me."

"Are you serious?" Kane asks. "You think the prince is just going to hand over a precious artifact?"

"Yes," I say, and my guilt is already weighing me down. "He cares for me, and he wants to make amends for his deception."

Pretha smiles slowly, and she nods. "The simplest path is usually the best. In the meantime, we'll train you as planned, and I'll look into the counterspell just in case. If the prince won't give it to you, we'll find a way for you to steal it."

"But ask nicely, Princess," Finn says. "Trust me when I say you don't want to have to do this the hard way."

CHAPTER THIRTEEN

I FIND SEBASTIAN IN THE TRAINING RING on the roof of the highest turret, shirtless, his bare chest glistening with sweat in the glow of the setting sun.

He's sparring with another shirtless male. I try to take note of the stranger's golden hair or the tattoo that runs down the side of his neck and over his shoulder — but I can hardly take my eyes off Sebastian long enough to catalogue anything about his partner. And worse? I can't get my mouth to form the words I need to let him know I'm here.

It's not just his physique that makes me nearly mute. It's the reminder of those days in Fairscape. The times I'd pretend to read while watching him train in the courtyard. The times he'd catch me watching and wink over his shoulder, and the way that simple gesture sent a flurry of butterflies through me. He and Jas were the bright spots in a dark and difficult existence; it's a struggle not to let myself cling to him when I feel like I've lost them both.

Sebastian spots me and gestures to his partner for a break. He grabs a towel and uses it to wipe the sweat off his brow. "Is everything okay?"

Words, Brie. Use your words. "I'm fine. I just . . ." I swallow. "I wanted to talk to you. But I can go if this is a bad time." I wince. Catching him up here seemed like a good idea, but now I feel presumptuous. Never mind that I don't want to draw too much attention to what I'm about to request from him. "I didn't mean to cut your workout short."

"Don't leave," Sebastian says. "We were just finishing up." He pours a glass of water and offers it to me. When I shake my head, he tilts the glass to his lips and drains it. I'm captivated by the movement of his throat as he swallows.

The other male catches me staring and his chest shakes in silent laughter. He winks at me knowingly before pulling a dark shirt over his head. "He can't keep up with me anyway," he says. "The prince went soft while he was in the human realm."

Sebastian grunts. "You lost three of five rounds. I wouldn't be too cocky if I were you."

"Before you left, I would have lost all five." He shrugs and smiles as he offers me his hand. "I'm Riaan. You must be the captivating and heart-stealing Abriella I've heard so much about."

My cheeks blaze — at that description and at the thought of Sebastian talking about me in those terms — but I manage a nod. "It's nice to meet you, Riaan. Do you two train together often?"

Riaan shakes his head. "Not nearly as often as we used to. This one's too busy for me. Preparing to be king. Choosing a bride." He shoots me a meaningful look, then adds, "Though if you ask me, he should just grovel until you agree to take the position."

I open my mouth, then snap it shut again, turning to Sebastian before I say anything incriminating.

"Riaan's my oldest friend," Sebastian says softly.

"Your secret's safe with me," Riaan says with a wink. He fills a glass of water and lifts it in mock salute before heading down the stairs and leaving Sebastian and me alone on the rooftop.

"I shouldn't have interrupted," I say, still thinking about what Riaan said. Maybe it would be easier to hold a grudge against Sebastian if I didn't know he returned the feelings I've harbored from the day we met, but every reminder tests my convictions.

He waves away my concern. "We were finishing up anyway. My mother wants him to accompany her to the north this afternoon."

"What's in the north?"

"Another palace."

I laugh.

"What?" he asks.

"You say that the way Jas might refer to *another dress* for my spoiled cousins." I look around, taking in the view of the expansive grounds around the Golden Palace. "I can't imagine having one place like this, let alone another."

When I turn back to Sebastian, he's frowning. "It's absurd, isn't it?" he asks softly. "So much excess here when so many suffer in Elora. I didn't realize . . . not until I moved in with Mage Trifen."

"Why did you do that anyway? You have magic — better magic than any human could dream of having. Why did you take an apprenticeship with a human?"

"Human magic is different, and I'm not arrogant enough to believe that I don't need it." He turns to the view beyond, and his gaze goes distant. "I know I'm going to need every advantage I can get if I want to be the best ruler for my people."

"When will that happen? When will you rule?"

He shakes his head. "Only the old gods know the moment, but I want to be prepared." He refills his glass and takes another drink, adding, "You didn't come up here to talk about my apprenticeship."

"No. I came about something else. But . . . it seems silly now."

He grins, sensing my embarrassment. "What is it?"

I grab a lock of my hair and twist it nervously. "I've been thinking about how we can find Jas, and I remembered legends of this magical mirror that would show you anyone you wished to see."

His eyes go wide. "The Mirror of Discovery?"

"I never knew what it was called." I smile to hide the lie. "But when you look into it, you can ask to see someone. Maybe we could use it to locate Jas."

"It's hard to know what you'd see if you used it." He frowns, thinking. "It can be unpredictable."

I swallow. *Please get it for me. Please.* "But wouldn't it be worth trying?" I blow out a breath. "Such an ancient piece of magic. I'm . . . curious."

He laughs. "It's the thief in you—don't make that face, I mean it as a compliment. But I can't have you breaking into my mother's sacred sunroom to appease your curiosity. I'll see what I can do."

———·———

"Won't the people at the palace think it's strange that I'm gone so often?" I ask the next day as Pretha escorts me through the front door of Finn's house in the form of Eurelody.

"They'll think you're studying with your tutor at her home. Finn paid the old scholar's family well for use of the place." She closes the door behind me, then shimmies her shoulders. The wings disappear and her body snaps back into the one I know as Pretha.

"Is this your . . . true form?" I ask, nodding at her.

"This?" She smiles slowly, and her face lights up. She's stunning. I wonder if she's Finn's wife or partner or—I squelch the errant thought. Why do I care who he's with? "Yes, this is my true form."

"Can you fly when you have the wings?"

She snorts and waves at me to follow her down the dimly lit hallway to the back of the house. "It depends on the form I take. I can't fly when I shift into Eurelody, because Eurelody can't fly. Other forms . . ." She shrugs. "Sure. Sometimes. Though it takes a lot of energy to shift so completely."

I follow her through a set of double doors into a massive library that has two-story ceilings and bookshelves lining every wall. In the middle of the room, a trio of fae males gather around a table, discussing something in low tones. I recognize Kane, and I think the other two were guarding the door to the office the night Kane carried me into the tavern. Finn isn't anywhere to be seen, but his wolves are napping in the shadows at the back of the library.

"Hell-ooo," Pretha singsongs, and the males straighten.

Kane grabs something off the table—a map maybe?—and rolls it up before sliding it into the back of his pants. "The princess returns," he grumbles.

I arch a brow. "If you don't want me here, then why does your prince keep sending *her* to retrieve me?"

"Ignore Kane," Pretha says. "He's perpetually cranky."

Kane scowls at her, and the other two chuckle.

Pretha points to the male with dark skin, short black dreadlocks, and silver webbing on his forehead much like Pretha's. "Abriella, this is Tynan," she says. He smiles as he offers his hand, and I shake it. "And Jalek," she says, pointing to the other, a pale-skinned male with buzzed white hair and dark green eyes. This one doesn't offer a hand. Instead he gives me a curt nod and takes a step back, as if he doesn't want to get too close to me.

I clear my throat. "It's . . . nice to meet you all."

Jalek grunts. "She's a terrible liar. You're sure she can dupe the prince?"

"Hush, you," Pretha says. "Abriella is the best chance Finn's court has."

I arch a brow. *Finn's* court. "You're not Unseelie?" I blurt.

She grimaces and exchanges a look with Tynan. "Not by birth." Sighing, she adds, "I was born one of the Wild Fae, but I pledged my allegiance to Finn long ago."

I look to the others. "And you three?"

"Unseelie born and bred," Kane says, pounding his fist against his chest.

"But don't worry," Tynan says. "Not all Unseelie are as ugly as that one."

Kane gives Tynan a vulgar gesture, and Jalek bites back a smile.

Pretha ignores them all. "Tynan is Wild Fae, like me. And

Jalek is Seelie by birth. Many years ago he was a courtier for the golden queen's father."

"Old ass," Kane mutters.

"I'd rather be old and wise than young and dumb," Jalek says, but his eyes remain on me, studying my reaction to this information.

I try not to gape. I was always under the impression that the fae were strictly loyal to the court they were born into, but Finn seems to have assembled a little band of misfits. "And you all work for Finn?"

"We work for the greater good for all of Faerie," Pretha says, pulling her long hair over one shoulder and beginning to braid it. "And since Finn is leading that charge, yes, we work for him. We work *with* him."

Jalek narrows those vivid green eyes at me. "Have you spent much time with Queen Arya at the palace?"

I shake my head. I haven't laid eyes on the queen since the day I went before her to pretend I wanted to marry her son. "No. She's not around much."

Jalek and Tynan exchange a look, and Kane mumbles something I can't hear.

"I think you all have somewhere you're supposed to be this morning," Pretha says pointedly, and instead of bristling at a female ordering them around, the three males nod and head toward the library's double doors. Females so rarely have any meaningful power in Elora, and I can't help but respect Pretha a little more.

Tynan is the last to leave. He stops in the doorway before

turning back to Pretha. "Misha and Amira have requested a meeting with Finn. Amira specifically asked for you to attend. I thought you might want to prepare yourself."

Pretha's smile falters, but she quickly pastes it back in place and nods. "Thank you for letting me know."

He turns away and lets the doors swing closed behind him.

"Who are Misha and Amira?" I ask.

"King and queen of the Wild Fae. They've been essential in our mission over the last two decades."

If they've been so essential, why does Pretha look shell-shocked at the news that she'll have to meet with them?

She draws in a deep breath and rolls back her shoulders. "How's your search for the mirror coming? Have you asked the young prince yet?"

I nod. "He's working on it."

Pretha gives me a tight smile. "Good. Now, let's work on your training, shall we?"

CHAPTER FOURTEEN

"Again," Pretha says.

Five hours into my third full day of training, and I am so bloody sick of that word I could spit. Except for a brief break for lunch, we spend the entire day in this library with her pushing me to create darkness. We started with drops at my fingertips and moved to a ball of it held steady in the palm of my hand. Bottom line? Despite Pretha's endless patience, I can make it appear, but I'm hopeless when it comes to commanding it, maintaining it, or generally doing anything *useful* with it.

I draw in a deep breath and focus on the palm of my hand, willing that darkness to appear. The moment I form a ball of shadow, it grows too big too fast and overflows, spilling like sand from between my fingers and then disappearing.

"Sloppy," Finn growls behind me.

I spin around, shocked at his sudden presence. Aside from my brief meeting with the three males that first day Pretha brought me to this library, it's just been Pretha and me during my training. Apparently Finn's decided to bless me with his presence today. "What did you say?" I ask.

"Finn," Pretha says. "How lovely of you to —"

He cuts her off with a sharp shake of his head. "Not today, Pretha. Leave us."

Pretha gives me an apologetic smile. "Don't let him push you around," she says softly.

"*Leave us*, Pretha," Finn says, his voice deadly quiet.

Her gaze hardens as she shifts it to him, still talking to me. "Don't take his moodiness personally. This one's been brooding for twenty years."

As she goes, the smarter, self-preserving part of my brain screams at me that I should follow her. But I don't. Finn doesn't scare me. Maybe he should, but . . . it was no coincidence that the darkness in my hand grew when he appeared. I don't know why or how, but my power responds to him. Even standing here, it hums, begging me to wield it.

I arch a brow when we're alone and bite out a single word. "What?"

"You're sloppy with your magic. You lack focus, and if you don't figure it out, your adoring prince is going to catch you sneaking around his palace."

I lift my chin, but his words hardly sting. He's right. Clearly, I'm capable of more than I ever realized in the human world, but I don't have the faintest idea how to control it. So far, practice is just making me tired. But if I could try with *him* nearby . . .

"Is that what you want?" he asks. "To be forced to abandon your quest so you can settle into your comfortable new life?"

The nerve. "I don't see *you* offering to teach me."

He cocks his head to the side. "That's a pretty passive-aggressive way to ask for help."

"I —" I clench one fist and release it. He is such an arrogant ass. "You're the one who insisted on helping me, but I come here and you leave me to Pretha."

"She's an excellent teacher. You should be grateful for her time, Princess."

"Why do you keep calling me that?" I snap. "I'm no princess."

"You're a few sweet promises and tender moments away from being that boy's bride, and everyone knows it."

I have to bite my tongue to keep from arguing. It doesn't matter what he thinks of me or my relationship with Sebastian. All that matters is getting the relics for the king so I can get Jas back.

But Finn's intent on baiting me. "Isn't life at the luxurious Golden Palace everything your mortal heart imagined?"

I sneer. "Why would you assume my *mortal heart* imagined anything?"

"Don't all mortal girls dream of marrying a handsome faerie prince?"

"You are such an arrogant ass!" A ball of shadow forms in my hand, and I curl my fingers around it. "*This* mortal girl never dreamed of it. I didn't want to come here. I was forced to come when the king of *your court* bought my sister."

"Pretha's wrong, then? You *don't* have feelings for the prince?"

"I . . ." I did. I do. But my complicated feelings for Sebastian are none of Finn's business. The ball of shadow pulses with my anger. "I have no desire to be a faerie princess. If I'd known Sebastian

176

was fae, we never would have become friends to begin with. He knew that."

Finn walks slow circles around me, and I feel like a horse at market, being appraised from every angle. "Surely you've forgiven him for his lies if you're hoping to marry him, to enter a bond with him."

"I'm not hoping to marry him," I snap. I have to splay my fingers to hold on to the writhing ball of shadow in my palm as it continues to grow. "I don't want to be a princess. I don't want to bond with a faerie — or with *anyone*."

He stops his circling in front of me and meets my eyes. "So you're not bound to anyone?"

I roll my eyes. "Not that it's any of your business, but no. I wouldn't allow that."

Finn's shoulders drop. If I didn't know better, I'd say he was relieved. But there's no reason why this Unseelie prince would care that much about me. "Sebastian will eventually ask to bond with you," he says.

"He knows how I feel about you faeries and your human-controlling bonds. It won't happen." I couldn't even bond with him if I wanted to. I can't give Sebastian that kind of awareness of me when I need to sneak around to save Jas.

"Mordeus will ask as well. Remember that the only way anyone can have it is if *you* allow it. If you value your mortal life, you won't do that — ever."

"Is that a threat, Finn?"

"It's a warning, Princess."

"There is no bond in our deal."

"There isn't *yet*, but beware of Mordeus's scheming."

Mordeus's scheming? What about Finn's scheming?

He lets out a breath. "I can try to help you. The truth, though, is that Pretha and I know nothing about mortals who have magic — or how the magic works with you."

"Why would it be different?"

His brows raise. "Because *you* are different." He walks forward and grabs my arm. He draws a fingertip from the inside of my elbow down to my wrist, just above where I hold the ball of shadow. A matching shiver shimmies down my spine.

His eyes lift and meet mine, and his lips part. For a moment I think he feels it too — the pulsing energy between us, this awareness that makes me feel more awake and alive than I ever have. *It's only the magic*, I tell myself, but I am a terrible liar.

He drags his fingertip across my skin again, and I take slow, measured breaths and wish he'd release me. He would if I asked — I'm sure of it — but I refuse to let on that he affects me.

"What happens if I cut you?" he asks.

"I bleed."

He nods. "And if you heal, your body will make more blood as you recover. But if the cut is too wide, too deep, if you bleed too much and cannot produce new blood fast enough to pump through your veins and tend to your body, you die."

"I'm familiar with how it works," I grouse.

He glowers. He traces that line again, and this time I can't hold back the shiver. "Magic is like blood for the fae."

"I don't understand. You don't bleed?" That can't be right.

I've seen Sebastian bleed — tended to some of his minor wounds myself at times.

"We bleed, but it's the magic in our blood that heals us, the magic that keeps us alive, not the blood itself. Your blood gives you life. Our *magic* gives us life." His gaze drops to my mouth, and my breath catches.

He releases my arm as suddenly as he grabbed it, and he backs away. Looking out the window, he drags a hand through his hair. He pulls it away from his face, tying it back like he's getting ready to spar. "It's not a perfect analogy, but it's the best I have. Magic isn't infinite. It's tied to our life source, and we have to learn what our capacity is so we don't overtax ourselves. But like blood regenerates after you lose a small amount, a faerie's magic should regenerate. How much a faerie can lose and regenerate without weakening depends on their power."

"What happens when a faerie bleeds too much power too fast?"

"In most cases, we would pass out before doing long-term damage, but if the magic is spent in an intentional, violent draining—" He turns back to me, and there's something like grief in those beautiful eyes.

"If it's spent too quickly, a faerie can die from using her magic?"

"It's a choice. A magical act so great and so dear to the faerie that the cost is considered worth it."

"Do you think *I* could die if I used too much magic too fast?"

He tilts his head to the side and studies me. "You haven't begun to find the depths of your power."

The shadow in my hand pops like a bubble and disintegrates.

179

Finn looks me up and down and shakes his head, disgust all over his face. "For someone who holds such a gift, it's almost impressive how little of it you use. Your power is as vast as the ocean, and you're limiting yourself to what you can hold in your hand."

"I was doing what Pretha *asked* me to do."

"You were failing," he growls, his nostrils flaring.

"What do you want with me?" I cling to my annoyance. I'm much more comfortable with this animosity between us than I am with those . . . *other* feelings he inspires. "Are you here to help or just to put me down?"

He folds his arms. "Fine. Show me what you can do. And none of that handful of darkness nonsense. *Impress* me." When I turn up my palms to signal that I don't know how to do anything impressive, he huffs. "The room is half shadow. There's plenty to work with here. Stop overthinking it and just show me."

Stepping away from the light, I focus and try to disappear, managing only to make my fingers fade in and out of existence. But I feel it — I always feel it when he's close — the power just simmering in my blood, begging to burst free. "Tell me how."

"You're fighting it. Just let it come."

I stare at my hand and try . . . not to try. When the darkness flickers again, I growl in frustration. "I think I might actually be getting worse."

"I have an idea," he says, looking out the window. "Follow me."

Without turning back, he heads outside — not toward the

front of the house where Pretha and I enter every day, but toward a back door I've never seen used.

I follow him out and across a furnished patio, down a dimly lit alley, and around a few buildings. When he finally stops, we're in a massive cemetery. The evening is clear and the rows of burial plots are beautiful, if a little morbid. "Why here?" I ask.

Finn pulls his attention away from a circling flock of ravens and arches a brow at me. "You tell me."

Because I feel most comfortable outside. Because the impending darkness of night always makes me feel inexplicably more confident. "The night feeds my magic, doesn't it?"

He shrugs. "You could say that. What were you feeling the times you successfully tapped into your power before?"

"Anger? Desperation? I don't know." I bite my lip and look up at him through my lashes. I hate feeling like a fool. "Can you use anger to make magic?"

He shrugs. "Sure. It's a weaker emotion, but it's a functional catalyst for less significant magic. But anger won't be enough to access the full depths of your powers."

I roll my eyes. "I suppose you're going to tell me for that I need *love?*"

His silver eyes light up, and I'm shocked to see him crack a smile. It might be the first time I've seen that smile when he wasn't mocking me. He's . . . stunning. I don't want to notice, but those sharp cheekbones and mesmerizing eyes, the full lips that part just so when he's watching me. Well, I can't imagine that anyone with healthy eyesight would fail to notice Finn's beauty.

"You might say that wielding full magical power feels a little like love," he says. "But it's more like . . ." Closing his eyes, he wiggles his fingers and takes a deep breath. "It feels more like hope."

"Then I'm doomed."

He opens his eyes and rocks back on his heels, studying me. "How so?"

I shake my head. "I don't hope. It's a waste of time. Dangerous, even."

He tilts his head to the side. "You're wrong about that. What's truly dangerous is not having hope."

I blow out a breath. "What if there's nothing to hope for?"

His lips twitch, and that mocking smile is back. "Are you lying to yourself or just to me?"

"I'm not lying."

He chuckles. The ass is *laughing* at me. "You live in that palace, searching for the Unseelie relics and holding your own with that two-faced court. You come here and train your heart out. Why do you do it all?"

"To save my sister."

He turns both palms up as if to say *There you go*.

"It's not the same. I'm acting logically, not desperately."

"Who says hope has to be desperate?" He steps forward and takes my hand, and that undeniable connection between us snaps into place as the evening sky darkens and fills with stars.

I gasp. The darkness soothes my ragged edges and cools my anxiety even as I realize it's not the whole night sky, but only a bubble around us. "You made it dark," I say. "It's beautiful."

"It's inside you," he says softly, almost sadly. "This isn't my power you're seeing here. It's *yours*. I'm merely a conduit, a tool to open the door, since you keep getting in your own damn way."

I reach my free hand up, and it blends with the darkness. As I fade into the night, as I become the darkness, I know I control it.

"Do you feel it?" Finn asks, pulling my attention back to him. His eyes scan my face again, as if he's looking for a secret. And I do feel it. Every brush of those silver eyes feels like an intimate touch. When he speaks again, his voice is lower, huskier. "Do you feel the potential humming in your blood?"

I meet his eyes and swallow. Is that what I feel when he touches me? Potential? Because it feels like . . . *lust*. But I'd rather spend another night in Mordeus's oubliette than admit that, so I nod.

Finn drops his hand, and the bubble of night falls away, replaced by the golden glow of the setting sun.

His attention has returned to the flock of ravens. "We should go back in."

"Why?" I ask. I don't want to go back in. Not yet.

"You see those birds?"

As if in reaction, one caws loudly, the sharp sound renting the peaceful evening breeze.

"Yes?"

"When ravens swarm like that, it's a sign the Sluagh are close."

"Slew-what?"

"Sluagh. They're spirits of the dead who've never been able to pass. For whatever reason, they're caught between."

"Are they ghosts?"

He grimaces, still studying the ravens. I wonder what he sees as he watches them. It's as if he's looking for answers in their movements. "Sort of, I suppose. They're the cursed dead, fae killed too soon and with too much power left. They're stuck wandering the realm until their deaths are avenged. Some will lure innocents to their death just to appease their angry souls."

A shiver of dread races down my spine, and I swallow. "Do they always linger in cemeteries?"

"They linger near wherever they were murdered, and unless you'd like to get a detailed lesson on these, I suggest we move quickly."

CHAPTER FIFTEEN

THE LATE EVENING BREEZE BLOWS in my window, a cool relief after a hot day.

I feigned a headache and skipped dinner with the other girls tonight. I'm mentally exhausted after my little training session with Finn, but I could have managed a couple more hours before retiring. In truth, I don't want to see all the other girls fawning all over Sebastian. I don't want to see him flirting with them. I don't want to see him smiling at them the way he used to smile at me, and I don't want to think about him having a future with one of them.

I'm staring into the star-studded night sky when someone raps on my door. *Three taps. Pause. Two taps.*

I smile at Sebastian's signature knock. "Come in."

The door cracks, and he sticks his head in. "Are you alone?"

I nod. "My maids have left for the night."

He pushes the rest of the way into the room. He's in russet leather pants and a white tunic that's open at his neck, showing off the golden skin of his chest. His white hair hangs loose around his shoulders, and his smile makes my chest squeeze with longing for things I can't have and shouldn't want.

He pulls something from behind his back with a flourish, and my eyes widen as I take in the silver gilded mirror. It's a match to the one I have waiting under my mattress. "Is that . . . is that really it?"

"The Mirror of Discovery." Holding it in both hands, he extends it toward me.

As I wrap my fingers around the cool metal, my heart races. *I'm one step closer, Jas.*

"You look . . . awed," he says.

I pull my eyes off my own reflection and look at him. "Who wouldn't be?"

He smiles shyly. "You surprise me. You've always spoken so poorly about my world. I never expected you to be interested in our holy relics."

Right. I swallow. "I guess the longer I've been here, the more interested I am in understanding your realm?" I can't manage to keep it from sounding like a question.

He's silent for a long beat. I give him an awkward smile and start to turn away when he says, "Is it so awful?"

"What?"

He extends his hands to the sides, indicating the room, the palace, maybe his whole court. "Being here. I know you never wanted to come, but are you . . . *unhappy?*"

"I won't be happy until Jasalyn is safe."

He ducks his head and rubs the back of his neck. "Of course not. I understand that."

I am the worst. "I'm sorry, Sebastian. I didn't mean . . ."

His expression turns tortured as he asks, "Didn't you?" I open my mouth to object, and he holds up a hand. "Do you want to try it?" He nods to the mirror. I hadn't realized I'd clutched against my chest.

Swallowing, I extend the mirror and study my reflection. I'd asked my maids to leave my hair down tonight, and my curls are a wild mess around my face, not the tamed, perfect curls they form them into when dressing me for the day. But my face . . . my face has changed since I arrived in this realm nine days ago. It's benefited from plentiful nutrition and regular sleep. The dark circles under my eyes have faded, and my cheeks are no longer so hollow. I've thrived here, but what about Jas? Until this moment, I didn't realize I was scared to know the answer to that question. "How does it work?"

"It shows you what you want to see. Or should. I don't know that a mortal has ever used it." His eyes soften, and he nods in encouragement. "Tell it what to show you."

"Show me Jasalyn," I say softly.

The air around the mirror shimmers with magic, and it seems to vibrate in my hand as my reflection fades away. The glass shows me a lavish bedchamber. It's like looking through a window. Jasalyn sits at a vanity, smiling at her reflection as her maids brush her hair. The sound that slips from my lips is half cry, half gasp. She looks *well.* Her cheeks are flushed with laughter, and her face

187

has grown fuller, as if she, like me, has eaten better while in Faerie than ever before.

"I miss my sister," Jas says, smiling at her maids. "She would love you two."

The one brushing her hair meets her eyes in the mirror and smiles. "I've no doubt you will be reunited soon."

Jas bites her bottom lip. "I hope so. I have so much to tell her."

The image fades, and I see myself in the mirror again.

"So?"

I drag my gaze up, and Sebastian's looking at me expectantly. "You didn't hear that?" I ask.

He shakes his head. "I can't see what you see. And if I hold it, you wouldn't be able to see what I see. Did it work?"

I nod, and I don't bother to hide the smile that stretches across my face. "She's okay. She misses me, but she's well and seems comfortable. She's not" — my throat tightens, and it feels like I have to push the word out through the smallest space — "alone."

Sebastian releases a breath. "Good," he murmurs, almost to himself. "So we have some time."

I clutch the mirror to my chest again. "Thank you, Sebastian. Thank you so much for this."

"You're welcome," he says softly. "I just want you to be happy here, to feel safe and trust that I'm doing everything in my power to get Jas back." He steps forward, his eyes intent on my face, and my heart pounds. "Will you take a walk with me?"

I draw in a deep breath. "Sure." I tell myself I'm just giving him the attention he needs so he'll let me stay, tell myself I'm doing what I need to prepare to retrieve the next relic for the king, but I've missed Sebastian over the last few days. I haven't seen him since I visited him in the training ring and asked for the mirror. I've been with Pretha while he's been gods know where, and I've missed his reassuring smiles. His warmth.

I lift the mirror. "I'll leave this here so no one sees it."

He nods. "Of course."

I pull open a drawer in my bureau and place the mirror gently inside. I notice my sleep clothes, and self-consciousness straightens my spine. "I should probably get dressed."

"You look fine."

I'm dressed for the hot summer night in loose, flowing pink pants that sit low on my hips and a matching scoop-necked sleep shirt that leaves my arms bare and is nothing but soft lace across my midriff. I arch a brow. "Won't the servants think it's odd for me to be walking with their prince in my pajamas? Anyway, I'm a mess."

His gaze drifts over me as slowly as a caress. "You're beautiful no matter what you wear." Warmth flares in my cheeks and pools low in my belly. He steps closer, and every cell stands at attention. "If you'd like, I could glamour us so no one can see."

"You . . . you can do that?" Aside from his attack on the Barghest and numbing my wound afterward, I haven't seen Sebastian use much of his fae magic.

Grinning, he snaps his fingers. "It's done."

I frown. "But I can still see you."

"And I you." His eyes skim over me slowly, as if to say he

wouldn't have it any other way. "But no one will see us or hear us when we speak. Do you trust me?"

It's a loaded question, and one I can't answer yet. Before I came here and found out who he was, I trusted him implicitly, and then he broke that trust. But now? He gave me the mirror so I could check on Jas, and he's searching for her. It would be easy to trust him again. Maybe too easy.

As if sensing the direction of my thoughts, he lifts his chin. "We'll get there. I'll earn it back. I promise you." He offers a hand, and I take it, aware of the warmth of his skin and the roughness of his fingers twining between mine.

We walk into the hall, hand in hand, past sentries and servants putting the palace to bed for the night. No one sees through Sebastian's glamour, and I have to wonder what he'd think if he knew I could do this too — if less effectively and inconsistently. Once, he would have been the first person I'd want to talk to about my powers. Now I'm grateful I didn't recognize them for what they were back in Fairscape. I would've told him, and my tasks here wouldn't have been possible.

"Care to walk through the gardens?" he asks.

I bite my lip and drop a glance to my bare feet. "Should I go back up for some shoes?"

"The gardens are pristine. It's perfectly safe to walk barefoot."

In truth, I can think of nothing lovelier than a moonlight walk on a warm night, the feel of the cool grass between my toes. I squeeze his hand and let him lead me through a pair of glass doors into a massive courtyard garden. There are countless like it around the palace, and I've passed this one, but I haven't visited before.

We wander to the center of the garden, and I pause under the sliver of a waning crescent moon. Closing my eyes, I breathe in through my nose, filling my head with the scent of roses and lilies. I'd almost swear I can smell the moonlight.

When I open my eyes, Sebastian is watching me. "What?" I ask, feeling a little foolish.

He swallows. "I love seeing you let go like that. You don't do it often, but when you do . . ." He lifts a hand and touches my neck. "You're breathtaking." His fingers linger at my ear, and for a beat, I think he might slide them into my hair . . . might finally lower his mouth to mine again. But he pulls away and turns to study a fountain that's gurgling in the center of a bed of roses.

Disappointment tugs at me. I bow my head, trying to pull it together and remind myself what I want—what I *need* from Sebastian—and it's not a kiss.

"I know you never wanted a life in Faerie," Sebastian says, still watching the fountain. "But . . . I need to know if you think you could be happy here. I need to know if . . . if I could be lucky enough to talk you into a life with me."

A life with him. In Faerie. Forever. Is he asking me to live as a pampered princess, locked up in her castle and ignoring the many human servants who make that life possible? Even if the servants at the Golden Palace have a better life than I ever could have imagined, how can I be part of a world that treats so many humans as commodities?

Is Finn right to think I'd be so easily swayed to accept this life?

No. Even if part of me wants Sebastian again — still? — that's not the life I want.

But if I want to stay in the castle, I might need to make Sebastian think I could want it. Even if lying to him crushes something fragile in my chest. "This is hard for me," I whisper, and the truth of those words resonates in my voice. "I would be lying if I told you I'm ready to accept a life in Faerie."

He bows his head. I wish he'd look at me.

"But I don't want to leave you either," I say. And even this is true, I realize. "Can you give me some time?"

Finally he turns and lifts his head, those sea-green eyes seeming to look right inside me. "I can do that. If you're willing truly to consider a life here."

My heart pumps hard, sending guilt trickling into my blood. I give him as much truth at I can. "It's easy to imagine a life with *you*, Bash. It's the other parts that are hard for me."

He shakes his head, and there's something like wonder in his eyes. "Thank you."

"For what?"

"For forgiving me. For being here with me now. I don't take this for granted."

I swallow. *I don't deserve you. You shouldn't trust me.*

When he takes my hand again, he leads me to a stone bench where we sit together, soaking in the moonlight, talking of nothing, and smelling the flowers. The night has always been my favorite time, but nighttime in Faerie makes my power tingle beneath my skin, makes me feel like I could fly. And here next to Sebastian, it feels like I could be *happy*.

"My mother loves these gardens," he says. "When she was younger, she spent every minute she could among the flowers. Father would find her out here in the middle of the night and drag her to bed."

"Your mother mentioned your father when I went before her. She said you got your tender heart from King Castan. I bet he'd be proud of you."

Sebastian bows his head. "I like to think that."

"What happened to him?"

"He was killed in an assassination attempt on my mother several years ago."

I gasp. "By whom?"

"A group of fae that defected from our court and took up arms with the Unseelie."

I shiver in the breeze, but it's guilt and not the balmy air that has my skin prickling. I shouldn't waste my time worrying whether I want a future with Sebastian. If he knew I was working with the Unseelie prince and his misfit band of friends, that future would be off the table. "I'm sorry," I whisper, but I know that an apology isn't enough for this kind of deception.

He sighs. "The war might be over, but the tensions between our courts are higher than ever. There are some who believe the solution is in taking out the monarchies of both courts and starting over."

"What do you believe?"

He studies me for a long beat. "I believe change is coming. And that the right leader could unite both courts." Shaking his head, he stands. "That's enough political talk for one night. Let's get you inside."

I'm quiet as we head back into the palace. I immediately miss the night air and the solitude of the courtyard.

Just inside, a group of girls dressed in slinky gowns head toward the ballroom. Since the queen's away and my attendance isn't required, I'd forgotten that there was a dance tonight. My maids are probably already in my chambers, waiting to see if my headache has improved so they can dress me like a doll.

"Shouldn't you be joining them?" I ask Sebastian, hoping he doesn't notice the jealous edge to my voice.

He cuts his eyes to me. "I think we both know I'd rather spend my night with you."

There go those stomach butterflies again, but I ignore the sensation and bump him with my shoulder. "You're a shameless flirt." I bite my lip, trying to hold back the question that's been bothering me all day.

"What?" he asks. "I know that look. What are you thinking?" He's smiling as he tucks my arm under his and leads me to the kitchen. When he looks at me like that, it's so easy to see the boy I knew from home. So easy to forget everything else.

"You said you were planning to come back to Fairscape for me."

"I meant it, too." He pushes into the kitchen. It's empty, like the last time we were here, but the smell of tonight's roasted chicken, squash, and stew hangs in the air — a bittersweet reminder of how pampered this life is.

"How would that have even worked, Bash? Were you planning to come home, pick a wife, and then return to Fairscape for me as a married man?"

He rolls his shoulders back. "I'm hungry. Are you?"

"Don't avoid the question."

"I'm not. But I need something to eat." He smiles and waves a finger toward the large cooler against the wall. "We have ice cream. It's fresh."

My mouth waters. I remember ice cream from my childhood. It's not a common treat in Fairscape. Fresh milk is expensive, and once the ice cream is made, you have to eat it right away, but the richest households in Elora have iceboxes where they always have frozen treats on hand. Is that what it's like to live in Faerie? Ice cream in every kitchen? Ending each day with that creamy sweetness melting on your tongue? I arch a brow and pretend I'm thinking about it rather than revealing that I'm already drooling. "What flavor?"

"We have many flavors, but if I recall, chocolate anything is your favorite."

Those words make me feel vulnerable, and for some reason they make me suddenly aware of my nightclothes and bare feet. Sebastian brought me chocolate for my birthday last year. Just a small portion purchased from one of the vendors at the market. It was such an indulgence, and it felt like too much, but the thoughtfulness of the gesture had made me fall even harder for him. "Chocolate sounds good."

He takes out two bowls and spoons, and I laugh.

He flashes me a grin. "What?"

"When it comes to tedious tasks like scooping ice cream, I always imagined faeries would use their powers." *Or their servants.*

"That would just be showing off," he says, winking.

And if magic is life the way Finn described, maybe they don't use it so carelessly.

Sebastian scoops a hearty serving of chocolate ice cream into each bowl before handing one to me.

We eat in silence, leaning against opposite counters like we did with our tea, and my bowl is half empty before he speaks again. "I planned to come back once I was in a position to free you from that contract. To be honest, I never let myself think it through too far. I knew you'd hate me when you learned who I was, but I promised myself that as soon as I had the power, I would help whether you wanted me to or not."

I want to point out that he's a prince, to ask why he didn't help us sooner, but given all he's done for me, that seems like the question of an ungrateful brat. Instead I stir my melting ice cream in my bowl. "When we get Jas back, can you find a way for her to stay here for a while? Maybe not right away, since you might still be in the middle of picking a bride, but . . . eventually? I want her to know what this is like, and when we return to the human realm, I won't be able to provide her with anything close."

I sense rather than see Sebastian step close to me. With one finger, he tilts up my chin so I'm looking at him. "When I am king, you and your sister will have an open invitation to stay at the palace." The rest hangs unsaid in the air: if I become his bride,

I won't have to wait until he's king. And maybe . . . maybe if I'm honest with myself, the possibility would be tempting. If it weren't for my bargain.

I finish my ice cream in silence, stuck in the loop of my own thoughts. When I'm finished, Sebastian puts our dishes in the sink and walks me back to my bedroom.

"Thank you for tonight," he says when we stop outside my door. "It was good to have you to myself, even if the minutes went too fast."

"It was really nice," I admit. "Thank you."

He drops his gaze to my mouth and his lips part.

Finn's words ring in my ears. *You're a few sweet promises and tender moments away from being that boy's bride, and everyone knows it.*

I step back. "Good night, Sebastian."

———·———

I sleep with the mirror under my pillow and half expect Mordeus's goblin to show up in my room during the night. He doesn't.

After breakfast the next day I feign another headache as an excuse to miss training with my "tutor" and wait in my room with the mirror. I want to get this to the king as soon as possible so that I can start looking for whatever's next.

But it seems that Mordeus's goblin operates on his own schedule.

I spend a lot of time using the mirror to see Jas, and as I lounge in bed waiting for the goblin, I allow myself to look again. She's sewing today, sipping tea, and laughing with her attendants.

I close my eyes and clutch the mirror to my chest. Could she really be so well cared for? I want to believe, but there's a niggling warning in the back of my mind that says I shouldn't be quite so willing to trust this magic. Even Sebastian wasn't sure it would work for me. How does he know I can trust what I saw? I need to know if Jas is okay.

I sit up in bed. This doesn't have to be complicated. I still have the mirror, so I can test it.

"Show me Sebastian."

My reflection fades away, and I'm looking at the golden prince. He's sitting at his desk in his chambers, his expression serious as he focuses on the book before him.

I jump off the bed and swap the mirror for the fake before rushing across the palace.

Halfway there, I second-guess myself. What if he moves before I make it to him? What if he recognizes the mirror I'm returning as a fake? With each doubt, I move faster, and by the time I get to his door, I'm out of breath.

When the sentry posted outside Sebastian's chambers spots me, he smiles and bows his head. "Lady Abriella."

"He's here?"

The sentry nods. "Yes, milady. I can show you right in. He said you're always welcome." He opens the door for me, and I step inside. I haven't been here since the night I was attacked by the Barghest. I'm more accustomed to the castle's opulence now, but even so, I never had the chance to fully appreciate the beauty of his room that night — the dark wood furniture, the sitting area as large as Madame Vivias's entire main floor, the floor-to-ceiling windows that line the far wall.

I find Sebastian at his desk, looking just as he did in the mirror, and I nearly melt with relief. It works. *Jas is okay.*

Sebastian looks up from his books and smiles at me. "Hey, you."

I don't bother trying to hide my grin. Knowing that Jas is well cared for is a massive weight off my shoulders. I want to dance. "Hey."

He closes the book he was reading and pushes out of his chair. "The servants said you were ill and canceled with your tutor today. Are you okay?"

I nod, giddy. "I was just tired."

He tucks the shorter lock of hair from my face behind my ear. It won't stay, but I don't think he minds the excuse to touch me. "I kept you out too late. I'm sorry."

"Don't apologize." I extend the replica mirror toward him. "I forgot to give this back to you last night."

"Right. I was ... distracted." He smiles and takes it from me, his fingers brushing mine. "I hate to cut this short when I have you to myself again, but I have a meeting I need to get to."

I step back. "Of course. I'm sorry. I didn't mean to keep you."

"I have a lead on Jas." He puts the mirror in a drawer. "I need to meet with one of my sources."

"What will you do if you figure out where she is?"

His sea-green eyes turn icy. "Whatever I have to do."

My heart squeezes. I'll keep doing what I must to free Jas, but if Sebastian can somehow free her before I've retrieved all three items, all the better. "Be careful," I whisper. "I've heard that the

199

king is cunning and can turn your own people against you. Watch your back."

"Careful?" He cups my face in one big hand and smiles down on me. "Could Abriella Kincaid possibly care about the fate of a wicked faerie?"

"You're not wicked," I say. Then I back out of the room quickly because I do care. I care too much.

I wish I knew how to contact the king. I've spent most of the day alone in my room, and his goblin hasn't shown up to take the mirror. Thinking that maybe the goblin can't come into the castle, I tell my maids I want to take a walk.

Heading out to the castle grounds and through the gardens, I wander to the area where Mordeus's goblin left me before.

I search. I pace. I lie on the grass and stare at the clouds, letting the setting sun warm my face.

He doesn't come.

CHAPTER SIXTEEN

"Who taught you to hold a sword like that?" Jalek asks with a sneer.

"No one." No matter how many times I adjust my grip on the bamboo training stick, I can't mirror the way the Seelie rebel grasps his sword.

After three days of waiting around the Golden Palace for Mordeus's goblin, Pretha insisted that I leave with her today. The goblin, she promised, would find me when he wanted to and not a moment sooner.

When I arrived at Finn's house this morning, I was given a change of clothes — *pants* for once, thank the gods — brought to a training room in the basement, and told that I was going to learn how to physically defend myself. "I have never held a sword before today."

Jalek's face is grim as he surveys me. "We should have started with her physical training on her first day here," he says, speaking to Pretha without taking his eyes off me. "Look at those arms. They're little more than twigs. She couldn't defend herself against a sprite."

"I can *hear you*," I snap.

"If she masters her power, she won't need swords," Pretha says, folding her arms across her chest.

"I have no intention of getting into a sword fight anyway," I mutter.

Jalek studies my stance. "Shoulders back, chin up. Feet shoulder-width apart." He taps my training stick with his sword, and I wobble to the side. "Keep your knees soft."

"Pretha!"

We all spin toward the sound of her gasped name to see Finn and Tynan on the stairs. Finn's face is pale and contorted with pain. He's slouched sideways as Tynan holds him up with one arm.

Jalek drops his sword, and he and Pretha rush toward their prince, helping Tynan get him to a chair in the corner of the room.

"I found him collapsed at the top of the stairs," Tynan says.

Finn is grasping his side, and his lids flutter like he's struggling to hold on to consciousness.

"What happened?" Pretha asks, kneeling before him.

"I let my guard down," Finn whispers.

"No shit," Jalek barks. "What the hell were you doing out there? You have something that needs taking care of, you send one of us. You sure as fuck don't go alone."

"I was with Kane." Finn's pants are bloody, but it's not until he leans back that I see the bright red blood coating his fingers.

"Kane?" Jalek barks. "Great. Our entire realm in the hands of *two* Unseelie idiots."

"We got a lead," Finn says through clenched teeth, "and none of you were available. I'm not going to sit on my ass until old age kills me."

"What kind of creature did this to you?" Jalek asks. "Is there any chance the wound is poisoned?"

Finn shakes his head. "Sword—" he coughs out. "Kane and I were smuggling a group out of the queen's northern camp. The sentinels posted around the perimeter were dressed like her royal guard, and we assumed they were Seelie. She's never deigned to dress Wild Fae in her sacred colors before, but it appears the old hag has wised up."

"One of ours did this?" Tynan asks, glancing toward Pretha.

Pretha sneers. "Dirty traitors."

Tynan draws in a ragged breath. "Where is Kane?"

"Kane made it out with the group while I brought down the guards," Finn says. "Dara and Luna are with him. They should be back in a few hours, after he gets the refugees through the portal."

"So the bastard who did this is dead?" Jalek asks, those dark green eyes blazing.

"By my own sword," Finn says.

Camps? Refugees? Traitor Wild Fae? "Why are Wild Fae more dangerous than Seelie guards?" I ask, understanding nothing.

They all ignore me. Pretha shoves Finn's hands aside to study the wound. Her expression is a study in tenderness and gut-deep worry.

I step forward to get a closer look at the wound. It's deep, but yesterday I watched Riaan slice his arm open when he was training with Sebastian. It healed so quickly I could practically see the flesh knitting itself back together, but there's no sign of that with Finn's wound. "Why aren't you healing?"

Finn ignores my question and lifts his chin in Jalek's direction. "I have a med kit in the safe. Grab it for me." His voice is rough with pain.

"Finn?" I wait for him to acknowledge me — my question — but he just closes his eyes and leans back.

Pretha chokes back a sob as she hovers a hand over the wound.

"Don't waste your energy, Pretha," Finn says softly. He gently touches her face, and something uncomfortable twists in my chest. I scowl. I shouldn't care about their relationship beyond how it affects my training and my bargain with the king. "This isn't a deathblow," he whispers. "I *will* heal."

Pretha swallows and nods. I can practically see her pulling herself together. "You're losing too much blood."

Jalek pulls a small table next to Finn's chair and puts the med kit on top of it. "We need to enlist a human healer to teach us how to use this mortal shit," he mutters, his eyes fixed on the ointments and salves.

Finn lifts his head and meets my gaze. "Do you have any experience stitching up wounds, Princess?"

"Some." I've stitched myself up a few times, but never anything this big. "But it will hurt, and my stitches are more likely to leave an ugly scar than a neat one."

Finn grunts. "You hear that, Tynan." His words are breathy, and he winces as if it hurts to talk. "Maybe mine will be uglier than Kane's, and he'll stop his gloating."

"I will never understand you males," Pretha mutters, pushing to her feet before turning to me. "What do you need, Abriella?"

I sort through the pile of ointments and find a disinfecting salve, a healing salve, and a numbing salve. Unfortunately, with a wound like this, none of them can be applied until after I stitch him up.

"Can you do something for his pain?" I ask her. "After the Barghest attacked, Sebastian numbed my leg until the healer could get to me. Could you do something like that?"

Pretha purses her lips and shakes her head. "I could try, but it wouldn't help."

"Finn's tough," Jalek says, showing his first hint of a smile since he spotted Finn on the stairs. "He doesn't need anything."

"I'll get you a drink," Tynan says, and a decanter of amber liquid and a tumbler appear on the small table. He fills it with shaking hands and passes it to Finn, who doesn't hesitate before draining the whole glass in two gulps.

"Do it, Princess."

I gather the thread and needle from the kit, but when I look down at my hands, I see they're shaking as badly as Tynan's. "Can you spare a bit of that for me?" I ask him. "Just to calm the nerves."

"Happily." Tynan summons another glass. He pours half the amount he poured for Finn and hands it to me.

I take one large swallow and cough as the burning liquor hits my throat. "That's enough for me," I mutter. I nod to Finn. "We need to wash the area."

Finn gingerly sits up, and Pretha returns to his side to help with the buttons and peel the shirt off him. His dark, muscular chest is covered with a smattering of rune tattoos. My mouth goes dry at the sight, and I turn away. Bad enough to gawk at him while he's injured, but worse to do it in front of his . . . What is Pretha? His wife? His mate? Just a friend?

Am I jealous? Not of her for having him, but of the connection they have, of the trust and honesty between them that I can't have with Sebastian even if I could trust him again. Thanks to my bargain with Mordeus, I can never have that.

Nevertheless, I turn away, using the time while Pretha cleans the area to prepare the needle and thread for stitching. My mother taught me to sew, but I never took to it the way Jas did. It was only through Jas's persistence that I learned how to make strong, clean stitch lines.

When Pretha's done prepping the area, I take her place and kneel at Finn's side. Now that he's cleaned up, the wound doesn't look as gruesome as before, but it is deep, and I hesitate before plunging the needle into his skin.

"Do it," Finn says. He flinches at the first slide of the needle, but he doesn't move.

My stomach churns at the sight of the oozing blood, but I blow out a long breath and keep stitching. *I can do this.* "Will someone tell me about these camps of the queen's?" I ask without looking away from my task.

I can sense them looking at one another as I stitch, sense that they're having a silent conversation and deciding what to tell me.

"Don't let the word *camp* confuse you," Jalek says. "They're prisons."

"For criminals?" I ask.

206

Jalek shakes his head. "Their only crime is being caught on Seelie land with Unseelie blood."

"What do you mean by prison?" I never bought into the idea that the Seelie were "good," since I never trusted any of the fae, but I have trouble believing that they would be cruel to their own kind without a good reason, even if the faeries in question were from a rival court.

"The adults are put into labor camps, forced to work eighteen hours a day with minimal provisions," Jalek says, his face so somber I can't help but believe him. "They're executed if they don't fall in line."

Does Sebastian know about this?

"Your prince has tried to get his mother to end the camps — at least as they are now," Finn says, grimacing through the pain and reading me like always. "But she refuses."

I release a breath, and relief courses through me. Sebastian might not be the male I once believed he was, but I could not stomach a world in which the kind and caring mage's apprentice I once longed for was responsible for such atrocities.

"*Tried* my ass," Jalek mumbles. "If he really wanted to see the end of the cruelty, he'd assassinate the queen himself, but he doesn't have the backbone. I thought he'd snap when he found out about the children, but —"

"What about the children?" I ask.

Pretha meets Finn's eyes for a beat, as if getting his permission before she explains. "They separate the children from their parents. They say it's to discourage families from crossing into Seelie lands, but they brainwash them, feeding them propaganda about the queen and teaching them that they are, by their very birth, beneath the Seelie and therefore meant to serve."

I still my hands. I have to close my eyes for a beat at the thought of those children. I know what it's like to be without your parents and forced to serve those who feed and shelter you. How naïve was I to think that all the fae led easy lives?

This time when my stomach heaves, it has nothing to do with the sight of blood.

"Well, look at that," Pretha whispers.

"Princess," Finn says, and I open my eyes to see that I've blanketed the two of us in darkness. The only light between us comes from those captivating silver eyes. "We find the children and get them to safety in the Wild Fae territory. Kane is transporting two dozen as we speak."

I hold his gaze as I coil my power back into myself. It hisses through my blood like a wild animal flailing inside a cage. "Why do any Unseelie come here if it's so bad?"

"Because their existence under Mordeus's rule is so grim that the risk is worth it," Pretha says. "He's greedy and selfish, and he doesn't care about taking care of his whole kingdom. His laws favor the rich and powerful and punish the less fortunate."

I let my gaze flick up to Finn's for a beat, and I can't help but think that the anguish I see on his face has less to do with the wound in his side or the needle in his skin, and more to do with the state of his kingdom.

"Many choose to flee rather than to stay in such conditions," Jalek says, continuing for Pretha. "But the Unseelie land is surrounded by vast and treacherous seas on every side except the one that borders the Seelie lands. Like Finn said, the Wild Fae will take in refugees, but the Unseelie have to get there—either by trekking through the whole of the Seelie territory or by finding a portal."

I continue stitching, but I have to focus to keep the rage inside me from filling the room with darkness. "Why don't they use goblins to transport them?"

Jalek grunts, clearly disgusted. "Those creatures are more selfish than Mordeus. There's nothing the refugees can offer that's worth getting on the bad side of both Mordeus and Arya."

"Anyway," Pretha says, "a goblin can transport only two at a time at best. The easiest path to Wild Fae territory for groups of any significant size is a portal."

Tynan's been so quiet, I'm almost surprised when he speaks. "The Wild Fae king and queen have been doing their best to welcome the displaced Unseelie—temporarily only, just until Finn can take his rightful place on the throne. But for their own border security, they can't allow portals directly from Mordeus's land to theirs. The usurper would use it against them and send his nastiest creatures through to torture Wild Fae innocents." The webbing on his forehead glows brighter and pulses until he rolls his neck and draws in a deep breath. "We've been setting up portals near the Seelie border and trying to get the Unseelie through before the queen's guard catches them."

"The portals have to be opened, closed, and moved frequently to dodge Arya's guard," Pretha says, pouring herself a drink. "It's draining on our forces, but it's the best solution we've come up with for the time being."

I finish the final stitches, and when I lift my gaze to Finn's again, he's watching me. I don't bother trying to hide my devastation from him. I quietly apply the necessary salves across the stitches, but my mind is reeling. *The children.*

"Is he going to die?" The tiny, tear-stained question comes from the stairs. I wonder how long the child's been standing there and whether she saw the extent of Finn's wound. I instinctively stand and step toward her.

I don't get far before Tynan scoops her into his arms. "Nah, kiddo. He's going to be just fine. See?" He carries her to Finn, who reaches up and tickles her bare foot. She giggles and wipes away her tears.

If she were human, I'd guess her to be five or six years old. She has light brown skin and silky dark hair like Pretha's. On her forehead, she has the beginnings of the silver webbing that Pretha and Tynan both have, but her big eyes are silver, and her smile — it's just like Finn's.

"Lark, I told you to stay upstairs when we have guests," Pretha says, glancing at me. Her meaning is clear. We might be helping each other, but I'm not to be trusted with knowledge of her child. Never mind that I just stitched up her — whatever Finn is to her.

"But I saw her in a fire," Lark says, and points to me. She cocks her head, as if trying to put together a puzzle. "Your sister isn't in there."

"Lark, stop!" Pretha pulls the child from Tynan's arms and buries her face in her hair. "What did Mommy say about using your sight?"

"Pretha," Jalek says, his voice gentle, "we might need to know about this fire if—"

"Then find a seer," she snaps. There are tears in her eyes. "Not my daughter."

"I'm sorry, Mommy." Lark puts her little hands on her mother's cheeks. "I don't try. I just *see*. And I don't want her to die in the fire. She did that already."

My heart squeezes hard at the worry in this sweet child's voice. "I didn't." I hold out my arms. "See? I was in a fire a long time ago, but I survived."

Lark isn't paying attention to me. She looks at her mom when she says, "Next time she dies, it has to be during a bonding ceremony. Otherwise, she'll never be queen."

My blood chills. *Next time she dies . . .*

"*Queen?*" Jalek barks.

"Please stop, baby." Tears stream down Pretha's cheeks. She's beyond distressed.

Jalek spins on me. "You *do* love the golden prince." He mutters a curse. "You must *tell us* before you promise him anything."

I ignore Jalek and pretend I don't notice Finn's piercing silver gaze on me. "I didn't die," I tell Lark. "And I'm not going to be the Seelie queen."

She giggles. "You could never be the Seelie queen."

This should be a relief. And yet the words are a little splinter in the wistful part of my heart that I keep hidden from the world — from myself. The part that wants Sebastian, the part that wants to be good enough to be . . .

No. I *don't* want that.

Jalek gives Finn a hard look before turning back to study the child's face. "You mean the *Unseelie queen*, Lark?"

Pretha shoots him a glare so angry, everyone in the room withers under it, but Lark smiles. "She could if she wanted, but she won't have a chance if she dies in the fire."

"Tynan," Pretha says, passing her daughter into his arms. "Take Lark to her room, please."

Tynan nods, and Lark wraps her arms around his neck. "You promised you'd teach me how to play your card game. Can we do that now?" Tynan asks as he starts up the stairs.

"Okay, but I'm really good," she says. "You can't get mad if I win."

"I promise to be a good sport," he says, and their voices fade away.

"Well, that was . . . enlightening," Jalek says.

Pretha glares at him.

"Lark can't help it," Finn says softly. "Her magic isn't like yours, Pretha. There's no on and off. It just *comes*."

"Are we going to talk about what she saw?" Jalek asks.

"Right, the fiery death." Finn looks at me, and his brows disappear into his mop of curls. "Thoughts, Princess?"

"I think she's just a kid and it doesn't mean anything." I hold my arms out to my sides. "See? I'm not dead. Humans don't get to keep walking around after we die."

Jalek grunts. I have no idea what that means.

Pretha wipes away her tears and drags in a breath, composing herself before she turns to Finn. "Ask your spies in the Unseelie Court if they know anything about an attack on the Golden

Palace. Maybe something with fire or explosives." She turns to me and forces a smile. "And you? Stop, drop, and roll, okay?"

I barely refrain from rolling my eyes. "Can we go back to the situation with the camps and the refugees?" Finn looks more ragged and tired than I've ever seen him, but I need to know. "This would stop if you were on the Throne of Shadows?" I ask him.

"I can't change Seelie law," Finn says, "but I could make life better in my court. I would do everything in my power to make it so my people didn't need to run. Everything I do I do to protect my people and give them a safe home." His eyes lock on mine, so intense you'd think I alone had the power to give him his father's throne. "That is a king's true responsibility."

I need Jas back, and that has to remain my first priority, but I can't stop thinking of those Unseelie children, stuck in veritable prisons and being told they're less worthy because of their birth. If Finn overthrows Mordeus, the bargain would be moot. Finn would give my sister back. I know he would. "Tell me how I can help."

Finn's face goes cold, and he turns to Jalek. "Help me to my room?"

"The girl wants to *help*," Jalek says.

Finn pushes out of the chair and flinches in pain as he straightens. "Or I'll get there by myself."

"Fine." Jalek studies me for a long beat before helping his prince up the stairs.

"Did I say something wrong?" I ask Pretha.

She shakes her head. "I think that was enough excitement for the day. Let's head back to the castle early."

213

CHAPTER SEVENTEEN

It's been a week since Sebastian gave me the mirror. A week of waiting around the castle and distracting myself with Finn's misfits, wondering if Mordeus forgot about me and our bargain. A week of obsessively asking the mirror to show me my sister. Seeing her happy and well cared for is the only thing that makes the wait tolerable. As crowded as the Golden Palace is, I feel lonely while I'm there. The only person I trust even remotely is Sebastian, and I can't confide in him.

I'm starting to wonder if the king ever intends to retrieve the mirror, but I won't miss any more training in the meantime. I may need these strange skills for the next relic. Though, if I'm honest, my preference for being with the Unseelie misfits is about more than this bargain. When Pretha brings me from the palace to Finn's house, I end my day smiling and feeling less . . . hopeless.

Today I spent the morning practicing fading myself into shadow and walking through wards and walls. I've gotten better at controlling that, but once Pretha told me to turn *her* to shadow, we hit a wall. Figuratively and literally.

"Let's take a break for lunch," Pretha says now, leading the way out of the library. "Jalek's making sandwiches."

When we enter the kitchen, Jalek and Tynan are already at the table with Finn. Three more plates are set, but I don't see any sign of their red-eyed Unseelie friend.

"Don't know where Kane is off to this morning," Jalek mutters when he notices me looking toward the foyer. "Too hungry to wait for him, so just sit."

Pretha cuts her eyes to me. "Ignore him. He gets irritable when he's hungry."

"I get irritable," Jalek snaps, "when Litha is this close and that bitch is still on the throne. I get *irritable* when the prince I've sworn fealty to has a fever and won't do what's necessary to heal himself."

My head snaps to Finn. I'd asked him how he was when we arrived this morning, but he blew me off and said not to coddle him. Now I see beads of sweat on his forehead that I hadn't noticed before.

"Well, you can't fix any of that if you're hungry," Pretha tells Jalek, taking the seat beside Finn. "So eat." She mops Finn's forehead, and he swats her away.

"I'm fine," he grumbles.

"You have a fever?" I ask Finn. "Have you been using the salve?"

"It's not from that." His jaw twitches; he's sick of explaining this. "It's a regular fever."

"How do the stitches look?" I ask. "Is there redness or swelling?"

215

"I looked at it myself this morning," Pretha says, avoiding my gaze. "We're dealing with it. Now sit."

Reluctantly, I sit next to Pretha, and Tynan passes around a platter of sandwiches while Jalek fills our glasses with a sparkling water that tastes like sunshine and lemons — a description I would have found ridiculous before coming to Faerie simply because I wouldn't have understood that it . . . fits.

I'm halfway through my sandwich and the guys are working on seconds when Kane walks into the kitchen, a woman by his side.

The conversation halts, and everyone stops eating.

Finn pushes back from the table and stands. The wolves I hadn't even noticed appear from the shadows and take their places on either side of him. "What's this?" His voice is dangerously quiet.

Kane bows his head. "I found you a tribute."

I've heard that word before. People in Elora are paid well to go to Faerie as tributes. My cousins would giggle about what they thought was involved, but the only thing that was clear to me was that tributes never came home. I push my chair back and head toward the girl, but Pretha grabs me by the wrist and holds tight. "Brie. Don't."

"I didn't ask for a fucking tribute," Finn barks. His anger radiates off every word. "Take her home."

"Finn." Kane's voice is hard and nearly matches Finn's. "Be reasonable."

The girl steps forward. She's not much older than I am and very pretty. Her long blond hair is swept back from her face with combs, showing off her high cheekbones and shining blue eyes. I wonder what her name is. I wonder if she has a family who will miss her.

I yank on my arm again, but Pretha holds me tight. "She's not doing anything she doesn't want to do, Abriella."

The girl bows her head. "Please, my prince. I escaped Mordeus's court. I've lived in Faerie all my life, and I've . . . I've seen enough to understand what I'm doing." She drops to her knees —bowing, I realize. "Please?"

Finn looks at her long and hard, then at Kane. With a sharp shake of his head, he storms out of the room, his wolves following quietly behind him.

Pretha winces. Kane mutters a curse under his breath. And the girl buries her face in her hands and sobs.

"I'll talk to him," Jalek says.

Pretha stops him with a hand to his chest. "No. I'll do it." She follows Finn to the library and shuts the door behind her.

"I'm sorry," Kane tells the girl. "Just give him a minute."

"Does someone want to explain what's happening here?" I give a pointed look to Jalek and Tynan.

Jalek shakes his head and begins clearing the table. Tynan stoops to help the girl stand up, murmuring reassurances.

"I'm going out back," I announce, not that they're paying me any attention. I follow the hallway to the back of the house and welcome the summer breeze on my face as I let the door bang closed behind me.

I'm so sick of being kept in the dark. I'm so sick of the people I'm forced to trust not trusting me with anything.

The library windows are open. I cross the patio to listen, but I can't make out the conversation happening inside. Pretha has likely shielded the room against eavesdroppers . . . against *me*.

I straighten. If I want to know what's happening in there, I'm completely capable.

I close my eyes and feel myself dissolve to shadow, to darkness, to nothing. I don't open them again until I've slowly slipped through the wall, through the wards they have around the house, through Pretha's shield, and into the library.

Finn is sprawled out on the couch, one hand hanging over the back and the other massaging his temples. "Abriella isn't ready. If I ask now, I risk her becoming suspicious."

Pretha paces before him. "Fine. Then you need to do this."

"Why? Because I have a small infection? You think *that* is what's going to keep me from winning this war?"

"No. I think your stubborn pride is what's going to keep *us* from winning this war." She swipes at her cheeks, and I realize she's crying. "Do you have any idea how hard it was for me to watch Vexius waste away?"

Vexius? Have I heard that name before?

"Do you have any idea how it feels to live each day knowing that it didn't have to be like this?"

"You act like it's so simple," Finn says, "but if I take tribute after tribute, am I any better than *him?*"

Who's *him?* Mordeus? Does he take tributes too? What do tributes do? And why?

"I think you're still grieving over Isabel, and—" She turns toward me and scans the shadowed wall of books.

218

Finn sits up. "What is it?"

"I just got the feeling that we aren't alone."

Shit.

She flicks her wrist, and an orb of light appears at her fingertips. With another flick, it floats toward me.

I slip back out through the wall before she can see me.

"I don't see anything," Finn says as I slip away. "Are you sure?"

"You shouldn't linger in the dark when she's around."

I'm not supposed to know that the girl is still here. I'm not supposed to see her step into the library, where Finn's brooded all afternoon. And I'm definitely not supposed to be using my shadows to sneak in behind her and spy on them.

Ever since Pretha taught me about wards and shields and made me realize I'd unwittingly been moving through them when I slipped into shadows, I've been more conscious of that extra wall of magic. I can feel it now as I slip inside — an additional shield that someone placed around the library.

The young woman stands before Finn with her head bowed. "Please don't send me back."

Finn tilts her face up to him and studies her. "You don't understand what you're offering."

"I do. I was born and raised in Faerie, and I know how this works. I am not a typical human."

"What if I sent you to the Wild Fae?" he asks, tilting his head to the side. "Would your life be so bad there?"

The girl swallows. "I do this for my brother — my half

brother. He was Unseelie, and the only person who truly cared about me."

"Where is he now?"

She ducks her head. "He died, my prince. He shouldn't have, but the curse . . ."

"I understand."

She pulls a pile of stones from her pocket. "Please?"

"What can I give you in return?"

She shakes her head. "I see all you do for the Unseelie. This is how I can help. I want to do this for you and for them."

"Surely there's something?" His voice is thick and scratchy.

She gives him a small smile. "There's nothing."

She reaches out to cup Finn's face and leans toward him, her lips inches from his. His eyes remain open as he slowly lowers his mouth to hers.

The moment their lips touch, something dull and ragged tears through my core.

I turn my back on them and leave the library. I tell myself I'm upset for Pretha. Not that I'm even sure they are . . . involved. But it's the only reason I should feel anything at the sight of Finn kissing someone.

I sit in the garden, looking up at the sun sinking low on the horizon. For the first time all day I want to return to the palace. I don't want to be here while Finn takes his . . . *tribute.* I want to ignore this feeling in my chest that I can't name. Is it jealousy? No. I don't want some broody fae prince.

I don't want him.

So why does seeing him touch someone else so tenderly hurt so much?

It would be easy for me to disregard my emotions as gratitude toward someone who is helping me when I desperately need it, but what about the connection I feel to him? What about how my power seems to surge when he's close or the way it feels when we touch?

What if all that *means* something? What if Finn is more to me than a teacher and a friend?

The thought feels like such a betrayal to Sebastian, I wish I could physically pluck it from my mind.

"Are you ready to head back now?" Pretha asks from the doorway. She's been trying to get me to return to the palace all afternoon.

"Do you not care that he's in there *touching* that girl?"

Pretha blinks at me, her shoulders seeming to sag in . . . *relief?* "I didn't even feel you move past my shield," she mutters. "Impressive."

"He kissed her. I'd think you'd care about that." I sound as catty and cruel as my cousins, so I shake my head and soften my tone. "I mean, I thought you'd want to know."

She frowns, and then realization strikes and she smiles. "You think *I'm* with *Finn?*" She laughs. "Where in the world did you get that idea?"

My cheeks heat, and I try to swallow my embarrassment, but it's useless. I've made assumptions, and now I look like a fool. "Lark has his eyes."

She shakes her head. "Lark has her father's eyes. Finn's her uncle, and he's free to kiss whomever he wishes." She mutters something under her breath that sounds a lot like *Likely thinking of someone else.*

"What are tributes? Why do you need them and what happens to them? Why did that girl have a handful of stones in her pocket?"

Pretha folds her arms. "We're trying to be your friends, Brie. Friends don't spy."

CHAPTER EIGHTEEN

"FIRE GIRL. WAKE UP," a raspy voice says by my ear.

When Pretha returned me to the palace, I went straight to bed — upset with myself for spying on people who have trusted me and more upset with myself for feeling . . . whatever it is I felt when I saw Finn kiss that girl.

"Fire Girl." A pointed nail grazes the shell of my ear, and my eyes snap open.

King Mordeus's goblin is crouched over my pillow.

Finally.

"What's taken you so long?" I ask in a hiss as I swing my legs over the side of the bed.

"The king has had matters to deal with, girl. He works on his own timeline."

I snort. *All* faeries seem to work on their own timeline. I blame immortality for their lack of urgency. "Let me get dressed."

He shakes his head. "No time."

I look down at my thin sleep shift. "Are you kidding me? I'm not going like this."

"Now or wait another week. It's up to you."

Glaring, I grab my satchel from where I tucked it beneath the mattress. Before I can turn back to the goblin, his cracked fingers wrap around my wrist. The room disappears around us.

When we appear at the Court of the Moon, I expect to find myself in the throne room. Instead, I'm in the entrance of a small sitting room. The king is lounging on a red wingback chair. The goblin releases my arm, the room spins, and I fall to the ground before I can get my feet under me.

Bile rises in my throat, and I put the back of my hand to my mouth.

"Abriella, you're looking lovely," the king says. He's dressed in all black today—from his pants to his crisp tunic to the velvet robe draped across his shoulders. Even his fingernails have been painted black. Three sentries stand on either side of him, forked tongues darting out every so often, as if they can taste danger in the air.

I lift my chin even as nausea grips me. I refuse to show weakness in front of this male—though in honesty I'd find some enjoyment in vomiting on the king. "I've had your mirror for a week. I don't appreciate being kept waiting."

"Nor I," he says, his tone bored. "And it took you longer than I expected. My spies tell me you ultimately asked the golden prince for it. That's so clever. I only wish they'd been able to see what payment he required for that favor. I certainly hope he made the most of it."

Nausea is replaced by anger in a flash, and cracks of darkness web out from my fingertips on the marble floor. The king's sentries reach for their swords, and I spare a glance at the endless depths revealed in the crumbling marble.

Whatever this power of mine is, it *blossoms* in the Unseelie palace.

"Well now." The king's eyes darken, and his nostrils flare as he looks at the mess I've made. "I see you haven't learned to control your magic yet."

I haven't even learned what it can *do* yet, apparently. I certainly didn't know I could do this. But I make a fist and concentrate on winding the power back into myself. I imagine it coiled in my gut, not dormant, but like a powerful snake — alert and ready to strike.

The king scans my face. "What I wouldn't give for such a gift."

I don't care what he thinks about my powers, and I don't want to stay here any longer than I have to. It's not the court I object to, but Mordeus. The way he looks at me — as if he wants to climb inside my brain and take a look around. It makes my skin crawl. I push myself off the floor and straighten my shift as best I can. "Let me see my sister."

"You know I can't do that."

"Let me see her, and I'll give you the mirror."

"As you've already discovered, you can see your sister *in the mirror*," he says.

I don't even want to know how he knows that. Images of his spies watching me in my chambers flash through my mind and make me shiver. But no. Surely he's just guessing. "That's not good enough."

He shrugs. "It will have to be. It's all I can offer. Have you enjoyed that this past week? Having the image of whatever you ask at your fingertips?"

I shake my head. "I want to see her. In person." It's been too long, and her absence is a constant awareness at the back of my mind.

"Have a seat." Mordeus waves and a decanter filled with dark red liquid appears in his hand. "Let's drink to your success."

Drink faerie wine. *Hard pass.* "No, thank you."

"I insist." He pours two glasses and nods to the empty chair beside him. "We drink, and then I will tell you of the next relic I need you to retrieve so that you may see your sister *in person* all the sooner."

Games. He's playing games with me. Clinging to the last of my patience only because I have no choice, I enter the room and sit. When he passes me a glass, I accept it, hoping to speed him along.

Mordeus lifts his glass. "To power," he says. I arch a brow, and he pauses with the glass halfway to his lips. "No?"

"In my world, power means the ability to cheat someone out of their life, their choices, and their free will." His piercing gray stare burns into me, and I feel like he sees too much. I roll the glass between my hands and study the liquid. "I don't care to toast to power."

"To what would you like to toast?"

I meet his gaze and let the silence hang heavily for a beat before I raise my glass. "To promises kept and delivered."

"Ah, yes. Your concern is still your sister." He nods. "I will toast to that, as I look forward to you delivering on yours." His smile sends an uneasy chill up my spine as he taps his glass to mine.

I watch him drink and sit with my wine untouched for several long minutes before he releases an exasperated sigh. "We won't be discussing the information you're waiting for until you drink, girl."

I want to argue, but what's the point? Everything's about power to this male, who's stolen most of his. He will not stand for even this small defiance. I take the smallest sip possible. The wine is sweet and velvety, and it spreads warmth through my chest. "The second relic?" I prompt.

He smirks. "Such a taskmaster you are. Don't you want to enjoy your wine for a moment?"

I glare at him. Hard.

Mordeus leans back in his chair. "The second relic is called the Grimoricon, and it will be much trickier to retrieve than the mirror."

Of course it will. I can't expect Sebastian to hand over everything I need to get my sister back. Though I'm beginning to believe he would — for me, for Jas. If only telling him wouldn't void my bargain with Mordeus. "What is the Grimoricon?"

"You may know it as the Great Book. It's the sacred text of Faerie, and it contains the earliest spells and magic from the Old Ones."

"A book?"

He takes another swallow of his wine. "Of sorts. Something that powerful cannot be contained by pages alone, so like all the greatest magical texts, it can change its shape and appearance."

"Into what?" I don't feel any ill effects from my sip of wine, so I brave another. It is truly delicious. Besides, if he wants me to retrieve this book, drugging me senseless won't help.

"Into *anything*, my girl. It can and will turn itself into anything if it senses danger."

A book that senses danger and changes form. Looks like we started out with the easiest of the relics. "Where is it?"

"That I cannot answer. The Seelie Court stole it during the war and has guarded it since, though it belongs to my court and its magic cannot be used by the golden fae."

"Then why did they steal it?"

He takes another sip and stares off into space, as if flipping through millennia of memories to find the answer. "The same reason they've taken everything else. To weaken us."

"You're saying you want me to find a book that could be anywhere in the Seelie Court and that could look like *anything*?" It's worse than a needle in a haystack. At least when you come across the needle, you know you've found what you're looking for. I could be sleeping next to the Grimoricon each night and never know it.

"I'll let you keep the mirror," he says, his gaze dropping to my lap, where I'm clutching the mirror in a white-knuckled hand.

Every time I thought about losing the mirror — my only connection to Jas — I pushed the thought away, unable to consider it. Now, knowing I'll be able to check in on her, my shoulders sag.

"Good luck."

———•———

Mordeus's goblin whisks me away from the Unseelie palace and back to the gardens surrounding the queen's castle.

"Why could you get me from my rooms, but you can't return me to them?" I ask him, fighting the nausea that goblin travel brings.

"Because you have a visitor in your chambers," the goblin says, "and I'm not interested in losing my head today."

"But how do you know that?" I ask.

The goblin gives me a wide grin, showing all his yellow, pointed teeth, then disappears.

It seemed as if I was at the Unseelie Court for only a few hours, but the sun is already high in the sky. The gardens are bustling with staff tending to the flowers, and the smells of lavender and roses call to me as I walk toward the palace entrance. It's so tempting to take a seat here, maybe close my eyes, let the sun warm my face and the sound of the birds lull me to sleep. But I resist. If there's truly someone in my chambers, I want to know who it is.

"He's been waiting there all morning," a syrupy sweet voice says behind me. "The prince might be suspicious if you show up in your pajamas." I turn to see "Eurelody" motioning me toward a carriage. "I've already sent word to your maids that you're training with me all day."

I grimace. "I'm too tired to train."

"And my ears are too pretty to listen to whining, yet here we are. Come on."

I don't argue — not when she's right about the pajamas. But when we get to the house, we walk into mass chaos.

"Get out of my way, Tynan," Jalek barks.

"No."

"You're being ridiculous. I'm going on patrol, not —"

"First of all, I don't believe you," Tynan says. "Second, it doesn't matter *where* you think you're going. You're safest if you stay here."

Pretha pulls me in the door and out of the way of the ruckus. It's not uncommon for this group to fight, but this isn't their typical bickering. Jalek is dressed in his leathers, his broadsword strapped across his back. He glares at Tynan, whose silver facial webbing glows with his emotions. Finn stands between them, legs wide as he looks from one friend to the other.

"Please, Jalek," Tynan says, whispering now. "Be sensible."

"It was a dream," Jalek says. He folds his arms and looks to Finn. "Please explain that I cannot be expected to sit in my room in perpetuity just because I had a nightmare."

"It wasn't just a nightmare. I *heard* her." Tynan nearly vibrates with frustration. "Look me in the eye and tell me you didn't wake up to the Banshee sitting on your chest. Look me in the eye and tell me you are no more nervous about going out that door than you would be any other day."

"You don't have to go, Jalek," Finn says. "I'll send Kane."

"Kane needs a break," Jalek says. "He was out half the night protecting the new portal."

"What's the Banshee?" I ask, and three heads turn to me.

Jalek glowers at Tynan. "It's nonsense."

"She's a woman who comes in your sleep and sits on your chest," Tynan says. "She appears both in this world and in your dream and —"

"A woman?" I ask.

"A spirit," Pretha says, sighing. "When she visits you, she sits on your chest and says your name over and over. It's considered a sign that your death is coming."

"It's a wonder that anyone ever dies if she *warns* them," Jalek says. But I can see the worry in his eyes. Maybe he doesn't want to believe the Banshee's call, but he's shaken.

"It's too close to the solstice," Tynan says, swallowing.

"That's exactly why I want to go," Jalek says. "She's weakest tonight."

"See! I knew you were lying," Tynan growls.

"I'm sending Kane," Finn says. "It's not worth the risk."

Jalek's jaw hardens. "Stop trying to coddle me. I'm not a child. I can make my own decisions."

"You are part of this group, and you've sworn fealty to *me*. It is *decided*," Finn says. His voice is so low I can barely hear his words, but the command in it is undeniable.

Pretha grabs my hand. "Let's get you changed and back to the castle. The prince grows impatient."

"If you just wanted me to change, why didn't we just do it in the carriage?" I ask.

"Forgive Pretha," Finn says, watching Jalek storm up the stairs. "She didn't realize it was going to be civil war in our home today. But it would be best if you'd go. Jalek's mood won't improve until after the sun sets on summer solstice."

———

My door is indeed ajar when I return to my rooms at the Golden Palace.

I press one palm against my satchel—the mirror still safely tucked inside—and the other to my thigh where my knife is strapped. "Hello?" I call, stepping inside.

Sebastian spots me and springs off the chair, crossing to me in three long strides. "Where have you been?"

I swallow and toss the satchel on the bed. "I was training with Eurelody."

"I came before breakfast, and you were already gone."

"She . . . wanted an early start."

He winces, and I wonder if he knows I'm lying. "I thought you might have decided to return to the mortal realm."

I press a hand to his heart and feel it racing beneath my palm. He's warm and strong, and I miss confiding in him, miss feeling like Sebastian's goodness was something I deserved. If only there were a way around these lies. My heart burns with hatred for the shadow king—for what he's done to my sister and my life. "I'm sorry I worried you."

Sebastian cups my jaw in one big palm and studies my face. "You're okay?"

"Yes. I'm fine."

He lowers his mouth to mine—a gentle sweep of his lips that quickly turns searching and intense. My breath leaves me in a rush, and I can't be bothered to find it again. It's the first time we've kissed since I discovered his true identity, and it's fierce. I feel every bit of his worry and terror in that kiss, feel it all the way down to my bones. Maybe I should pull away. Maybe I should tell him he has no right to kiss me. Maybe I should still be angry with him for lying to me for two years. But the truth is, his kiss is a balm to my loneliness and fear.

The heat and breadth of him make something inside of me cut loose. I'm safe here in his arms. As long as he's close, no one can hurt me, and I can't hurt him. If we never end this kiss, he'll never have to know I used him, lied to him, betrayed him.

His mouth softens against mine, and his hand slips from my hair to my neck, one big thumb stroking along my jaw as his other hand goes to my waist and pulls me tightly against him. I press closer. He groans in approval, and I smile against his mouth, feeling powerful and loving it. I need to feel every inch of his strength, want to memorize every ragged breath he takes.

I don't know how long we kiss, but it's not long enough. He's the one who pulls away. He leans his forehead against mine and we're both left gasping for air. I look down to the hand at my waist, where he's bunched my skirt into his fist, exposing my thighs and the knife. If Sebastian notices, he doesn't say.

Blowing out a breath, he opens his hand and steps back. "Sorry." He drags a hand over his face, closes his eyes, and curses softly. "I didn't come here to seduce you. I came to invite you to tonight's Litha celebration."

A celebration, meaning more gowns and dancing and pretending I have nothing better to do than watch other girls flirt with Sebastian. Girls who don't already know how they'll lose him. "I think you know which of those options tempts me more." I extend a tentative hand, brushing a finger along his knuckles. "You don't need to apologize for kissing me."

His lips twist into a lopsided smile. "I don't?"

"I kissed you back."

"I know, but . . ." He blows out another breath and puts another step between us, as if he doesn't trust himself. "Everything's gotten so complicated."

I can't argue with that. And yet . . . "Why do you say that?"

"That first night I saw you in the gardens, I was so happy. I knew you were here for Jas, and yet . . ." He swallows. "Just seeing you on my lands was more than I ever imagined. Then, when you ran from me, I realized I needed to give up whatever hope I felt in that moment. You hated my kind too much — and right then you hated me too."

"I didn't hate you," I whisper. "I was shocked and hurt. Maybe I wanted to hate you, but I couldn't."

He swallows hard and backs away. Just one more step, but it feels like a mile. "When you said you wanted to stay here, I couldn't let go of the hope that you might change your mind. And every day I see you here in my palace with my people, it's harder to ignore."

I close the distance between us and take his hand, unwilling to accept what he's trying to say, even if I need to.

He toys with my fingers. "I know you never wanted to be my bride. I know that's not what keeps you here. When you were missing this morning, it was a painful reminder that you've always intended this stay to be temporary — a means to an end. But I can't imagine spending my life with anyone else. You're the one who's always made me laugh. You're the one who makes me feel like I can still be *me* without letting my duty to my crown swallow me whole. And yet that same duty might require losing you."

My gut twists with guilt. Does he know something? Does he suspect that I am stealing from his kingdom? "How . . . why would you say that?"

"My mother is pressuring me to choose my bride," he says, his eyes downcast, as if he's confessing something shameful. "She informed me last night that I have until the next new moon to make my decision."

"That's just over three weeks away." My chest aches. It hurts to take a full breath. He'll be choosing a bride, and while I should be focused on what this means for my access to the castle, jealousy burns a hole in my gut and demands my attention. "Why so soon?"

"She wants me to have a queen. Someone who can support me. Ruling . . ." He shifts his gaze to the window, staring out across the gardens. "It gets lonely. And she wants me to have a partner before she begins to transition her power."

"Have you made a choice?" I don't really want to know. I have no right to feel anything about Sebastian's future bride, yet this jealousy feels as if it might tear me apart from the inside.

Finally he lifts his head and meets my eyes again. "I tell myself it doesn't matter. Among the nobility, marriages are more often about power and alliances than about love. But then I think about you leaving and . . . Brie, if there is any chance that you could be happy living here, that's what I want. I want *you* as my queen."

I feel like the room is closing in around me. I can't imagine what that life would look like — life as a princess of a kingdom that imprisons people fleeing a hostile land. But if Sebastian and I ruled, we would change all that.

Could I possibly be a force for good in this world? Not just another queen never wanting for anything and ruling over others, but a queen of change? But no. That's not even a choice. When Sebastian knows the truth, he won't want me anymore. Lark's vision assured me of that.

You could never be the Seelie queen.

And there's the evidence of just how despicable I am. He thinks he wants me *forever,* and part of me is considering it even as I'm betraying him. I'm the thief who's stealing from the kingdom he'd have me rule by his side. And then there are these things I feel for Finn — the way my power surges when he's close, the attraction I don't want but can't deny. Would Sebastian want me if he knew any of that? Even if he did, doesn't that prove I don't deserve him?

I'm silent too long, and Sebastian closes his eyes. The hurt that flashes across his face is a punch to the solar plexus. "Right," he whispers. "Well, at least now you know where I stand." He turns on his heel and heads out the door.

"Bash," I call, following. He stops, keeping his back to me. I don't trust myself to look at his face, so I speak to his broad shoulders instead of asking him to turn around. "I never wanted to marry a prince." I want to press my palm between his shoulder blades, to feel the reassurance of his strength, his heat. Or maybe wrap my arms around him, press my front to his back and rest my palm on his chest to feel the reassuring beat of his heart. I do neither. "But I would have married Sebastian, the mage's apprentice, in a heartbeat."

He hangs his head. "You can't have one without the other, Brie."

"Ah," I say softly. "But the prince is growing on me."

When he turns, the hope in his eyes cuts me deep, and I don't know what I hate more: that I'm manipulating him or that what I said is true.

236

CHAPTER NINETEEN

After my heart-to-heart with Sebastian this afternoon, urgency and guilt weigh heavily on me as I pull out the mirror to begin my search for the Grimoricon. If Sebastian must choose a bride by the new moon, I have only a few weeks to find the second and third relics for Mordeus and get Jas back.

My eyes flick to the locked door for the tenth time before I lift the mirror and stare at my reflection. "Show me the Grimoricon," I say, careful not to speak too loudly.

The mirror shows me a grand, brightly lit library unlike any I've seen before. It's massive, with a domed stained-glass ceiling and row upon row of books fanning out from a dais in the center of the room. There, on that dais, a pedestal holds a thick leather-bound book.

When the image fades, I ask again, and it shows me the same thing.

Why is the queen hiding the sacred book in a library? If it were in the stacks, I might think this was a case of hiding the book in plain sight, but it's right there, on display, the centerpiece of the room.

I tuck the mirror away and ring the bell by my door to call for my maids. I've searched every inch of this palace and have never seen a room like the one I saw in the mirror. Maybe it's hidden, or maybe the library lies within the queen's well-guarded sunroom. It would make sense for such a valuable item, but it makes this all the more complicated for me.

"Lady Abriella," Emmaline says, curtsying as she steps into the room. "What can we do for you tonight?"

I never call for them, so the surprise on her face is expected.

"The prince told me there are some special festivities tonight."

"Yes, milady. Tonight we celebrate Litha."

"I would like to go. Would you help me dress?"

Emmaline blinks in confusion. I can't blame her. In my two and a half weeks here, I've never cared about the seemingly endless dances happening around the castle. I go only when I'm required, and I'm usually so full of excuses that the twins have stopped trying to convince me otherwise. "Of course. I'm so sorry. We should have asked."

I wave off her apology. "I only decided moments ago." She beams, and I force myself to return her smile. "I suddenly feel like dancing."

I wasted time with the mirror, but I won't make the same mistake again. I can't afford to. I will lock my guilt away tight and get whatever information I can out of Sebastian. And if he hates me forever once he learns how I used him . . . well, if that's the price of saving Jas, it's one I'm willing to pay.

By the time my maids dress me in a bell-sleeved gown of lightest purple and pin my hair into ringlets atop my head, the music and revelry are so loud, I can easily follow the noise to the celebration on the palace lawn.

I exit the palace and stop at the top of the stairs, awestruck by the sight below.

Litha, I learned from my maids, is a celebration lasting from dusk to dawn the night before summer solstice. Bonfires are lit all around the castle to honor the sun and bring in the longest day of the year. Smaller celebrations like this happen in the human realm, but I never bothered about them or understood why the masses would celebrate blessings in a world that seems to bless so few. But under the cool glow of the crescent moon, with food and wine aplenty and so much music and laughter, I can almost understand the need for such a spectacle of gratitude.

Slowly I descend the castle steps and venture onto the lawn. The fires are massive, with heat rolling off them. Just as a fine sweat breaks out on my brow, a server thrusts a cold glass of wine into my hand and walks away before I can decline.

"You came," Sebastian says softly behind me.

Tensing, I turn to him, all too aware of the hurt I caused him earlier. "I can go back to my rooms if you want."

"I'm pretty sure my problem lies in the fact that I don't want that at all." He looks me over slowly. "Though it seems you're bent on torturing me with your beauty." There's no bite to the words, and he's smiling when he meets my eyes again. "I'm glad you came."

"I'm glad you're glad." I look him over and swallow. He's not the only one feeling tortured. His white hair is swept back, tied at the base of his neck, and his golden tunic makes his shoulders look impossibly broad. My gaze dips for a beat, but I don't dare let myself linger on the sight of his powerful thighs in his leather pants.

"I'm sorry about earlier. I had no right to —"

"No. *I'm* sorry," I say. And it's true. It might not change how I feel or what I must do, but I hate hurting him. Hate knowing that what I'm doing now will hurt him more. "I know I came here with prejudices, and I see now how unfair they were. I'm realizing that Faerie isn't exactly what I thought it was."

He searches my face. "Is that a good thing?"

"Mostly." I try to find the words to explain the shift in my thoughts, and I'm not sure how. "I have trouble trusting people here, but trust never came easily for me back home either. Faerie might have its own problems, but the fae are no more cruel and selfish than humans."

He studies my face, as if he might find all my lies and secrets written there. "And what does that mean for us?"

I step closer to him. When I take his hand, I feel every bit the traitor I am. "It means, I hope you won't give up on me yet."

His eyes widen and his nostrils flare. "I don't know how to give up on you, Abriella."

I'm too much of a coward to hold that beautiful gaze, so I drop his hand and look down at my wine. "This is Litha, then?" I ask, if only to fill the silence.

"It is. Though as you noticed, we'll use any excuse to dance and drink wine to excess."

"Can I ask why a celebration of the day is held at night?"

He scans the crowd, the fires, the musicians. "Because you can't have the longest day of the year without the shortest night. And because we honor the sun by bringing the fires into the night. They're lit before the sun sets and will burn until she rises, symbolically lighting even the short hours of darkness."

"And what do the wine and dancing symbolize?"

"Our zest for life." He grins, his gaze dropping to the untouched wine in my hand. "Is it bad?"

"I haven't tried it." I consider it a moment. The bubbles cling to the sides of the glass and sparkle in the firelight. "Doesn't faerie wine make mortals lose their inhibitions?"

He laughs. "Much like mortal wine, that depends entirely on how much of it you drink." He reaches for my glass and our fingers brush as he takes it. The single touch sends me back to my chambers, his hand on my waist, his mouth pressed to mine, and tingles race down my spine. He swirls the contents and sniffs it before handing it back to me. "It's safe if you'd like to try it."

It's my turn to sniff the golden liquid. It smells like sun-ripened cherries. I hold Sebastian's gaze as I bring it to my lips. The sweetness and flavor explode on my tongue, and warmth immediately fills my chest. I hum appreciatively and drain half the glass. "Wow. It's so good I want to *swim* in it."

Sebastian chuckles. "Summer solstice wine is my favorite too."

We watch the fires and the guests as I finish the rest of the glass. Worried that my curiosity will seem suspicious, I don't let myself ask about the library yet. Spending time with Sebastian is no hardship, and surprisingly, no one bothers us. Not even when the music turns slow and couples start dancing all around the lawn.

I frown suddenly. "I expected the other girls to drag you away from me." As my maids dressed me tonight, they told me that of the original dozen who were invited to stay at the castle, six have been sent home. I wonder if Sebastian's interested in the girls who remain. Once he discovers my deception, will he be happy to choose one of them?

He tears his gaze off a group of dancers and looks at me. "I have us glamoured so the humans can't see that we're here." He grins at me. "I wasn't about to miss out on spending tonight with you."

I want to shake him and tell him I don't deserve the adoration in his eyes. I'm the worst. A liar. A thief. A manipulator. Instead, I give my empty glass to a passing servant and loop my arms behind Sebastian's neck. "Then perhaps we should dance while we have the chance."

He slides his hands around to the small of my back and pulls me closer. I rest my head on his chest and sway to the music. My first night in Faerie, the music was a syncopated, drugging rhythm that lured me into its thrall. This is different. If anything, this music reminds me of home. It reminds me of my mother playing the piano while Jas and I played with our dolls. It reminds me of the dances my cousins attended while I was busy cleaning and trying to make my payment to Madame V. It reminds me of what

242

I could be building with Sebastian if I didn't need to trick him to save my sister.

It is precious memory and missed opportunity. It is the bitter and the sweet.

Sensing the shift in my mood, Sebastian pulls back to look down at me. "Tell me what you're thinking."

There's your opening, Brie. I hesitate, wanting to be Bash and Brie for a little longer. But I don't have time for hesitation. "I was thinking how, after a night like this, I might like to spend an entire day in bed reading." I hate myself for exploiting this moment, but I make myself smile up at him. "Do you think you could show me the libraries? That way I can lose myself in a book next time you have to leave me for days."

His eyes dance with amusement. "You know I don't actually *like* leaving you, but I can't avoid my responsibilities either." The humor leaves his face, and his hand rubs small, gentle circles at the small of my back. "Even if our time together is limited."

Limited because I don't want to marry him. Limited because he needs to choose a bride by the next new moon.

I bow my head and shut my eyes against the pain of it. I never imagined my heart would ache for a faerie, yet here I am.

"I can't have you looking so distressed on Litha. That won't do." Before I can appease his worries and pretend that I'm fine, he takes my arm and leads me back into the palace.

"Where are we going?"

"You've asked so little of me in your time here. If you want to see the library, I'm going to take you to it right away."

My heart races, and I don't bother to hide my smile. I didn't expect him to take me tonight. Maybe I could snag the book while everyone else is distracted by the party.

"You know," he says as we walk, "you were reading the first time I saw that terrible closet you called a bedroom in Fairscape."

"You remember that?" I know *I* remember. I hadn't known Sebastian long and was mortified that Jas brought the handsome apprentice down to our cellar. I didn't want him to see the reality of our lives.

"You were curled in the corner of the bed, completely absorbed in that book, as if it didn't matter that you lived this brutal existence and had only a tiny room to call your own. It didn't matter that you had to work so hard for everything. When you were reading, you were somewhere else. You were some*one* else."

He'd noticed so much more about me than I ever realized.

"My mother taught us to read and to appreciate the power of stories," I say. "After she left, stories were the only thing that helped Jas when she missed our mother. Stories helped both of us work through that."

He cuts a curious look to me. "I'm surprised you haven't asked about your sister lately."

"I . . ." I watch my feet as we walk. *Right.* Since he thinks I returned the mirror, he has no way of knowing how obsessively I use it to check on her. "I guess I try not to think about it."

"Hey." He squeezes my hand. "I didn't mean to upset you. I just wanted you to know I'm still working on it. My spies have narrowed her location down. I have soldiers heading there now. I don't want to get your hopes up, but . . ."

I stop walking. I'm not sure when I gave up hope that Sebastian might be able to rescue her. So typical of me. "Really?"

His expression is grim. "The king is cunning. He wouldn't have taken your sister if he didn't believe she was valuable, so he won't give her up easily. Though I feel like we're closer than we've been before, until Jas is home safe and under my protection, everything can change in a heartbeat. He's too powerful."

The king *is* powerful. I've seen it for myself. Whereas I've never seen Finn use his powers. Is Finn's magic suppressed somehow because he's not on the throne where he belongs? Is that why he didn't heal after fighting the Wild Fae traitors?

"Do the king's powers come from the throne?"

Sebastian frowns. "The king's powers are his own."

"If another took the throne, would that power transfer to him?"

He shakes his head. "You're thinking of the crown, but Mordeus hasn't been able to find it. In fact, he can't even sit on the throne without the crown, and until he gets the crown, he can't tap into the power of either."

The missing crown. Could Finn have powers but choose not to use them? Is he saving them for when he recovers the crown? None of this makes sense to me, and I know I'm missing some vital piece of information.

"Here it is." Sebastian pushes open the tall wooden doors that lead to the queen's library. The one I've already seen *and* explored several times.

"I've been to this one," I say, going for breezy. "It really is amazing, but if you're all about spoiling me tonight, how about taking me to a bigger one?"

He shakes his head and laughs softly. "There isn't another — bigger or smaller. But if you love books so much, perhaps I'll have the palace architects construct a new library wing." His smile wavers, as if he too is thinking of how few days I have left here.

Ignoring the guilt that stabs through me, I take his hand and wander into the library and into the stacks. I said I wanted a book, and since there are thousands in here, he'd be suspicious if I didn't pick one. Luckily, this little bit of play-acting is easy. I do love books, and I instantly spot half a dozen I can't wait to dive into.

"May I take a few?" I ask Sebastian, running my fingers across the spines.

"Take as many as you want," he says, his voice a little rough.

I limit myself to four, but when I turn back to him, he's staring at me with something like wonder in his eyes. "Why are you looking at me like that?" I ask, smiling.

He swallows. "Before all this, I couldn't imagine how you could fit in here, but now that you've been part of this life, it's going to be so much harder to let you go."

I tighten my grip on the stack of books. I can't imagine a life without Sebastian. In Fairscape, he was the color to my black and white existence. He filled me up when I was empty. When every day seemed to be an endless slog of work, thievery, and failure, I still had seeing him to look forward to. "I don't want to leave you either," I admit. *I just wish a life with you didn't have to happen here.*

The truth is, I couldn't stomach a life under the same roof as the queen. I don't want to be the kind of person who can turn a blind eye to her brand of cruelty, and no matter what I feel for Sebastian, I refuse to let go of that part of who I am.

Sebastian takes the books from my hands and sets them down on a nearby table. When he looks down at me again, his expression is soft, tender. "Close your eyes."

I look around the library. I hope he doesn't have some sweet surprise waiting in here for me. My guilt is already near paralyzing. "Why?"

"Just do it."

I can't even fake a smile. "Okay." I close my eyes and sense him bending closer.

"Keep them closed." He blows a stream of soft air into one ear. I arch my back in pleasure but keep my eyes closed. He blows into the other, and then I hear it — soft at first, then louder. A sweet melody fills my ears — fills the whole room. "Do you hear it?"

"Where is it coming from?" I ask.

"The library pixies. They love books and live among them. If you know how to listen, you can hear them sing."

Library pixies that live among books and sing. I wonder if I ever could have hated faeries if I'd known such a thing existed.

"Why can't we hear them with our eyes open?"

"I can hear them fine, but you're mortal. Your ears aren't as sensitive as ours."

He's used his magic to let me hear a special part of his world that my human ears would have never picked up.

"Dance with me?" he asks, sliding his arms around my waist.

With my eyes still closed, I rest my head against his chest and sway to the ethereal sounds of the library pixies. Maybe it's the pixies' song, but I somehow feel closer to him while we sway. I let myself imagine, just for a moment, that I could accept what he's offering me, that I could be his wife and have a life of stolen kisses and dancing in the library.

"Prince Ronan."

Sebastian stills, and I reluctantly step out of his arms as he turns to Riaan, who's stepped into the library.

"My apologies, Your Highness, but you asked to be notified if there was any news about . . ." His eyes flick to me for a beat before returning to his prince's face. "About the traitor."

My entire body goes cold. *The traitor.*

Sebastian bristles, his own reaction likely the only thing keeping him from noticing mine. When he turns to me, I try to keep my face neutral. "I need to step out for a few minutes. If you'd like to stay here, I can return for you, but it might be a while."

I look around the library and at my stack of books waiting on the table. All I want to do now is find out what Riaan means by *the traitor.* "I think I'll go to bed."

"Your rooms are on my way. Let me walk you."

He offers his arm, and I slide mine through it, falling into step beside him and trying to keep my movements relaxed when every part of me is wound tight with tension. Riaan stays behind us but never too far away.

Sebastian stops at my door. "Good night." He lifts my hand to his lips and kisses my knuckles. "Sleep well."

"Good night, Seb—" I realize that Riaan is watching, his eyes mistrusting. Can he hear my pounding heart with his sensitive fae ears? Sebastian, at least, seems oblivious, and I give him a smile as I nod my good night. "Your Highness."

"Sweet dreams." Sebastian winks at me.

I back into my chambers without closing the door and watch as they walk away to deal with a traitor.

As soon as they're far enough that I don't think they'll notice, I slip into the shadows and follow.

CHAPTER TWENTY

"You're sure it's him?" Sebastian asks Riaan as they turn into a back hallway that is blessedly dimly lit. *If they head toward the queen's quarters, I'll have to abort my mission.*

"Yes. And the queen has identified him as well."

Sebastian rolls his shoulders, then turns down a hallway I've never seen before. *The queen must keep it glamoured.* "We'll make an example of him."

It's less hall and more tunnel, with ceilings so low the males have to duck their heads as they walk. It quickly leads to a dark staircase, and Riaan summons a ball of light to guide their way. I stay a safe distance back and focus on blending with the shadows.

With each step down, the air grows cooler, and the hair on my arms stands on end. Sebastian stops at the bottom of the stairs and stands with his legs wide, his arms folded as he looks into a barred cell. I can't see inside from here, but I'm close enough to hear them speak.

"Jalek," Sebastian says, and my already unsettled stomach clenches tight. *Could it be Finn's Jalek? The male who's been* teaching me to wield a sword? "How nice of you to return home for the holiday."

The male behind the bars spits at Sebastian. "Fuck off," he growls, and I know it's him. I know that voice.

"That's no way to treat the man who holds your fate in his hands."

Jalek huffs out a laugh. "Am I supposed to believe there's any chance you might free me?"

Sebastian tucks his hands into his pockets and leans back against the wall opposite the cell. "I might, if you tell us about who you're working with and where we can find them."

"I work alone."

Sebastian grunts. "I'm not a fool. I know you work with Prince Finnian. Did he send you? Tell me his plans, and I will protect you from punishment."

"I don't betray my own — unlike your queen." He says *queen* like it's an insult, and Sebastian lunges forward, grabs his shirt through the bars, and lifts him off the floor.

"You treasonous bastard."

Jalek gasps for air, his mouth opening and closing like a fish out of water. His face turns red, then purple, as if someone is choking him. I want to look away. I don't want to see this side of Sebastian. I don't want to believe he's capable of cruelty against a male I've come to know as good and kind. But I force myself to watch every moment.

Sebastian still holds him off the floor, but Jalek suddenly wheezes and sputters as if the pressure on his windpipe's been released.

251

"Give me a reason not to kill you right now," Sebastian growls.

"Kill me, and she'll never give you the crown."

Why would the queen refuse Sebastian his birthright for killing a traitor?

Sebastian drops him and steps back, his nostrils flaring. "What do you know about it?"

Jalek laughs. "Enough to know that you don't have her fooled."

A blast of light slams into Jalek, knocking him to the floor.

"You sleep there tonight," Sebastian growls. "If you have a change of heart by morning, perhaps we can make a deal. If not, I will make an example of you. I'll show the whole kingdom the consequences of threatening my family."

Sebastian storms up the stairs and right past me, Riaan following.

I wait until they turn down the hall at the top of the stairs and are no longer visible. Only then do I release my grip on the shadows and find my physical form again.

I approach the cell and rub my arms. It's so cold down here. "Jalek?"

He straightens at the sight of me. "Brie. How long have you been here?"

"Long enough."

His face pales. "How much did you hear?"

"Enough to understand that he's likely to kill you if you don't betray Finn." And I can't risk that for too many reasons to count. "I have to get you out of here." I run my hands over the bars, looking for the lock.

"It's a magical cell. The entry appears and disappears as Prince Ronan wills it."

I shiver. "You'll freeze before morning. There has to be a way. What about your magic?"

He chuckles — low, dry, and . . . hopeless. "The first thing they did was inject me with a toxin that blocks my powers." His head rolls to the side, and he closes his eyes. "It kind of feels like having lead injected into your veins."

"Will it wear off? Maybe I can distract Sebastian in the morning so you can —"

"I appreciate the offer, but no. You could distract the prince for days, and they'd still keep me pumped full of that poison."

"It's hard for me to imagine Sebastian like that. If I hadn't seen for myself . . ." I swallow my confusion.

"War brings out the worst in all of us." Jalek shakes his head. "Tell Finn I'm sorry. Tell him . . ." He cradles his head in his hands, muttering a string of curses. "Tell him he was right about the queen. She is dying, but not fast enough."

I wrap my hands around the bars, wishing I had something to say to reassure him. But all I have are questions. "Will the queen really keep the crown from Sebastian if he kills you? If that's true, maybe he'll keep you alive as long as she lives."

He meets my eyes and gives me a sad smile. "You know too much and not enough."

"Then tell me what I need to know!"

He closes his eyes again and seems to curl into himself as he whispers, "Curses are made of secrets and sacrifice. We will suffer as long as she pays the price."

When I sneak out of the palace, the Litha celebration is still in full force, and it's easy enough to sneak a horse from the stables. I've been escorted between the palace and Finn's enough times that the route is ingrained in my memory.

I ride quickly, sticking to the shadows and not allowing myself to think about what lurks in the darkness beyond the trees.

When I arrive at Finn's, I tie the horse up in front and don't bother knocking. Instead, I cut through the alley and shift into shadow to walk through the wall and into the back of the house. Low voices are coming from the library and getting louder.

One belongs to Finn, and when I get closer, I realize that the second is Pretha's. I could slip inside and spy — see what they're saying when they don't think I'm here — but I don't have it in me tonight. Seeing Sebastian nearly strangle Jalek and then watching Jalek curl into himself in that cell, seeing the defeat in his eyes, like that of a man awaiting his execution, it broke something inside me.

I can't bring myself to deceive these people who are my . . . Pretha said they were trying to be my friends. Are they? I don't know. I don't know if anyone is my friend anymore, but I can't leave Jalek there. Even if he won't betray me or Finn, I couldn't live with myself if he died. So I emerge from the shadows, open the library doors, and walk inside.

Finn and Pretha stop talking and turn to me.

"What happened?" Pretha asks.

"Jalek. He was captured. Sebastian's threatening to . . ." I realize I don't exactly know what Sebastian will do if Jalek doesn't give him the information he wants. Kill him, I assume. Maybe worse. "Sebastian said he'd make an example of him."

"We know," Pretha says softly, throwing a long look at Finn. "We were just discussing how to find and free him. No one knows how to get to the queen's dungeons."

"I do." I swallow. "I followed Sebastian there tonight, but I couldn't free Jalek. There is no door on his cell — only bars."

"Only mortals are foolish enough to give their prisoners doors, Princess," Finn says.

Pretha chews on her thumbnail. "We'll trade something for him."

"Like what?" Finn asks.

"I think I have an idea," I say.

"Information," Pretha says, continuing as if I never spoke. "There has to be something."

Finn shakes his head. "There's no information I can give Prince Ronan that he would think was worth the trade."

"I know what we can do," I try again.

"But there is," she says, looking at me quickly.

"No," Finn growls. "We've worked too hard."

"Listen to me," I shout, my voice loud enough to echo in the high-ceilinged room.

Finn raises a brow. "Pardon, Princess. We didn't mean to upset you. Tell us your idea." Condescension drips from his words and I almost want to walk away just to spite him, but . . . *Jalek*. I can't leave him there.

"We can't open his cell, so we walk him out through the walls."

Pretha's eyes light up, and she turns to Finn. "Could you —"

"No," he says, cutting her off. "Not even on a good day, and definitely not right now."

"I think . . . I think *I* can."

Pretha steps forward, her brow creased. "Then why didn't you do it when you were there tonight?"

Finn scoffs. "Because she *can't*." He turns to me. "Your optimism is charming, but we aren't deep enough into your training yet. You can hardly control the smallest bit of your power, and if you lost your hold on it while slipping through the queen's wards, you'd have the entire royal guard on your ass."

My cheeks burn. I feel like a fool for what I have to admit, but I force myself to say it. "You're right. I can't. Not by myself, but my power . . . it's stronger when you're around. And when you touch me . . ." I immediately regret my words. They sound far, *far* too intimate. My face is on fire, but I lift my chin and go on. "I think if you go with me, the boost I get from you will give me the power and control I need to do this."

Finn stares at me.

Pretha shakes her head. "It's too risky. What happens if you get inside that cell and you can't do it. Then all three of you are stuck. Putting aside the trouble that would mean for us, Brie, do you really want to risk your prince discovering what you've been up to?"

"Let's show her." Finn steps forward and offers me his hand.

I put my hand in his and arch my back as my power awakens inside me. The room goes wholly dark, and Pretha mutters a curse right before I take her hand and the three of us walk through the wall and into the back alley.

"Wake up, you lazy bastard," Finn says, nudging Jalek with his boot. "Unless you want to be the queen's breakfast this morning."

I cringe at Finn. In the pitch black of the cell, I can hardly make out his features, even with my excellent night vision. "Her *breakfast*? Is she a cannibal?"

"She's a monster," Jalek says, pushing himself off the ground and scowling at us. "How the hell did you two get in here? You have a damned death wish?"

Finn tilts his head in my direction and shrugs. "The princess insisted. I didn't want to disappoint her when she was in the mood for an adventure."

"If you end up sacrificing yourself for me," Jalek mutters, "I'm gonna kill you before the queen has the chance."

At the sound of feet scuffing on the stairs, I turn toward the bars and try to see who's coming, but the angle makes it impossible. When we snuck past the party roaring outside and into the castle, there were two guards stationed in the hall with the glamoured doorway and another two at the top of the dungeon stairs. "Someone's coming," I whisper.

Finn's head snaps to the stairs, and before I can even follow his gaze, he's yanked me to the back corner of the cell. There, we become the darkness.

Jalek's eyes widen. "Gods above and below," he mutters.

I see the light before I see the sentry. He's dressed in the traditional attire of Arya's guard and holds an orb of light in the palm of his hand.

"Are you talking to yourself, traitor?" the uniformed sentry asks.

Jalek's face becomes a mask of indifference as he turns to face the bars.

The sentry flashes the orb over Jalek's face and then around the cell. Finn keeps ahold of my hand as he pulls me against him so my back is flush with his front. My breath catches at the contact, and my body stiffens.

"Shh," Finn whispers, his breath hot against my ear and his free hand flat against my stomach.

I close my eyes and swallow. I hate that I react to him this way. Hate even more that part of me wishes he'd move that hand, stroke the skin that burns beneath his touch. "You're enjoying this far too much," I whisper.

His chest shakes against my back in a silent chuckle, and his lips brush my ear. "You have no idea."

The sentry paces down the corridor past Jalek's cell, but we stay hidden, waiting for him to return to his post at the top of the stairs.

Finn's thumb circles ever so slightly against my stomach.

"Stop that." The protest is too quiet to sound sincere.

"As you wish."

But the feel of his splayed fingers flattening against my stomach is almost worse, and I have to swallow back a contented groan. The darkness pulses around us.

"Easy, Princess, focus on the magic. When we're out of here, you can go back to imagining all the ways you want my hands on you."

I open my mouth to tell him he's a disgusting pig who is absolutely wrong about the direction of my thoughts, but I snap it closed when the sentry returns. He casts light into the cell again. When our back corner remains blanketed in darkness and he returns his attention to Jalek, unaware that anything's amiss, I release a breath.

"I remember your sister," the sentry says with a sneer. "It was a shame to see such a pretty thing pay the price for her brother's crimes, but you didn't care, did you? I got to put her into the fire myself. I'll never forget the sound of her screams as the flames melted her skin."

Finn grips me tighter, as if he's afraid I might lunge at the guard. Jalek's entire body goes rigid, his fists balled at his sides, but he doesn't reply.

His sister, burned alive. My heart aches for him, and I feel more conflicted than ever about these supposedly "good" fae.

The sentry narrows his eyes at Jalek, his lip curling in a sneer. "I hope she lets you rot down here." Then he turns back to the stairs, and we all hold our breath as we count his steps to the top.

Finn releases me, his fingers skimming across my abdomen slower than necessary. I spin and shoot him a glare.

He only smirks before turning his attention to Jalek. "When we get you out of here, you're going to have to walk right past him."

Jalek whips around, and even in the darkness I can see the torment in his eyes.

Finn crosses the cell to look his friend in the eye. "I know

259

you'd like to tear him apart, but that is going to have to wait for another day. Do you understand?"

Jalek swallows and gives a curt nod. "How do we do this?" His voice is low but raw.

Finn takes my hand, then offers his other hand to his friend. "Just hold on and let us lead the way."

CHAPTER TWENTY-ONE

By the time we get back to Finn's, I am exhausted in a way I haven't felt since my mother left. I've never used so much magic at once, and the events of tonight have left me feeling emotionally wrung out.

While Jalek reunites with his friends, I go outside and sink into one of the chairs on the patio that runs the length of the back of the house. Dawn will come soon, and I need to get back to the palace before someone notices that I'm gone, but I can't bring myself to go. Not yet.

I tilt my face up to the stars and close my eyes. I've known for a while now that the Unseelie aren't the devils mythology makes them out to be, but tonight opened my eyes to the cruelty of Sebastian's court. Burning an innocent alive to punish her brother? I can't think of it without feeling sick.

I hear the click of the back door, and without turning to look, I know it's Finn. I *feel* him . . . something else I don't want to think about too much.

"Are you okay out here?"

Okay? What is okay? "Yeah. I'm just tired." I roll my shoulders back. "Do you think I was at risk of burning out tonight? I feel completely drained."

He shakes his head. "You've barely begun to tap into what you're capable of. You just need practice. You're not used to using that much power. You might feel . . . *off* for a few days. In fact, I'll tell Pretha that you're not training tomorrow. You should rest."

I study the moon that's sinking toward the horizon. "You mean today."

"I suppose so. Today, tomorrow . . . take as much time as you need. You did great tonight. As soon as we get you past this block of yours, you'll . . ."

I cut my eyes to him. "I'll what?"

His face is solemn as he meets my eyes. "You'll be unstoppable."

"Why did Jalek leave the Seelie Court?" I ask. "If he let them burn his sister so he could —"

"He didn't *let* them do anything. He didn't know what they'd done to Poppy until it was too late." When I stare at him, waiting for an answer to my question, he sighs. "He left because he didn't want to serve the queen. He left as protest but also because he wanted to help me get her off the throne."

"How long ago was that?"

He lowers himself into the seat next to mine and leans back, tilting his face to the sky. "Twenty years ago."

"And still she rules," I whisper. It's not a judgment, and when Finn nods, I think he knows that. "I don't know how I'm supposed to act happy in that palace when I've seen how cruel she can be."

Finn grunts. "You've barely seen anything."

"When Sebastian was talking to Jalek, Jalek said that the

queen would never give him the crown if Sebastian killed him. But then it sounded like the queen planned to kill Jalek herself, so I don't understand."

Finn finally pulls his attention off the sky and studies me instead. "Are you so sure he was talking about Arya?"

"Yes, he . . ."

Finn arches a brow, waiting for me to remember.

But no. He said *she,* not *the queen.*

"Then who?"

"You impressed my entire team with what you did tonight," he says, "the risk you took."

I should make him answer my question, but I already know it's futile and I'm too tired for the fight. "You all would have done the same if it had been me in that cell."

He draws in a breath, and his brows knit together. "I don't know if that would have been true before tonight, Princess. You may be better than all of us."

I frown, remembering my night in King Mordeus's oubliette and my dream of Finn. Did he come to me? Is that his power? The question sits on my tongue, but I swallow it back. The last thing I need to do is reveal what an impact he's had on me since the first night we met. I think I'll die with that secret, if for no other reason than to save myself the embarrassment if it turns out it was just a dream.

"Are you ready to go back to the palace?"

I shake my head. "Not yet, if you don't mind. I just . . ." I pull in a deep breath and blow it out. "I need a few more minutes."

"By all means."

I half expect him to get up and go back inside, but he stays, and when I look over to him, he's toying with the curls at the back of his head and staring at the night sky.

"I used to sit outside with my mother at night," I say. I don't know why I'm telling him this, but I want to remember her right now. "She loved the darkness, the moon, the constellations. She'd tell me to pick a star and make a wish."

Finn doesn't look at me. He closes his eyes, as if picturing it. "She sounds amazing."

"Sometimes I wish she hadn't been. If she hadn't been so wonderful, maybe it wouldn't have hurt so much when she left." I blow out a breath. "What about your mother? Is she still living?"

"My mother died birthing my younger brother many, many years ago. I imagine she was like yours in many ways." His voice goes rough. "She too loved the night, and put her children above all else."

My mother didn't, though. She left us. But I don't correct him.

He takes my hand and squeezes my fingers. Power ripples through me from whatever his connection does to my magic, and the stars seems to glow brighter. "Pick a star," he says. "Make a wish."

I shake my head. Even with that surge of power from his touch, I am so damned tired and the tears are too close. I don't want to cry. "I'm not sure I believe in that anymore."

"Oh, but you do. I'm fae. We have an instinct for these things."

"When I was a little girl, I had so many reasons to believe, so many reasons to hope. Then each day, week, year that passed after

Mom left . . ." I swallow and pull my hand out of his. This — whatever I feel when he touches me — it's too confusing. I don't want to deal with sorting that out along with everything else tonight. "After she left, I could still see the stars, but it seemed that fewer and fewer of them were for me. Wishes were for girls who had parents, for people who weren't stuck in impossible contracts. If I lose Jas, I don't think there will be a single star in the sky that feels like mine." But in this moment, sitting here and looking up at the stars next to this male who helps me tap into a power I don't even understand, a power that may very well allow me to save my sister, I can understand hope. I can understand wishing on stars. I can almost believe I'll be doing it for a very long time.

When Finn stands, his gaze locks on the hand I pulled away from him. "Abriella, every star in that sky shines for you."

It's not until the door swings closed behind him that I realize he called me by my given name.

———

The days after we rescued Jalek from the queen's dungeons stretch long. Finn makes good on his promise to give me a break from training, but being stuck at the palace all day feels more like a punishment than a reprieve, especially without Sebastian around. When I found Riaan training on the roof, he told me his prince was "away." Since I haven't seen Sebastian since Litha, I don't know what he or the queen thought about their prisoner disappearing — not that Sebastian would tell me anyway.

The second evening after Litha, I'm pacing my room, bored out of my mind and frustrated that I'm at a standstill on the book. I'm wondering how to contact Pretha when I decide to ask the mirror to show me Jas again. My chest goes tight at the sight of my little sister, as it does every time I see her through the mirror.

She's sewing and telling the story of the faerie princess who fell in love with the shadow king. "When the golden princess's parents learned their daughter was meeting the shadow king in the mortal realm, they combined their magical powers to lock all the portals between the human world and Faerie — keeping their daughter from reaching her lover and preventing the shadow king from returning home."

When the image fades, I start to put the mirror down but decide to try something else.

"Show me my mother." I stare at my own reflection for so long I think it's not going to work, but then she appears.

I haven't seen my mother in nine years, but the woman in the mirror looks exactly as I remember her — tall and graceful, with the same chestnut hair as Jasalyn. It's braided and wrapped into a coronet atop her head. She's walking through a cemetery, and she stops at one gravestone and sinks to her knees. The setting sun makes the red highlights in her hair shine, and my chest aches a little with unexpected longing. She was such a good mom. We laughed together, and she told us stories. She always wanted to play games and take long walks with us. She always put us first.

Until she didn't.

That's the real reason I need to guard my heart against Sebastian. Loving a faerie can make you lose yourself. It can make you forget what matters most. My mother did.

Why is she in the cemetery? Could that be the grave of the faerie she loved? I scan the image in the mirror over and over. Something about this looks familiar. Then I realize what it is. This is the same cemetery Finn took me to when he wanted to show me what my power could do. It's not far from here at all.

The image in the mirror fades, and I make a quick decision. I loop a leather satchel over one shoulder and slide the mirror inside. Then I run toward the cemetery, a golden stripe of the evening sun the only light left along the horizon.

If my mother is so close, maybe she can help me get Jas back. I know the faerie she loved was important — a noble fae, she said, a male who loved his people and cared for them enough to sacrifice his own happiness. Maybe he has some sort of connection to the Unseelie king. Maybe she could get him to release Jas before I finish retrieving his artifacts. Even if she doesn't have pull, it would be a relief to have her close. To have someone to confide in and know I'm not alone in this.

My soft dress shoes weren't made for running on this rough stone ground. The rocks bite into the bottoms of my feet, but I don't slow down until I reach the graves I saw in the mirror.

The cemetery stands empty, and I spin around, hoping to see where she may have gone.

"Mother!" I call. "Mom?" My voice cracks, and with it something in my chest leaks out.

I pull the mirror out again. "Show me my mother."

The image shows a tomb, a rotting corpse lying in darkness, her arms crossed over her chest.

I drop the mirror as if it burned me. "No." I back away from it.

No. Sebastian said it might not work for mortals. Just because it's worked until now . . . No. This means nothing.

A cold breeze whips through the gravestones, and the last of the sun disappears, but I'm not ready to go back to the palace.

I swallow hard and force myself to pick up the mirror and shove it into my satchel. *That image meant nothing.*

"Brie!" My name comes from a cry in the woods and it sounds like— "Brie! Help me!" Even as I move toward the call, I try to convince myself that the voice isn't familiar— isn't one I know better than my own.

I hear the cry again—a cry and a terrified sob. At the sound of my little sister's desperate shrieking, I run as fast as I can into the trees. The forest floor is dense with brush, twigs, sticks, and leaves. My skirt snags on a bush, and my useless shoes tear away, but I keep running.

"Help! Brie? Brie, help me!"

Racing toward the sound of Jas's voice, I swing around trees and through underbrush, following her cries as they grow louder and more panicked. I run until my legs are burning and my throat is raw. I'm not even surprised when I see my childhood home— the one we escaped from almost ten years ago. The one where my father died.

Flames whip around the walls, licking at the roof and reaching higher and higher. Just like that night.

I back up a step. *This isn't real.*

The fire crackles and snaps, and smoke shoves itself up my nose while the heat of the flames burns my cheeks.

"Brie, please!"

I race inside without letting myself think.

The next time she calls my name, my ears are filled with the roar of the fire and I can barely hear it. I know that her voice will get quieter and quieter. I know because I've been here before. And I know she'll go completely silent before I reach her. She'll be unconscious on the floor beneath her bed.

Part of my mind tells me this is an illusion. The house is gone. It can't be here. But I can't leave her. If I'm not the girl who runs into the fire to save her little sister, then I am nothing.

Jas screams again, and a loud crack rends the air as the ceiling joists crumble.

The smoke is unbearable. It fills my lungs, leaving no room for oxygen as I scramble around fallen debris and dodge the flames. A beam falls on my leg, and I collapse on the burning floor.

"Jas," I whisper.

"Abriella!" The roar of a deep voice comes from the front of the house. "Abriella!"

"Back here." The words are weak, my lungs too full of smoke. There's no way he heard me above the sound of the house burning around us.

I push and shove at the beam, but it doesn't move. My nose fills with the smell of my own burning flesh. I can't keep my head up. I can't even hear Jas anymore.

"You foolish mortal!"

Unconsciousness falls over me like a heavy blanket. I try to surge out from under it, but I can't.

"I was supposed to save her," I whisper. And then everything goes dark.

CHAPTER TWENTY-TWO

"WHAT HAPPENED TO HER?" The low voice barely enters my consciousness, drowned out by the pain that's so intense it's become a beast screaming inside my brain.

"The Sluagh lured her into the woods. She was surrounded by flames and smoke. Her leg is in bad shape, and her mind . . ."

"She fought us, even after we chased them off," another voice says. "She said she wouldn't leave her sister."

I force my eyes open, grasping for reality. "Jas?" My voice is hoarse. Too much smoke in my lungs. *It was real.* "Did you get my sister?"

"Shh. Don't talk." Silver eyes study my face. *Finn.* He turns away. "Heal her."

"Are you fucking kidding me?" another male voice asks. Kane? "This is a blessing. A gift from the old gods. *Take it.*"

Finn growls a low warning I can't quite make out.

"Do what you want, but I won't stand here and watch you throw everything away." Footsteps. A slamming door.

"I don't want to see her hurt either," Pretha says. I want to open my eyes, but it takes more strength than I have. "After what she did for Jalek, none of us do, but you need to stop making the same self-righteous mistakes that made me a widow."

"I am not Vexius."

"And *she* is not Isabel."

"Don't you dare," Finn growls.

"Your kingdom is doomed without you, don't you get that? And these injuries—"

"Don't tell me about my kingdom, Pretha. Letting her die when we have the means to save her is as good as murder. Do you want the magic to turn against us?" Finn asks. Then silence, so much heavy silence I nearly manage to open my eyes. "Heal her. *Now.*"

I force my eyes open, and Pretha is kneeling beside the bed, one hand on my brow, the other on my chest. "Sleep now," she says. "You'll feel better when you wake up."

———·———

Voices cut into my dreams. Finn. Pretha. They're arguing again.

"She'll be fine," Pretha says. "She just needs to rest."

"Thanks to you," Finn says. His voice sounds ragged, exhaustion hanging on every syllable.

"We need to talk about this decision you made tonight," Pretha says.

"We don't," he says. "It's done."

"Are you sleeping with her?"

"No," he snarls.

"But you're falling for her. I saw the way you were looking at her when you returned with Jalek. I watched you two on the patio, and I saw—"

271

"You saw nothing."

"Are you sure about that? Because you're supposed to be focusing on —"

"I know my duty. Now maybe it's time for you to remember yours."

Sleep begins to pull me back under when I hear Pretha say, "You're not the only one who has something at stake, Finn."

———•———

I dream of a faerie child with big silver eyes and a mischievous smile. We're in a field of flowers, and she has a lollipop in her mouth as she skips along beside me. The sunshine is lovely and the flowers smell like heaven. She looks so cherubic with her chubby cheeks, I wonder if this is it. I died in the fire — just like Lark warned me I might.

"Did I die?" I ask.

"Only the once, but not this time." She beams at me, her mouth pink and sticky with candy. "I'm glad. The other path is better for everyone."

"The *other* path?"

"Well, one of them. Some of them are bad. You die forever sometimes, and the golden queen rejoices. But other times you become fae. Other times you become *queen*." She tosses her lollipop to the side and a puffy pink ball of cotton candy appears in her hand.

"What kind of queen?"

She smiles. As if she's been waiting for this question. "A different kind. A new kind." She closes her eyes for a moment, and her face grows serious, as if she's trying to concentrate on something.

"And sometimes a bad kind. Sometimes the anger is too much and you let it make your insides ugly. Don't do that. I don't like you like that. Finn will explain if you let him."

She talks in riddles, and I can't make right or left of them. "What if I don't want to be fae or a queen?" I ask.

"Why wouldn't you want to be a faerie?" She frowns around a bite of cotton candy. "Would you rather be dead?"

I don't know how to answer that question. "I don't know anything about being a queen. I don't like the idea of having so much when others have nothing."

"I guess this is perfect then," she says. "Because you'll lose everything." She plucks a chunk of cotton candy off the ball and offers it to me.

I decline with a shake of my head, and she happily pops the sugar into her mouth. "Are you always right about the future?" I ask.

"Not possible. Because sometimes the future is wrong about you." She turns around. "I have to go. Don't tell my mom I was here."

CHAPTER TWENTY-THREE

I'M IN A LARGE FOUR-POSTER BED in a room I don't recognize. The curtains are drawn and the room is dark, but as my eyes adjust, I see Finn sitting in an upholstered chair on the opposite side of the room, his wolves on either side of him.

I draw a deep breath and painstakingly push myself up. "What happened?" My voice is hoarse. I remember the fire. Going after Jas. The old house that couldn't have been there because it was burned down when I was eight. It had all looked so real. Judging by the rawness in my throat, the fire certainly had been.

I sweep aside blankets to look down at my legs, prepared to see bandages, burns, or worse, but there's no sign of injury. I shake my head, trying to weed out illusion from reality.

"The Sluagh lured you into the woods by the Golden Military burial grounds."

I swallow past the burn in my throat. "How?"

"Mind games. Illusions," he says. He closes the book I hadn't noticed on his lap and tucks it under an arm as he stands. "They tap into your worst memories and trap you inside them." He lights a candle on the bedside table and studies me as I study him. His dark skin looks paler than I've ever seen it, and as he makes his way back to the chair, I notice that he's limping.

Did he get hurt rescuing me? Somehow I know he wouldn't want me to ask. "How long was I out?"

"A full day. Pretha healed you as best she could, and then we brought in a true healer to do the rest. Your leg was broken and you were covered in burns — mostly superficial, thank the gods. That level of magic is taxing for a human, so the healer put you into a deep sleep to help you recover."

Pretha healed me, not him. Does he have no magic or does he just choose to let others do the work for him? For someone who seems to hold so much sway over the magical creatures around him, I can't imagine him having no abilities of his own.

"How'd you find me?"

"Dara and Luna sensed you were in trouble. They led me to you."

I nod, as if this all makes perfect sense. As if running into monsters who can recreate my worst memories is something that happens every day, as if it's totally normal to have a pair of wolves acting as my guardian angels.

"You're lucky. A few more minutes, and —"

"I know," I blurt, cutting him off. I don't want to hear the rest. I know what would have happened. Mom's healer friend may have taken away the burns nine years ago, but he hadn't erased the memory of the flames licking my skin or the smoke in my lungs. I know all too well how it feels to be dying in a fire. I shake my head again. "But . . . It wasn't real? Or was it?"

"The Sluagh's illusion becomes real when you engage with it.

The fire was very real because the Sluagh became the fire when you believed it was. And you ran right into it."

"I heard screaming."

"Your sister?" he asks. "That's why you ran into the flames?"

I nod. "It seemed . . . real." I'm glad I'm still in bed, lying against pillows, but my hands tremble nevertheless. "So the fire was real, but she wasn't?"

"There was no one else in the forest with you. When we chased away the Sluagh, you were alone."

"My satchel?" I ask, moving to stand.

"Stay where you are." He bends to get something from under his chair. When he returns to the bed, he places my satchel gently in my lap. "I warned you not to use that mirror."

"You did." I lift my chin, but I'm not feeling very confident in my decisions now. The mirror tricked me into going to the cemetery. It led me right to the Sluagh's trap.

"You can't trust it," he says.

"I know," I grit out. Though I don't. Not really. It seems to work sometimes, but obviously not always. It showed my mother alive and well and showed her as a corpse in some sort of tomb. Both cannot be true.

"Then why were you out there?" He holds my gaze and waits. "What were you looking for?"

"Nothing. It . . . it doesn't matter." I look away. I've proved myself to be a careless, human fool, and part of me wishes he would leave so I could hide under the blankets. Another part of me would cry out if he walked away. *He saved my life. Again.*

"The mirror hasn't worked properly in years," Finn says. "It was created eons ago, when the Seelie and Unseelie rulers had an alliance. They made several magical items with their combined powers and divvied them up between the courts as a show of good faith. But the magic was corrupted when the Seelie Court stole it for themselves."

"It works sometimes," I say, sounding like a petulant child.

He shakes his head. "You can still ask it to show you someone or something, but you can't trust what you see. Corrupted magic is dangerous. The things it shows you can lure you into danger."

"Maybe you could've mentioned that sooner?"

"I didn't realize that *Don't use it* was a complicated order." He sighs and softens his tone. "A mirror like that is dangerous for someone like you."

I roll my eyes. "A human?"

"No. Someone with so much hope in her heart."

So much hope? Does he not know me at all? I'm the least hopeful person I know.

Then suddenly I'm aware of where I am. In a bed. In his house. "Is this *your* . . . room?" I almost say *bed* but catch myself. Somehow that's even more embarrassing.

"Yes. It was the easiest place to watch over you, and the bed is big enough to give the healer room to work. But now that you're awake and more or less healed, I can get you moved to the spare room."

Why is he being so kind to me? I think he hates me half the time, and the other half . . . I don't like to think about what I feel between us then. "I need to get back to the palace." I push myself out of bed, and the room spins. I sit down again and fall back onto my pillows.

"Stay put," Finn says. "You're healed, but you'll be weak for a few days."

"I can't just disappear. They'll come looking for me."

"Pretha has taken care of it."

I don't like this. I could miss something important and make the queen angry. What if she won't let me remain at the palace and makes me go home before I've gotten the final artifacts for Mordeus?

"As your *tutor*," Finn explains, "she was able to get permission to take you away from the palace for a few days of training. You are currently visiting a city to the south that's known for their musical performances."

"Oh." I sag into the pillows. I really am very tired, and the idea of returning to the palace and pretending I'm well? I don't think I could pull it off just yet. "She told me about your brother. Vexius? I'm . . . I'm sorry."

He nods, but his eyes avoid mine. "Me too."

What was it Pretha said when Finn was commanding her to heal me? *Stop making the same self-righteous mistakes that made me a widow.* I want to know what she meant, but I know Finn won't answer.

"Do you have any other siblings?"

"None I care to claim." He rolls his shoulders back as if suddenly realizing how stiff he is from hours of sleeping in the chair.

278

"Rest, Princess," he says. "All your problems will still be here tomorrow."

I don't want to listen like an obedient pup, but I settle into my pillows anyway and feel my eyes drifting closed.

"You must be hungry. I'll call for a tray."

"Finn?" He stops at the door and turns. "Thank you. For saving me. Again."

His throat bobs as he swallows. "I hope that whatever you were looking for was worth it." His gaze dips to the satchel in my lap. "Don't trust that mirror."

———•———

"Any leads on the Grimoricon?" Finn asks the next morning. We're in the library, and his wolves are sleeping on the floor on either side of him — where they seem to prefer to stay.

Considering that he just saved me from the trouble I got into by following the mirror, I don't want to tell him about the library it showed me. "Not really. Do you have any ideas?"

"The Grimoricon scares the queen, so I don't think she'd keep it close to her. My sources tell me it's never been at the Golden Palace."

Great. "Well, tell your *sources* that it would be helpful if they could be more specific."

He grunts. "I'll do that."

I'm feeling well enough to be playing with my power, though Finn won't let me do much. So far all I've done is learn to wrap items in shadow so I can hide them on myself. I want to practice turning others to shadow, but Finn said that's too draining, so I've

279

been working up to bigger and bigger objects. I sheath a sword at my side and wrap it in shadow before looking at Finn.

"Well done," he says, but he doesn't sound impressed. Nothing I've done with my magic impresses the shadow prince. Not that I care. "How's the boy treating you? Does his schedule allow him time to woo you?"

I frown. "What boy?"

"Prince Ronan, the golden child — I believe you call him *Sebastian?*"

I snort. "Why would you call Sebastian a *boy*? He's twenty-one." Finn ignores me, but I consider my own question. "How old are *you?*"

"Older than he is."

"That's not an answer."

He absently scratches the head of a sleeping wolf. "Old enough that I fought in the Great Fae War and young enough that I don't remember a time that our courts weren't determined to destroy each other."

That puts him somewhere between fifty and five-hundred years old. Also not an answer, but more information than I had before. I tilt my head to the side and study him. He's obviously older than Sebastian, but he looks the same age. Whereas Arya and Mordeus look older. If they were human, I'd guess they'd be my mother's age. Then there's Lark, who seems to be aging like a human child. "How does aging work with the fae anyway?"

He sighs. "It depends on the race. Some have very short life spans. Most sprites, for example, live less than five years. Other fae can live for thousands of years."

Why must he always be so obtuse? "I'm asking about fae like you, and you know it." When he seems reluctant to answer, I say, "If you don't answer, I'll just have Sebastian tell me."

"The elven fae, *like me*," he says, "typically age much like humans until puberty, then age significantly slower after that. Several hundred years between us might look like a decade to your human eyes."

"Typically? When do you age in a nontypical way?"

He shrugs. "Arya, for example, is closer to my age than to Mordeus's."

"Jalek said she's dying. That's why she looks so much older?"

"It's your turn to answer questions," he says. "How's the golden prince treating you?"

"*Sebastian* is fine," I say. I frown, realizing I don't know much about how he spends his time. "It's true he's busy, but if you think I'm going to tell you something that can be used against him, you don't know me at all."

"Oh, I already know you'll protect him," he says, his silver eyes narrowing. "You've made that abundantly clear. To be fair, he's been protecting you too." He nods at my wrist, where my scar remains glamoured away. It used to startle me to see it missing, but I forget about it most of the time now.

"How is hiding my scar protecting me?"

He stiffens, then shakes his head. "I meant the Barghest attack."

But did he?

"Has he gotten you to change your mind about becoming his queen yet?"

"*No.* Why do you assume I will?"

"Because you're in love with him."

"What does one have to do with the other?" I form a soft ball of shadow in my hand and throw it at his chest.

He grabs it and holds it in the palm of his hand before setting it spinning. "Typically, when you love someone like that, you find a way to be with them."

"Once he realizes that I've been stealing from him, I'm pretty sure he's not going to want me anyway."

The spinning ball of shadow disintegrates. "Ah. So the truth is revealed. It's not that you don't want to be with him. It's that you think he can't forgive you for what you're doing to save your sister."

"Why are you pushing this? Do you *want* me to be his queen?"

"I don't want any surprises," he bites out, standing and heading to the door. "Pretha will escort you back to the palace."

"Why don't you ever use your magic?" I blurt before he can leave.

He turns slowly back to me and cocks his head to the side, making one of those dark curls fall in his eyes. "I use my magic."

"I've never seen it."

"My gifts are not meant for your entertainment, Princess."

I roll my eyes. I understand his response for what it is — an evasion. Finn has no desire to reveal why he doesn't use his powers. And why would he? If, for some reason, he truly isn't able to use them, that would be an incredible weakness. One that could get him killed if his enemies found out.

I still can't help but think it has something to do with

his father's crown and the wrong male ruling the Court of the Moon.

"Finn, you deserve to be on that throne. Once I find my sister and get her home safely, I'd like to help you find your father's crown."

He steps back, eyes flashing. He opens his mouth, and I think he's going to scold me, but he snaps it shut again, then turns on his heel and storms from the library.

His wolves rise from where they were sleeping, and I swear there's disgust in their eyes as they look at me before following their master.

I sink into a chair and swallow back tears. I want to help, but they don't trust me enough to let me. Sure, I'm gathering the relics that will supposedly help his kingdom in the long run, but I'm being kept in the dark about so much, I don't even understand how that will help.

I pull out the mirror and stare at my reflection. I've known that the crown was missing, so why did I never think to ask the mirror?

Because you can't trust it.

But sometimes it's right. And maybe this will be one of those times.

"Show me King Oberon's crown," I say softly. But the image in the glass doesn't change, and no matter how many times I ask, I remain staring at my own reflection.

CHAPTER TWENTY-FOUR

"GUESS WHO'S BACK AT THE PALACE and asking to see you?" Emmaline teases me as she brushes my hair.

I turn to look into her big blue eyes. "Sebastian?"

I had returned to the palace yesterday afternoon, but when I found out that Sebastian had been gone since Litha, I began to worry — that he'd been hurt, that he'd somehow discovered that I'd freed his prisoner, that he knew I was staying with Finn. No one knew where he was, and my mind was more than happy to supply me with terrible possibilities, however unlikely, paranoid, and self-absorbed they may have been.

Emmaline grins. "Yes, of course Sebastian. He asked that we tell you he'll be coming by your room after sunset and he'd like to go on a *walk*." The way she squeals, you'd think *walk* was code for something much more scandalous.

"Did he seem . . . excited to see me or serious?"

I watch Tess in the mirror over my vanity as she makes my bed. "Seriously excited," she says with a wink.

Okay, so he's not angry. It's a start — especially since I know where the book is and need to ask him another favor.

"How much of Faerie have you seen during your time with the queen?" I ask Emmaline.

Emmaline smiles as she twists my hair back from my face. "We serve the Seelie Court, so we go where they go." She frowns at the short lock of hair at the base of my neck. "I wish I could get my hands on the incompetent drudge who cut your hair."

"I told you it was an accident," I say, dodging her usual complaint. "Just leave the back down and it won't show. So does the queen have *other* palaces?"

"Of course she does," Tess says.

"Many," Emmaline says, nodding.

This should have been obvious to me, but only yesterday, when Finn said that the book wasn't in this palace, did it occur to me that the library I'm searching for isn't either.

On the one hand, after my run-in with the Sluagh, I shouldn't trust the mirror anymore. On the other hand, I have no other leads on the Grimoricon, so I don't have much of a choice. New strategy? Use the mirror but proceed with caution.

When I asked the mirror again this morning, I studied the image more closely than I did the first time, and the answer was right in front of me. Waves crashed just beyond the library windows. If I'd noticed that the first time I looked, I wouldn't have wasted time thinking that there was some secret second library in this palace. From everything I've seen here so far, we are nowhere near the sea.

Tess pours me a cup of tea, and Emmaline continues to fight my curls into submission while hiding the choppy pieces. "The queen has several palaces throughout her territory. This is her primary residence, and the location of all the most formal events, but she only spends about half the year here. The other half she splits between her three other palaces."

I give my best attempt at a dreamy sigh. "I think if I were a powerful queen, I'd want to spend my day by the sea."

The twins laugh. "Maybe because it would remind you of a certain prince's *eyes?*" Emmaline says.

"*When* you're queen," Tess says, "you'll be able to choose where you spend your time."

"Serenity Palace, the seaside castle, is lovely, but it's not meant for the full court. It's more of a retreat for the royal family," Emmaline says. "But I suppose you could change that."

"There *is* a seaside palace then?" I ask.

"Of course. The southern shore is thought by many to be the most beautiful part of the Seelie territory. Rumor has it that the queen's parents were partial to Serenity Palace."

"Perhaps that is why she rarely visits," Tess says.

Emmaline shoots her a sharp look, and Tess bows her head.

"Why wouldn't she want to visit a place that reminds her of her parents?" I ask. There's something more than grief here if they aren't supposed to talk about it.

Emmaline shakes her head. "We wouldn't know, milady. We've only been in her service for ten years. The queen's parents died twenty-one years ago."

They exchange another worried glance. I'm sure they know more, but they're too afraid to say it, and I decide not to push.

———•———

"I have an idea," I tell Sebastian as we walk through the gardens that night. "Promise you won't laugh at me?"

The hot day turned cool with the setting sun, and I shiver in my sleeveless sundress. Sebastian tucks me closer to his side, warming me with his body heat. "I suppose that depends on the idea," he says, grinning.

This morning he told me he'd been away for some important meetings. I think I believe him, but I can't help but wonder what he thinks about the missing prisoner. I don't want to believe he truly would've killed Jalek, but the uncertainty is getting to me.

"Tell me your idea," he prods.

"The maids mentioned a beautiful seaside palace that your mother rarely uses. One that sits on the southern shore? I was thinking it might be nice for you and me to get away from all the pressures and demands of the court. To actually spend a couple of days where we can focus on each other."

He smirks and wriggles his brows. "Oh, really?"

I nudge his side with my elbow. "That's not what I'm talking about, and you know it."

"That's a shame," he says, chuckling.

"Says the man who barely wants to kiss me," I tease, and when the amusement falls off his face, I'm reminded that he's not human. So strange that when we're alone together it's easy to forget. "Male, I mean. Sorry." I cover the awkward moment with a smile.

He sighs. "Man, male, whatever. After two years living as a human, the label hardly matters to me. It was the *other part* . . ."

I frown, not understanding, and he explains. "You think I don't *want* to kiss you?"

"Well . . ." I bite my bottom lip, and his eyes follow.

"Half the time I can't think of anything else."

"But you don't," I say softly, thinking of my conversation with Finn, of his revelation that I *do* want Sebastian but I don't want to risk his rejection when he finds out the truth. He was right, even if I don't want to admit it.

Sebastian smirks. "Can't you tell I'm playing hard to get?"

I laugh. "Oh, I noticed. Playing at it for two years, it seems."

He cups my jaw and drags his thumb across my lips. The contact is like the first sip of sparkling wine — sweet, heady, and leaving me wanting more. "Is it working?"

I swallow. "Maybe."

"You really want to go away with me? Just the two of us?"

"Wouldn't it be nice to go to a place where there aren't so many eyes on us all the time?"

"Brie, the reality of my life is that there are always people watching. I'd like to tell you that I can give you anything, but the truth about ruling is that you don't get a private life."

And if I'm going to stay with him, this is a reality I'm going to have to accept. *That's the least of our problems, Bash.* "Even getting away from the hordes of courtiers would be something," I say. "I always loved the ocean, and I'd love to see what it's like in your world."

His eyes soften, and he presses a kiss to the top of my head. "If I'm honest, the idea of having you to myself for a couple of days is incredibly appealing. Let me see what I can work out. I have to leave first thing in the morning, and I expect to be away all day."

My heart sinks, but I don't know if it's because I'm that anxious to get to the book or because I don't want him to go away again. "Where do you go this time?"

"We've had some trouble at the eastern border." He frowns. "Our security isn't what it once was."

"You mean the camps?" When his expression hardens, I hesitate, but the words are already out there, so I go on. This is too important. "You don't help them lock up those innocent people, do you?"

"What do you know about the camps?"

"I . . . not much. Just that it's Unseelie who are trying to escape Mordeus's oppressive rule and . . . They're just trying to find a better life, Bash." I can see in his eyes that there is no way I should know even half that much. "I didn't believe you would have anything to do with it. I thought you wanted to help people — no matter what court they're from."

"Of course I do. But you need to understand that —" He shakes his head. "It doesn't matter. You don't need the details. Who told you about this?"

"I've just . . . heard people talking."

"What people?"

The anger in his eyes worries me — not for myself, but for anyone I might implicate. After seeing him with Jalek, I'm not entirely sure who I'm dealing with. "I don't know."

"I can trust you, right, Brie?"

289

You can never trust a thief you've welcomed into your home.
"Of course." The lie is bitter on my tongue.

His shoulders relax. "I do, you know. For better or worse, I do." He brings my hand to his lips and kisses my knuckles before leading me back to the palace and my room.

I lie awake half the night, the bitter taste in my mouth making my stomach cramp.

———

Pretha gets me from my chambers shortly after breakfast, and guilt dogs me with every step to the carriage and every turn toward Finn's.

I can trust you, right, Brie?

He can't trust me, and I have to keep that secret until Jas is home safe. When I consider the choice between Sebastian's feelings and Jas's freedom, the choice is obvious. It's easy. So why do I feel this way?

"What's wrong with you?" Pretha asks as the carriage stops in the village.

"Nothing." I climb out behind her and we walk along in silence toward the house.

She stops at the front door. "Don't lie to me, Brie. It's a waste of time."

"I just want my sister back. I want to find the damn book so Mordeus can tell me what's next. I'm sick of everyone acting like we have all the time in the world. I want to finish this and get my sister and go home." But my voice cracks on the last word. *Home?* Is that what it is? We can't stay in Fairscape. Gorst will never stop hunting me down for stealing from him, and going back to Elora

290

in any capacity means saying goodbye to Sebastian ... and to Finn and Pretha and the whole misfit faerie crew.

When I look up, Pretha is studying me. Maybe it's just the nature of Eurelody's form, but her expression seems almost sympathetic. "Are you and Sebastian fighting?"

"Not at all." I shake my head and look away. Across the cobblestone street, a faerie with angelic translucent wings and curled horns sweeps her front porch. "The problem is that he trusts me and I need him to, but I feel like garbage every time I exploit that."

She frowns. "You've been put in an impossible situation."

I wait for her to give me some sage advice on helping said impossible situation, but she just pushes inside and gestures for me to close the door behind me. She shifts back into her own form and leads the way to the library.

The doors at the back of the dark hall are closed, and Kane stands guard, arms crossed in front of him, his red eyes glowing in the dim corridor.

Pretha looks between him and the closed doors and frowns. "My brother's here early?"

"The king and queen are speaking with Finn and Tynan now, but the queen is expecting you to join them for lunch." Kane grimaces. "Do you want me to make excuses for you?"

Pretha shakes her head. "I knew this was coming. Lunch, dinner? Does it really matter?" Her tone is causal, but her gait, as she turns on her heel and storms to the sitting room, is anything but.

I look helplessly between Kane and the dark doorway where Pretha disappeared. "Should I leave her alone or ..."

Kane turns up his palms. "Can't you do the female thing?"

I arch a brow. "The *female* thing?"

He waves a hand. "You know, where you say the nice things and make her feel better even though she's heartbroken and love's a bitch?"

"Oh, I . . . Why's that a *female* thing?"

He grunts. "You think *I'm* a good candidate for that job? I can't even tell someone to have a good day without sounding like I secretly wish they'd die."

He has a point. I frown, thinking this through. "She's heartbroken? Over whom?"

He rocks back on his heels. "If you want to know, you should go do the thing." I can tell by the way he looks after her that he hates not being able to be that kind of friend for her, but I'm not sure I'm a great candidate either.

Nevertheless, I find myself heading into the sitting room. Pretha's standing at the front window, staring out at the street, her face blank, her eyes cold.

"Do you want to talk about it?"

She tenses. "To admit there's anything to talk about feels like a betrayal to my husband."

Oh. Well, then . . . "When did Vexius die?"

"Four years ago. He was injured while taking a group of Unseelie refugees to a portal to the Wild Fae territory." She swallows. "He didn't recover."

No wonder she looked so stricken when Finn was hurt under the same circumstances. "Four years is a long time. Surely you can forgive yourself for developing feelings for someone."

She tears her gaze off the street and meets my eyes. I've never seen her look so old or so tired. "What I feel for Amira I felt long before I met Vexius. Long before either of us married."

The name niggles at my memory. This is the meeting she's been dreading. "Amira is the queen of the Wild Fae?"

Pretha nods and looks away again. "And my brother's wife."

"Oh." My stomach sinks as I try to imagine this. "Oh, Pretha, I'm so sorry."

"Yes, me too." Her puff of breath leaves a foggy patch on the window.

"Amira and I were both your age when she was brought to my family's palace. She was there to prepare to be Misha's bride, but I fell in love the first time I laid eyes on her."

"That's beautiful." My voice is heavy with sadness. I know where this story is going. "Then she chose him over you?" I wince at the sound of my own question. If Kane were here to witness my ineptitude, he may have handled this himself.

Pretha scoffs. "Hardly. There wasn't ever a choice given, not to either of us. The Wild Fae are more accepting than the Seelie of people like Amira and me. My parents raised us to believe that love is beautiful in all forms, but I always knew that this acceptance stopped at the palace doors. To be in the royal family means living by a different set of rules."

"Why?" I ask. "What's the difference?"

"They would tell you it's about the power of bloodlines, but it's really about appearances. And about their own discomfort with the idea of their daughter loving another female." She sighs. "But for three years Amira and I got to be together while they groomed her for her life as the queen. Misha didn't care. He wasn't marrying her for love, only to strengthen the alliance between our families. But when our *parents* found out?" Her lips twitch — in amusement? Irritation? Old anger? Maybe a combination of all three. "You can imagine my horror when they sent me away to marry the young brother of the Unseelie Prince."

"Vexius," I say softly. I can't imagine what it would be like to be expected to marry someone for political reasons. Can't imagine love having so little weight in the list of reasons you decide to spend your life with someone. Yet this is exactly what Sebastian will deal with if I decide not to stay with him. "But you eventually grew to care for him?"

"Some days I wish I hadn't," she says, pressing a fist to her chest as if she's trying to stave off the ache there. "But he was so damn easy to love."

———

"You're getting better," Finn says.

I gape at him. "Was that a compliment?"

We're upstairs while Pretha takes lunch with her brother and the queen of the Wild Fae. Although I didn't expect to be welcomed to that meal, I assumed that Finn at least would be there for moral support for his sister-in-law. But no. The king and queen requested privacy.

"Just focus," Finn says.

Tynan folds his arms and lifts his chin in an I-dare-you pose.

The goal is to wrap him in shadow — not like I would to bring someone through a wall with me, but to *trap* him in my shadows. A defensive maneuver Jalek swears is my only hope in combat, since I'm pathetic with a sword.

Unspooling my magic, I zero in on Tynan and wrap him in shadow — only to have it fall away when he shrugs.

"Should work fine," Tynan says, his eyes dancing. "As long as your enemies stay *perfectly still*."

I flash him a vulgar gesture but laugh. I might still suck at this, but I'm making progress.

"Finn." Kane stands in the bedroom doorway. "We have a problem. Prince Ronan's at the door."

That one name, and my good mood is gone. My stomach clenches hard. This is what I was afraid of. He's going to find out I'm betraying him. How did he find me here?

Finn seems to have the same question. "Did you tell him where you're spending your days?"

I shake my head. "No. He just knows I'm with my tutor."

"We planned for this," Finn tells Kane. "That's why we're here, right? So send Eurelody to talk to him. Amira and Misha will forgive the interruption."

"We would, but . . ." Kane clears his throat. "He has the real Eurelody with him. He tracked her down, and she admitted that she left the queen's service years ago."

Finn mutters a curse.

Tynan grimaces. "We need to get him out of here before he realizes that Misha and Amira are on the premises."

"I can go talk to him," I offer, though I have no idea what I'll say. I just want to get rid of this sick feeling in my stomach. What will happen to Jas if Sebastian sends me home?

Finn's brows disappear into his curls. "You want him to know without a doubt that you're here? That you're working with us?"

I flinch.

"That's what I thought. Stay put." He follows Tynan out of the room and shuts the door behind him.

I listen to the muffled sounds of the males downstairs.

I hear Finn's low voice and Sebastian's, but I can't make out their words.

There's another low rumble, and then suddenly silence. I can't stand it anymore.

The bedroom door squeaks as I open it, and I flinch and quietly pad toward the top of the stairs.

"Let me in—" Sebastian's growl practically shakes the house. He stands toe to toe with Finn, who has Tynan at his side. The two princes are a formidable sight, broad-shouldered and menacing, glowering at each other. "I know you have her here."

"Maybe your magic is failing you, Prince. I'm sure you'll fix that soon enough, what with all those ripe opportunities waiting at your palace." I can't see Finn's face, but I can hear the sneer in his voice.

"Shut up," Sebastian snarls. "Don't act like you're any better than I am."

"Leave, boy. Go back to the castle and your doting mother. Go back to your herd of human women desperate to hand their lives over to you." Finn takes two steps back, retreating into the house, but Tynan stays put, his chest puffed out like he's ready to strike.

"Finnian, you're a bigger ass than I remember."

Finn gives a mocking half bow, and Sebastian turns on his heel and stomps away. Tynan slams the door shut behind him and turns to Finn with a tight jaw. "I thought we could trust her."

"We can," Finn says.

"Then how do you explain *that?*"

Finn shakes his head. "Don't assume anything. I'll take care of it."

I realize that Finn's headed to the stairs, and I rush back to the bedroom, pulling the door shut behind me. At the window, I search the street for Sebastian, but he's not there. He must have come here with his goblin and had him take him back to the castle.

The bedroom door creaks as it opens. "Trying to catch a glimpse of your true love?" Finn asks.

I don't turn around. "Do you knock?"

"Not in my own house."

"Then maybe I should just—" I don't get the chance to finish my empty threat before he spins me around and pulls my amulet from where I keep it tucked beneath my dress.

"Why didn't you tell me about this?" Finn spends more time irritated and moody than happy, but I've never seen him like *this*. Anger blazes in his eyes and turns the silver nearly white around his pupils.

"It's none of your business."

"Bullshit. If I'm going to keep you here, if I'm going to risk *my people* to protect you, this is completely my business. Where did you get it?"

I can't risk giving this up. I've nearly died twice since arriving in this godsforsaken realm. Any protection Sebastian's amulet offers me, I need. "My mother gave it to me."

He makes a fist around the amulet and yanks hard, breaking the chain before turning on his heel and heading toward the door.

"What the hell do you think you're doing?" I stalk toward him. His friends might be afraid of him, but I'm not. "That's mine. You have no right—"

"No right to destroy Prince Ronan's *tracking* amulet? No right to keep him and the queen from knowing where you've been spending your time?" He grips the amulet so tightly his knuckles whiten.

"You don't know what you're talking about. It's an amulet of *protection*."

"Is it? How well did it protect you when the Sluagh got you in their claws? How do you think your prince found you the night the Barghest caught you in the forest?"

"I—" The fight drains out of me and I'm shaking as I lower myself to sit on the bed. I never questioned how Sebastian found me that night. I was just so relieved to be saved, and I figured . . . I figured he was a magical creature, and it wasn't so hard to believe he'd be able to track me.

Finn opens his palm so I can see the amulet. Once lustrous and sparkling, it's turned the color of dirty water since Finn tore it off my neck. "He was tracking you with this, and he followed you right to my door."

"I'm sorry," I whisper. *Tracking me.* He'd told me it would protect me, but all he'd intended to do was keep tabs on me. A terrible thought occurs to me, and I snap my gaze to Finn's. "The

Unseelie Court. I was wearing the amulet both times I went to speak with Mordeus." If Sebastian realizes I'm tricking him, if he knows I'm working for Mordeus to steal from his court —

"This amulet is too weak to work over such distances." Finn shakes his head. "He won't know you went to Mordeus — at least not from this." He heads to the window. "I'll have Pretha take you back to the palace soon. Sebastian will be looking for you now that he suspects you've been with us, and I can't risk him knowing about our alliance. Pretha will glamour one of the other tutors to make them believe they've been working with you all this time."

I nod. Of course. We have to address this. But will that be enough to convince Sebastian?

"Don't come looking for us. We'll need to relocate. Pretha will come to you when it's safe."

He's going to have to move. To uproot his people and Lark. All because of me. "I'm sorry."

He shrugs, but I don't miss the weariness in his expression. "This was a temporary home anyway. It's part of a life in exile. Nothing we haven't done before."

"You and Sebastian . . . you didn't fight."

When he turns, exhaustion tugs at his shoulders. "You think that was a *friendly* encounter?"

"No, but I was under the impression that you hated each other. I thought you might try to kill each other if you were ever in the same place."

He studies the amulet in his palm. "I don't know what he's told you about me, but I don't wish your prince any ill will. His mother, on the other hand —" He tilts his head side to side, stretching his neck. Anger washes over his face, but then it's gone just as fast. "Sebastian isn't my enemy."

It's a relief to hear, and as I return to the palace, I can almost convince myself that everything will be okay.

But when I open the door to my chambers, Sebastian is waiting by the windows. "How is Prince Finnian?"

CHAPTER TWENTY-FIVE

I CAN TELL BY THE SET of his shoulders that he's angry. "Bash?" I say softly. Guilt and shame wash over me. They're always there, lapping at my feet, trying to slow me down, but now they're a rising tide threatening to drown me. "Wha—what do you . . ."

"*Prince. Finnian.* I know you've been spending time with him." His voice is raw—as if he's been screaming.

I wrap my arms around myself. "I . . ." Do I try to deny it, or would that make it worse? "Does it matter? He's a friend."

Sebastian's eyes are red, his jaw set. How long has he been waiting in here in my empty bedroom, knowing the truth about where I was? "Are you in love with him?"

"What?" I gasp. "Why would you even ask me that?" But maybe the question hits too close to home because it makes me want to run away. From Sebastian. From those sea-green eyes that seem to see too much. From my own confused feelings. I *love* Sebastian. I might not ever be able to marry him, but I do love him. It kills me to think that he feels like he has to stand before me and ask me if I'm in love with another male. It kills me because even if I don't love Finn, I do feel *something.* I feel more than I should.

"He is my *enemy*, Abriella."

"Well, you're not his, so maybe you should rethink that," I snap. Part of me knows that now isn't the time for this, but I don't want the secrets anymore. I don't want to feel like I'm betraying one prince for the other when they are both good males who want what's best for their people.

"Is that what he's been telling you? Is that how he convinced you to trust him? By pretending that we're friends?"

"I didn't say you were friends. I'm not that naïve. But he's not the monster Mordeus is, and if you want what's best for your people, you should do everything you can to put Finn on the Throne of Shadows where he belongs."

He flinches. *Flinches.*

"Sebastian." He doesn't look at me, and I move slowly as I cross the room to him. When I put my hand on his arm, he closes his eyes — relishing my touch or enduring it? I can't tell. "Look at me. Please."

"I can't." His jaw hardens. "You've been spending your time with my *enemy* while living under my roof and making me believe . . ." He shakes his head and keeps his gaze averted when he asks, "Are you even considering my proposal, or are you just pretending to so you can feed him information to bring down my court?"

"No." I shake my head. I may be awful, I may be guilty of deceiving Sebastian and betraying him, but I would never try to help Finn destroy the Seelie Court. "I wouldn't. But that's *not* what Finn wants." My voice shakes.

"Then what are you doing with him?"

He's so wrecked, and it breaks my heart. *You don't know the worst of my betrayals, Sebastian. I don't deserve you.*

Because of my agreement with Mordeus, I can never tell Sebastian the full truth of what I'm doing with Finn — the how and the why of his help. Even if I could, I don't know if I would. Sometimes I believe Sebastian would do anything to help me get Jas to safety, but other times . . . Nights like Litha, when I saw him throw Jalek around in that cell, I realize there's still so much I don't know about this world and the role Sebastian plays here. There's so much I still don't understand about the dynamics between the courts and within them.

Sebastian spins to me, and anger and desperation flash in equal measure in those beautiful eyes. "Answer me."

"He's training me," I blurt. "He's helping me learn to use the powers that manifested when I came to Faerie."

"Powers." Some of the anguish leaves his face. "Tell me what you mean."

I lick my lips, eager to explain in a way that will allow him to forgive me for spending my time with his enemy. "You know I've always been good in the dark, but when I came here, I could suddenly become the darkness and the shadows. I could disappear into them."

He searches my face, his expression unreadable. "Do you know where these powers came from?"

I shake my head. "No. They're just *there,* though I'm not very good at wielding them. Finn offered to help."

"In exchange for *what?*"

I close my eyes. I can't answer that question without forfeiting my bargain. "I don't know," I whisper, and as the lie slips past my lips, I realize there is no lie I won't tell, no object I won't steal to save my sister.

"Why didn't you ask *me?*"

Because I didn't want you knowing about my powers. I didn't want you knowing that I have abilities that let me sneak around your palace, that let me steal and spy and free prisoners. I bow my head. "I'm sorry."

He strokes my cheek and nudges my chin up until I'm looking at him again. "I am *mad* with jealousy. I've been losing my mind here thinking he might be stealing your heart. I tried to tell myself that all I really care about is the security of my kingdom, when in truth" — he bends over and touches his forehead to mine — "in truth, I've put you before my kingdom for a long time now." He traces the line of my jaw with the rough pad of his thumb, and I lean into that touch — the warmth and comfort of it. "Can I truly trust you, Abriella?"

If he could, he wouldn't be asking again. But nothing's changed. I need Sebastian's trust. I need him to take me to the summer palace, and I need him to continue allowing me to stay here so I can retrieve the third artifact. "Of course."

"Really?" He sighs heavily. "Maybe you don't understand what it's like between Finn and me, what it's like between our families, the centuries of animosity. I've been protecting you all this time, and meanwhile, you've been spending your time with him. I can't pretend this isn't a betrayal."

"Bash, you can trust me. How can I prove that?" *How can I make you believe this awful lie?*

"You—we could—" Swallowing, he seems to consider his words, but then he shakes his head. "I won't rush you into anything you're not ready for."

I slide both hands behind his neck and lift onto my toes to press my lips to his. If I ever questioned what I feel for Sebastian, this kiss is the answer. A simple brush of his lips and I want to wrap myself around him.

But again, Sebastian is the one who pulls away. His eyes are hazy with desire, but he takes a deep breath, steeling himself, then steps back.

I grab his hand. "Where are you going?"

His lips quirk into a crooked smile. "If I stay here, I'm going to kiss you again."

I step closer. "That sounds nice."

His eyes darken. "Don't play games with me, Brie. I can't handle it."

I take another step and press my palm to his chest. "I'm not playing games." And maybe at any other moment that would be a lie, but in this one, right now, it's true. All I want is his kiss, his touch, his affection. I want to soak in as much of him as I can before he learns the truth about me and pushes me away.

Slowly, he lowers his mouth to mine. "My heart is in your hands, Abriella," he says, a breath before our lips meet.

I don't know if it's his words or the gentle way he parts my lips with his, but I let everything else go in that moment. My mind goes fuzzy and my body comes alive. Sebastian's hands stroke down my arms and back up, and every pass of his callused fingers sends an electric pulse through me. It would be so nice to hand everything over to him. He's doing everything in his power to get Jas back, to protect me. I don't want to deceive him anymore or sneak around. I don't want to carry this weight alone.

Soon. It's a promise I'm making to myself. One I'm secretly, silently making to Sebastian. As soon as my bargain with Mordeus is complete and my sister is safe, I won't keep any more secrets. I'll find a way to be worthy of this love he offers me. If he'll have me.

I plunge my fingers into his hair, and the leather tie that binds it comes loose. I stroke my tongue against his, and he groans into my mouth — the vibration of the sound sending lightning flicks of pleasure down my spine. The kiss goes rough, deeper, and claiming.

He kisses his way down my neck, kisses the swell of my breasts, dips his tongue beneath the fabric of my dress. My skin burns with the need for more, the need for *him*.

He backs me up until the back of my thighs hit the side of the bed. I lower down onto it, my hands at his hips guiding him to follow.

"I can't think straight when it comes to you, Brie," he says, his breath hot against my neck. "I have duties to my family and to my people, but one taste of you and I want to forget everything."

I hold his face between both hands and guide him to look at me. His eyes are dark and foggy with pleasure, his lips parted as he searches my face. "Then let's forget. Just for these moments. Let's pretend nothing else exists."

His nostrils flare, and he lowers his mouth and sucks my bottom lip between his teeth. Groaning, he grabs the hem of my skirt, and I lift my hips to help him drag it up until it's bunched around my waist. He settles between my legs and I can feel how much he wants me. I lose myself in the sweet weight of his body on mine, in the aching pleasure of his hand on my hip, his thumb brushing maddeningly over my skin.

He dips his head to suck at my breasts right through the fabric. I cry out and arch into him. My hands are everywhere — on his shoulders, then against his powerful chest and down his sides, then to his belt. I can't feel enough of him at once.

He draws back and meets my eyes again. "Tell me you'll be mine," he murmurs. "Tell me you'll stay here with me."

"I'm here with you now." Sadness muddles with passion, and my words crack as I offer the only promise I can. "I'm yours tonight."

He tears himself away, and suddenly he's off me and sitting on the side of the bed, breathing hard, head hanging. "I'm sorry."

I prop myself up on my elbows. "Why? What's wrong?"

He swallows hard and stands. "That was too fast. We're moving too fast."

Are we? It didn't feel too fast. In fact, it felt *right*. Easy. And I know if he hadn't stopped, I would have let him keep going as long as he wanted. Would that be so bad?

I push off the bed and straighten my dress before standing in front of him. "Hey." I press a hand to his cheek, and he turns his head to press a kiss to my palm. "I didn't mind. Come back to bed."

He looks into my eyes for so long I'm sure he can see all my secrets. All my betrayals. "I want more than your kisses, Brie."

I bite back a smile. "I'm positive if you climb back into that bed with me, I will offer you much, *much* more than my kisses."

His nostrils flare, and his eyes go dark. "Gods above and below, you tempt me, woman."

I sigh. "Not enough, if you're going to walk out of here."

He looks to the door, then back to me. "I don't want to go, but I have a meeting." I try not to let the disappointment show on my face, but it must because he says, "I'm sorry I'm always so busy. I'll make it up to you." He pinches my chin between his thumb and index finger. "How about we take that getaway to the summer palace you want so badly."

My mind is fuzzy from his kisses, and it takes me a moment to remember why I want to go to the summer palace and what I need to do there. "Really?"

"Really. I think you're right. It would be good for us to get away and have time for just the two of us." He sweeps a sweet kiss across my lips. "When I finally lie with you, I won't be rushed."

My stomach flips, then twists miserably. He wants time with just the two of us, wants to spend our time at the summer palace making love and connecting, when I'll need it to search for and steal a sacred item from his mother's library.

Sebastian must see the torment on my face. He frowns. "If you've changed your mind about the palace . . . or about . . . us being together —"

"No," I blurt. "Neither. I'm . . . impatient, but you have things to do. It's fine. Thank you." For Jas, I will deceive him a little longer. For Jas, I will be less than the woman he thinks I am.

But *soon* I will be better. *Soon.*

He studies my face as if he's trying to piece together what he sees there. "Maybe the wait will give you a chance to think about . . . us. To think about the future."

"Sebastian . . ." I bite my lip. *Tell me you'll be mine.* I don't want to tell him no. I don't even want to tell him I don't know. Because I know what I want to say, but it's at odds with what I need to do. So I can't say yes. Not yet.

Soon.

With a stifled wince he puts a finger to my lips. "You don't need to say anything. I know you're not ready." He leaves my room, shutting the door behind him.

———

Sebastian is going to take me to the summer palace, and until then there's nothing I can do . . . nothing but train.

After Sebastian's gone, I shift into the shadows and explore the palace like I've done so many times before. I pass Riaan and a few members of the royal guard arguing about something in low tones. I consider stopping, but I'm not interested in spying on Sebastian's sentinels tonight, not when I my guilt is gnawing at my gut. But I do need to test my ability.

I never go to the east wing of the castle, where the royal family's chambers are. They're always too brightly lit, but I need to push myself and try using my gifts in brighter areas. If I can darken the brightly lit corridor that leads to Sebastian's rooms, I might find the courage to try something even harder.

I smile as I pass a second guard and slink closer to his door. Then I smile even more when I remember that Sebastian knows about my powers now. *One less secret.* Maybe I'll leave him a little note to let him know I was there. Maybe I'll suggest that I can meet him when he returns from his court business.

I hear voices inside and slip through the door without opening it. Or I'll just surprise him now.

Just as I inch into the room, female laughter greets me, and a matching voice says, "Prince Ronan, you're a devil."

The sight before me slams into my chest. I gasp but can't breathe. There's no room for my lungs to expand when they're surrounded by the shrapnel of my shattered heart. Sebastian and a human girl are tangled up together. His voice is low and husky as he murmurs something into her ear. Her skirt is hitched around her waist, and one of her pale legs is wrapped around his hips. His mouth opens on her neck, and she moans in pleasure.

"No." The word blurts out before I can stop myself, but they're too focused on each other to hear. I back away and slam into the door I never opened.

I've lost my grip on my shadows, and it takes all my focus to turn to shadow again and slip back into the corridor, all my control to hold on to my magic as I race back to my chambers. I barely make it to the guest hallway before I'm corporeal again, and when I get inside my room, I don't bother shutting the door behind me before I sink to the floor, shaking.

It couldn't be. He wouldn't. That wasn't Sebastian.

Maybe some shape-shifting faerie is pretending to be him to get to the girls — or maybe . . . maybe . . .

Maybe Sebastian doesn't think I'm going to agree to marry him, and he's doing exactly as he told me he would. Maybe he's trying to find a bride. Trying to do his duty to his kingdom.

But somehow ... somehow it never occurred to me that when he's not with me, wooing and kissing me, he's with one of them. Is he sleeping with the other girls? Was I so incredibly naïve to think he wouldn't? I knew he'd be preparing for the possibility of another bride, but this ache I feel isn't because he was kissing her, but because he looked like he didn't want to stop. What I witnessed wasn't some *duty* of the crown, but passion and pleasure — the very thing I was offering him when he left me for a "meeting."

My heart feels like it's been eviscerated, and I can't decide if I want to cry or storm back into his room and scream at him. All I know is that I can't do nothing. I cannot just sit here and be a sad little girl until he comes back to explain why he lied and why he ran from my bed to meet with another woman.

It hurts. I press a balled fist to my chest, wishing I could tear out the organ inside, desperate for a way to be done with this pain. I don't want to be a girl who falls apart over a male, but I don't know how to feel okay with what I just saw. I draw in one gulping breath after another. I won't let Sebastian turn me into a sniveling idiot. I thought he wanted *me*. I was such a fool, thinking I was special.

Once I found out who he really was, I didn't expect to ever want him for myself. I didn't realize that the idea of him with someone else would hurt so much. By the time I realized my feelings hadn't disappeared with the knowledge of his deception, I took his word when he told me I was the one he wanted. I never doubted it for a moment.

I should talk to him. At the very least, I should tell him how I feel, but I can't afford to fight with him. I can't afford to have him cancel our trip to Serenity Palace or suspect why I'm staying and pretending everything's okay. Sebastian *knows* me. He'd never believe that I'd see him with another woman and look the other way.

I push off the floor, determined to pull myself together. I'm here for one purpose, and that's to save my sister. Maybe I was beginning to think that more could come of it, that Sebastian and I might someday—

It doesn't matter. If Sebastian wants to walk away when things are hot and heavy with me just so he can go kiss other girls, it's his loss. We're headed to Serenity Palace and that's all that matters. In the meantime, I won't be the girl who stays in her room and cries about a boy.

All I need is a little dancing and faerie wine. I'll give myself one night to shake it off. To lose myself. And tomorrow I'll be ready to refocus on my task. It's better this way. Better that I know where I stand. Better that I'm not distracted by Sebastian and an impossible future.

When I step into the ballroom with its raucous music and crowd of dancing bodies, I see Riaan and force a smile for Sebastian's golden-haired friend. "Good evening."

"Abriella." He beams. "So good to see you. Where's Sebastian?"

"With another woman." The words are out before I can stop them, but I cover them with a smile, as if they aren't a blade currently twisting in the center of my chest. Every time I blink, I see Sebastian's hand sliding up that girl's skirt. It's like being hit in the same place over and over again. An open wound that grows deeper and more tattered with every strike.

His smile falls away. "I'm sure he'd rather be with you."

"Not at all." I scan the party, avoiding those piercing, knowing eyes. "He left me to be with her. But it's fine. At least I know where I stand."

"You don't, though." He shakes his head. "He would give you anything. Abriella, look at me." When I do, he stoops a bit so we're eye to eye. "My prince wants you *desperately*. If he's with another woman right now, it's because he was so hurt to discover that you've been spending time with Finnian."

I balk. Riaan knows too? Have I kept no secrets?

"He tells me everything," he says. "If you care for him, if you don't want to lose what you two have, you have to regain his trust."

"I want to," I say, but it's not a want. My heart doesn't give a damn about Sebastian's trust right now, but my mission . . . I *need* his trust. "But when I asked Sebastian how, he said he didn't want to push me into anything I wasn't ready for."

"There is only one ultimate show of trust between a human and a faerie."

"The bond," I whisper. That's what Sebastian had meant. He wants me to share a life-bond with him. But I can't. Not until I retrieve Mordeus's artifacts. Not when the bond would mean Sebastian's knowing — even in a vague sense — where I am and what I'm doing. But after Jas is safe, when I can finally tell Sebastian the truth, would I be willing to bond with him to prove I can be trusted? Yet it's not just an issue of him trusting me. After what I saw tonight, I'm not sure *I* trust *Sebastian* enough.

"Don't be afraid of it," Riaan says, giving me a soft smile. "It's a kind of intimacy you simply can't imagine. A connection deeper than any other I've ever known. Just . . . consider it." He straightens as someone calls for him from the other side of the room. He waves before returning his attention to me. "Now, tell me what I can do for you so you can enjoy this fine party."

I wave him off. "Go. I'm fine."

He studies me for a beat. "You're sure?"

"I'm going to *dance*," I say, forcing a smile.

"Thatta girl." He bops me on the nose and turns away to find his friends.

There are parties in the Seelie Court nightly. It seems like most of the palace residents spend their evenings dancing and drinking, but with the exception of Litha, I've never cared to attend. I've always made excuses. If my presence was required, I made a polite appearance and then slipped out moments later. But tonight I don't refuse the faerie wine that's offered to me. I snatch it from the waiter's hand and down it in two gulps before grabbing another.

I want the untethering I felt when I danced on my first night here. I want the comforting warmth I felt when I drank Mordeus's wine. I want to forget this worry and heartache. I welcome the drink to steal my hours so I don't have to endure this feeling of being crushed beneath the weight of disappointment—in Sebastian and in myself.

By the time the second glass touches my lips, I'm already

dancing. My limbs feel lighter, and my head clears of the constant worry. In this moment, I am free. I am the birds swooping through the night sky. The kite cut loose and floating on the breeze, just above the waves.

I'm vaguely aware of cheers, smiles, and laughter of the people around me, but mostly I'm somewhere else. I'm at once here and nowhere. I'm free.

I don't know how long I've been dancing when I find Riaan at my side again. His smile is broad. "How do you feel, Abriella?"

Letting my head loll to the side, I grin. "Beautiful."

He lowers his mouth to my ear and whispers, "Don't deny yourself the male you want. Don't be afraid of this life."

I stretch my arms above my head and let my hips undulate to the beat. "I'm not afraid of anything tonight."

"Good." He takes me by the waist and turns me toward the ballroom doors. "He sent the girl home. He's alone in his chambers. Maybe you can both have what you want tonight."

I squirm out of his hold and turn back to him. "You mean the bond?"

His eyes flick over me suggestively, and the corner of his mouth hitches up in a crooked smile. "Among other things."

"But I can't," I whine. My words are slurred. I think I'm still dancing. I don't know how to stop. Don't want to. "I can't even tell you why, or I'll lose my sister forever."

Something flickers across his features, and those eyes turn too serious for a beat. "Sebastian will always find a way to give you what you want."

"I want to *dance*." I grab another glass of wine from a passing waiter.

"Then dance." Riaan taps his glass against mine. "It is my pleasure to serve my future queen."

Those words bring back memories of Sebastian and the girl tangled up in the shadows in his room. I don't want those thoughts. I don't want the bad feelings that come with that memory, so I throw back the third glass, drinking it so fast I cough.

The music changes . . . or maybe that's me, and my weightless body suddenly feels very different. I'm hyperaware of my limbs moving through the air, my hips swaying to the beat. Why have I never noticed how nice it is to have a body? To have arms and hands? To feel the air on my skin?

I want *more* of that.

I reach back to unlace my bodice, but someone stops me.

"Abriella, stop," Emmaline says, taking me by the shoulders.

I blink at my handmaid a few times, but she flickers in and out of focus, and when I squint, she isn't one of the twins, she's *Pretha*. "Preeetha," I crow, dragging out the first syllable. I stroke my hand down her smooth face, trying to see the beautiful faerie's true form. "You're so beautiful. Why do you always shift to be someone you're not?"

"We're leaving," she says. "Stop it." She smacks my hands away from the laces on my bodice.

"We should take off our clothes and feel the air on our skin," I whisper conspiratorially. "It's lovely having skin that *feels* so much. I just want to feel with my skin and not with my stupid heart."

"You've been drugged," she says. "You don't know *what* you want."

"You're right about that." I let her guide me out of the ballroom, mostly because it's easier to follow than to fight her. Why would I want to fight and ruin this wonderful feeling?

We've always left the palace in a carriage, but today she takes me through a new door in the hall. "Where'd this come from?" I ask, but she's already pulling me inside, and we're suddenly in the quiet sitting room of a warm home.

CHAPTER TWENTY-SIX

"MAGIC TASTES LIKE RAINBOWS," I say, swaying on my feet.

"Gods above and below," Pretha mutters.

There's a rug on the floor and candles burning from sconces on the walls. It would be a great place to read a book, but I don't want to read tonight. I want to *feel*.

I grip her arm. "Is this your new house? I'm so sorry you had to move because of me. I'm sorry that he's kissing another woman because of me."

She shakes her head and turns away. It's too bad. She looks like herself again, and she's so pretty, but then I see who she's looking at, and I understand.

"Finn," I say, stumbling toward him. "You're beautiful too. So beautiful it distracts me when I'm around you. Did I ever tell you that? Sebastian would be so mad if he knew that." I giggle. "Maybe we should go tell him. It would serve him right."

"She's been drugged," Pretha says.

"Clearly," Finn says. Those stunning silver eyes crinkle in amusement. "Bring her up here."

Finn leads the way up a large staircase, and Pretha holds me upright as we follow him to the top and into a large bedroom. I take in every detail I can — the big, worn rugs, the candlelight, the massive bed. My gaze snags on the bed and stays there until my mind starts painting pictures of Finn stretched out on his side, propped up on one elbow. He'd smile down at me, and I'd feel those crisp white sheets against my bare skin, a contrast to the heat of his fingertips trailing over my stomach the way they did when we were hiding in the back of that cell.

My eyes float closed again as I let the fantasy wrap around me. I'm vaguely aware of sinking to the floor.

Heat presses into my side as I'm jostled into someone's arms. Finn's scooped me up off the floor, and the smell of him so close flips a switch inside of me. That dull sexual ache winds tighter and more insistent until it's a pressing need. I wrap my arms behind his neck and bury my face in his chest.

He stiffens and mutters a rough, "Thanks."

Did I say something? Maybe about how good he smells or how sometimes I think about those big hands of his, wonder how those hypnotic eyes might change when he's aroused — no, not that. He wouldn't thank me for that.

"What did you drink? And how much?"

The sound of his voice makes me open my eyes — when did I close them? His face is so close when he's holding me like this. Those lips hovering above mine. "Just one, two, three," I say. "I'd like more, please."

"I'm sure you would," he grumbles, then takes his eyes off mine. That makes me sad. I don't want him to look at anyone but me. "She's too far gone for the elixir."

"Am I dying?" I must be dying, because Finn has me in his arms and he's touching me so tenderly. He has one hand on the small of my back and the other is stroking down the side of my neck.

"You're not dying. You're *high*." But he doesn't even look at me.

"The prince wasn't around," Pretha says. "And the queen hasn't returned to the palace since Litha, though we still have no reason to believe she knows who Abriella is."

"Then who did this?" he asks. There's an edge of violence in that voice, and I know it should scare me — *he* should scare me — but instead the sound turns up the volume on the thrumming pulse between my legs.

High. Drunk. Drugged. Whatever this is, I'm grateful for it because I'm different right now. *This* Brie isn't afraid. *This* Brie doesn't have to deal with a broken heart and stupid guilt. She gets to say and do whatever she wants, and she wants to feel her fingers in Finn's hair.

"Your curls are soft." I twirl one around a finger.

Finn curses. "She's overheating."

I shift in his arms, sliding my hand from his hair to behind his neck and lifting my mouth to his ear. "I need to tell you a secret."

"Is she going to be okay?" Pretha asks.

I feel his deep inhale. I'm pressed so close to him that I move with every breath he takes. "I'll take care of her. Go find out what you can."

My skin burns to be touched, and I nuzzle his neck.

"Brie." His voice is low and deep. The husky timbre rakes

along my sensitive nerve endings even as some distant part of my mind registers the warning.

"I saw her with you."

"What are you talking about?" He's carrying me somewhere. Somewhere away from the bed, I realize with disappointment, but he's still holding me, so I don't protest.

"She was in the library with you. You kissed her. I saw."

"Who? Kyla?"

"Is that her name? What happened to her?"

He carefully sets me on my feet. "Spy much, Princess?"

"I was trying to get answers. Not that it worked." I giggle and stumble on the edge of a rug. He pulls me upright, his thumbs grazing the underside of my breasts. I lean in to the touch and look into his eyes — more gray than silver tonight. I reach up and trace the curve of his lips. "You're beautiful. I think I want to kiss you. Just once."

His expression changes, and for a breath, I think I see something there. Is that heat? But then it's gone. "You've been drugged. This isn't you."

"You're right. It's not me. I'm Abriella, the responsible one. The tough one. The *boring* one." I close my eyes and settle my hand over his, leading it across my stomach as I whisper, "The lonely one."

"We have to cool you off."

I love the sound of his voice. It's like a gentle massage across my skin. He's saying more — boring nonsense about body temperature and water and blah blah blah — but I nuzzle into him, guiding his hand across my stomach.

"Brie! Abriella!"

My eyes snap open. We're in a massive bathing room. How did we get here? When?

He's turning the dials in the shower; then he nods. "Get in."

I keep my eyes on him as I unlace my dress. I let it float down my body into a puddle of satin around my feet, leaving me almost naked. His eyes remain on my face. "You're no fun," I tease, walking a circle around him. "What did Kyla have that I don't? What did Sebastian's girl have that I don't?"

A muscle twitches in his jaw. "Get in the shower."

I step forward to obey, weaving slightly. I still have my undergarments on, the fussy, lacy ones Emma and Tess always give me, but I'll leave them. I want *him* to take them off. I want him in there with me, the hot water on our skin, his hands all over me. Sebastian's not the only one who can find companionship elsewhere.

But when I step into the tiled showering chamber, ice-cold water hits my skin, and I jerk back.

Finn blocks my exit. His legs wide, arms crossed.

I shiver. "It's freezing."

"It's not. Your body temperature is too high."

I blink at him as the water cascades over me, drenching my hair and my undergarments. "Let me out."

"I can't."

"Fine, then." I reach forward, tuck two fingers behind his belt, and tug him in with me.

His eyes close, and I see the truth in his strained expression. He wants me. Finn *wants me* and is fighting it.

With his shirt wet, I can make out the tattoos beneath the fabric. I trace the runes on each pectoral with my thumbs. "I love your tattoos."

His eyes fly open and he stiffens. "Don't."

Does he mean don't touch him or . . . "Don't what?" Testing, I trace a tattoo shaped like a flame. "Don't do this?"

He shivers, and his chest rises and falls quickly, over and over, as if he's running. "Don't love my tattoos," he whispers. "Don't romanticize something you know nothing about."

"*There's* my grumpy shadow prince." I let my fingers graze the hard planes of his abdomen and all the markings there. "You don't like them?"

"Not particularly."

"Then why do you get them?" I lift his shirt and study one that dips beneath his waistband. It looks like a five-pointed star with a swerving line through the middle. I press my thumb against it and lift my eyes to meet his. "I want to taste this one."

His nostrils flare. With a low grunt, he takes me by the wrists and pins my hands to the shower wall above my head. "Brie. Be still."

"Why? Finn . . ." I whisper his name like a secret. With my hands trapped, the only way I can touch him is if I arch my back to press my body against his, so I do. "Please. I want to be wanted. With no strings, no expectations. A kiss without demands for a promise I can't make. Just once."

He frowns at me. He looks younger when he frowns like that. Less serious, which is bizarre. Who looks *less* serious when they frown?

"Sebastian wanted the girl he was kissing. He doesn't want me, though. Not like that."

"Trust me. Sebastian wants you. Desperately." There's a sneer on his face at these words, but when I circle my hips to press my body closer to his, it disappears almost as quickly as it appeared. His throat bobs as he swallows.

I shake my head. "Everyone wants something from me, but nobody wants *me*. He always leaves when I kiss him. I think it's because I won't promise to be his bride. But he didn't want to leave *her*. He wanted to *keep* kissing her."

His jaw ticks. "He's an idiot."

That makes me smile, but I try to bite it back. "But you . . . sometimes you look at me like you want me — that is, when you're not looking at me like you hate me. Finn . . ." I let out a breath and it sounds like a whimper. "Touch me."

"I'm not going to take you to my bed just because your prince hurt your feelings."

I try to free my hands, but he tightens his hold. "Can you just pretend?" I ask. "For a minute? Kiss me like you kissed her."

"Who?" His chest rises and falls with his heavy breaths, and his gaze returns to my mouth no matter how many times he tears it away.

"The human girl Kane brought for you. The tribute. I saw her in your arms and . . . I wanted it to be me."

Finn freezes for a long beat, his only movement the bobbing of his throat as he swallows.

My skin is so hot. Too hot. And the water is too cold. And the only places on my body that feel right are the parts that are touching him. And if Sebastian knew these things I feel for Finn, if he knew that part of me *wants* Finn, he'd never forgive me. But what's one more transgression against him? Would it matter in the end? He didn't choose me tonight. Why would he ever choose me after learning the truth?

"He'd still choose you," Finn says, frowning. How much did I say out loud? I can't bring myself to care about any of it right now, not when my skin tingles like it was made for touching. Not when Finn's adjusted his grip on my hands and his thumbs are lightly stroking the insides of my wrists.

"Let me touch you." I squirm against him.

Finn uses his body to press me against the wall to stop my movement, one powerful thigh thrust between my legs. He lowers his mouth to the crook of my neck. My skin is so hot, his breath is a cool caress. "Just . . . be still. This feeling will pass."

I rock into him, needing release. "I ache." I don't care that I sound pathetic. *Desperate.* Nothing matters but the coiling heat low in my stomach and the need burning in my blood.

"I know." He keeps his face buried in my neck, and I can barely hear his muffled words over the roaring in my ears.

"Is it me?" My voice cracks. *It's me. I'm not enough.*

"Never."

"Prove it."

The sharp sting of his teeth against my neck makes me gasp, but then his tongue flicks across my skin, turning the pain to pleasure. My blood pulses there, silently begging for more attention.

I let instinct take over — instinct and this need to escape my own spiraling thoughts. My hips move, rubbing my center against his muscled thigh, begging with my body for *more,* but his grasp remains firm on my wrists, his mouth and tongue moving up my neck to nip my ear, hot and delicious. I focus on that point of friction between us with every ounce of my awareness, chasing my pleasure until it pulses through me.

Finn groans against my neck. "Brie," he whispers, his hot breath caressing my skin. "Fuck."

I collapse against the wall, limp and shivering, and Finn carries me to bed.

CHAPTER TWENTY-SEVEN

I ROLL OVER AND PRESS my hand to my forehead. My mouth feels like it's full of sand. Every muscle aches. I curl onto my side and whimper.

"Don't be dramatic," Finn says.

My eyes fly open, and I sit up so fast the room spins. Images come at me in waves. The party. The dancing and the wine. Emmaline's — no, *Pretha's* hand on my wrist as she dragged me away.

Then Finn. The shower. The *begging*.

Gods above and below . . . *so much begging.*

My face burns, and Finn smirks. "Problem, Princess?" he asks, rocking back on his heels.

I wanted it to be me. I hadn't even admitted that to myself, but last night I told him. I threw myself at him, and he denied me. Held me in place as I begged for his touch. And even through my humiliation, the thought of his lips on my neck makes my skin heat.

I collapse back on the bed and cover my face with both hands. "Go away."

He chuckles. "You didn't want me to go away last night. In

fact, when I tucked you into this bed, you were begging me to stay. I have to admit, you made some pretty intriguing promises."

I peek at him between my fingers, and just as I expected, the ass is smiling. He never smiles, but of course this most mortifying morning of my life would be the occasion of his shit-eating grins. "I hate you."

"Also not what you said last night."

I roll over and bury my face in the pillow. "I was drunk on faerie wine. I didn't mean it." My words are muffled, but judging from his chuckle, he heard them anyway.

"That's not how it works, Princess. It lowered your inhibitions, made you aroused, yes, but you'll notice you didn't pull *Pretha* into the shower and beg her to touch you."

No. I'd very specifically wanted *Finn*, and he had endured my pathetic pleas. "If I had any taste at all, I would have," I mutter. I roll to my back and frown. "Faerie wine never affected me like that."

"The wine isn't to blame. Whatever was *in* the wine is your culprit." He places three vials on the bedside table. "If anything ever makes you feel like that again, take one of these at the first sign and get somewhere safe. The elixir will counteract the effects of the drug, but you must take it right away. By the time Pretha got to you last night, it was already working its way through your system and we had to wait it out. Many fae would have taken advantage of you if they'd found you in that condition. They could've gotten you to . . . make decisions you might not be ready for when sober."

But not Finn. "Thank you," I say, but I can't get the scowl off my face.

He tosses clothes on my bed. "Quit feeling sorry for yourself and get dressed."

I throw my pillow at his face. He catches it in one hand and smirks at me. No, not smirks. *Smiles.* Something's changed between us, so I risk a question. "Who's Isabel?"

His light brown skin pales, but for once he doesn't evade. "Isabel was the woman I loved. I planned to marry her and give her children." He swallows. "But she died."

"What happened to her?"

His silver eyes look haunted when he says, "She was mortal."

"I'm sorry, Finn."

"But not sorry you finally got some information out of me?" I roll my eyes, and he nods at the clothes in my lap. "You should get dressed."

"Why?"

"The prince is planning to take you away to the summer palace tonight."

I don't want to know how he knows more about my plans with Sebastian than I do.

He cocks his head to the side. "You still want to go, don't you? Go to the palace, find the book, free your sister?"

"Of course."

He folds his arms. "So get dressed."

I point at the door. "After you leave."

His perfect lips quirk into a mocking smile, and I remember

the way they felt against my skin — soft against the sharp sting of his teeth when he bit me. "You didn't mind stripping in front of me last night."

"Out!"

The house is unfamiliar to me, but it's easy enough to find my way to the kitchen. Finn's waiting with Kane when I come downstairs. They're dressed in leather riding pants and vests, with swords strapped to their backs and knives to their thighs. It's all I can do to keep my eyes off Finn's powerful legs — all I can do not to remember how intimate I got with those corded muscles last night.

Finn lifts his mug, amusement dancing in his eyes. "We have coffee."

Embarrassment, guilt, and shame all mingle in a cocktail that makes my cheeks burn even hotter than they did last night.

I nod. My head's still aching, my thoughts fuzzier than I'd like. "Thank you." I cross the kitchen and pour myself a cup of the steaming dark brew.

"Heard you had an exciting night," Kane says, wriggling his brows at me. "Now I regret going out on patrol when Finn wanted to take the shift. I would've happily helped you through the worst of it." He winks, and Finn shoots him a look.

I meet Kane's lewd stare. "There aren't enough drugs in the world."

"Your loss," he mutters. "At least I know how to take care of someone who's been dosed with faeleaf. A good male wouldn't have left you begging."

I spin on Finn, gaping in horror, and he holds up both hands. "I didn't say a word," he says.

Kane smirks. "Jalek could hear you through the walls. Old house."

When I woke up, I didn't think the memories of last night could be any more mortifying than they were. I was wrong.

"What do you remember?" Finn asks.

My gaze flies to him and then to Kane. I open my mouth to shut him down—because, seriously, thin walls or not, I don't want to have this conversation in front of anyone, especially not Kane. But then I see that no one looks amused anymore.

"*Before* Pretha brought you here," Finn says. "Who gave you the wine?"

I sip on my coffee and wait for my memories from last night to come into focus. They remain blurry at the edges, but . . . "There were so many people there. I got my wine from a waiter just like everyone else." Unless all the wine was drugged.

He seems to see the thought on my face. "I haven't heard of anyone else suffering ill effects from the wine," he says. "If anyone else was drugged, it was kept quiet, which certainly couldn't be done if everyone at the party was dosed."

I draw in a sharp breath as a thought occurs to me, but I shake my head, willing it away.

"What?" Finn asks. "You suspect someone. Tell me."

"Sebastian's friend Riaan talked with me at the party."

Kane mutters a curse. "Of course. Keeping his prince's hands clean."

"What? No. Bash would never have wanted me drugged, but Riaan found me after I'd had a couple of drinks and . . ."

"And what?" Finn asks gently.

I shake my head. "It's personal."

Finn's brows disappear under his hair as if to say *And last night wasn't?*

"It doesn't matter."

Kane grunts. "But it does. What did he do?"

"He didn't *do* anything." My cheeks heat, remembering the conversation and Riaan's suggestion that I go make everything right between me and Sebastian. "He was trying to be a good friend."

"What did he *say?*" Finn asks.

"I was upset because I'd seen Sebastian with another girl — one of the ones he's considering marrying."

Finn folds his arms. "You mentioned that last night."

"I went to the party to get my mind off it, but I saw Riaan and told him what happened. He found me later and let me know that the girl was gone and that it was a good time to . . . regain Sebastian's trust."

Kane gapes at me. "Why the hell do you need to regain *his* trust when he's the one who was with another female?"

I bow my head. "He's supposed to be choosing a bride. Since I won't take the position, it's not exactly fair that I was upset about this."

Kane snorts. "How convenient for him."

A thousand excuses for Sebastian's behavior sit on the tip of my tongue, but each tastes a little sour even in the light of a new day, so I swallow them back. Yes, I wish he'd been more up-front with me about his physical relationships with the other girls. Yes, it hurts that he left my room and took someone else to his. But my complicated feelings for Sebastian are even more complicated by what happened last night with Finn . . . or what didn't happen but easily could have.

"Did Riaan suggest that you bond with the prince?" Finn asks, his jaw ticking.

"Yes, but I was hurt, and of course I can't do that without risking my mission where Jas is concerned."

Finn's brows shoot up. "Interesting. That's a different tune from the one you were singing before about *never* wanting the bond."

"Of course," Kane mutters. "The golden prince has her right where he wants her."

I bristle. "Screw you, Kane." I turn my glare on Finn. "Why do you care so much about who I bond with . . . or if I ever do?"

"Because, Princess," he says, and the bite of anger in his voice stuns me, "bonds have consequences. If you think for one minute—" He's cut off by the front door slamming.

Pretha rushes into the kitchen, Lark in her arms. The child has blood running down one leg, and she sobs as her mom slides her onto the counter.

Finn puts a hand on his niece's shoulder. "It's okay. It's just a scrape. It'll heal." Lark nods but lets out another hiccupping sob. Finn wets a towel and gently presses it to the girl's knee.

Pretha sees me watching and folds her arms. "She doesn't *heal.*"

"She'll heal just fine," Finn says over a shoulder. He turns back to his niece and gives her a reassuring smile. "Won't you?"

The child nods and wipes her tears, clearly determined to put on a brave face for him.

"She heals like a *mortal*," Pretha says, spitting the word *mortal* from her tongue like it has a foul taste.

Finn shoots her a warning glare before returning his attention to Lark's cut. "Does that hurt?"

"It could get infected — like yours did — and what then, Finn?" Pretha says. I've never heard her sound so panicked.

"Abriella, do me a favor and take Pretha outside while I get Lark cleaned up?"

I want to stay and see why a banged-up knee is making Pretha so sure that her immortal child's life is in danger, but I understand why Finn needs me to take her away. With every panicked word out of Pretha's mouth, Lark's face grows more stricken and more tears fall.

"Come on," I say, gently taking her arm.

"I'm fine," Pretha says. She lifts her chin, and I can tell that her need for bravery in this moment is greater than Lark's. "I'll calm down."

"Take a walk," Finn says, his eyes on Lark's knee. "I've got this. It's just a bleeder. Not that deep at all."

I tug on my friend's hand and lead her out the back door. She

334

follows reluctantly, but not without throwing a final desperate glance at her daughter before we leave.

"Why?" I ask Pretha when we're alone on the patio. She knows what I mean — *why does Lark heal like a mortal?*

"It's . . . like a disease. She's been this way her whole life." As someone who's always healed quickly and easily, it must be terrifying to see her daughter heal as slowly as a mortal.

"Is there a cure?"

She barks out a laugh, but there's no humor in her eyes as she swipes at her tears. "What do you think we're doing here?"

I shake my head. I guess I don't know. I *thought* they were searching for King Oberon's crown so Finn could take his rightful spot on the throne. What does that have to do with Lark? But then I see the obvious connection, and my heart sinks. "This disease — Finn has it too, doesn't he?"

Pretha slowly lifts her head. She studies me for a long beat, as if she's trying to decide something very important. "Abriella, all the shadow fae age and heal like mortals. They have for twenty years."

"But I'm sure I've seen fae who heal quickly."

She nods, calmer now, if more desolate. "Yes, but not Unseelie."

"Is that why Finn doesn't use his magic? And why you tell Lark not to use hers? Because it's dangerous somehow, and they're now . . . mortal?"

"Yes and no." She shakes her head. "For fae, magic and life are one. There is not one without the other. As long as the Unseelie are aging and healing like mortals, using magic is just too costly."

Life is magic. Magic is life. Finn tried to explain this to me when we first started training together. No wonder Pretha panics when she catches Lark using magic. The child is unknowingly shortening her own life.

"Why? How did this happen to them?"

Pretha steps closer, and the silver webbing on her forehead glows as she grips my shoulders. "I wish I could tell you more, Abriella, but I cannot."

"How am I supposed to help if none of you tell me *anything*? How many times did I ask about Finn and his magic? Or why he doesn't heal?"

"We've brought you into our home even though you live with and love a man who would like to see the entire Unseelie Court taken down. How could we trust you with the truth? How could we share that vulnerability?"

"But now —" I say. "Now you trust me?"

She loosens her grip on my shoulders and strokes her hands down my arms. "Even as I stand here knowing you may give your heart and your life to the wrong prince, I trust you. And Abriella, you should know this is no small thing."

The wrong prince? That implies that *Finn* wants my heart. Does he? It shouldn't matter. I love *Sebastian*. But . . . "Tell me more. Explain this. *Please.*"

"I can't. If I try . . ." She opens her mouth, but no sound comes out, and she wraps her hands around her throat as if she's choking.

I step forward. "Pretha? Are you okay?"

She drops her hands and does a full body shudder. "Like I said," she says, her voice hoarse, "I cannot."

"Are you somehow spelled to not be able to speak of it?" I ask.

She doesn't nod, but I see it in the way she holds my gaze. She physically cannot say more.

"Okay." I don't want her to hurt herself again. "I understand. Tell me what I can do to help."

"Find the Grimoricon and return it to the Unseelie Court."

The Unseelie Court. *Mordeus.* "Mordeus has magic," I say. "I've seen him use it again and again. Does this disease not affect him?" Because surely he wouldn't shorten his own life by using his magic on things so trivial as making a decanter of wine appear in his hand.

"Mordeus has proven he'll go to any length to maintain his power — and even greater lengths to get more. Magic is a big part of that."

"I don't understand."

"I know." She sighs and turns toward the door. "I used to think it was better that way, but now I'm not so sure."

"Pretha," I say as she wraps a hand around the knob. "After I get the final relics for Mordeus, I have a lot I need to figure out, but whatever I decide, I hope you . . . I hope everyone understands that this isn't easy for me. I've had feelings for Sebastian for two years, but Finn . . ." I swallow. My gaze slips to the kitchen window. Inside, Finn is cleaning Lark's knee and making her laugh. I think of the way he refused me last night when I was drugged out of my mind and begging. Of his cocky grin this morning. "Finn is my *friend.* I don't want to lose either of them."

When she turns back to me, her smile is sad. "In the end, you will have to choose."

I think of Sebastian and how badly it hurt me to see him with that other girl. I think of how tempting it is to excuse it, just so I don't have to sacrifice the little time I have left with him before he finds out that, of the two of us, my betrayals might run the deepest.

Pretha doesn't realize she's wrong. There will be no choice for me.

CHAPTER TWENTY-EIGHT

I SNAP A THREAD ON MY BRACELET, and before I can prepare a lock of hair for Bakken, he's sitting in my bedroom in the Golden Palace, legs crossed, eyes closed, and palms turned up on his knees. I think I caught him *meditating*.

He sighs heavily, then flashes those pointed teeth in a horrific grin when he sees me. "Fire Girl. I told you not to summon me inside the queen's palace."

Indeed he did, but I'd forgotten. I shrug. "Too bad."

He stands with surprising grace and extends a hand. "Payment, then?"

I grab a lock of hair from the back, pulling it from along my hairline near where I cut the last one. I shear it off quickly and hand it over. "What do you do with it?"

"Is *that* what you wish to know today?"

"No!" What a waste of hair. I don't actually care. I probably don't want to know, truly. "I have another question. Tell me about the disease that makes the Unseelie age and heal like mortals."

"There's no disease."

"Then tell me *why!* Why do they heal like mortals?"

He strokes my orange-red hair between two fingers, saying, "She grows wiser."

"She grows *impatient*," I say, watching my bedroom door. I'm supposed to leave for the summer palace with Sebastian tonight. When I returned to the palace, I sent my maids down to tell him I was preparing to go and needed another hour. I can't risk Bakken being here when Sebastian comes to my door, but I can't wait any longer for answers either. "Tell me."

"Twenty years ago, when King Oberon returned from the long night in the human realm, Queen Arya rushed to him, desperate to be reunited with her first and only love. But Oberon rejected her. While the king was locked in the mortal realm, he had fallen in love with a human woman. He said he couldn't be with the queen when his heart belonged to another. Heartbroken and angry that he would choose a weak mortal over her, the queen cursed the Unseelie king and all his people. Under the curse, they were no longer immortal, as before. They would age and be weak like humans."

"Then why does Mordeus have so much power? Isn't he Unseelie?"

"Ah, but the queen was vindictive. She wanted mortals punished alongside Oberon and his people. So she provided the Unseelie with a way to maintain their powers and their life. If the king didn't want to die or become weak, he would have to take the life of a human — *many* humans if he wanted a long life, and many more if he wanted to use his magic during that life."

The hair stands up on my arms. Why do humans wish for

magic when this is what is done with it? I can't imagine a world in which the greediest of my kind could wield that kind of power.

Then the implications of this click into place, and I have to wrap my arms around myself. They have to take human lives to heal or have access to their powers, and that was why the tribute showed up when Finn was sick. But no. Finn wouldn't do that. He's not a murderer. He must have found some work-around for the curse.

I lock the thought away and rub my hands over my arms, trying to find warmth. "Why don't they just . . . curse her back?"

"Their power is too weak, even as they sacrifice human after human." His eyes grow distant — as if he's not even there. As if he's looking far into the past and not at me.

"How is this even possible? Why hasn't this happened before if it's so easy to cripple an entire court?"

He shakes his head. "Because the cost of such power is too great. The queen was mad with jealousy when she made this curse, and alongside her summer solstice sacrifice, she gave something else to bend the magic to her will. She made the Seelie powerless to hurt the Unseelie — thus the end of the Great Fae War."

"That can't be true," I say, shaking my head. "Finn was hurt by one of the queen's sentries. I stitched him up myself."

"Perhaps the sentry worked for the queen, but the Seelie cannot wound the Unseelie."

I remember what Finn said about assuming that the guards were Seelie when they were actually Wild Fae working for the golden queen. I couldn't understand why the Wild Fae were more dangerous to him than the Seelie. Now I know. "Why did no one tell me any of this?"

"The curse prevents the fae from speaking of it—a clever loophole the queen included to keep humans from learning the truth."

"Then why can *you* speak of it?"

"Goblins are the keepers of realms. We gather the secrets, the histories, and the stories. No curse or spell can keep us from gathering or sharing any information we wish, though my kin and I know better than to anger the queen by sharing her secrets widely. Her wrath is great. Just ask the Sluagh that lurk about the seaside palace." He grins at this.

"Why would she allow them to use humans to get their powers back? Why give them that opportunity when the fae have so little regard for human life as it is?"

"Because the queen wanted the Unseelie to become as evil as they're rumored to be. She *wants* them to kill humans. It's her way of punishing all humans for the one who stole King Oberon's heart."

"And yet she wants her own son to marry a human." I've never *liked* the queen. I may have pitied her that first night when I saw the emptiness in her eyes, but when I learned about the camps, I began to hate her. But it is still hard to imagine the sweet mage's apprentice I fell for coming from someone so spiteful. So diabolical.

"She wants her son to *thrive*, to continue on after her and to be more powerful than even she could be. It is her son who wants to marry a human — a very specific human with the loveliest fire-red hair."

He tucks my hair into the pouch at his waist. "I've given you more than is fair for your offering." He lifts his hand, his fingers pressed together to snap.

"Wait!"

His hand drops to his side. "Yes?"

"Can the curse be broken?"

He shakes his head. "You push your luck. Good night, Fire Girl."

"Stop." I pull another lock forward from the back of my hair. "If I give you more hair, will you tell me how to break the curse?"

He merely extends a hand and slowly opens his palm.

I close my eyes as I shear away another lock. My maids will have a fit when they see what I've done to myself. But if I can save Finn and those children in the camps, if I can save Lark and keep Pretha from having something as simple as a scrape cause that look of terror on her face . . .

I place the lock in the palm of his wrinkled hand.

"*You* can break the curse. For twenty years the Unseelie have tried and failed, but you are unique in that there are two paths to end the Unseelie's torment."

He starts to tuck my hair away, but I grab it before he can. "How?"

His eyes blaze in anger, and he yanks the hair out of my grasp. "The curse comes from the queen's blackened bitter heart. As long as she sacrifices one of her own each year to feed the curse, it stands."

"Sacrifices one of her own?"

"On each summer solstice, a golden fae must be offered to the fires to feed the curse."

My stomach heaves. *Jalek's sister.* Who did she sacrifice this year? The Unseelie refugees can't afford to wait another year but ... "If the sacrifice could be prevented, would the curse be broken?"

"Weakened, yes, but not broken."

I hate the way goblins talk in circles. "Tell me how to break the curse and give the Unseelie their powers back."

"Fire Girl, you have two paths. Which do you desire to know? The one where you die or the one where you live?"

A cold specter slinks over me, and I swallow. "The one where I *live.*"

"If that is what you choose —" His smile is wicked. "To end the curse and live, you must kill the queen."

There's a knock on my door. *So much for my hour.*

I open my mouth to tell Bakken to leave, but he's already gone. "Abriella?"

The sound of Sebastian's voice on the other side of the door warms and cools me all at once. I've been dreading the moment I'd see him again after last night, but despite any residual heartache, I need him more than ever.

Does Sebastian know about the curse? He must — it seems all the fae do — but does he know his mother is responsible? Does he understand that a whole host of faeries want her dead — not just because of feuding courts but because she is literally killing them? I can't imagine he'd sanction the death of one of his own simply to keep this curse alive. Then again, there's so much about Sebastian that I never would have imagined, which is exactly why I can't trust him.

I tuck the Mirror of Discovery under my skirts and wrap it in shadow. Drawing in a fortifying breath, I open the door and am met with the sight of Sebastian's deep eyes and smiling face. All thoughts of curses and sacrifices scatter from my mind as it fills with images of Sebastian with his hands all over that other woman.

Keep it together, Brie. Focus.

Swallowing hard, I gesture him inside. "Hi." One word, and it wobbles. I don't know if I'm capable of pretending last night didn't happen.

"We need to talk."

"Okay . . ." I drop my gaze. I'm so sick of keeping secrets from him, but if I get the Grimoricon from the summer palace, I will be that much closer to the end of these lies and all this deceit. That much closer to helping Finn and his people — and I'm realizing that's something I really want to do.

I don't have to look up to know that Sebastian's moving closer. I am always *aware* of him when he's close. He tilts my face up, guiding me to meet his eyes. "I heard about last night," he says.

Everything inside me stills as images flash before me. The shower, so cold on my hot skin, and the firm, unrelenting press of Finn's body against mine, his mouth on my neck. The way I *begged* him . . .

"Riaan just told me. He would have told me sooner, but for some reason he assumed that when you left the party last night, you came to my room." He shakes his head. "I wish you would have."

Oh. *Oh.* I can only stare. My mind's a mess of questions and hurt and justifications I know I shouldn't tell myself. But as I lose myself in those sea-green eyes, I feel the temptation of easy forgiveness. Everything would be so much easier if we could just go back to how things were when he left my room yesterday.

"I'm sorry about the other girl," he whispers. "I never meant to hurt you."

"Bash, minutes before, you'd been in here kissing *me*." Pointing this out makes me feel like a complete hypocrite. Only hours after *that*, I was begging Finn to touch me, to kiss me. It hardly matters that it didn't happen. I would have welcomed it if he'd been willing, and that is betrayal enough. Yes, I could blame the cocktail of drugs and heartbreak, but . . .

Sebastian's eyes flash as he steps back. I see so much in that beautiful face — frustration, anger, maybe a hint of self-loathing. "I told you I'm expected to choose a wife, and while you try to talk yourself into even considering it, there are women who *want* the position."

"I invited you to my bed and you walked away and found *her*."

He squeezes his eyes shut. "I think I was trying to convince myself that what I felt with you wasn't special. I wanted to believe I could feel it with one of them too."

The words hit like a dull blow. "Did you?"

His gaze drops to my mouth, and he slowly shakes his head. "No. I never do, no matter how strongly I wish it."

I turn away and walk to the window, hating that he wishes he didn't feel so much for me and understanding it all the same. That's the worst part of this: *I get it.* I don't understand the rush to find a wife or a world where those decisions usually *aren't* emotional ones, but trying to connect with someone he may marry while his mother's deadline looms? I can sympathize. "You looked like you felt it just fine," I say.

"I wanted to, but I *didn't.*" He blows out a breath. "If I felt for her what I feel for you, I wouldn't have sent her home."

"Okay." Right alongside my hurt, guilt ravages my chest. I spent last night begging Finn. I spent this morning loving the laughter in his eyes when he teased me, and the entire afternoon trying to figure out how to save him. And I don't know where this puts me and Sebastian.

"Can we put all that aside for the night?" he asks. His warm hand slides down my arm until his fingers wrap around my wrist. "I want to focus on us for the next two days. I don't want to think about you training with Finnian or my mother pressuring me to choose a bride or how soon I'll have to take my position as king. Can we just focus on *us* for a while?"

"I'd like that." *Liar.* While he thinks he's taking me to Serenity Palace so we can have some quality time together, my focus will be on finding the Grimoricon and getting it back to Mordeus.

He smiles. "Are you feeling okay?"

I narrow my eyes. Does Sebastian know someone drugged me last night? *Was* Riaan involved? "Yes, why?"

"I came to your room after breakfast, and your maids said you were still sleeping. That's not like you."

Pretha must have put some sort of glamour on my room to make my maids think I was here and sleeping . . . or glamoured someone to look like me and play the part.

"I had a few glasses of wine at the party last night," I say.

"I'm glad you went." His eyes soften. "I like seeing you take part in events around the palace."

But maybe a little more honesty would be better. "Bash, I think I was drugged."

His faces pales, and those beautiful eyes turn as violent as a raging sea. "What?"

"I didn't feel right. Hot all over, low inhibitions." My cheeks heat in embarrassment. Thank the gods only Finn witnessed the worst of it. "When my — my maid found me at the party, I was trying to take my clothes off."

His jaw is hard, and his eyes glitter with anger. "I need to ask you something, and I need you to be honest with me."

How can he and I ever stand a chance when simple honesty is something I can never agree to?

Sebastian takes me by the shoulders, his face solemn. "Did you see Finn or any of his people last night?"

"You think *they* drugged me?"

"I think Finn would like nothing more than to gain your trust, then lower your inhibitions so you'd do something reckless . . . like agree to bond with him."

"I didn't bond with *anyone*."

"I know." He squeezes my shoulders gently. "I want to know if they *tried*."

The only one I was tempted to bond with last night was Sebastian, and my bargain with the king kept me from indulging that wish. "But . . . why? Why do you all care about this bond so much? You act like it matters more than . . ." *More than me.* That was at the root of my begging in the shower, wasn't it? It seemed that Sebastian couldn't want me without a promise of the bond, and I wanted to feel like I'd be enough even without it. I can't blame the drugs for that.

"Because it does matter." He searches my face. There's more he's trying to tell me. Maybe he can't. Maybe something about the curse? "I wouldn't put it past Finn and his crew. A simple bonding ceremony, and he could take you away from me forever."

Didn't Finn give me a similar warning about Mordeus when I first came here? Why would they both warn me this way? And Finn was *angry* this morning when I admitted that the bargain with Mordeus is truly what keeps me from bonding with Sebastian. What else would he have said if Pretha hadn't come in with Lark?

I can't afford a fight with Sebastian now, and defending Finn and his friends will only prolong this argument, so I swallow back the urge and shake my head. "I don't know who drugged me."

He squeezes my hand in his. "If we were bonded, I'd know when you were in trouble. I would have found you last night and made sure no one could use your inhibitions to their advantage. I hate knowing how vulnerable you are."

"I'm not vulnerable — not like I once was. I'm getting better at using my powers."

But he doesn't look reassured. "Sometimes it's your power that makes you so vulnerable."

"Why do you say that?"

"It doesn't matter." He gathers me against his chest, and I can hear his heart racing. "All that matters is that you're safe."

"Is it truly so rare for a human to have magic?"

He huffs out a laugh. "Indeed." He leans his forehead against mine. "You're so damn special, and Finn knows it." He swallows. "Even if he's not responsible for you being drugged last night, he *will* try to convince you to bond with him. But whatever you do, refuse him. No one can force the bond on you. It has to be entered into freely by both parties."

"Why would Finn want that? What could he possibly gain from that?"

Shaking his head, he slides his hands down my back and to my waist, tugging my hips flush with his. "He'd have . . . access to your power."

And since Finn can't use his own without shortening his life or becoming a serial killer of humans, he *needs* my power. Is that why he flirted this morning, was so good to me last night? Is that the real reason he's been training me? Is this all a long game to gain my trust so I can be his puppet?

I can't bring myself to believe it. Then again, Finn once told me that everything he does, he does to protect his people. Why would I think his actions with me were any different?

"I wouldn't bond with Finn," I say, almost to myself.

Swallowing, Sebastian gives me an insecure smile. "When you're ready, I will be honored to bond with you. I would use the bond to protect you. I wouldn't let anything happen to you." He lowers his mouth to mine and brushes a soft kiss there. "Are you ready?" he asks.

I swallow. "Bash . . . I can't. I need more time if—"

"To go to the summer palace." He brushes his knuckles along my jaw. "The bond can wait. For now." He turns toward the hallway and lets out a low whistle.

A goblin hobbles into the room. His bowed head jerks sharply to the side and his nostrils flare. He sniffs, then looks at me, accusation in his eyes. Can he smell Bakken? Does he know his kin was here?

"Take us to the summer palace," Sebastian says.

"Yes, Your Highness," the goblin says, but as he reaches for my hand, he smirks at me—a dangerous creature who holds my secret. Sebastian takes the goblin's bony hand in his own, and then I do the same.

Before I can take a breath to brace myself for the free fall of goblin transport, I hear the sounds of the sea crashing on the shore. Then I see the light of the moon twinkling in the water and feel the sand beneath my feet.

Salty air tickles my nose, and the sound of the waves invades my senses just as the summer palace comes into view. I wouldn't call it small by any stretch of the imagination. Its many spires seem to loom over the sea, but right before me are the grand windows that I know lead to the library. And the Grimoricon.

CHAPTER TWENTY-NINE

"THANK YOU," SEBASTIAN SAYS, releasing the goblin's hand.

"I'm here to serve, Your Highness." The goblin purses his lips and gives me one final knowing smile before disappearing.

There are beaches in Elora, but I'd seen the sea only once when I was young. I almost can't remember that trip, riding on a horse with my mother, my father riding beside us, then my first tentative steps into the water, laughing as the waves knocked me over.

Sebastian's white hair blows in the breeze as he looks out toward the horizon and the sun sinking into the sea. "Walk with me?" he asks.

I turn away from the palace and toward the sea. "I would like that."

He leads me down the beach, clutching my arm to his side the whole time as if he's afraid I might disappear. "This is my favorite spot," he says, walking slowly. "The sound of crashing waves has always brought me comfort. The Golden Palace is continually bustling with servants and courtiers. I preferred it here from a young age, but didn't get to come nearly as often as I'd like."

"It's beautiful. Very peaceful."

He nods. "I've come out here a few times in the weeks since you came to the palace." He cuts his eyes to me for a long beat. "I've had a lot to think about."

I swallow, my eyes burning. I feel so close to saving Jas, and more than ever I'm terrified that the moment I save her, I will lose everything else. Or worse, that Mordeus will somehow get out of the bargain and I'll lose her.

Hadn't Lark said that, when I saw her in my dream? I told her I didn't want to be a queen with so much when others have nothing, and she said I'd lose everything. Was that really the child visiting me or just a dream?

"Hey," he whispers. "Why the tears?"

I swallow. "Jas would love it here."

He bows his head. "I'm sorry I haven't been able to get her. Mordeus . . . He's used his essence to hide your sister." He says this like it's terrible news.

"What does that mean?"

"It means that as long as he's alive, we will not be able to physically reach her." He rolls his shoulders back. "It means the only way I can save your sister is if someone kills the king."

"But you can't," I blurt. "The Seelie can't harm the Unseelie." His eyes go wide, and I realize what I've said. "Isn't that true?"

His breath quickens, and he licks his lips. "Tell me what you know."

Can it hurt to admit what I've learned? I hate lying to Sebastian, and pleading ignorance after blurting what I did is pointless. "I know that the Unseelie lost their magic and immortality to the curse your mother put on them."

I watch him as I say this, but he has no reaction. No denial or confirmation. *He can't talk about the curse.*

"I always believed the Unseelie were evil," I say, continuing, "but I don't believe that anymore. Some shadow fae are evil and some are good. And some golden fae are evil and some are good. But maybe . . . maybe the Unseelie who seem evil are just trying to make the best of a bad situation."

Sebastian stops walking and turns his head toward the ocean. "I never told you this, but there was an assassination attempt on my mother on the night of Litha — made by a member of my grandparents' court who defected after my mother took the throne." He shakes his head. "The traitor was captured before he could hurt her, but somehow . . . somehow Finn's people were able to infiltrate the castle, get past my guards and our wards, and free the traitor who'd planned to put a blade in the heart of his own queen."

I bow my head, but I'm terrified that he can smell my guilt.

"But . . . apparently you knew about that," he says. The hurt in his voice grates against my conscience. "You knew Jalek wanted to kill my mother, and you didn't say a thing to me."

"I *didn't* know about Jalek's plans." It's true, and yet . . . I soften my tone before I continue. "But I won't pretend I would have stopped him if I had." I lift my chin and look him in the eye. "I know what it's like to work nonstop and still be a prisoner of your circumstances. Your mother's *camps*? It's hard to not wish worse than death on someone who would do that to innocents."

"I won't defend those camps," he says, his voice shaking. "But with so many Unseelie fleeing Mordeus's rule, our court has been overrun. *Our* people are suffering, and the queen is putting her subjects first, protecting them from the shadow fae."

"What if the shadow fae are the ones who need protecting?"

"Finn told you about the camps, but did he tell you about the hundreds in my court who've been slaughtered in cold blood so those running from the mess in *his* could take over their homes?"

And because of the queen's curse, those golden fae wouldn't be able to protect themselves from the Unseelie. It's a sickening image. "I won't argue that all the Unseelie are good," I say, "or that terrible situations don't sometimes bring out the worst in people, but —"

"They still have free will. They make their own choices, and through those choices they've proved who they really are."

"But you can't define a whole court on the actions of the worst of them. I believe Finn is good."

Sebastian's eyes blaze as he turns back to me. "If you think he's so good, you should use those powers of yours to find his catacombs in the Wild Fae Lands. See what he keeps there and tell me if you still believe him so noble."

What could Finn keep in his catacombs that would prove he's as evil as Sebastian wants me to think?

"I can't stand how he's gotten to you, made you think you can trust him."

"He's become . . . a *friend*."

"That's what he wants you to think. I'm begging you not to fall for it."

"I don't understand. Why are you so against Finn and his people when your own mother is the cause of their suffering?"

"I'm not against the Unseelie." He shakes his head. "Not at all, Brie. I hate what is happening to them under Mordeus's rule. Faerie can't exist without the light and the dark, the sun and the shadow. My mother knew that, and if it weren't for her, thousands of fae would continue to die every day in the Great Fae War."

"She ended the war?"

"Through *her* sacrifice, the fighting stopped."

He wants to believe she's good. Can I fault him for that? She's his mother. But he's too smart to turn a blind eye to all she's done. "I don't see it the way you do."

"You don't know the whole story."

"Then tell me — tell me what you can."

He swallows. "Once, my mother was the golden faerie princess. Young and inexperienced, she was seduced by King Oberon. She fell in love with him, but their kingdoms had battled for hundreds of years, and her parents were sworn enemies of the king and his kingdom. As long as the golden queen and golden king ruled, the princess could never freely be with her shadow king. But when they were able, they would sneak away from their lands and disguise themselves as humans to meet in the mortal realm. There, they wouldn't be condemned for their love. Their power was so great and their magic so intense that their love could move the sun and the moon, creating what the humans called an eclipse."

I know this story. My mother used to tell us the story of the shadow king and the golden princess. When he doesn't continue, I continue for him. "And one day Oberon came to the human realm, but Arya couldn't make it. Her parents had discovered what she'd been doing, and they combined their magical powers to lock all portals between the human world and Faerie — keeping their daughter from reaching her lover and preventing the shadow king from returning home. The humans sacrificed innocents in an attempt to appease their gods and get the sun back."

Is that what Bakken meant when he referred to the long night? The same long night I heard stories of when I was a child?

Sebastian waits as his eyes will me to go on.

"But no matter the prayers or the sacrifices, the humans couldn't end the long night. They had no power over the portals, and the shadow king remained locked outside his world, searching for another way home. His magic grew weaker with every day, until he could no longer disguise his true form. With no magic to protect him from the humans and their prejudice, he was beaten and brutalized, the tips of his ears cut off and his face pulverized with their fists. It was then that he met the human woman. She found him outside her house and took pity on him, giving him the healing tonics she had. She couldn't stand to see any creature suffer. She gave him a place to stay, tended to him, and used her potions to heal him. As the long night dragged on, they fell in love. He never forgot the golden fae princess, but his love for the woman was too intense to deny. When the portals reopened, he knew he had to return home, but the human refused to join him. She didn't want to leave her world. Even so, the shadow king knew he could no longer be with the princess. His heart belonged to the human."

Sebastian's eyes flash with anger, and he picks up the story for me. "Meanwhile, in the Court of the Moon, the shadow king's brother had swept in to take over his empire, capitalizing on his brother's absence. Oberon returned to find that his brother had won the allegiance of half of the Unseelie court, and Oberon couldn't return to his throne without risking a civil war his people couldn't afford as the Great Fae War raged on.

"On the other side of the realm, my mother had taken her place as queen of the golden fae. She begged the shadow king to marry her as they once planned — if not for love, then for the good of their kingdoms. She promised that if they married, she would help him get his brother off his throne and then they could unite their courts and end the war between them. But Oberon refused. He wouldn't even do it for peace between their peoples. He was no longer in love with her, and he still believed he might one day convince his mortal love to join him in his world."

Sebastian stops his story there, so I finish it for him. "Then the queen cursed the Unseelie."

I wait for him to confirm it, but he only freezes.

"You *do* know about the curse," I say, "but you can't speak of it."

Again, it's as if he can't even nod in confirmation. "The most powerful magic in Faerie comes from its rulers," he says. "My mother was the most powerful queen to ever take the throne, but wielding such great magic comes at a cost, one far worse than having an entire court hate her."

"How could they not?" I ask, trying to keep my tone gentle.

"She ultimately saved thousands of fae lives by ending the war," Sebastian says. "Oberon cared more about himself than about his people. He could have ended the war by marrying my

358

mother, such a small sacrifice, but he refused. Whereas my mother's sacrifice was enormous and saved thousands, but now she is dying to pay the price of . . ." He flinches, then swallows.

By *cursing* the Unseelie and making her own people helpless against them, I think, but I keep my mouth shut. The queen is his mother, and she's dying. I can't blame him for being blind to her mistakes if he feels like he's losing her and powerless to stop it. "Why doesn't she just lift the curse?"

When he only stares at me and doesn't answer, I remember that he's not able to speak so directly to the curse. The torment in his eyes weighs on me, and I wrap my arms around his waist.

His hands slide into my hair, and he pulls back as his fingers tangle with the shorter locks I hide beneath my thick curls. "What happened back here?" I lower my gaze, but he tilts my chin up so I'm looking at him. "You don't have to hide anything from me."

I already told him what I know about the curse, so I might as well explain how I learned it. "I gave Bakken some of my hair so he would tell me about the curse." Again, the word *curse* makes him flinch — as if the word's a knife in his back every time.

He slides his hand up the side of my face and toys with the locks of shorter hair framing my face. "And these?"

"Back in Elora. He told me that Mordeus bought Jas." I shrug at his frown. "There are things you cannot tell me, and there are things I didn't want you knowing I was doing." *There still are.* "And I trust Bakken."

"Goblins' secrets aren't usually so easily bought. He must . . . he must believe he has something to gain by staying on your good side. But be careful that you don't rely too much on their kind. If they discover your weaknesses, they'll take and take until you find you've given everything."

I pinch his side gently. "Don't look so worried, Sebastian. I have more where that came from."

"Not all secrets can be bought with a lock of hair, Brie."

I thread my fingers through his and smile sadly as I tug on a lock. "I wish they could."

Sebastian scans the horizon where the golden and red fingers of dusk stretch low across the water. "We need to move inside." There's a note of urgency in his voice.

"Why?"

He nods down the beach, and I see a cluster of ravens swarming.

"The Sluagh?" I ask.

"Yes. They roam the beach at night. It's one of the reasons my mother doesn't come here much anymore."

"Why would there be Sluagh here? Who died on the beach?"

Something flashes in his eyes. When he doesn't answer, I realize it's not because he doesn't know, but because he can't or won't tell me. Still so many secrets between us, but at least it's clearer now that there are at least some that he doesn't keep by choice.

"Come on." He tugs me toward the palace and I follow. I know better than to linger with Sluagh about.

———•———

Sebastian tells the servants he'll show me around while they prepare our dinner.

"King Mordeus doesn't belong on the Throne of Shadows,"

Sebastian says when we're alone, picking up where we left off outside. "And all of Faerie suffers for it. But he will do anything to wear the crown so the throne will accept him."

He takes my hand and leads me down a brightly lit staircase. As he pushes through a heavy door, I realize he's brought me to some sort of armory. My eyes go wide as I take in all the weapons — the variety of knives and swords, the rows of armor, and the racks of wooden bows.

He goes straight to the far wall and selects a shining black dagger before turning back to me. "This is made of adamant and iron." He offers it to me. "It was sharpened with diamond blades by the queen's own blacksmith, and its magic will leave traces of iron behind in anyone you use it on."

I take it. It's heavy but not clumsily so. When I wrap my fingers around the hilt, a strange jolt of power rocks through me. It feels like it was made for my palm.

"Only this can kill the king," Sebastian says. "Keep it on you at all times."

My eyes flick up to meet his. He doesn't know I've been working for the king, so why would he think I need a dagger than can kill him?

"Riaan told me that you two talked last night," he says softly. "He said you admitted to having secrets. Secrets that you're forced to keep or risk losing your sister." He pulls a scabbard from a drawer and unbuckles the small belt attached to it. "Maybe the same secrets that made you give me a fake and keep the Mirror of Discovery for yourself."

I gasp. "You knew?"

"Yes. And I waited for you to explain — to trust me — but now I understand that you can't."

"I . . ." *He knew.* "I can't believe you didn't say anything."

"I trust you, Brie. Whether or not you trust me in return."

Heart heavy, I watch as he kneels before me, lifting the hem of my skirt from the ground. His fingers brush my skin as he wraps the scabbard around my calf and buckles it in place. When he turns a palm up for the dagger, I gently hand it to him by the hilt. "Keep this on you at all times for protection. Use your magic to hide it if you can."

"I . . ." How much does he know about my magic? About my secrets? "I can. I've gotten better."

He slides it into place, and there's something comforting about the hug of the belt, the weight of the blade at my calf. When he stands, his face is solemn. "This blade will also work against Finn."

I swallow hard. Maybe that's why he gave this to me after all — not so much because he thinks I'll need it against Mordeus but because he hopes I'll use it against Finn. "You said you don't want Mordeus on the Throne of Shadows, but who would you have take his place if not Finn?"

He shakes his head. "Faerie has been divided too long, and it's time the halves unite under one ruler."

I bite my bottom lip. I don't want to argue about Finn or who should or shouldn't be on the Throne of Shadows. All I care about is saving my sister.

But that's not true anymore. Maybe it hasn't been true for a while.

I care about the realm I once sneered at and the creatures that reside here, and now I'm torn between warring kingdoms when I never wanted to feel allegiance to either.

"Would you like me to show you the rest of the palace?" Sebastian asks.

I nod, but through his whole tour I'm thinking about the adamant blade strapped to my leg and Sebastian's hushed words, *This blade will also work against Finn.*

I'm so distracted that I'm unprepared when he leads me into the library on the top floor of the palace.

"This is the jewel of Serenity Palace," he says just inside the doors. "It's best seen when the sun is shining through the skylights, so I'll bring you back tomorrow."

But I like it as it is now, with the silvery moonlight dancing off the glass and barely illuminating the center of the room. I could explore the stacks of books in the darkness. I imagine it would feel like going to the library with my mother when I was a child — that feeling of safety and endless possibility.

I stroll into the room, looking around and letting my gaze skip over the pedestal at the center of the space. I don't want to seem too interested in it, but Sebastian seems to sense it anyway.

"That's the Grimoricon," he says. He takes my hand and leads me to the center of the room until we are a single step from the book. So close I could reach out and touch it.

"What is it?" I ask, as if I don't know.

"It's the great book of our people. The Court of the Moon once claimed it as their own, but I'm loath to imagine the havoc Mordeus would bring to our world if he had it."

My heart sinks. I may be confused about many things, but I am clear on Mordeus's character. He is evil, cruel, and conniving, and Faerie will not fare well if a male like that has even more power. I've been on a mission to save Jas at any cost, but for the first time, I see that I'm endangering the fate of an entire realm in exchange for my sister's life. But the alternative? It's unfathomable.

I tamp down my newfound doubt and focus on the book. "What's inside?"

"It holds the spells of our Old Ones and guidance for tapping into their powers. Once I take the throne, this is the book that will lead me in ruling my kingdom. My grandparents went to great lengths to retrieve it, and they lost many good faeries in doing so. Now it may be the only thing keeping my mother alive."

I whip my head around to look at him. "What?"

"Magic is life. And this" — he nods at the book — "this is some of our most powerful magic. My mother's been dying for years now. She's probably only alive today because her life has been magically linked to this book."

Slowly, I reach out, but he grabs my hand before I can touch it.

"Don't." His eyes are wide, his pulse fluttering quickly in his neck.

"Is it dangerous?"

"I don't know what would happen to you if your mortal skin came into contact with such great magic. And if the book is disturbed . . ." He swallows. "If the book is disturbed, I fear what would happen to my mother."

Is this why Mordeus wanted me to steal it? Yes, for the

powerful magic, but also because he knows it's tied to the queen's life? Is that why *Finn* wants me to steal it?

I swallow back the uncomfortable lump in my throat. "You really love your mother, don't you?"

He blinks, and his expression is pained. Conflicted. "I'm not blind to her faults, but she is my mother, and she's sacrificed so much for our court . . . perhaps even more so for me."

If I give the book to Mordeus and Arya dies, the curse will be broken and Jas will be safe. But Sebastian will never forgive me. And if Mordeus uses the book to destroy the lives of more innocent fae, I may never forgive myself.

———•———

When the palace staff serves us dinner, I'm still thinking of Finn and the Throne of Shadows and Sebastian's warnings that whatever Finn keeps in his catacombs will prove his true nature.

"Brie?"

I lift my head at the sound of my name and find Sebastian staring at me across the table. How long has he been waiting for me to answer? Judging by his half-empty plate, I've been zoning out for a while.

"Where is that mind of yours?"

I blow out a breath. "I'm so sorry, Sebastian. I'm lost in my thoughts tonight." I look around the dining room and realize that I haven't even taken in the details of the romantic dinner that was probably prepared to impress me.

Candles line the table, and day lilies overflow from vases in every corner of the room. I've pushed my food around more than eaten it, and I'm more than a little disgusted with myself. The old me would be disgusted too. Not only am I eating mouthwatering dishes while children in the human realm go without, I'm here with Sebastian. How many times before entering the portal did I wish we could have more time together? And it seemed we never were alone. If Jas wasn't with us, my cousins were close by, ready to report anything they heard or saw to my aunt.

"What are you thinking now?"

"I'm thinking how quickly I've come to take these luxuries for granted." I wave a hand, indicating my plate. "I know better than to disregard the blessing of a full belly, yet after only a few weeks, I can sit here feeding myself and not even taste the delicious flavors. Meanwhile, my sister . . ." My throat squeezes tight at the words.

Sebastian reaches across the table and takes my hand. "Despite all he does to maintain his power, the king is weaker than ever. It's only a matter of time until we're close enough to act. I haven't given up."

But what happens to us after Jás is safe? I don't give voice to the question. He's as eager for an answer as I am, and I don't have one yet. Do I want to stay with Sebastian? Do I want to live in a castle with the queen who is responsible for the curse and the horrible treatment of the Unseelie in her camps? If what Sebastian says is true and she's dying, perhaps that means the curse will soon be broken. If her possession of the Grimoricon is the only thing keeping her alive . . .

To end the curse and live, you must kill the queen. The memory of Bakken's words makes my stomach heave. If I kill his mother on top of everything else, I will truly lose Sebastian.

"I can practically see you drifting away on your thoughts." Chuckling, he wipes his mouth with his napkin, then reaches for a decanter of wine, tilting it to fill our glasses. "Drink with me and let go for an hour."

After he goes to bed, I will have to go to the library and make a plan for the Grimoricon. I initially planned on taking it immediately — it kills me to wait — but Sebastian might be suspicious if it's missing when he takes me back to the library tomorrow. And since I have no replica of this relic, I will need to wait.

I can give him an hour. After all he's done for me, all he's endured and is likely to endure, he deserves that and more. And maybe I deserve it too. *An hour.*

I lift my glass to my lips and drink. Within minutes, my worries fall away.

CHAPTER THIRTY

SEBASTIAN SPINS ME AROUND and presses my back against a tall wooden door. "This is your room," he whispers against my lips.

My skin is warm, my cheeks flushed from the wine, and my heart full from the conversation. One hour turned to two, and it was like old times — just the two of us, talking and laughing.

"This is where I'm supposed to say good night." His hands drift slowly down my sides — fingertips leaving a burning trail in their wake. When he reaches my hips, he squeezes gently.

I slide a hand behind his neck and study his face. I love the strong lines of his jaw, the piercing beauty of those sea-green eyes, his slightly parted lush lips. "So soon?"

Smiling, he brushes those lips over mine. Once, twice. The third time, his tongue sweeps across my bottom lip, and I melt a little. "Thank you for this. I know nothing's simple right now, but I'm glad we're here."

Me too. I know it's the wine, but right now I'm glad for everything, from the heat of his body to the fact that there's a bed on the other side of this door. "I need to tell you a secret," I whisper.

He pulls back, his eyes searching mine, his face solemn. "Yes?"

"I don't deserve you." I thought I could make a joke of it, but tears prick my eyes. "And one day you're going to realize that." *You're going to realize I've used you to give Mordeus what he wants. You're going to realize I've weakened your kingdom to save my sister. And you're going to know that even as sorry as I am that it will hurt you, if it means saving Jas, I would do it all over again.*

"Hey." He strokes his thumb along my jaw. "None of that. We were having a good time, and these tears are gutting me. I'm the one who doesn't deserve you, but I'm too selfish to let you go."

I bury my face in his chest and shake my head. "Don't let me go. I need you to hold on."

His swallow is the only sound in the quiet hall. "I thought I could walk away until it was safe, but I was wrong."

I lift my head. "Until it was safe?"

"You are in danger every moment you remain in my realm, yet I can't bring myself to . . ." He searches my eyes. "You don't understand yet, but I *need* you."

"Bash . . ." I lift to my toes and press my mouth to his.

I want to drag him to my bed and beg him the way the drugs made me beg Finn. When Sebastian touches me, it feels like walking into the sun after a week stuck in Madame V's cellar. I forget all about my conflicting feelings for the Unseelie prince. About Finn's secrets and his tributes. About the queen and the book. About a little girl's prophecy and a goblin's glee at telling me I have to kill the queen if I want to break the Unseelie curse without dying.

Sebastian kisses me back with more intensity than before. His hands plunge into my hair, and he tilts my mouth to his. I want to soak him up. To revel in these moments until I'm covered in them. Whatever my life is after he finds out the truth, I want to be able to remember this feeling — being loved and protected by Sebastian. Not Prince Ronan, not the next Seelie king, but *my Bash*.

When he pulls away, his breathing is ragged. He leans his forehead against mine. "I can go to my own chambers or I can go in with you." He swallows. "But if I stay, I need you to ask. I need to know this is what you want. That you're ready."

I graze my fingertips along his jaw, relishing the short stubble I feel there. My feelings may be as complicated as my loyalties, but what I want from him right now isn't complicated at all. "I want you to come inside. I want you to stay."

His chest rises and falls with a deep breath and maybe something more. Maybe, like me, he's navigating emotions that are heavier and more complicated than the stories teach us love should be. I take his hand and lead him into my room.

He waves his hand, and a soft breeze closes the door behind us. "You're sure?"

"Yes." Maybe I'm selfish. Maybe this will make everything worse when he finds out the truth, but . . . "I want this."

Stepping forward, he reaches around me and slowly unlaces my dress. I let it fall from my shoulders and stand still in front of him in nothing but a flimsy lace camisole, matching underwear, and the dagger he strapped to my calf. I let him look at me, and when he lifts his eyes to meet mine, they're hot, dark. I feel beautiful. If guilt nags at me from a corner of my mind, I lock it away to focus on him.

"You're perfect," he whispers. "You have no idea how long I've wanted to do that."

"Then why didn't you?"

As soon as I say it, I see the vulnerability in his eyes and hate myself for the question. He didn't kiss me until that last day in Fairscape because he knew I hated the fae. He believed I would hate *him* when I found out the truth.

I don't have long to dwell on the realization because he's taking me in his arms and cupping my face in his hands. He kisses me long and hard, hands trailing up and down my back, over my shoulders and my breasts, across my stomach. He grips my hips in his big hands and kisses his way down my neck, nipping and sucking at the sensitive flesh, setting my wine-warmed skin ablaze with every kiss, every scrape of his teeth and flick of his tongue.

His fingers are rough where they curl under the top of my camisole. The thin strap snaps when he tugs it down, baring me to his mouth and his wicked tongue. My eyes float closed and my head falls back. Nothing matters but the feel of his kisses, his hands on my body, the tingle of his teeth scraping across that sensitive peak. My core tightens with pleasure, with need, and I press closer, telling him what I need with the arch of my back and the soft sounds that spill from my lips.

I tug on his hair until his mouth finds mine again, and our tongues seek and stroke. He's never kissed me like this. Raw, feral, ravenous. I unbutton his tunic and slip it from his shoulders. I want that sun-kissed skin all over me. But then he steps away, and I whimper in protest.

His lips quirk into a cocky grin. "I'm not going far. I promise." He presses a single finger to my breastbone, and my skin tingles as his hand flares with light. He trails a finger down between my breasts, over my stomach, over each hip, leaving a glowing path in the wake of his touch. As the light fades, the fabric falls away, even my scabbard and dagger fall to the floor with a *thud*, leaving me completely nude, my undergarments in tatters on the floor.

He devours every inch of me with his gaze, lips parted, breath jagged.

"Magical showoff," I say, grinning as I reach for him.

His deft fingers stroke down my back, over my hips, and back up. "What good is magic if I can't use it to impress the woman I love?"

My heart squeezes at the words, and I freeze. I've known I loved Sebastian for a long time, but I'm not sure I ever believed he could return those feelings. I didn't believe I was worthy of his love, and he's giving it to me now, when my actions prove I'm not.

"I do love you, you know." His eyes are hooded as he looks down at me. "Does that scare you? Knowing . . . who — what I am?"

Guilt breaks out of its cage and slices through me. "I was so ignorant, Sebastian, and so much of my prejudice came from my mother's choices. But *you* . . ." I trace his ear with my fingertip, lingering at the pointed peak. He closes his eyes and shudders against me. "I loved you in Fairscape, loved the mage's apprentice who kept me from despair, and I love you now. The golden fae prince who loves his family and wants to find a way for feuding kingdoms to find true peace." I look into his eyes and send up a

372

rare prayer to the gods: that whatever happens after this night, whatever comes of Sebastian and me, he'll never doubt that I meant these words. "I'm so sorry I ever thought I wanted you to be different. I love you as you are."

He opens one palm and a pile of shiny jewels appears there. Then the other opens and silky red rose petals spill to the floor. "Anything you want, Brie. Anything I can give you is yours."

I sweep away the contents of both hands, sending the jewels clinking to the floor and the petals scattering around us. With a step forward, I guide his arms back around me. "I don't need flowers or jewels. I want only you." I press my mouth to his and slide my hands up his back, relishing the feel of his warm skin under my hands and against my breasts. "I want this."

He nuzzles his face in my neck and breathes in deeply. "Have you done this before?"

I nod. It was last year, and only a few times with a young man who worked at one of the houses I cleaned. There was no real emotion between us, just physical connection. Escape. It was good, but with Sebastian, it will be so much more. "Is that okay?"

He chuckles, a low and warm sound that fills my belly with want. "Sure. Just don't give me any details, okay?"

I shake my head. "None of it matters."

He cups my face, but he's shaking almost violently.

"Sebastian." I take his hands in both of mine. So big and broad, rough with calluses. "Have *you* done this before?"

"No. Yes, I mean —" Shaking his head, he takes a deep breath. "I've done this, but never with someone I love." He swallows. "I've never felt like this about anyone, and it scares me a little — how I feel about you. How much I need you. It scares me how . . . how this has all come together."

I smile. "Here we are. Against all odds." I release the button at his waist, and our hands tangle as we work together to free him of his pants.

I'm not shy when I look at him — at his tanned skin and strong chest, at the tight muscles of his abdomen and his powerful thighs and . . . the rest of him. I do blush at that, but I don't turn coy. I know what I want. I walk to the bed. Keeping my eyes on him, I settle onto the feather-soft mattress and crook a finger, beckoning him to join me.

He takes me in again and again, and my skin grows warmer with each pass of his eyes. When he finally climbs onto the bed, he lies at my side and props himself up on one elbow. With his free hand, he strokes down my body, dipping just below my navel and making my breath catch, then back up, between and across my breasts.

I hold his gaze and arch under his touch, guiding his fingers where I want them. "I imagined this," I whisper, reaching for him. "Imagined you like this. I never thought it would happen. Don't walk away now, okay?"

"I couldn't if I wanted to." His eyes darken, and he shifts and settles over me. The weight of him sends a delicious pleasure pooling low in my belly. I draw my knees up and lead him to settle between my thighs, gasping at the press of him against my sensitive center.

"You're okay?"

374

I nod, but *okay* isn't the right word. I'm desperate and needy. I'm grateful for this moment and scared of what comes next. I'm in love and loved and undeserving. I'm not *okay*, but I want this. "You?"

He smiles at that. "Better than ever." Sadness darkens that smile, as if he senses the undercurrent of my thoughts. "I want more than this, but if tonight is all I get, I'll take it."

"I want more too," I whisper, then echo his words back to him, back to the gods who've granted me this moment of happiness. "If tonight is all I get, I'll take it."

I slide my hands into his hair and hold his gaze as I shift my hips to guide him inside me. My body tightens, and his breath hitches. His hands frame my face, and he slowly begins to move, but I can sense him holding back and I need more than these tentative touches. I guide his mouth down to mine and kiss him until he's helpless to do anything but let go and give us both what we need. Soon enough any guilt or sadness is gone and we become our pleasure, become nothing more than the connection between us — and a kernel of hope that this love might be enough.

———

Can't. Breathe.

My eyes fly open, and the specter of a woman peers down at me. I open my mouth to scream, to gasp for air, but she's sitting on my chest and my lungs refuse to expand.

She leans forward, like a lover leaning in for a kiss. I can't stop her. My arms won't move. I want to turn, to flail, to kick and push, but my body isn't my own. I'm paralyzed. Trapped.

"Abriella," she says, her breath dancing along my cheek. My name is a song from her lips, and her silver hair floats around her face like she's in water. "Abriella, Abriella, Abriella."

The song of my name is haunting but beautiful. I'm so transfixed, I forget that I need air. I forget that I can't move. I watch her lips and let the melody fill my ears.

I feel consciousness slipping from me, and I let it. She continues to sing my name as the world goes black.

———·———

Lark stares at me with big silver eyes. We're underwater in a deep, dark abyss, and her hair floats around her like the Banshee's did. The only light emanates from her glowing silver eyes as she strokes my face. I'm still not breathing, but I'm not sure I need to.

Someone in another world is calling my name. Not the Banshee. *Sebastian.* Calling my name from above this abyss, begging me. I look up, but the surface is too far away to see.

Lark's small fingers trace a path from my temples to my chin and back. When she meets my eyes, I sense her words in my mind more than hear them. "I see three paths before you. In each, the Banshee's call is clear. Don't be afraid."

My body jerks in the water as if some invisible hand has shaken me. Lark's eyes flick up to the surface. I see it now — ripples of light as the surface grows closer.

"Remember your deal with the false king. He will be true to his word. Choose your path wisely, Princess." Her eyes sparkle in delight as she leans forward and whispers in my ear, "Now breathe."

CHAPTER THIRTY-ONE

"BREATHE!" HANDS ON MY SHOULDERS, shaking me, Sebastian's commanding voice fills the room. "That's right, Abriella, breathe!"

I pull in a breath, and it burns—like breathing water or drowning on air, but I take another breath. And another. Each hurts a little less.

He gathers me against his chest and strokes my hair. "I heard her," he says. His arms wrap around me, almost too tightly, but his fear is palpable, and I can't deny him this embrace. "I heard her singing your name."

The Banshee. It wasn't a dream. "Sebastian." My voice sounds like crushed glass.

"Shh, I've got you." He rocks me, but I can feel him shaking. I can feel the grief rolling off him. As if he's already lost me. "I've got you. I won't let death be the end. I promise you."

"What?" I flatten a palm against his chest and push him back. "What does that mean?"

"Did you see her?"

I nod. "Does it really mean . . . Sometimes she's wrong." We saved Jalek. He didn't die.

Sebastian shakes his head. "I don't know. I just . . ." He swallows, anguish in his eyes. "I don't know."

"You said you won't let death be the end. What did you mean by that?"

He looks away.

"Sebastian?"

When he meets my eyes, his shoulders sag. "I never imagined how helpless I would feel, loving a mortal. But it cuts at me, Brie. Every time I don't know where you are, every time I don't know if you're safe. I could lose you so easily. And then I woke up to the sound of her singing your name and —" He squeezes his eyes shut. "If you die, I can't bring you back. Once you're gone, I can't give you the Potion of Life."

"You mean you can't turn me fae." My voice is tired and brittle.

He cups my face in his hands. "I heard her sing your name," he whispers. "And all I could think was that the potion wouldn't work, because we're not bonded."

I stiffen. "Humans have to be bonded to the fae to use the Potion of Life?"

He blows out a breath. "Whoever created the potion believed that humans might steal the magic if the bond wasn't required."

"I . . ." I just want to be me. To be enough for him without becoming a faerie. I never wanted to be fae. I didn't think I'd ever want that. But with the sound of the Banshee's voice in my head, the world looks a little different. "Bash, I'm scared."

His eyes go shuttered. "Of the bond?"

Of what I need to do. Of losing you. Of the sound of my name on the Banshee's lips. Of never having the chance to give you the bond you want so badly.

He doesn't wait for an answer but settles back onto the pillows with me, stroking my arms and pulling me closer and closer. Reassuring us both.

When my heart rate returns to normal, I turn in his arms. "Tell me how it works, the bonding ceremony."

He holds my gaze for a long time before he answers, and I get the impression that this conversation is a little heavier for him after hearing the Banshee. "The ceremony is elegant," he finally says, "in the way that only what is pure can be. It begins with us selecting the rune that will symbolize our bond, and then I'd say some words and you'd repeat them."

"Is there an audience?"

"Not typically, though my parents chose to perform theirs in front of a crowd in conjunction with their wedding vows." He smiles. "I was five, and I remember being so embarrassed when they kissed and kissed, waiting for the bond to solidify."

"You were five when your parents were married and bonded?"

His smile falls away. "My father always said it took him years to convince my mother he was worthy of her. Lately I've begun to sympathize with his plight."

I nudge him with my elbow and almost smile. "Would *you* want an audience?"

"No. I'd want it to be just us, if only because we have to maintain a . . . a physical connection until the bond snaps into place."

I bite my lip. "You mean sex?"

He grins and pinches my side. "Not necessarily. The magic demands a physical representation of the empathic bond. Some bonded pairs will simply hold hands, but when the connection is romantic, most couples let the intimacy of the moment guide them. The magic — it's . . . intense. Powerful."

"I hope someday I get to experience that." I'm surprised by how much my feelings about being bonded have changed, but I mean it. I just want to be there with him — to be past everything else so I can. I might never have that. When I said I'd take tonight if it was all I could have, I meant it.

"It is my greatest wish." He presses a kiss to the top of my head. "Until then . . . stay close. I'll protect you."

He holds me tighter, and I realize he thinks I'm worried that death will come between us. Soon he'll understand that my secrets will tear us apart faster than the threat of a Banshee call ever could.

———

I don't close my eyes again. When I'm sure Sebastian is in a deep sleep, I slip out from under his arm and climb out of bed.

I pull on my silky pajama pants and the matching top my maids packed. Everything else they sent has a skirt, and I'll need to be able to move as freely as possible.

Every time I close my eyes, I see that ghostly woman in her tattered white dress, her hair floating around her. Even with my eyes open, I hear her. The sound of my name in her voice is a macabre song stuck in my head.

Sebastian fell asleep holding me. He wants to protect me, but I can't allow him to stay close enough to try. A ticking clock clangs in my head right alongside the Banshee's song.

I know what I need to do, and I have never been more terrified.

Now more than ever, it's tempting to put Jas's fate in Sebastian's hands. If he could get someone to kill Mordeus, his men would be able to retrieve Jas. I want to believe he can get it done — but now I know that the Seelie cannot harm the Unseelie, and too much time has passed for me to not act.

I hate that my actions might take Sebastian's mother from him, but I feel no remorse over what my actions will do to the queen beyond her son's grief. She tortures and enslaves an entire race of faeries. Her curse is the root cause of the sale and murder of countless humans, all because one male broke her heart. Sebastian will grieve, and for that I am sorry, but I know what I have to do.

I unwrap the mirror from my shadows, returning it to its solid form, and take it into my hand. "Show me Jasalyn." I need to see her. I need the reminder of why I'm betraying Sebastian. Why I'm undoubtedly heading to my own death.

I see my sister laid out on a stone floor, her head lolling to the side in sleep, her lips chapped. I grip the mirror tighter, and the image ripples like a reflection in a pond. When it clears, it shows Jas tucked into a big bed. She's sleeping on her side, draped in fluffy blankets, her arms curled around one pillow while her head rests on another.

Which image is real? Which can I trust?

Either way, I need that book. I tuck the mirror away and slip into the shadows to head to the library. If I'm lucky, I'll be back before Sebastian wakes, and I'll be able to pretend I didn't have anything to do with the book's disappearance. If I'm unlucky, I'll understand the Banshee's call soon enough.

I sneak out of my room and past the sentries guarding the end of the hall. My mind goes over my plan again and again. *Please don't suspect me, Sebastian. And when you find out the truth, please forgive me.*

The library doors are closed, locked, and no doubt warded, but I slip past them as shadow and into the library. Does Sebastian know I can do this? Will he realize it had to be me when he finds the book is gone and the doors still locked?

Moonlight casts a cool glow across the beautiful space. I can't hear the pixies singing here, but if I close my eyes, I know I'll be able to remember the sound of the library pixies at the Golden Palace and what it felt like to have Sebastian hold me in his arms and sway to the angelic melody.

I don't close my eyes.

I don't let myself remember.

I head straight to the book.

Before I can second-guess myself, I reach out and place my hands on the open pages, aware of Sebastian's warning. I feel nothing. No magical jolt in my blood and no danger. Carefully, I close the book with a soft *thwap*. I'll tuck it into shadow and go to Mordeus.

But the moment I lift the book off the pedestal, it shifts in my hands — squirming and twisting. I nearly drop it out of instinct alone.

The book in my hand has turned into a massive, hissing serpent, so big I can barely keep my hands around it. I'm desperate to get away from those fangs and that darting tongue, but I think of Jas and hold it tighter. I knew the book could shape-shift. I should have considered what form it might take when I tried to steal it.

It snaps at my face, but I refuse to loosen my grip. *It's a book. Just a book. A book cannot hurt you.*

Then it strikes. Pain is like a gong echoing through me as its teeth sink into my shoulder. Every vein in my arm burns as its venom pumps through me.

The library doors fly open, and light pours from the ceiling as half a dozen sentinels rush toward me. I must have triggered a silent alarm.

"Drop the book!" a sentinel calls as he draws his sword.

The serpent releases its massive jaws from my shoulder, and if possible, the skin throbs more than before. I block out the pain and loop the creature around my neck, lunging for the shadows, willing myself to disappear, but even in the rows of darkness between the stacks, my magic fails me.

I turn back, ready to run, and find myself face to face with the tip of a sword.

"Drop the book now, milady."

I can see the confusion in the sentinel's face. He's been commanded to protect me by his prince, no doubt, and commanded to protect the book by his queen.

"I can't." I remember what it felt like to cast a room in darkness with Finn at my side, and I conjure that feeling. I ignore the blinding pain in my shoulder and focus on darkness. On the cool soothing of pitch-black night.

The room goes dark, and the sentinels shout in confusion. Not even moonlight from the skylights makes it through my shield of darkness.

I run in the direction of the windows, and suddenly I'm free-falling. All I can do is keep my hands around the serpent and soften my knees. My jaw clacks and my head jerks back as I land in the sand, but I ignore the pain and run away from the palace as fast as I can, leaving chaos in the castle behind me.

Once the ocean laps at my feet, the serpent shifts in my grasp. I grip tighter, but it's no longer looped around my neck.

A little boy tugs on my hand. He has silver eyes and dark hair —a child of the shadow court. Tears stream down his face, and I feel the compulsion to kneel before him and hug away his sorrow. "Take me home, Fire Girl. Please take me home." He clutches his chest with his free hand, and blood oozes between his fingers. "You're killing me."

The book. This is the book. Do not let it manipulate you.

Easier said than done when the throbbing in my shoulder proves it isn't *just* anything. I snap a thread on my goblin bracelet. I speak before Bakken is fully corporeal. "Take me to the Unseelie Court."

"I told you I cannot save you from mortal peril."

Sentries storm the beach, coming straight at me, and I catch sight of Sebastian among them. I uncoil my power from deep within me and throw a blanket of darkness over them, trapping them. "What mortal peril?"

The goblin smirks. "Payment, Fire Girl."

The boy is bloody and growing paler by the minute. "She's killing me," he sobs.

I don't dare let go, but I know Bakken won't do anything without payment, so I grab a lock of hair with my free hand. "Cut it."

With a smile, he does. The sentries are breaking free from my darkness, but then we're gone, and I'm standing before the king. In my grasp, not the hand of a little boy, but a heavy, ancient book.

The king's silver eyes go wide with shock and pleasure, and I thrust it at him. "Take it."

He retrieves it on a magic breeze and strokes the cover. His eyes float closed, and he pulls in a deep breath. His skin glows, and I can feel the power reverberating from him. Did I look like that when I touched it?

"Let's drink," he says. He snaps his fingers, the book disappears, and suddenly he's holding a bottle of wine and there's a glass in my hand. He smiles at me as he fills both glasses, and he hoists his in the air. "To my beautiful thief."

With shaking hands and a throbbing shoulder, I tap my glass to his, but I don't drink. My adrenaline is waning.

"Oh come now. You know I won't tell you the next relic until you drink with me. It's our tradition."

Unwilling to play games, I drain half the glass in one pull. "Tell me the third item you want. I need to get back to Sebastian." Get back — and what? The Serenity Palace sentinels saw me with the book. Even if that wasn't Sebastian I spotted running toward me on the beach, I'm sure his guard has filled him in by now. I bow my head, remembering the way he looked at me as he made love to me last night. The grief on his face after he heard the Banshee sing my name. The sincerity in his eyes when he spoke of his mother.

She's sacrificed so much for our court . . . perhaps even more so for me.

My shoulder throbs, and that useless broken thing in my chest makes me feel like I'm moments from caving in on myself. I finish the wine, but it does nothing to numb either pain.

"You are so close to finishing your tasks," the king says. "Why do you look like you have a broken heart?"

I lift my chin. I've let him see too much. "The prince might not allow me back into the castle. I will do my best to retrieve the third relic, but—"

His grin stretches across his face, and his eyes sparkle. "You won't need to return to the castle, my girl. The third relic I require is King Oberon's crown. Without it, I can never heal the damage Queen Arya has done to my court."

I nearly laugh. That's what everyone wants—what everyone needs so desperately. How does he expect me to get it when even Finn—the Unseelie prince and rightful king—can't find it. But I've lost so much at this point, I feel half crazed. "Okay. Tell me where the crown is, and I'll go grab it straightaway." *Just end this. Just give me my sister back and send us home.*

"This is one thing you won't have to steal. You already have it. Where do you think your power comes from?"

Now I do laugh. *I* have the crown? How ridiculous. The laughter spills out of me. It comes and comes until I fold in half with it, imagining both Mordeus and Finn having it within their reach all this time. "If only Finn had known," I say, still laughing.

"Oh, but he does. So does Prince Ronan. Why do you think they both care so much for your welfare? Why do you think they're both working so hard to steal your heart?"

I lift my arms. "Okay. Where is it?" I'm so over this. My heart is breaking as I imagine Sebastian back at the Golden Palace with his dying mother — or perhaps she's already dead. How quickly would stealing that book kill the queen? I've never killed someone. Am I a murderer now?

I don't want to think about any of it anymore. I just want to be *done*.

The king's eyes sparkle. "Where else would you carry a crown but on your head?"

I laugh harder, and it rolls out of me in a snort. "Well, in that case" — I mime taking the invisible crown from my head and handing it over — "here you go."

"If only it were that simple." He snaps his fingers, and my laughter clogs in my throat when the throne room goes dark. "Look at yourself in the Mirror of Discovery."

"In the dark?" He doesn't answer, but I oblige, retrieving the mirror and expecting to see a pitch-black room. But when I look at my dark reflection, chills race down my arms at what I see. There, on my head, is a string of starlight that weaves through my hair to form a glowing . . . a glowing *crown*.

CHAPTER THIRTY-TWO

THE CROWN SITS ATOP MY HEAD, twinkling in shades of purple and blue and everything in between.

I lift a shaking hand to touch the top of my head — to try to grasp the crown I see in the mirror — but I can't. I watch my reflection as I try to push the crown from its spot, but it stays.

"It's a magical crown," King Mordeus says. "This kingdom is dying so long as it's worn by a human. Only one with Unseelie blood can rule here."

"I . . ." I stare, transfixed by what I see in the mirror. The crown isn't just beautiful. It's mesmerizing. "How?"

"My brother, Oberon, loved your mother."

I nearly drop the mirror. "What?" It's so dark I struggle to make out Mordeus's expression, but this has to be some sort of joke. All of it.

Mordeus snaps his fingers, and the candles in the wall sconces flicker to life, leaving the room cast in long shadows and changing my reflection. I see no crown now. "He was once trapped in the mortal realm and fell in love with your mother," he says. "But when he was finally able to return to Faerie, she refused to go with him. While he tried to reclaim his throne from me, she remained in the mortal realm, met your father, and fell in love. By the time Oberon had fortified the portals and could safely return to her, your mother was already married and had two little girls — you and your sister."

Once upon a time the king of the shadow fae was trapped in the mortal world, and a woman fell deeply in love with him . . .

My mother wasn't just telling us bedtime stories. She was telling us *her* story.

"Oberon gave her a wind chime," Mordeus continues. "He told her that if she ever needed him, all she had to do was hang it in the midnight breeze and the music would call him to her. She never forgot Oberon, but she was happy with her life in the mortal realm, with her husband and her daughters. Then one night while you all slept, your house was consumed by a terrible fire."

I close my eyes, remembering. The heat. The crackle of the wood burning in the walls. The way my lungs burned as I tried to get enough air. The feel of Jasalyn in my arms. My father died in that fire, and we nearly did too.

"You girls were badly burned in the fire, but you had endured the worst of the injuries while protecting your sister, and you were barely hanging on. Your mother hung the chime and begged her old lover to help. It was Oberon who healed your sister and left her without a single scar. But your wounds were so profound that it was too late for even the greatest healer. My brother was blind with love for your mother." Mordeus's voice is filled with disgust.

"He didn't want her to suffer the heartbreak of losing her child, so he saved you with the only option available to him."

I stare at the spot where Sebastian's glamour still covers the scar on my wrist. It was the only mark from a fire I've always known should have killed me. "How did he do it?" I ask.

"The moment of your death, he surrendered his own life to save yours."

I remember the sound of my mother pleading with the healer with the deep voice. *Please save her.*

How desperate she was, how heartbroken when she seemed to understand the price. *I do this for you.*

All these years, I've hated the fae, never knowing that their magic is the only reason I'm alive.

"What does that have to do with his crown?"

"When a Faerie king dies, he chooses which of his offspring will take his throne. When he makes that choice, his power passes to the heir, and it is only with that power that the land truly recognizes the new king or queen. But Oberon didn't pass his power to a son or daughter. He gave it to you — it was the only way to save you, to heal you, and to protect your mother's mortal heart."

I brush my fingertips across my scalp, and this time I can feel it — not a physical object, but a hum of power, the vibration of the crown itself. It's too much to take in. I can't wrap my mind around the reality of it or the idea that a faerie — a male I would have assumed selfish and cruel — loved my mother so much that he died to save me.

But with the awe of the truth comes the pain of what he's not saying. Mordeus is here telling me he needs the crown. Asking me for it. Which means that all this time when Finn pretended to help me, pretended to be my *friend*, his true purpose was to get closer to his crown.

"If you all want this crown so badly, why has no one taken it before now?" I've stayed at Finn's — been injured and unconscious, even drugged. He's had plenty of opportunity. "Why not just kill me for it?"

"The ancient kings who forged the Crown of Starlight had it spelled so that their offspring couldn't kill them for their power. It can only be given, never taken, as my brother gave it to you.

"I cannot kill you for it, or the crown will refuse me. But you can *choose* to give it to me — your crown, your power. Understand me when I say that you will never know peace if you keep wearing the crown. But if you give it to me through a bonding ceremony, the crown will shift to me, and you will save your sister in the process."

"Just . . . bond with you and it's over?" A lifelong bond with the darkest, ugliest soul I've ever encountered. *Never.*

"Yes, my dear."

The bonding ceremony — Sebastian warned me about it just last night when trying to convince me that Finn wanted to bind himself to me. *A simple bonding ceremony, and he could take you away from me forever.* He knew. He knew that Finn was really after the crown. No wonder he insisted that Finn wasn't my friend.

But Sebastian wasn't the only one who warned me against bonding with a member of the Unseelie Court. Finn warned me against bonding with Mordeus. *Remember that the only way anyone can have it is if* you *allow it. If you value your mortal life, you won't do that — ever.*

It wasn't a threat but a *warning*. A warning that neither prince could speak of directly because of the curse. But Finn also warned me not to bond with Sebastian. Because that would ruin Finn's chances of bonding with me . . . or because Sebastian could steal the crown? But no, Mordeus said that only someone with Unseelie blood can rule here.

"Summon your goblin," I tell the king.

His eyes narrow. "Why?"

"You want this crown? You want to me to consider bonding with you? Summon. Your. Goblin."

Mordeus snaps his fingers, and his goblin appears before me, sniffing delicately. "You reek of my kin," he mutters.

"Do humans die when they bond with faeries?" I ask the creature.

The goblin looks to his master, whose jaw is tight.

"Answer the girl's question," Mordeus says.

"Not always," the goblin says, stroking its patchy white hair. "But sometimes."

Not always, because not all faeries are cursed. "When a human bonds with the Seelie, do they die?"

The goblin glares at me. "No."

"And when a human bonds with Unseelie fae?"

The goblin looks to Mordeus again, but I don't need him to answer. Now I understand the truth. That is the pure evil of the curse. To prevent Oberon from bonding with his human love, the queen cursed the Unseelie so that bonding with a human would kill the human.

I spin on Mordeus. "You say I must bond with you, but you really mean I must *die.*"

The goblin cackles softly, and Mordeus scowls at him until he disappears in a flash of light.

"Oberon's crown saved your life," Mordeus says. "It *gave* you life when yours was gone. So, no, you cannot continue this mortal life without the crown. Through the bond, you would shift the crown to me the same way humans have shifted their life force to the Unseelie for the last twenty years."

That's what Finn wanted from me — what Sebastian was warning me about, why he said Finn could take me away from him forever if I bonded with him. Because a bond with Finn would mean my death. I shake my head, and the room spins. "Even if I was willing to die to fulfill my side of the bargain, how would I know you freed my sister?"

King Mordeus smiles. "I swore that promise on my magic, so you can be sure it isn't one I will break."

I stare at my feet. I need to *think*, but between the pain in my shoulder and the countless implications of this new information, my mind is fuzzy.

"Since you're so clever," Mordeus says slowly, "I could offer you an alternative. A gift."

I lift my head. I fear my desperation for another solution is all too clear in my face.

"If it's death that bothers you, but you're planning to make good on your promise to return the crown . . . What if you didn't have to end your existence, only your human life?"

"What?"

"Surrender your life to me, and with it the crown, and I will revive you with the Potion of Life." He steps down from the dais and takes my hand. I'm so stunned by all this information that I let him. "This doesn't have to be the end for you. This could be the beginning." A pile of rune-marked stones appear in his open palm. "All you have to do is bond yourself to me."

My head spins, the room blurring around me. Mordeus smiles, and I sway toward him.

"Choose the stone that will represent our bond and accept your fate, my girl."

It's so simple. *Choose a stone. Accept my fate.*

I reach for the pile of runes in his hand and feel like I'm floating. So familiar, this feeling. I've felt this before . . .

At the Golden Palace. When I was drugged.

"I need the restroom," I blurt.

Irritation flashes in the king's eyes, but he smooths it away quickly. "Of course. My servant will assist you."

I nod, careful not to let on that I know I've been drugged.

A young human servant with a scarred face appears and leads me out of the throne room under the watchful eye of a dozen of Mordeus's sentinels. She keeps her head bowed as she opens the door and steps in behind me.

"Could I be alone, please?" I ask.

The girl darts a glance over her shoulder, hesitating. "I shouldn't . . . I mean, the king wouldn't like it if . . ."

"I will only be a moment," I promise, fighting to stay steady on my feet.

"Okay." With a bowed head, the girl backs away.

When the door swings shut, I pull Finn's elixir from my darkness. With a quick look at the door, I drink. I drink, and then I sink to the floor and try to figure out how to fix this mess I've gotten myself into.

I can't give Mordeus the crown. I can't do that to Finn or to Sebastian. If the two are united in anything, it's the belief that Mordeus will bring nothing but destruction to Faerie. But I can't abandon Jas either. Even if . . . even if she has been safe thus far. Maybe she could wait a little longer. If I just had more *time*, I could figure out a solution that doesn't end with this crown on Mordeus's head. After all, the conditions I've seen in the mirror showed Jas —

The mirror.

I've spent all this time believing that my sister is safe and happy in his care, but I've believed that because of what I've seen in the mirror. But once, for just a flash, I saw Jas in that dungeon. But then the image shifted to what I desperately wanted to believe. And then, when I wished so desperately to not be going through this alone, the mirror showed me my mother — not because she was there, but because I *wanted* her to be.

Didn't Finn tell me not to trust the mirror? He said it was dangerous for someone who had so much hope in her heart, and I disregarded the warning. But hasn't it shown me what I hoped to see more than anything else?

I believed it when it showed me that Jas was safe and happy —because I *wanted* to believe. But for a beat tonight, the image it showed of my sister was dire, not joyful.

I'd thought that Finn didn't know me at all to think I had hope, but he was right. For my sister, even for my mother, I *did* have hope. But now it's gone.

Before, I needed to see that my sister was safe, and the mirror gave me just that. With shaking hands, I lift the mirror, stare at my reflection, clear my mind of expectations, and focus on my desire for the *truth*. "Show me Jasalyn."

There's no lavish room with lush bedding. No laughing handmaidens. There are no trays of food and picture windows that overlook beautiful vistas. All I see now is Jas, chained in a dungeon, a pallet of hay on the ground and a bucket in the corner. She's thin, pale, and sipping at a cup of water with chapped lips.

I clamp my hand over my mouth before my gasp escapes. Sinking to the floor, I stroke my fingers across the image until it floats away. I've been eating like a queen and making friends. I've been dancing and laughing and falling in love. And all the while my sister . . .

Mordeus knew I'd want to believe she was in better conditions. He knew the mirror would show me what I hoped to see.

Another sob rips from my chest.

"I'm so sorry, Jasalyn. I'm so, so sorry."

The mirror helped me find Sebastian once when it was inconsequential. It showed me Sebastian at his desk and later showed me the book. But I didn't know enough about the book or even about Sebastian's life to have any hope for those things — unlike my hopes for my family. Even my mother, who I believed abandoned me, I hoped even for her.

"Show me my mother," I whisper. When I'm shown the tomb with a corpse inside, I'm not sure what I feel crumbling in my chest, but I fear . . . I fear it's what little hope I have left.

I take slow, measured breaths and wait for the elixir to set in, but my mind won't stop spinning. *I wear the crown.*

I pull myself off the floor and square my shoulders. I didn't need the Banshee to visit me last night. I didn't need Lark visiting my dream and telling me her call was inescapable. I knew how this would end when I entered the portal. Part of me . . . part of me knew I wouldn't be going home.

The woman who escorted me to the restroom sags in relief when I return to the hall. I want to ask her why she works for the king. I want to ask her if she counts the days until she becomes his next tribute and if whatever she sold herself for was worth it.

How ridiculous that I once believed I'd live long enough to save women like her. How ridiculous that when Lark talked about me being a queen, I thought it might mean I'd have a chance to make a difference.

I'm numb as I follow the girl back to the throne room, but it's not from his poisoned wine. No. I must have taken the elixir in time because I no longer feel the effects of the drug. This numbness is something else.

Resignation.

Disappointment.

A hopeless heart.

The king's eyes are cautious as he watches me approach his throne. Does he see the sobriety in my movements? In my face?

I sway a little on my feet, unwilling to let him know he doesn't have the advantage. "If I do what I must to fulfill my part of our bargain, you will be true to yours?" I ask.

His eyes glow so brightly the silver looks almost white. *Greedy.* "Yes."

My eyes flick to the throne he never sits in. The throne that denies him its power as long as he doesn't wear the crown.

"This can all be over by sunrise," he promises me. "The ceremony is simple. We choose a rune, we say a few words, and I have the Potion of Life waiting."

In my dream, Lark told me to remember our bargain. She said that Mordeus would be true to it. What were the words of our bargain, precisely? Return the artifacts to him and . . . no. Not *to him.* I'd specifically twisted his original offer on some hunch that his court was more worthy than he was.

Once the three artifacts are returned to my court where they belong, I will send your sister back to a location of your choice in the human realm.

Where they belong.

I take a step toward the dais and then another. "The Grimoricon has been returned to its rightful place in the Unseelie Court," I say.

Mordeus's greedy eyes dilate with excitement. "Yes."

I offer him the mirror. "And this? Where does it belong?"

398

He snaps his fingers, and it floats from my hand through the air to a glass case behind the throne.

"Now all that needs to be returned to the court is Oberon's crown," I say, my heart racing. "But I am not going to die today."

He opens his palm, offering me that pile of runes again. "You will make a beautiful faerie, but we must complete the bonding ceremony first. Otherwise, the potion won't work."

I lift my skirts and climb the three steps of the dais.

Mordeus beams at me. "Good girl."

Drawing in a breath, I offer a prayer to the gods above and below that I am right about this. Then I make a quarter turn away from the false king and take a seat on the Throne of Shadows.

CHAPTER THIRTY-THREE

THE POWER OF THE THRONE and the crown and *the court* pumps through me.

The crown has been returned to its rightful place in the Court of the Moon.

Mordeus's eyes go wide. He steps back and stumbles down the stairs. "What have you done?"

"Your turn," I say, mustering all my bravado. I still don't know if this will work. "Return my sister safe and alive to the mortal realm — send her to Mage Trifen's so he can tend to her."

His mouth twists with rage, but he snaps his fingers as he glares at me. "It is done." He steps toward me, but I'm still too numb to object to his nearness. "You think you're so clever," he says. "But you never said I had to return *you* to the mortal realm, and now you have signed your own death sentence. I would rather see my peasant-loving nephew on this throne than let a human *woman* take charge of my court."

"I'm not afraid of you."

Mordeus straightens and opens one big hand. Suddenly the scar-faced servant girl who took me to the restroom is between us. He holds a blade to her throat. "You're not. But *she* is," he whispers. "And I hear you're like my nephew in your fondness for protecting the weak."

A thin line of blood appears on the blade where it bites into her skin, and her soft whimper is more piteous than the loudest cry for help.

He goes on. "You think you can trick me, but your unskilled magic is no match for my power. Your mortality and empathy make you weak. Bond with me, and she will be spared. Refuse me and watch countless others just like her lose their lives because of you."

More blood trickles across the blade.

"Release her," I say, my voice broken. I'm floundering. The throne room is lined with Mordeus's sentries, all looking ready to tear me apart at the first order. If this worked, maybe Jas is safe now, but I might be the reason that this innocent girl dies. "Please."

"You'll take the bond?"

I can't die without knowing Jas is okay, and I can't allow the bond and give someone so cruel control of this power. I can't abandon the innocent Unseelie who've already suffered so much from his rule.

"Bond with me," he growls. "And this ends."

"No." My voice shakes three times on the single syllable, but my chin is high.

Mordeus slices the blade across her throat, and blood burbles from her mouth and neck, covering his hand before she falls to the floor.

When he opens his hand again, his magic flares, and another girl appears in the first girl's place. This one can't be more than twelve. She fights his grip, and the knife at her neck bites into her skin as she looks desperately around the throne room.

"I have dozens upon dozens of humans at my disposal, all bought and paid for thanks to the greed of your kind," he says. "How many are you willing to sacrifice for your own selfish reasons? How many lives is your stubborn pride worth?"

The girl's blue eyes are wild before landing on me. I watch the moment she takes me in. Then I see it there in a flash: hope.

Hope.

Even with another girl dead on the floor before her and a blade digging into her throat, she has hope.

I tap into that feeling and blanket the room in darkness. It's Mordeus's element but mine too, and I'm stronger than before. Invisible tendrils of power tether me to the throne and the court. I draw on all of it as I mentally wrap the night around each of his guards, locking them into little boxes of shadow just as I disappear into my own. The king loses his grip on the girl as he lunges forward to stop me, but I reappear behind him, the adamant knife Sebastian gave me in my hand. The moment he spins to face me, I plunge it into his heart.

Mordeus roars in pain, and everything moves in slow motion — his snarl as he grabs a handful of my hair, the hot, sticky blood from his chest pouring onto my fingers, and the keening cry of the young girl who's fallen to her knees behind him.

Mordeus strikes with his bloody blade, aiming for my gut and finding his mark, but he falls to a heap on the ground before he can drive it home.

With shaking, bloody hands, I help the girl to her feet. "Do you have a safe place to go until I can get back to you?" *Countless humans,* he said. All just waiting to feed Mordeus's power and extend his cursed life.

She nods. There are tears running down her face. "My sister," she chokes out, and I realize she's looking at the body of the first girl on the floor. The one I didn't think fast enough to save.

"I'm so sorry," I whisper. I've sacrificed so much to save my sister, but I let hers die. "So very sorry."

She sinks to the floor to smooth her dead sister's hair from her face, and the sight threatens to tear away my numbness. I don't have the luxury for the pain or the terror that want to claim me. I have to go.

I snap a threat on my goblin bracelet.

Bakken's eyes go wide when he surveys the scene before him, his gaze locking on the false king who is dead on the floor in a pool of his own blood.

"Take me to Finn's catacombs." I wipe my hands on my skirt, my stomach roiling at the smell of blood and the feel of it under my fingernails and soaking the silken sleep clothes that cling to my skin.

Bakken steps back and shakes his head. "You ask too much."

"I always pay," I say between clenched teeth. I squeeze the handle of the dagger in my hand so hard the threads in the hilt bite into my palm. "Take me to the shadow prince's catacombs."

"The location is a highly guarded secret. This isn't your average information."

Without thinking, I wrap my fist around my hair and use the bloody knife to sheer it all off. I shove the handful of hair toward him. "Here."

His eyes bulge, and spittle drips from the corner of his mouth as he takes it from me. "Yes, Fire Girl."

I close my eyes, prepared for the nausea that comes with moving through the world with a goblin, but it doesn't help. When the world stops weaving beneath my feet and I open my eyes, I'm surrounded by darkness so deep even my eyes can't quite make out where we are.

"I leave you now, Fire Girl."

I sense more than see Bakken disappear, and I don't try to stop him. The air is cold and smells of damp earth. We must be deep underground.

Mordeus thought he could drug me to convince me to bond myself to him. Then he thought he could use innocents to force me. Which means that Mordeus is as untrustworthy as everyone said and as devious as I feared. But I was prepared for Mordeus to be devious.

I wasn't prepared for the same from Finn.

All this time, that's why Finn helped me. He was hoping I would fall for him and eventually trust him enough to bond with him. He planned to claim my life force and with it the magic crown I didn't even know I carried.

I believed I had friends here, actually felt *less* lonely than I did in Fairscape. But Sebastian is the only real friend I have, and I have broken his trust too many times to count.

Slowly, my eyes adjust and I have to bite back a sob. I don't know what I expected to see. These are his *catacombs.* Of course the dead are kept here. But even so, I never expected this.

The catacombs hold row after row of glass coffins. I rush forward. The woman inside the first one is young — probably my age — and her long blond hair is pulled over one shoulder, her eyes closed. Her hands are folded across her stomach.

She wears a soft white gown of lace and looks like a bride ready for her wedding. I put my hands on the glass — to push it aside, to wake her up, to . . . Save her? — it won't move.

I press my hand against the glass. "No."

I step to the next and see a young man. He has sunken cheeks and sallow skin. He was probably starving when he offered himself to Finn. Maybe he was like me and had a younger sister relying on him. Maybe he handed his life over so someone he loved could survive.

Coffin after coffin, human after human, these catacombs tell a story of a monster who was willing to take the lives of men and women to protect his own. When I come upon a coffin with a familiar face inside, I lean on it and choke back a sob.

Kyla. I *watched* as she offered herself to him. Sacrificed herself because whatever life she'd been living had been worse than this fate — eternity in a glass coffin.

I wanted to believe that Finn was good. When Bakken told me about the curse, I wanted to believe that Finn would never take a human life, that he'd let go of his magic and sacrifice his own immortality before falling victim to the awful choice offered by the curse. Part of me knew — part of me has known for a long time — just what it means to be a tribute.

I wanted to believe we were friends and that the connection I felt when we touched *meant* something. Instead, the connection was nothing more than a crown I don't want. A crown he needs. A crown he planned to kill me to take.

"I keep them here to honor them."

I spin around in the darkness. Finn stands behind me, the orb of light floating at his side illuminating that criminally beautiful face. That lying mouth. Those deceiving silver eyes. "Are you going to finally ask me to bond with you? Or maybe you're too much of a coward to take the crown you and your friends have been grooming me to hand over."

He leans one shoulder against the stone wall and closes his eyes as if he is very, very tired. "Then you know everything now?"

"I know you planned to kill me from our very first dance." I can't keep the pain from my voice. "Everything you did to win me over you did for the crown — to get me to bond with you so you could be *sure* the crown would be yours."

Straightening, he drags his hands through his hair in frustration. "I can't solve the problems of my court from exile."

My hands shake, but I'm not scared. I'm ... hurt. My gaze scans across the row of coffins, and the room tilts around me. I press a hand to my stomach and feel the sticky warmth of Mordeus's blood. Of my blood, still oozing from the dagger's shallow strike.

"And while you worked to manipulate me, you were killing all these innocent people because you believed *your* life was more important than theirs."

When I turn back to him, he doesn't deny it. A mask of resignation covers his face, and sadness glistens in those silver eyes. No, *not sadness.* That's what he wants me to see, and I won't be manipulated. Not anymore.

I swallow hard, but it does nothing to push down the ache in my chest. "Did you kill them all?"

"No, but enough." He walks to the first coffin and gently presses his fingertips to the glass as he studies the woman inside. "Too many."

"Do you even know their names?"

"Every single one."

I nod to the coffin his hands are resting on, the one holding the bride. "Who's that?"

"Her name was Isabel." His voice cracks, and he lifts his head to meet my eyes.

I remember asking him about Isabel — who she was, what happened to her. I remember the anguish in his eyes when he replied, *She was mortal.*

"You killed her," I whisper. "You killed your own betrothed."

"Yes." It's hard to hate him when he looks so broken, but the facts make it easier. He is *not* the male I was beginning to believe he was.

"The king is dead," I say. I want him to know what I'm capable of — that I'm not so easily manipulated or bested. I want *myself* to know.

"I know."

I pull my dagger from my calf but keep it wrapped in shadow in my palm. "I killed him."

"I know. He underestimated you from the beginning. But your mother didn't."

An image of her smile flashes in my mind. "Don't talk about my mother."

My eyes burn. I can't think about that. Not when I've spent the last nine years so angry with her for abandoning us. I can't think about all the anger I've felt that she didn't deserve. I can't think about how much she sacrificed for me. *Not yet.*

"I could have forgiven you for the deceit, but this?" I wave my hand toward the coffins. "I've lived my whole life in a world that thought humans could be bought and used. I will *never* give the crown to someone who is part of that problem."

His jaw twitches as he flicks his gaze over me. "You should make use of the dagger you're hiding in your hand and kill me then. Because as long as I live, I have an obligation to my people. So as long as I live, I will fight for that crown you wear."

My hand shakes as I adjust my grip on the hilt. Killing him wouldn't bring back all these humans, but he would be one less shadow faerie taking innocent lives.

I take a step forward and he doesn't move.

Would he even fight me, or would he just let me end him?

I *trusted* him.

And I betrayed Sebastian. For my sister, yes, but for Finn too. For his kingdom. For his chance to take back his throne.

I try to grip the dagger for a proper strike, but I can't. My fingers refuse to tighten. So I run. I find the stairs and run up and up and up. I feel him watching me, but he doesn't follow. My lungs and legs burn as I climb, but I'm driven by something more than oxygen, and I keep going until I smell the fresh air of day and see the light of the sun peeking in from a door beyond.

I scramble into the sunlight and collapse onto the pine needle carpet of the clearing. I can't catch my breath, and it's not just because my heart is pounding so fast or because the pain from the serpent's bite and the gash in my gut are finally catching up with me.

Finn betrayed me, I betrayed Sebastian, and it all hurts more than I can handle.

CHAPTER THIRTY-FOUR

"LADY ABRIELLA," EMMALINE SAYS SOFTLY. "I'm sorry milady, but you need to wake up."

I try to open my eyes, but it's too hard. I roll over and put my pillow over my head. "No. I need to sleep."

Emmaline squeaks, and I'm vaguely aware of her and Tess having a low conversation as sleep claims me again. "Just found her here." "Bleeding too much." "Find the prince."

"Brie?" Sebastian's voice. The smell of leather, salt, and sea. Sunshine on green grass. "Brie, wake up."

I don't want to open my eyes. I'm in a soft bed, wrapped in blankets. I can smell him all around me, and I don't remember why, but I know I don't want to leave this safe place.

"The healer needs to look at you," Sebastian says softly.

With those words, everything slams into me with the clarity of someone pulling the curtain to reveal a sunny day. I don't want to face the reality of what I've done. I can't handle the thought of Sebastian hating me.

"Abriella, open your eyes." Why does his voice sound so gentle? Doesn't he know? His hand is warm and rough against my cheek, and I lean into it as he runs his thumb along my jaw. "You scared the shit out of me. You know that, right? Please just open your eyes so I know you're okay."

But I don't want to open my eyes. I don't want to end this dream where he still cares for me.

His soft breath flutters against my lips, and then his mouth is on mine, gentle and coaxing. My heart squeezes. *Sebastian.*

"I'm so sorry," I whisper against his lips, finally opening my eyes.

"Sorry?" His face is lined with worry, but he's still bowing close to me, his eyes scanning my face again and again.

"For stealing the book. For deceiving you. I couldn't tell you about my deal with Mordeus. I had to save Jas." I close my eyes before adding, "I'm sorry I trusted Finn when you warned me I shouldn't. I'm sorry. I'm so sorry."

The mattress shifts as he sits on the bed next to me. He pulls me into his arms, his touch and warmth such a relief that tears stream down my face. "Let the healer look at you, and then you can tell me everything."

So I do.

———·———

We spend most of the night talking. I tell him about my deal with Mordeus, about the mirror and the book. I tell him about training with Finn and about the night I was drugged and Pretha dragged me away from the castle. I tell him about the crown and finding the trick in the bargain. I tell him about Finn's catacombs and what a fool I'd been to believe that Finn wanted to help me.

Sebastian listens to every word without judgment, without

411

any of the anger I deserve. And when I'm drained—when the story is told and my words are all gone, when my body feels weak with relief and exhaustion, I let him hold me and I fall asleep.

———·———

I don't wake again until light is streaming into the bedroom. Sebastian's still in bed with me, still holding me, watching me.

"Did you sleep at all?" I ask.

He nods. "A little. How do you feel this morning?"

I sit up in bed, rubbing my eyes. "Better." Tilting my head, I study him. "Still a little surprised that you can tolerate the sight of me."

"You were in an impossible situation, and you did what you had to do." He strokes my cheek with the back of his hand. "My love isn't so fickle that it fades under stress."

I snuggle closer to him. "What would have happened to the crown if I'd died without knowing I wore it? Who would have gotten it if I'd never bonded to a faerie?"

"We don't really know," he says. "This isn't a situation my realm has ever encountered, but any Unseelie who tricked you out of that crown could take the Throne of Shadows."

"And what if I bonded with a member of the Court of the Sun and passed it to him upon my death?"

Sebastian draws in a sharp breath and his eyes flash with hope. My Bash somehow still wants a life with me after all I've done. "Only one with Unseelie blood can rule from the Throne of Shadows, but all any shadow faerie would need is that crown and the throne would be theirs. I hope you understand now why I didn't want you to come here."

412

He *warned* me. Sebastian warned me about this world, about Finn, and I didn't listen.

"I spent so many years being angry with my mother," I say, tired all over again, "and I'm beginning to believe she sacrificed everything for me." Even after sleep, my voice is raw and my throat hurts. "That's why she left us, isn't it? Somehow she left to protect me?"

Sebastian tucks my hair behind my ear. "After Oberon saved you and passed his crown to you, she realized very quickly that there would always be fae chasing you — looking for the crown and trying to trick you out of it."

"Is there any way I could . . . get rid of it? If I don't want it, could I somehow . . ."

"It is tied to your very life, and it remains a part of you until the moment of your death." He swallows, and I remember Mordeus saying the same thing. The crown gave me life, and it is tied to my life. "Your mother did the only thing she could and sold herself to protect you. For the price of her life, she was able to hide you from them for seven years. That's why she left you with your uncle Devlin. She believed that by the time seven years had passed, you'd be clever enough to outwit anyone who would try to steal it from you."

"And I've been angry for nine years."

"You didn't know." He slides his fingers through my hair, examining the ragged ends. "I can't believe you gave that goblin all your hair."

Self-conscious, I run my fingers through my short, wild locks. I've never been particularly vain, but my hair was one trait I always believed was beautiful. "I'm sure I can't compete with those other girls now."

He grabs my hand, stopping me, and squeezes my fingertips. "I sent the girls home."

"What? But I thought . . ."

"For weeks I've been trying to convince myself I could do it. I talked with them, danced with them and . . ." He releases a breath and seems reluctant to say the rest.

"What?"

"They're not you. They never will be you. And I'm done pretending I can live with that."

Warmth fills me, and I lean against his chest. "Bash . . ."

"And if you're not ready for a wedding, my mother will have to deal with it."

My breath catches at mention of the queen. "How is she?"

"Mother? Stronger than anyone realizes. No one in the shadow court knows the book is linked to her life, so they haven't used it against her."

"What will happen if they figure it out?"

He slides his hands around my waist and buries his nose in my hair, taking in a deep breath. "She has the best healers in the realm. They will find a way to fortify her powers, and if they don't . . ." He's quiet for so long that I pull away from the heat of his chest so I can see his face. What I see there isn't grief but thoughtfulness.

"If they don't?" I prod.

"Mother made choices knowing their consequences."

"But what about you? She's still your mother."

He releases a long breath. "I've had years to prepare for this. All I can do is make arrangements to take care of her kingdom as best I can."

"You seem wiser than your years, Prince Ronan Sebastian. I imagine you'll make an incredible king when the time comes."

He gives me a sad smile, and I can almost see the question in his eyes—he will be king, but will I be his queen? I don't know what's next for me, and I've run out of time to deliberate. But when he opens his mouth, a different question comes out. "Do you want to go see your sister?"

I draw in a sharp breath. "Yes. Can we? Is it possible?"

"I'll have my people prepare a portal and we'll go to Nik's first thing in the morning."

I frown. "I asked Mordeus to send her to Mage Trifen's."

"I had to find somewhere else for her to stay," Sebastian explains. "Mage Trifen doesn't do charity."

No kidding. "I'm sure Nik will make room for her until Jas can afford a place on her own."

He's silent for a long beat. "You say that like you're not planning to stay with her."

I open my mouth to object, but there's no objection to make. I take his face in my hands. "I'm so sorry about all the terrible things I've said about you and your people." I swallow. "I love you, Sebastian. I can't live in Fairscape. It's no longer my home."

His expression is guarded as he studies my face. "And where is home?"

"I'm not sure I have one anymore."

He dips his head and brushes his lips softly against mine. "I'll make one for you . . . if you'll let me."

I curl into him, relishing his heat, his protective strength, and I think I just might.

CHAPTER THIRTY-FIVE

EVERYTHING ABOUT FAIRSCAPE SEEMS GRAY after weeks in Faerie. From the sky to the houses, the grass to the trees — everything is less vibrant, as if a film of dreariness has been thrown atop the human realm.

Nik's building looks just as I remember it, and Sebastian squeezes my hand as we approach her unit. Does he know how much these conditions sicken me?

Nik meets us at the door. She grabs my hand and pulls me inside, immediately shutting the door behind us. "They're still looking for you, Brie."

"Who—" *Gorst.* It seems like another lifetime that I broke into his vault to steal money to pay Madame Vivias.

"I've been so worried about you. I would've thought Gorst's men got you if they weren't still looking." She pulls me into a tight embrace. She smells like soap and rose petals, just like I remember. I'm not sure I realized how much I missed her until this moment.

When she pulls back, she keeps holding my shoulders and looks me up and down. "You look amazing. I told you there were good things in Faerie." Her gaze lands on Sebastian, and she

frowns before looking back to me. The question is on her face —
what does he know?

I almost laugh. Sebastian glamoured himself to look human
for our visit to the mortal realm, and Nik doesn't know that he's
fae, let alone that he's the Seelie prince.

"I know everything," he says softly, and I nod in confirmation.

"How is she?" I ask.

"She's okay. She was pretty dehydrated and confused, but
she's doing better. Mage Trifen helped while she was at his place."

"Thank you so much."

She turns toward the bedroom. "She's sleeping, but I'm sure
she'll want to wake up to see you." Before I can object, she opens
the door and lets the light from the living room pour into the tiny
bedroom. "Jas? Your sister's here."

My throat is tight as I walk forward. How many times in the
last weeks have I asked the mirror to show me my sister just so I
would feel less alone? How many times did I want to give up but
kept going for her? I rush forward as she leaps from the bed, and
we meet in the middle of the bedroom.

Jas shakes as she curls into my chest, sobbing quietly. "I knew
you'd come. I knew you'd find me."

"I'm sorry it took me so long." I pull back and study her. She
looks different — still a girl but one who's seen too much. There
are dark circles under her eyes, but unlike the last time I saw her
in the mirror, there's color in her cheeks. "I have so much to tell
you."

Jas looks over my shoulder. "Sebastian," she says with a smile.
"You helped too?"

"Your sister did it on her own." His voice is thick with emotion. "She would have done anything to save you. Would have given anything." There's sorrow in those words and a bit of heartbreak.

Sebastian stays by my side as I explain everything to Jas. I tell her who he is and how I found out. I tell her about my deal with Mordeus and my misguided friendship with the exiled prince and his band of misfit faeries. I tell her about our mother, and Sebastian squeezes my hand a little tighter when I explain the curse.

If it's all too much for her when she's still recovering from weeks as Mordeus's prisoner, she doesn't let on. When I'm done with my story, Sebastian kisses my forehead and releases my hand. "I'll leave you two to talk."

He leaves the room and shuts the door behind him. I press my palm to the tug in my chest as I watch him go.

"Have you told him yet?" Jas asks.

I turn back to my sister. "Told him what?"

She smiles weakly, but I see an echo of my hopeful little sister in the upward tilt of her lips. "That you're in love with him?"

I swallow. "He knows."

She tilts her head to the side. "Then why do you look so sad?"

Because I never believed I'd trust a fae prince, let alone two. Because I finally made some friends and found out they were using me. Because I hurt Sebastian and it's going to be hard to forgive myself for that.

"Brie," she says, squeezing my hand. "What is it?"

"I don't think I'm staying in Elora."

"What? Why? Surely if we leave Fairscape, Gorst won't—"

"I'll never be safe here, not so long as I wear this crown."

"You're returning to Faerie?"

Weeks ago, I was the one who said the name of the magical realm with disdain and Jas was the one who wanted to go there. Today our roles have reversed.

"I'll be with Sebastian," I say, trying to make it sound like I'm not just hiding. "I want to do what I can to . . . help with things there." I bow my head before risking a look back at her. "Would you go with us?"

Her eyes go wide. Her fear is so palpable I can almost smell it. I can't blame her. All she knows of Faerie is her experience being a prisoner of the Unseelie Court. "Brie . . ."

"To the Court of the Sun. We would keep you safe."

Her hands shake harder and harder until her whole body is vibrating with fear. "The things I saw in the dungeons . . . the horrible things I heard—"

"You don't have to," I blurt. I hate being the cause of the pain on her face. "I love you so much," I whisper. "If you need me here, I will stay."

"I love you too." She wraps her arms around my waist. "You deserve to be happy, Brie. You've worked so hard for so long. You've done everything to protect me, and I can't handle seeing you sacrifice yourself one more time for me."

"But I don't want to leave you."

"Just give me time. I need to stay here awhile, and when I'm better, I'll join you." She tries to smile, but the shaky curve of her lips doesn't hide the lie from either of us.

"I'll visit you as often as I can," I say, but I already know it won't be as often as either of us would like. The hot tears on my cheeks are barely a hint of the grief I feel at telling her goodbye.

There's a knock at the door, then Nik opens it a crack and sticks her head in. "Brie, it's time. I'm sorry, honey, but I can't risk Gorst finding you here."

I nod but don't take my eyes off Jas.

"Go," she says. "I'll be fine."

"I'll miss you every day."

"Visit me in my dreams like you did when we were kids." She grins and waves goodbye, but as Sebastian hurries me toward the portal, I remember the old joke. After we moved in with Uncle Devlin, Jas would wake up some mornings and thank me for the adventure I took her on in her dreams. Were they just dreams, or did I have access to that part of my power even as a child in the human realm?

CHAPTER THIRTY-SIX

WHEN WE RETURN TO THE GOLDEN PALACE, my mind is still in Fairscape with Jas.

Sebastian escorts me to my room, and when I stop at the door and turn to him, he studies me. "I'll take you back to see her soon," he says.

"Thank you, Sebastian."

"It's nothing."

"No, thank you for . . . everything. For standing by me through all this when anyone else would send me away." I close my eyes. "For forgiving me for taking the book and for . . . understanding the choices I made."

I feel his fingertips on my chin, sliding along my jaw and into my hair, and when I open my eyes, his are full of anguish. "I love you, Abriella. All that matters to me is that you're here with me now. We'll figure out the rest. Together."

I search his beautiful eyes, his strong yet fine features. "I want to be bonded with you."

Sebastian swallows, and his eyes widen. "You're sure?"

I nod. I can't stop thinking of the Banshee — of death sitting on my chest. Or of the crown that sits on my head and the false king and the Unseelie prince who tried to trick me out of it. The prince who was willing to let me die so he could claim this throne. "Mordeus was right about one thing. As long as this crown is on my head, my life won't be my own. If it's not Finn after the crown, it will be another Unseelie. Until we can figure out how to get rid of it safely, I need the bond so you can protect me."

"I thought you were against humans bonding with faeries."

I take both of his hands in mine. "I trust you."

He brings my hands to his lips and kisses them each twice. "I vow to do everything in my power to give you a good life. To make you happy and protect you."

———•———

Sebastian chose to do the bonding ceremony on the balcony outside his chambers at dusk, and my maids are giddy as they prepare me for the occasion, styling my ear-length mess of curls as best they can and taking extra time on my makeup.

When they bring out my dress, my breath catches.

"Sebastian gave us your sister's muslin mockup, and we did our best from there. Is it what you wanted?"

"Yes." I take in the thin emerald-colored velvet, and my vision goes blurry with tears. Only Sebastian would have thought to let me wear something designed by my sister on this special night. The dress isn't a dress at all, but the outfit Jas had designed for me to wear to Faerie. The one she wasn't able to finish because Madame V sold her.

"No crying now," Tess says, wiping at her own eyes. "You'll make me start."

I step into the loose-legged pants, and the velvet feels decadent against my skin. Emmaline helps me into the fitted top with its deep V.

She places a matching emerald necklace around my neck. "Also from the prince," she says.

I close my eyes. Has he been holding the muslin mockup of this dress all this time? Saving it for this occasion?

"Why are you so sad?" Emmaline asks. "You look stunning."

"I'm not sad." I draw in a ragged breath. "I'm ready."

———•———

The view of the sunset from Sebastian's balcony is breathtaking, but nothing compared with the man who stands in front of it.

Sebastian's resplendent in a white tunic and pants of the finest linen. There are no weapons on him tonight, only a single day lily in his hand. His eyes fill with tenderness as he tucks the flower behind my ear. "You're so beautiful."

I duck my head, feeling inexplicably shy, and look up at him through my lashes. "Thank you for the dress. And the necklace."

He offers me a glass of wine from a nearby table, and I take it, grateful to have something to ease my nerves.

"I had the staff hold back a bottle of solstice wine. Typically, it's only served on Litha, but since you liked it so much . . ." He lifts his glass and taps it to mine. "Here's to you, Abriella. I've only dreamed of being bonded to such an incredible woman."

Tears prick at my eyes again. "And to you," I whisper. "And a new beginning for both of us."

We both drain our glasses, but my hands are still shaking when we return them to the table.

Sebastian summons a pile of runestones in his open palm and extends them to me.

I hesitate before reaching for one, all too aware of the magnitude of what we're about to do. I'm ready for this lifelong bond, and yet —

No. No more doubts and no more secrets. I trust Sebastian, and I need to allow him this bond so he can protect me through whatever comes next.

Before I can change my mind, I reach for an oblong alabaster stone. The moment my fingers touch it, the rest disappear. I turn it in my palm to study the symbol. One long, thick line stretches from top to bottom of the longest side of the stone, another line angles off it to the right, and a swirl crosses the middle.

"It's beautiful," I whisper, stroking my thumb across the imprint. I flick my gaze up to Sebastian. His eyes are locked on the stone, and his face has fallen. "What's wrong?"

He swallows and shakes his head. "Nothing. It's fine."

"What does it mean?"

"This symbol can mean sorrow and loss." He clasps his hand over mine, pressing the stone tight between our palms. "But it can also mean rebirth after those things. New beginnings, like you said." He bows his head and brushes his lips against mine, keeping our hands clasped. "Are you ready?"

I search his face. I love that he's not rushing this, that he understands what it means to me. "I'm ready."

"Abriella Kincaid, I bond my life to yours. I will feel your joy and know your pain. Near or far, we will always be close in heart, connected in spirit."

"Prince Ronan Sebastian," I say, repeating the vows as I was instructed. "I bond my life to yours. I will feel your joy and know your pain. Near or far, we will always be close in heart, connected in spirit."

His lowers his head, brushing his smile across mine, his hand still holding mine tightly, almost as if he's afraid I'll pull away.

"Is that it?" I ask. I thought I might feel different somehow, but I don't.

"It takes a moment," he says. He sprinkles whisper-soft kisses down my neck and pulls my body close. Pleasure and anticipation shimmer through me. We kiss and kiss until the evening air wraps around us, like a band holding us together.

Then it's there — a connection between us, something snapping and electric, a power pumping through me to him in an infinite loop.

"Sebastian," I whisper. The rune is no longer between our palms. "Where did it go?"

He shifts the green velvet at my décolletage to the side and smiles. There, inked on my skin, is the rune that disappeared from our clasped hands.

The sight reminds me of Finn's chest and all those runes inked there. Does each represent someone he bonded with? A life he stole?

I push the thought from my mind. Tonight is about Sebastian and me. About *us.* "Do you have one too?"

Swallowing, he nods and turns our joined hands to show me the inked symbol on the inside of his wrist. "We are bonded."

My vision blurs, and my knees go weak under me. "I think I need to sit down."

Sebastian's face pales, but he takes my arm and leads me to a chair just inside his chambers. "I'm going to need you to drink this," he says, pulling a vial from a pouch at his side.

Pain stabs through my chest, and my lungs seize. "Sebastian . . ." I gasp and draw my knees to my chest as the pain rips through me again. "I think someone poisoned the wine."

"I need you to drink." He keeps a hand on my arm. When I'm able to open my eyes, he's watching me, concern all over his handsome face. "I'm here, Abriella. I'm right here."

"What's happening to me?"

"It's a reaction to the bond. *Now drink.*"

The pain rips through me. Sebastian's lips are moving, but his words are little more than a soundtrack to my torture. I try to listen, try to focus on anything except this excruciating pain ripping me apart, but I can't. I just want to sleep until the pain is gone.

The world flashes — bright with the sunset coming in from the balcony, then the comforting darkness of unconsciousness. Light, dark, light, dark. It's like I'm being asked to choose — life and pain or relief and nothingness.

"Brie."

I drag my eyes open.

Sebastian's pressed the vial to my lips. "You're dying. This is the only choice we have."

"Dying?" I always imagined that death would seize me and pull me under. I never thought it would sink jagged claws into my chest and fight me down. I never imagined I'd have a chance to fight back.

"Please drink. The Potion of Life is the only way I can save you." I hear his tears before I can force my eyes open long enough to see them. "For once in your life, stop being so damn stubborn."

The Potion of Life.

The room spins. My lids are so heavy, and it's hard to stay here when I want to slip away. *Light or dark. Dark or light.* Lark's words echo behind the pain.

Next time she dies, it has to be during a bonding ceremony.

I see three paths before you. In each, the Banshee's call is clear.

The vial is cool against my lips. If I drink, this pain ends? If I don't drink, death awaits?

"Please." Sebastian's voice is a ragged sob. "This is the only way." He's hurting, and that's worse than these claws tearing through me. I'd do anything to ease his pain, so I part my lips. I drink.

The potion is silky on my tongue and feels like it sends me flying. Every swallow pushes another claw from my chest, lifts me away from this pain.

"Good girl," he whispers. "You have to drink it all. That's my girl."

With my last swallow, the claws are gone, and warmth races along my veins, then heat, then— "Sebastian!"

My veins flood with fire, and I writhe in his arms. Please gods, not fire. *Anything but fire.*

"What's happening?" he asks.

"This is the transformation," an unfamiliar female voice says. "One cannot become fae without some pain."

"Fix it," he growls. "Do something to save her from this agony."

"Magic has a cost," the female says. "And so does immortality. She must endure or the potion will not take. She must endure or you lose her forever."

"I'm here," he whispers. "I have you."

But he doesn't. Nothing can save me from this pain. Time lurches forward, then stands still. I see my childhood in a flash, relive the fire in slow motion. Time teases me as seconds pass, fly by, then holds me captive as it stills again.

The world goes black again. I push away from consciousness and welcome the darkness, wrapping myself in a soft blanket.

CHAPTER THIRTY-SEVEN

THE STARS HAVE NEVER LOOKED SO BRIGHT, the night sky never such a velvety black. Cool night air whips around my skin, brushing across my ears and cheeks like the lightest, sweetest kisses.

A tall male with broad shoulders and dark curls has his back to me, his face tilted up to study the stars, as if he too depends on them for answers.

"Finn?"

When he turns to me, I'm struck anew by his beauty. He's wearing a black shirt, the top two buttons undone, and his soft leather pants are as dark as the night beyond. Some distant thought nags at me. I'm not supposed to be here with him, but I can't remember *why* . . .

"I think . . ." I look around us. There's no landscape. Only vast night sky. "Is this real?"

I lift a hand, skimming my fingers over the sharp point of my new, elven ears. "I died," I whisper, remembering now.

"Died and were born anew. You're sleeping now. The metamorphosis . . . it is never easy, but your mortal flesh fought it harder than most."

Because I never wanted to be fae.

A reaction to the bond. Sebastian was prepared with the Potion of Life, prepared to save me when the bond ended my mortal existence. Nothing in the curse included danger to mortals who bonded with the Seelie. But how could he have known? As I try to wrap my mind around the thought, it falls away, lost in the never-ending darkness.

I look down at myself. I'm dressed in the green gown Jas designed, but there's nothing beneath my bare feet. We're floating with the stars. "This is a dream." Even if the lack of landscape didn't give it away, I'd know it was true because I feel none of the anger and frustration I know I'm supposed to feel toward Finn. I feel . . . *peaceful*.

He nods and rolls back his shoulders as he surveys the sky. "A dream. One of the best I've had in years."

"I don't want to go back." I bite my bottom lip. "So much pain."

"The pain will be gone when you wake." His silver eyes look sadder than I've ever seen them. "Are you happy?"

"I'm not sure I know how to be happy. It's been so long since I've had the luxury."

"Now you have your whole immortal life to figure it out."

I look around the starry night sky that seems to cradle us here — outside of reality, outside of time. Even my thoughts feel suspended in this moment. "What happened?"

"After you left my catacombs, I had Pretha get you back to the Golden Palace. I knew you wouldn't go with us, but I couldn't leave you alone and bleeding in the Wild Fae Lands."

Finn. Finn was the one who got me back to safety. I feel no surprise at this news. "I mean what happened after that?"

"You'll understand the rest soon enough."

"More secrets," I say, but I'm too relaxed for the words to sound angry.

"I am sorry—for what it's worth. I never expected . . ." He squeezes the back of his neck. "I tried to find a way out of involving you. Even after your mother's protection ran out and I knew where to find you, I searched for a way. I saw you in a cellar, saw you work until your fingers were bloody, paying your debts and caring for your sister. I searched and searched for another way. My father put me in an impossible position when he gave his crown to a mortal girl."

I ponder this. I never thought of it that way. Finn had an entire kingdom to think of . . . all those refugees. *The children.* "Do you hate him for it?"

His lips twist into a semblance of a smile. "I did once." His gaze flicks to mine. "Before I knew you."

I study the stars again. "I thought I had no hope, that there was nothing to believe in anymore, but when I think about your people and the camps . . . I hope. And still I believe you can help them."

Swallowing, he closes those hypnotic silver eyes and bows his head. "Despite all I did to you? Before you?"

"Despite that." Sighing, I let the stars sing to me. "I like it here. It reminds me of something my mother used to tell me when she took me outside at night." Something I'd forgotten until now.

"What?" he asks. "What did she say?"

"That no matter how hopeless I feel, there's always a little more hope inside me. That no matter how faithless I think I am, there is always something to believe in." When I turn to look at him, he's staring at me, eyes soft, jaw a bit slack. "Maybe that sounds foolish to an immortal."

"Not at all." He swallows hard. "May you always have a star to wish on, Abriella, and a reason to believe." He begins to fade into the darkness.

"Finn, wait." He rematerializes before me and waits, silently. "Why are you using your magic to visit my dreams? What of the cost?"

"Ah, what are the shadow fae good for but foolish dreams and ghoulish nightmares?" His eyes flick over me — from my eyes to my collarbones, down my gown, and to my bare feet before bringing them back up and settling on my wrist. I follow his gaze. My scar is gone. Not glamoured away, but *gone*. Its absence is an echo in my mind. Because it wasn't a scar at all but the mark of the one who wears the Unseelie crown. "There is no cost now that the curse has been lifted, but it's not my power that brought us here. I'm not using my magic."

"Then how?"

"You're using yours." Then he disappears, and the dream fades to nothing.

"The healer said she needs her sleep."

Puzzle pieces swirl in my head, weaving and shifting. Answers just out of my grasp.

433

"Well certainly, but she can sleep after the coronation."

"The prince will want her there."

The prince. *Sebastian*. Sebastian's sudden appearance in my life two years ago. He moved in next door and charmed me from his first smile. Seven years after my mother left. Almost to the day.

"These are the first days of these new times. If she's to be his queen, she should be by his side."

"She's been through too much. I don't think she's ready to wake. The potion takes a toll."

The potion. The potion Sebastian had with him. The one he somehow knew he'd need.

I feel something important there. Like a word on the tip of my tongue. But consciousness slips through my fingers alongside the answer that's just beyond my grasp.

"She's coming out of it. Just look at those eyes."

"Princess Abriella?" There's a gentle shake on my arm. "Princess, you need to wake up. We have to get you ready for the coronation."

I drag my eyes open, sit up, and look around the room. I'm still in Sebastian's chambers, but everything is just a little different. Brighter? More . . . defined?

"Oh, Prince Ronan will hate that he's missing her first look at the world through her fae eyes." Emmaline says, practically squealing. "Someone send for him."

"You make a beautiful faerie, milady," Tess says.

"As if you were born that way."

Faerie. I'm a . . . *faerie?* It all comes back to me in a flash.

Choosing the rune, saying the bonding vows with Sebastian, the ever-weakening pain of death . . . *The Potion of Life.*

"I'm so sorry to rush you, Your Highness, but if you're going to make it to Prince Ronan's coronation, we need to get you in the bath quickly now."

Died. I died. But why? How did Sebastian know I'd have that reaction to the bond? He *knew* the bond would kill me. He *knew* he'd have to make me fae or lose me forever.

One of the servants takes my hand and leads me from the bed. I waver on legs that don't feel like my own.

Another servant holds up a dress. "You will look beautiful standing by the new king's side in this."

I'm still woozy from sleep. From the potion. What they're saying doesn't make sense. "The new king?"

The ladies laugh. "Prince Ronan, your Sebastian, will take the throne today with our lady by his side. So many reasons to celebrate."

I close my eyes to that blow. In my dream, Finn said the curse had been lifted. *The queen has died and it's my fault.*

There's too much to take in.

I open my eyes again and give a start. Emmaline and Tess aren't the women I knew. They're faeries, with pointed ears, glowing skin, green vines tattooed down their arms. "You aren't human?"

"The prince had us glamoured," Emmaline says. "To make you more comfortable."

"But now we can be our true selves with you," Tess says. "Why do you look so sad? You will make a wonderful queen."

"Beautiful too," Emmaline adds.

Why do *I* look so *sad?* Why do *they* sound so *joyful?* "Queen Arya," I say, swallowing. "She passed while I slept?"

Emmaline's eyes go wide, and she and Tess share a long look before she looks back to me. "No, no, milady. The queen is well. Prince Ronan will take the Throne of Shadows."

I stumble backward until my legs hit the bed. I sink into the mattress, shaking my head. Oberon's crown would have shifted to Sebastian when I died, but . . . "I don't understand. I thought only a fae with royal Unseelie blood could take the Throne of Shadows."

"Yes, milady," Tess says. "And Sebastian is both Seelie and Unseelie royalty."

Emmaline nods. "We were unable to speak of it until he wore his father's crown and the curse was broken, but now we can celebrate who he is."

"A joyous day," Emmaline says, and all the other servants in the room chorus in agreement.

His father's *crown?* Anger surges, even as I grapple with this information, trying to reorder the puzzle pieces, make sense of them. "I thought King Castan was the prince's father."

"King Castan, rest his soul, raised the boy," a servant behind Tess says. She has horns, and her wide blue eyes glow like a summer sky. "But Prince Ronan is Oberon's blood. Conceived in the mortal world during the eclipse, our prince brings day and night together. Light and dark. He is the new king who has been raised to unite our kingdoms."

Sebastian is Unseelie.

He's Unseelie, and he knew I'd die when I bonded with him.

436

He knew I'd have no choice but to take the Potion of Life, even though I never wanted to be a faerie.

"A prayer answered," another servant says. "He and his mother have searched long and hard for his father's crown. Then he found you."

"He . . ." I swallow, remembering his whispered promises to me.

I vow to do everything in my power to give you a good life. To make you happy and protect you.

He lied to me. *Manipulated me.* He let me believe that Finn was the only one trying to trick me into a bond, let me believe that he only wanted to *love* me, to *protect* me. "He knew." My words are sharp and hard, but they don't hold a fraction of the anger that's surging through my blood.

"No one could speak of it until his father's crown was returned to him," Tess says. Her joyful expression has shifted to one of worry. "Should I . . . get him for you?"

"It's time to dress now," Emmaline says. She approaches me slowly, extending a hand like she might toward a frightened animal. "After the coronation, you and the new king will be married. You will be a beautiful bride and an honorable queen."

Queen to a male who appeared in my life right after my mother's protection ran out. To a male who's been planning for *years* to trick me out of the Unseelie crown. A male who stole my power and lied to me about his own.

Something in my chest cracks open, and the servants scream as darkness floods the room. *My* darkness.

Sebastian may have the crown, but somehow this power — the

437

power that came with Oberon's life, with his crown — it remains my own. *Magic is life. Life is magic.* Maybe in choosing to give me the Potion of Life, Sebastian unknowingly tied these powers to me.

The servants scramble for light. Someone calls for the sentinels in the hall, but I silence their screams, wrapping them in shadows.

They expect me to dress pretty and show up to be his queen.

I am not a pretty thing to be manipulated. I am darkness, and the power rushing through my veins is stronger than ever. *This* is what it's like to be fae and have magic. *Magic is life.*

And with the darkness swirling about the room and my shadows becoming one with it, I feel more alive than I ever have.

I walk past panicking servants, past guards scrambling to summon fae light. I walk past Riaan and the royal guard as they command light to fill the halls. I walk and watch their magic fail next to the might of mine. Rage pulses through my blood, demanding vengeance, retribution.

But . . . *there.* Beneath that rage is something else. An emotion that is not mine. A thread of panic, a tightening bond that tells me Sebastian will be turning the corner a second before he does.

Sebastian races down the hall, runs toward me. In the darkness I've cast upon the palace, the crown of twinkling starlight is visible atop his silver-blond hair. I see him more clearly now than ever, and I stare at the tattoos on his chest and neck. *Dozens* of rune tattoos I've never seen before. *Another glamour. Another way to deceive the human.*

He stops near me and spins in the darkness. "Abriella." His

panic hums in my blood. He *feels* me, but he doesn't see me. I see him, though. I see him and I *feel* him. I am shadow and darkness and stronger than the girl he sacrificed for that crown. "Stop this, Brie. Lift the darkness. We need to talk."

But he can't make me stop. And he can't keep me from walking away from the Golden Palace with nothing but my darkness and the betrayal that has wrapped itself around my immortal heart.

ACKNOWLEDGMENTS

Thank you to my writer friends, who encouraged me with this project — for squeeing with excitement rather than warning me off of diving into a new genre and for cheering me every step of the way. Mira Lyn Kelly, my bestie, my brainstorming buddy, queen of hair stroking and reassuring — thank you for being there for me while I drafted this book and for batting down my insecurities. Carrie Ann Ryan, Jeffe Kennedy, Kyla Linde, Lisa Maxwell, Meghan March, Sawyer Bennett, Zoe York, and everyone else I pestered when this story wouldn't leave me alone, thank you for your enthusiasm. Thanks to Rhonda Merwarth, who provided feedback when this book was just a proposal. Thanks to my Goldbrickers, who blow me away every day with their work ethic and support. I am better for being around you all.

Thanks, too, to my real-world friends, those of you who might not understand publishing but cheer me on anyway. A special thanks to Lisa Kuhne, who has the dubious honor of being both my dear friend and personal assistant, and who is a master at handling my neuroses; and to Emily Miller, my own personal elf-advisor and fellow lover of all things fae.

Thanks to my family — my mom for worrying about me when I work myself ragged and always giving me permission to rest when I won't give it to myself; my sisters, Deb and Kim, for texting with me and "getting me" in a way no one else likely ever will; and of course my four big brothers, Eric, Aaron, Danny, and Josh, who taught me to believe in magical elves, dragons, and monsters in the forest. Aaron, thank you for the map of Faerie; I love it so much.

To my agent, Dan Mandel, who was enthusiastic about this book from when it was nothing but a single sentence pitch in an email and a few rough scenes on my hard drive. Thank you for always believing in me and my work.

I am grateful to have found such a wonderful editor in Nicole Sclama. Every editorial note she gave me resonated so true with my vision for this story. She helped me make this the book I wanted it to be and one I'm so proud to share. I've been honored to work with the whole team at HMH Books for Young Readers, notably Gabriella Abbate, Emilia Rhodes, Helen Seachrist, Andrea Miller, Samantha Bertschmann, Nadia Almahdi, Tara Shanahan, Margaret Rosewitz, Erika West, Rebecca Springer, Maxine Bartow, and Romanie Rout. Thank you for all you do!

A huge thank-you to all my readers! To my romance readers who had to adjust to fewer books a year while I made time for this passion project, thank you for your endless enthusiasm for anything I put out there. I am humbled by your support. Thank you to all the bloggers and early reviewers who took a chance on this book. I appreciate your time and was renewed by your sweet messages — shouty caps and exclamation points give me life!

441

Finally, and most importantly, I need to thank my husband, Brian, and my children, Jack and Mary. Brian, my rock, my voice of reason, my sounding board, thank you for supporting me through every book and the endless highs and lows this career delivers; everything feels possible when you're holding my hand. And to Jack and Mary, the coolest kids ever, thank you for reminding me that I am more than a writer. I used to believe the best parts of me would end up in my books, but now I know they're really in you.